ACKNOWLEDGMENTS

This book and my vision of Atlantis lived in my imagination for years, and it would never have come into being if not for the constant support of a few important people. From my husband, who always respected my writing, to my agent, Lucienne Diver, who believed in the story from conception, to Heather Osborn, who bought the series for Tor, and to Melissa Frain, who edited it.

No writer truly writes alone. Thanks to the other writers who were there for me: The Alphabet Gang: Alison Diem, Beth Yarnall and Charity Hammond; The Hotcakes: Jenna Kernan and Susan Meier; and Shannon Donnelly, wonderful friend and fantastic writer/brainstormer/editor.

But the most important dedication goes to Ryan Manning, the inspiration for Rafe Montana and his Hunter counterpart, with much love. Always use your powers for good.

PRODIGAL SON

PRODIGAL SON

DEBRA MULLINS

A TOM DOHERTY
ASSOCIATES BOOK
NEW YORK

PRODIGAL SON

Copyright © 2013 by Debra Mullins

A Tor Book
Published by Tom Doherty Associates, LLC
175 Fifth Avenue
New York, NY 10010

www.tor-forge.com

Tor® is a registered trademark of Tom Doherty Associates, LLC.

The Library of Congress Cataloging-in-Publication Data
is available upon request.

ISBN 978-0-7653-3686-6 (trade paperback)
ISBN 978-1-4299-7098-3 (e-book)

Tor books may be purchased for educational, business, or promotional use.
For information on bulk purchases, please contact Macmillan Corporate
and Premium Sales Department at 1-800-221-7945, extension 5442,
or write specialmarkets@macmillan.com.

First Edition: October 2013

Printed in the United States of America

0 9 8 7 6 5 4 3 2 1

Prodigal Son

CHAPTER ONE

The diner had seen better days.

The smells encompassed Rafe Montana as he walked in: fresh coffee and the lingering aroma of bacon, burgers, and fries served twenty-four hours a day. At this hour of the night, fluorescent lighting glared off the red vinyl of the empty booths, emphasizing without pity every rip and patch. A Formica counter stretched the length of the far wall, and a waitress nursed both a steaming cup and a magazine near the coffee machine at the end. She looked up at the sound of his booted feet on the worn tile, her heavy mascara failing to disguise the fatigue in her eyes.

"Getcha something?"

"Sit anywhere?"

"Sure." She waved a hand in the direction of the empty dining room, then dropped her eyes back to her magazine. "Menu's on the table. Let me know when you're ready."

"Thanks." He slid into the booth facing the restrooms, on the side where the door would swing toward him. He took a menu from the holder and opened it to block his face. And to give his damn hands something to do so they wouldn't shake like some rookie's.

He had to do this. He was the only one who could.

His gut clenched. He kept thinking about the job, tied himself in knots over it. He gritted his teeth, his fingers tightening on the menu before he blew out a deep, slow breath and forced himself to relax. If he wasn't the one to do this, it would be someone else. And he had to look Jack Needham in the eye to find out the truth.

Literally.

Seeing the truth was just the smallest part of what he could do, along with the way he sometimes knew things, like nuggets of information dropped into his mind by the universe. And he could focus on a person and immediately see that person's location. If the image was in color, the person was alive. Black and white, dead. All gifts, the family stories said, from some ancient ancestor in Atlantis. He could find anyone, anywhere.

He was a Hunter.

He'd used his power earlier to Hunt Jack. The vision he'd gotten had exploded with color and put his quarry right here in this run-down diner near the Nevada-Arizona border. When Jack came out of the men's room, he would find Rafe waiting.

And Rafe would know for certain if Jack really was dirty.

When Rafe had first come to Vegas a few years ago, he'd had big dreams about using his truth-seeing gift to play professional poker. But nowadays the players usually wore sunglasses to hide their eyes, and the mojo wouldn't work if he couldn't see the eyes. So he went to plan B and became a bounty hunter. After a couple of years as a PI, he'd aced the training, gotten his license, and jumped right in. That's how he'd met Jack.

His friend. His mentor. Now his prey.

None of these fellas would have any trouble with me if they hadn't broken the law. They made the choice. Jack's voice, about mellow as a rusty hinge, echoed in Rafe's memories even now. How many times had he echoed Jack's motto? Considered it gospel?

Rafe shook his head. He should have known better than to get caught up in the whole team thing. He was better off alone.

"You made the choice this time, Jack," he murmured, his throat tight. "You broke the law."

The restroom door swung open with a creak, momentarily blocking Rafe from Jack's view. He had five, maybe ten seconds before Jack's training would have him looking this way.

The door started to swing closed, and Rafe used the resulting squeak to cover the sound of his movements as he slid from the booth. He rose to his feet just as Jack turned his head. Their eyes met.

Rafe gave him a short nod. "Jack."

"Damn, kid." The older man swept a quick, assessing gaze over him, his dark eyes sharp. A half smile quirked his mouth. "Long time, no see."

Yeah, Rafe hadn't seen Jack in a while and was shocked by the tiny differences in his appearance. Deeper lines around his mouth and eyes in a face tanned by Nevada sun. More gray in his black hair than there used to be. A leaner, hungrier look that made his wiry body appear even thinner and, for some reason, made him look older than his fifty-nine years.

"So, did you do it?"

Jack jerked his gaze up, challenged him with his rigid posture. "Hell, no."

Lie.

Disappointment unraveled through him, merging with his churning misgivings and promising misery later. "You've been taking bribes to let skips go. Willie the Fish. John Allen. Martino Sanchez. And now you blew off your court date to make a run for Mexico."

Surprise flickered across Jack's face for just a second, before he squared his jaw and narrowed his eyes. "Where do you get your info, kid? I haven't even left the state, much less thought about Mexico. And I thought the court date was tomorrow."

Truth, lie, and *lie.*

Rafe wouldn't allow himself to be fooled by the cajoling tone. His powers had never failed him, and he could see the cunning, the calculation, lurking in Jack's gaze. He'd never thought Jack would lie, not to him. Betrayal sliced deep, shredding any lingering hope with cruel finality. In his book, there was never any excuse for screwing the people you cared about.

In a way, it made the situation easier. With friendship and trust destroyed, now there was only the job.

"The *coyote* is supposed to meet you here at two A.M.," he said, responding to the inner prompt that suddenly fed him the information. "You were going to ditch your truck and ride with him to Naco, where he would hand you off to another *coyote* who would get you across the border." He shook his head. "Bad plan. I don't think a guy your height would fit behind the dashboard."

Jack had stiffened more and more as Rafe laid out the scenario in a calm, sure tone. "You don't know shit."

"I know this." Rafe took out his cuffs. "I know I have to take you in, Jack."

"Like hell." All pretense melted away. Jack leaned toward him, pointed a finger. "You don't know, Montana. You don't know what it's like to work for years perfecting skills to get to the top, only to have some punk like you roll in and take it all away without breaking a sweat."

Truth.

Rafe flinched at the vicious attack. "What the hell are you talking about?"

"What's the matter, rich boy? You get bored with corporate America? Needed to slum?" Jack took a step toward him, his familiar face a rictus of rage. "I worked my butt off making a name for myself, and then you show up. I decide to be a nice guy, show you the ropes. Then what happens? You start snagging all the good cases out from under me like some goddamn Vegas Mountie who always gets his man. Zero percent failure rate. What the hell? Your rich family got a bunch of PIs on the payroll or something?"

Truth and lies, tumbling over each other like dirty laundry, but Jack believed every word. Of course he'd checked out Rafe's background, found out about his family. Rafe would have done the same thing. He didn't discuss his family; he hadn't seen or talked to any of them in years. That was safer for everybody. As for his success rate, what could he say? *Hey, Jack, I have this psychic thing that tells me where all the skips are.* Cold crept through him. He'd relaxed too much, used his powers too freely. Just like before. But at least no one had gotten hurt this time.

Lie. Jack had gotten hurt, however inadvertently.

Guilt pinched. But then again, Jack had made the choice to go bad. He could have found another way. That was on him, not Rafe.

"Say something." Jack opened and closed his fists at his sides. "You ruined me. The money dried up. My girlfriend left me and took my bank account with her. No one wanted to hire me anymore, not for the good stuff. They had me chasing DUIs and deadbeat dads. That's not me. I'm better than that." He sucked in a shaky breath. "I had to find some way to survive."

Rafe gave him a hard look. "By taking kickbacks? C'mon, Jack."

"You'll see what I mean." Jack lifted his chin, glared. "This job burns the hell out of guys like us. A pace like you've been keeping? A couple of years from now, when you're sitting alone in an empty house with your bones aching and all the innocence beaten out of your soul, easy money for looking the other way will seem like salvation."

"No." Rafe shook his head. "I won't let it happen."

"That's what I said, too, kid." Jack gave a hard laugh. "Just wait until some young hotshot shows up and muscles you out of the top spot." He paused, his lips curving ever so slightly. "Unless you screw up before then. Like you did back in Arizona."

The verbal sucker punch stole the breath from his lungs. He fought to keep steady. How the hell did Jack know about *that*? It wasn't in any public record anywhere.

"Told you I'm good." Jack narrowed his gaze, studying Rafe's reaction with apparent satisfaction. "You got no woman, no friends, and a family you turned your back on. All you've got is the job, Montana, and when it's gone, what are you gonna do? What will you have left?"

Nothing. Harsh truth, echoing down to his bones. Looking at Jack, Rafe realized he could be gazing at the reflection of his future self: lonely, bitter, fading into the shadows like some dusty legend.

Is that how he wanted to live his life? Is that how he wanted to go out?

Hell, no. But he had no choice. He couldn't take the chance of risking any more lives.

Jack had a choice.

"You're gonna dry up and blow away, just like the rest of us," Jack sneered. "Better get used to it." His gaze flitted to the windows, then back to Rafe.

The small movement triggered alarm bells. All it took was a thought, and the Hunter kicked in, showing Rafe a vision of a Latino guy in jeans, blue shirt, and a hat parking his ancient pickup at the far end of the parking lot outside. The *coyote* sat in the truck, engine running, and lit a cigarette before glancing at his watch. Rafe pushed the image away, focused on Jack.

The job *was* all he had, at least for now. And he was going to do it.

"Your *coyote* is here, Jack." His ex-mentor jerked. Alarm flickered across his face before he masked it. Rafe pushed a little more. "So how long's he going to wait for you? Five minutes? Ten on the outside?" Seconds ticked by in heartbeats and drips of sweat. "If you want out of this place, buddy, you're going to have to get through me."

Jack narrowed his eyes. "Fine." And charged.

Rafe reached for the Hunter, channeling energy through the clear crystal he always wore beneath his shirt. His senses flared into battle mode, adrenaline flooding his system. His eyesight sharpened. His hearing heightened. He met Jack's attack, shoving him in the chest with both hands. Jack flew back, skidding along the floor and crashing into a booth. His face hit the corner of the seat with a wet smack.

Rafe stalked down the aisle after him. The Hunter prowled in the back of his mind, not satisfied with just a taste. His muscles hummed with the strain it took to keep that side of himself at bay. He didn't want to hurt Jack if he could help it. He opened up a little more, let some of the raw power ripple along his flesh in a blatant show of intimidation. The crystal grew hotter against his chest. Maybe the old man would pick up the energy and back down.

Jack got to his feet, his gaze calculating as he wiped blood from his mouth. "Not bad, kid."

"Give it up, Jack. Don't make it harder than it has to be."

Jack curled his bleeding lip. "I never run from a fight."

Stubborn old man. Rafe flexed his fingers, hungry for a little carnage. Taking Jack down was starting to seem like a good idea. Was that his thought, or the Hunter's? Logic warred with raw instinct. "You won't win."

Jack flexed his shoulders. "I got a few tricks left."

"Yeah?" Rafe opened a little more, let the predator show in

the bared teeth of his smile, the narrowing of his eyes. "You haven't seen all mine yet, either."

The pickup outside revved its engine. Jack's eyes widened. Panic flared in his expression, and he whipped out a knife. "Get out of the way, Montana."

"Can't do that, Jack." The Hunter snapped at the leash, smelled the desperation in the air. Wanted to take down the prey—for good.

That would not, *could* not, happen. He was a civilized human being, damn it, not a wild animal. And blood always cost a price no one wanted to pay.

"I don't want to hurt you, kid."

Rafe saw the truth in his eyes. "Yes, you do. What you *don't* want is to do time for murder."

Jack blinked, then shrugged, his mouth curving with scorn. "Got me there. But I'll take the chance if it means getting out of here."

Truth.

Him or me. You know he'll kill you and not lose any sleep over it.

"Sorry, Jack." With no other choice, he unleashed the Hunter completely, the power surging through the crystal, overwhelming Rafe Montana, making him something different, something other. His mind winked out. . . .

. . . . .

He came back to himself with a snap, disoriented, worried, a little sick to his stomach. The crystal seared like a brand. How long had it been this time? Seconds? Minutes?

Jack lay on the floor, his face battered. His nose looked broken, blood seeping everywhere. The copper tang scented the air, filling Rafe's nose and lungs, coating his tongue. Slowly he removed his boot from Jack's throat, his heart pounding, his labored breathing straining his aching ribs. The knife lay on the floor several feet away.

No, no, not again. Bitter bile rose in his throat. He opened his clenched fists and crouched down, pressed battered, bleeding fingers to Jack's neck. Nearly keeled over when he felt the steady beat. Alive. He squeezed his eyes closed. Sent quiet thanks to the universe.

Outside, the screech of tires drew his attention. He rose and glanced out the window as the pickup peeled out of the parking lot. He blew out a slow breath and turned back to Jack. He had no beef with the *coyote,* not today.

A shuffle reminded him he wasn't alone. He turned to look at the waitress. She froze in her tracks, halfway around the counter with her purse over her shoulder. He didn't need any special powers to read the terror in her eyes.

Damn it. He'd forgotten she was there. He took a deep breath and tried to smile. "It's okay. Don't be afraid."

She drew back, wariness plain on her face. "I didn't see anything."

"I hope that's not true, ma'am." He reached into his pocket.

She screamed and crouched down, covered her head with her arms. "Don't shoot me! I won't say anything, really!"

"Hold on, hold on." He yanked out his ID and held it up. "It's just my wallet. Look, I'm a bail enforcement agent, and this man is a wanted fugitive."

She peeked out between her arms, then slowly lowered them as she straightened. "What do you mean, bail enforcement agent?"

He shook his head, blamed Hollywood. "A bounty hunter. This is my ID. I'm one of the good guys."

She tilted her head, considering him. "A real life bounty hunter, like on TV?"

"Yes. Like I said, I have ID. And my gun is still holstered."

She gave a cynical laugh. "Pal, from what I saw, you don't need no gun."

He ignored the whisper of self-loathing that curled in his gut at the distrustful way she watched him. Very few had witnessed the Hunter in full action, and she seemed a little freaked. But he didn't know how long Jack would stay out, and his cuffs had slid under the table during the fight. He had to take care of business before the burnout kicked in. Already his legs trembled with the beginning of the reaction.

You never got something for nothing in this world, and the price he paid for full-throttle Hunter equaled total physical shutdown for about twelve hours. He needed to get Jack in custody, and he needed her help to do it . . . before she had another unconscious body on the floor.

"Look—" He paused, flashed her an expectant glance.

"Vivian," she offered.

"Vivian," he echoed with a smile. "This guy is going to wake up eventually. You saw him pull a knife on me, right?"

She nodded.

"He's dangerous, and I need to get him cuffed so he can't hurt anyone. You can help me out by calling the cops while I do that."

She considered for a moment longer, then nodded. "Okay. But you stay over there, got it? I don't need you doing some crazy ninja moves on me like you did on that guy. I've never seen anything like it." Her voice quivered, and he could see the doubt in her eyes as she remembered what had happened earlier. "I sure hope you're the good guy you say you are."

So do I. He smiled, trying to project reassurance. "Thank you, Vivian. I appreciate the help." He ducked beneath the table and stood up again, holding the handcuffs where she could see them. "I'm going to cuff old Jack here, and you can call the police for me."

"Guess a bad guy wouldn't want the police, huh?" She went behind the counter, dumped her purse on the Formica and picked up the phone. Then she paused, her finger poised above the buttons. "So . . . you got a name or badge number or something I should give them?"

"My name is Rafe Montana." He grabbed Jack's arms and snapped the cuffs in place. "And Vivian, make sure you tell them we're going to need an ambulance."

"Sure thing."

As Rafe straightened, the diner tilted, then steadied. He groped for a booth, half fell into the seat. Vivian's voice seemed to increase in volume as she reported the incident to the cops, though he knew she wasn't shouting. Then the handset hit the cradle like a sonic boom. The ancient vinyl beneath him creaked like thunder as he started to slump into it. The crystal around his neck faded to warm, then cool.

"Hey, Rafe Montana, you all right?" Her voice scraped like sandpaper over his whacked-out senses.

"No," he muttered, shading his eyes against the suddenly blinding fluorescent lights. "I'm not."

Burnout slammed over him.

CHAPTER TWO

"I won the pool."

Cara McGaffigan frowned, pressing her cell phone closer to her ear as she dragged her wheeled carry-on down the airport Jetway. Already the desert heat of Nevada had turned the enclosed passageway into an oven despite the air conditioning, and she was baking in her jeans and sweatshirt. It had been chilly and raining when she'd left New Jersey. "What pool?"

Maisie, her friend and coworker, chuckled. "The one where we bet how long it would be after you landed before you called the office. I won."

Cara stopped. Passengers pushed past her, and she automatically moved to the side, out of the way of traffic. "Are you kidding me?"

"Nope. I am now eighty dollars richer, thank you very much."

Cara sighed, rubbing her temple. She'd been up since four in the morning and hadn't slept a wink on the plane. "Am I really so predictable?"

"You are to me, but only because I'm your best buddy in the whole world."

A businessman rushed by, jostling her. She scowled after him, then began moving forward again. "Then I guess the margaritas are on you next time we head over to Don Jose's."

"You got it." Maisie's tone grew more serious. "So you're in Las Vegas. Now what?"

"Get my luggage. Get a cab to Danny's place."

"Are you sure it's okay to crash there? I mean, I know Danny is your stepbrother and all—"

"Practically blood," Cara reminded her.

"I know. But is it safe? He's been missing for a while now. What if he was running away from someone, and whoever it is comes looking at his apartment while you're staying there?"

Nothing she hadn't thought of herself. Her throat grew tight. Her stepbrother had been missing for almost three weeks already, but despite the ominous implications, she couldn't *not* come, even though the plane ticket had cost her more than she could really afford. She'd put up her condo for his bail, and now he'd disappeared. She'd find him. She had to. "It's cheaper than staying at a hotel, and Danny might come back. Don't worry, Maisie. I won't do anything stupid."

"Like you ever do. Did you bring the pepper spray I gave you?"

"Yes, it's in my luggage."

"Make sure you put it in your purse the minute you get a chance."

"Yes, Mom."

"Ha-ha. Listen, I care about you."

"I know." The sincerity in Maisie's words brought a lump to her throat. She let out a shaky breath. Her emotions had been skating close to the surface these past few days. She had to keep it together, at least until she got to Danny's place. Then she could lose it . . . when she was alone.

"Cara? You still there?"

"Yeah." She glanced past the bank of slot machines in the middle of the terminal—such a weird sight—spotted the sign

21

for baggage claim, and started in that direction. "Sorry, I'm really beat. I was up before the sun this morning."

"I bet. Listen, I was thinking. You sure Danny didn't just hit the jackpot and take off for Fiji or something? That would be like him."

"You're right. It would." Despite the grim circumstances, her mouth curved as she thought of her stepbrother—always out for the bigger, better, flashier, get-rich-quickest way to anywhere.

"So that's it then. He's living it up on some tropical island and just forgot to tell you."

"I doubt it. He would have called. Especially since August nineteenth has come and gone." The lump in her throat grew bigger, and she struggled to keep her voice even. "He would never miss that, no matter how big the jackpot." *And I refuse to believe he'd skip out and let me lose my condo.*

"You're right. I'm so sorry, Cara."

Maisie's sympathetic tone almost destroyed Cara's fragile control. With relief, she noticed that the baggage claim signs stopped at a monorail. "Listen, I have to get on a train to get to baggage claim, and I'll probably lose the signal."

"Okay. Keep me posted."

"I will."

"Oh, just one more thing." Maisie paused. "Warren came back today."

Her gut tensed. "Oh, yeah?"

"Yeah. He was not pleased to find out you'd taken a leave of absence."

Too bad. "I talked to Mitch, explained it was a family emergency."

"And since the three of you are partners, it shouldn't be a big deal, I know. But I still get the feeling he's ticked off about it." Maisie lowered her voice. "I think he promised you would do a custom job for that new client, the Kirby Company. You know, personally."

"He knows he's not supposed to promise things like that. Things don't always work out." *Like our engagement.*

"I agree," Maisie replied. "Family comes first. And Mr. Big-Shot Salesman should know that. I mean, he's certainly living that philosophy. He handed out invitations to Ashley's baby shower today—personally! Can you believe that?"

Cara couldn't answer past the clog in her throat. She visualized Warren's wife—five years younger and nearly eight months' pregnant. *That should have been me.*

"Cara? Cara, you still there? Oh, man, I shouldn't have mentioned that. I'm really sorry. I was just so astonished by his gall."

"It's okay, Maisie." She took a calming breath. "I don't have time to think about Warren right now. I have to concentrate on Danny."

"That's a girl. Listen, keep me posted, okay?"

"I will. Thanks, Maisie. You're the best."

"Remember that the next time I need you to watch my dog." With a laugh, Maisie disconnected.

Cara shook her head as she slipped her phone into her bag. What would she have done without Maisie, especially during the past year when she had struggled to work side by side in the same company with the fiancé who'd rejected her? The same fiancé who'd promptly married their hot young receptionist Ashley and gotten her pregnant within two months of marriage?

Cara had always longed for a family of her own, and she'd thought she'd found that with Warren. Knowing he'd used her to get partnership in the company, then dropped her to marry someone younger and prettier, had hit her confidence hard. But Ashley getting pregnant so soon—and trumpeting it all over the office—had decimated her fragile self-esteem to ash. Maisie and her Friday-night margaritas had gotten her through the worst of the nightmare. Ashley had eventually quit her job to be a full-time mom, so at least Cara wouldn't have to watch her bloom with child with each passing day.

And be reminded of what she'd lost.

But Danny was missing, and her problems with Warren shrank in comparison. It was good to have something else to focus on. Her instincts screamed that her stepbrother was in trouble, big trouble, and that she might be the only one who could—or rather, would—help him. She'd learned to listen to her intuition, and now she just prayed that she was in time to bail Danny out of whatever mess he'd gotten into.

And that his latest fiasco wouldn't cost her the last living member of her family.

Las Vegas was Danny's kind of town, an adult playground that encouraged the breaking of rules and the shedding of restrictions. A place of luck and risk—not her style at all. She needed her rules, her habits. She'd never had any interest in Sin City, even for a vacation. The idea of losing her hard-earned money to pure chance didn't really appeal. But Danny? He'd thrived on the thrill.

He'd messed up this time, gotten arrested, and she'd bailed him out yet again, this time literally. But this disappearing act? She couldn't believe he would let her lose her condo, leave her homeless. He was irresponsible, not cruel.

The monorail arrived, and she shuffled onto the car with the rest of the crowd, finding a corner with a handrail. The train jolted into motion, shooting out of the terminal into the bright, alien landscape of Nevada.

Back east, September signaled the change of the seasons, and soon the flame of maple leaves turning orange or yellow or red, the advent to cooling temperatures. Here in the desert, the dry, stark heat of September signaled high summer and made a hundred degrees Fahrenheit sound like a pleasant memory.

Compared to the lush greenery of western New Jersey, the Nevada landscape stretched beige and barren, an emptiness that echoed across her throbbing emotions. The only green here came from the palm trees lined up along the walkways and roads; otherwise earth-toned houses and businesses clustered together amid miles of vast, open sand. Jagged mountains in every shade of brown and tan rose in the distance, the famous Las Vegas strip glittering in front of them, all luxury hotels and snazzy casinos.

She blew out a long breath. "Definitely not in Kansas anymore."

The shuttle ride took only minutes. She got off with the rest of the crowd and made her way to baggage claim. As she scanned the wide area for her carousel number, she spotted a dark-haired man holding a sign with her name on it.

What the . . . ? She hadn't called for a limo. She'd set aside those luxuries after the drop in the stock market a few years back had eaten up most of her available cash. Heck, she'd even had to take a pay cut to keep her small computer consulting company afloat. Her budget for this trip sure didn't include a luxury like a limo or rental car. It was cabs or walking for her, and Danny's apartment instead of a hotel.

Maybe someone at the office had set this up? Well, it wouldn't take more than a moment to clear up the misunderstanding.

She walked up to the guy, noticing as she got closer that he looked more like a successful businessman than a limo driver. He was attractive in a sleek, urban sort of way, and his suit seemed way too well cut to have been bought off the rack. She stopped in front of him. "Hi. I'm—"

"Cara McGaffigan?" He smiled, a quick flash of ultra-white teeth in an olive-toned face. "My name is Adrian Gray. I work at the Mesopotamian Resort. Mr. Bartow sent me to pick you up."

"Bartow? Artie Bartow?" She took a step back. The guy's hundred-watt smile and silky baritone overwhelmed her—the same feeling she got every time she walked through a department store and a salesperson ambushed her with a spritz of perfume. "Why would Danny's old boss send someone to pick me up? And how did you know I was coming, anyway?"

"We called your office. Why don't we collect your luggage?" He swept a hand toward the baggage carousels.

Called her office? Why hadn't Maisie said anything?

"Look, I appreciate the offer, but I'd rather just catch a cab." She smiled, hoping her intense desire to flee didn't show in her face. "I can stop by and see Mr. Bartow later. Or maybe tomorrow."

Gray's smile didn't dim. "I understand your caution."

"Yeah, a girl can't be too careful these days." She darted her gaze around. Weren't there supposed to be security people in the airport?

"Mr. Bartow wants to talk to you about Danny, about joining forces to find him. Surely that's worth your time?"

"Joining forces? I'd think your boss would be really ticked off at my brother right now. Why would he want to join forces?"

"That's what he wants to discuss." Gray indicated the baggage carousels again. "I believe your flight is on number three."

"Listen, I'm not going with you, okay? I'm going to take a cab. If your boss wants to talk, I'll come to the resort to see him. Sorry you made the trip for nothing." She turned away.

That honeyed voice wrapped around her. "You will come with me to the resort."

A wave of dizziness swept over her. She shook her head to clear it. The early morning flight had really taken a lot out of her. What had she been saying? Oh, yeah. "Sure, I'll come with you to the resort."

Mr. Gray swept an arm toward the baggage carousels. "After you. Carousel number three."

Cara moved past him toward the carousels. "My bag is on number three."

He fell into step behind her. "Why should you pay for a cab when you can take the limo for free?" he murmured. "Let's get your bag and go see Mr. Bartow."

"I mean, why should I take a cab if you're offering a limo ride for free?" She stopped at carousel number three and smiled at him. "Let's grab my bag—the gray one, right there—and go see Mr. Bartow."

"My thoughts exactly." He snagged her suitcase, then steered her toward the exit.

. . . . .

Late-afternoon sun had colored the sky the pinks and oranges of imminent sunset when Rafe walked into Sal Fellone's bail bonds agency. He'd slept all day since apprehending Jack yesterday, and he'd cleared his frayed senses with a meditation before heading over.

"You don't look so bad for a guy who had to be taken away in an ambulance." Sal came out of his private office and held out a hand to Rafe. "Rumor is you and Jack about killed each other."

Rafe's mouth curled in a half smile as they shook hands. "You should see the other guy."

"I did, and he don't look so good." The balding Italian gave him a quick once-over. "Still, you look okay for someone who collapsed and had to spend a day in bed."

Rafe shrugged. "Sinus infection," he lied.

"Really?" Sal shook his head. "Those things will knock you on your ass."

"Yeah. That's exactly what happened." He glanced at the envelope in Sal's hand. "That for me?"

"Oh, yeah." Sal handed Rafe the envelope containing his fee. "Sucks that you had to be the one to bring in Jack."

"Someone had to." Without looking at the amount, Rafe folded the envelope and tucked it away in his shirt pocket. "How's he doing?"

"Out of the hospital. In custody waiting for his day in court. No bondsman's going to touch him after this fiasco."

"He made the choice." Even as he said the words, Rafe realized they had lost their potency. Not words to live by anymore. Just a fact.

The desperation and self-deception he'd seen in Jack's eyes last night had shaken him. Jack was right. Rafe lived and breathed the job, and if it were taken from him tomorrow, he would have nothing left, not even the motto that had gotten him through every case. But this was the life he had to live. He couldn't make the choice, simply because he didn't have one.

"So, you ready to go back to work? Or you need a couple more days to rest up?"

"Depends." Rafe grinned at the flash of alarm that flickered across Sal's face. "Don't panic, Sal. I'm fine. Got any hot ones?" He glanced at the pile of manila folders stacked on the desk of Sal's currently absent secretary, Darlene.

"Take a look." Sal waved a hand. "The open cases are right there. But I don't know if you'd call any of them hot."

Rafe shrugged. "Interesting then."

"Pal, with your record you can pull any case you want." The phone rang. "Damn it. The phone always goes nuts when Darlene's at lunch. Look through those files while I get this." He scooped up the phone. "Hello. Badda Bing Bail Bonds."

While Sal talked on the phone, Rafe settled on the corner of Darlene's desk and reached for the top file folder. He flipped it open to the mug shot and opened his newly charged senses. *Where is he?* The crystal warmed against his flesh. A color image formed in his mind of the skip snoring away in a tiny, weatherworn house. More information rippled in, gifts from the universe. The house was near Laughlin and belonged to the guy's girl-friend. The skip himself spent all day passed out drunk in front of the TV; it would take about thirty seconds to apprehend him. No challenge there. He tossed the file aside with a mental note to drop Sal a hint about the guy's location. He sorted through the stack, discarding several more as too easy, a black-and-white vision as dead, and setting aside two others as possibilities. Opened another, looked at the photo.

Nothing. His mind stayed blank.

Where is he? He stared harder at the face of the alleged car thief, gazing deeply into the dark eyes that looked so guileless in the police mug shot. But nothing changed.

What the hell? He'd never before looked at a photo or person and seen *nothing*—except with his own family. What was wrong with him?

He scanned the information in the file, anxious to see any hint of a vision. Name, address, phone number, employment record, next of kin—

The image roared into his mind like an ocean wave. It was a woman, with eyes like melted caramel and honey-colored hair that curled in a ponytail. She was dressed in a simple shirt and jeans, but the way she filled out the clothes snagged his interest and would not let it go. She smiled, beckoning to him, a hint of mischief in her eyes. *Come with me. Let me make you whole.*

The vision shimmered and dissolved like smoke, and he found himself staring at her name in the file: Cara McGaffigan. Relationship: stepsister. He glanced back at the picture of her stepbrother. Still nothing. What was going on here?

He tensed his fingers around the manila folder before shutting it, blocking out the unresponsive face of Danny Cangialosi. He should shake this off, leave the case for someone else, but he couldn't force himself to set the file down on the pile of discards.

Sal hung up the phone. "Something wrong, Rafe?"

"No. Nothing's wrong." Rafe hesitated a moment, then tossed the file on top of the other, more lucrative skips he had chosen to bring in. Who was this guy? And why could he see the stepsister but not the fugitive?

Sal glanced at the name on the file tab. "Danny Cangialosi? Isn't that a little small time for you, man?" He eyed Rafe, one bushy brow raised.

"Maybe I need an easy one after Jack." Rafe scooped up the short stack of files.

"But Danny Cangialosi?" Sal gave a laugh. "You'll get paid beans on that one, pal."

Rafe tucked the file folders under his arm. "Money's money."

Sal shrugged. "You're the best agent I got, Rafe. You wanna chase down small time, knock yourself out."

"Thanks, Sal. This is why we work so beautifully together." He offered his hand.

"Come back when you want some real work." Sal shook his hand, then turned back toward his private office, chuckling.

Rafe headed for the exit, eager to be alone. His abilities had never failed him before, not once. He was a Seer, descended from an ancient line. His talents came to him as easily as breathing. Why now?

You know why.

The idea seized hold and would not let go. He had known all those years ago that abandoning his birthright was a risk, but over time he had become confident that as long as he continued to observe most of the ancient customs, he would be okay. Besides, he had good reasons for what he had done.

But now . . . Maybe there was something wrong with his powers, maybe a delayed consequence of that rash choice to walk away from his family and never look back. Maybe because he'd been making money from using those powers, a big no-no in the family tradition, even though he brought in the bad guys. Or maybe he'd been gone from his own kind for so long that his powers were disintegrating. He didn't know enough about how it all worked. He was supposed to have completed the Soul Circle when he was twenty-four, but he'd left before he could finish training for the ritual.

Was he losing his gifts? If so, then what would he do? Would he end up like Jack, alone and bitter?

He reached for the handle of the door and nearly bumped into Darlene as she came in from the street.

"Rafe! You scared me. I was just coming back from lunch." Darlene smiled at him, her blue eyes innocent as a babe's.

Truth. He could see it in her eyes, plain as day. The ability to see the truth was a gift that every Seer had—and one that was apparently still working for him.

Some of the tension drained out of him. He hadn't lost the old superpowers after all. He could still tell lies from truth, and he'd been able to locate the other skips in the files without a problem. He'd seen the stepsister, for whatever reason, though he preferred not to think too much about that provocative vision. So why the big blank screen for a small-time punk like Danny Cangialosi?

The only way to know, it seemed, was to find him.

· · · · ·

Cara clenched her fingers around her purse, then looked Artie Bartow straight in the eye with what she hoped was calm inquiry. Her energy flagged from both the five-hour plane ride and the hundred-plus degree heat. She wasn't sure how she'd ended up in the limo—she distinctly remembered saying no— but nearly half an hour ago she'd climbed out of the luxury car in front of the Mesopotamian Resort and Casino with Adrian Gray walking beside her to his boss's office.

Jet lag dragged at her. All she wanted right now was to head to Danny's place and crash, but she was here already, so she might as well take the opportunity to get some answers to questions she'd intended to ask anyway.

"Let me get this straight, Mr. Bartow," she said. "You're the one who had Danny arrested, and now you want to find him since he skipped his court date?"

The resort owner nodded. He flattened his hands on the desk, his pudgy face creasing into an expression of sympathy. "I'm sorry you have to hear the sordid details this way, Miss McGaffigan. I had high hopes for Danny. Thought he would go far. Didn't I, Mr. Gray?"

Her tall, dark-haired escort from the airport stood near the closed door of Bartow's luxurious office and nodded, arms folded in front of him. His smile had disappeared once the door shut behind them, and his sober gaze never shifted from Cara. The tailored suit he wore made him look like the cover of a fashion magazine, but it also emphasized his powerful, athletic build. Though she longed for a shower and change of clothes, he had somehow convinced her with just a few words to go see Bartow immediately rather than continue on to Danny's apartment.

Now he stood across the room, looking much less charming. The mantle of danger around him made her think he could move fast as a snake and be just as deadly—though neither of these guys struck her as Eagle Scout candidates, especially since they'd somehow talked her into coming here when she'd had no intention of doing any such thing.

Why *had* she allowed him to bring her here? That piece of the puzzle still eluded her.

She focused on Bartow again—short, chubby, and balding. Her stepbrother's boss. Or at least he had been before Danny had stupidly borrowed the man's Lamborghini, been arrested, and then jumped bail. Casinos didn't keep criminals on the payroll, and Danny had crossed the line. But now he was gone without a trace.

She knew it had to be bad, whatever he was into. Nothing but death or the threat of it would have kept him away from New Jersey on August nineteenth, the anniversary of their parents' accident. And she refused to believe he was dead.

"Miss McGaffigan," Bartow said, bringing her attention back to the present. "All we want now is for Danny to turn himself in, for this whole terrible ordeal to be over."

"That's what I want, too."

"Of course you do." Bartow spread his hands, grinning with all the congeniality of Marlon Brando playing Santa Claus. "That's why we've offered to have you stay at our beautiful Mesopotamian Resort and Casino, courtesy of the management. Perhaps your stepbrother will contact you, and you can convince him to do the right thing."

The right thing? She glanced from one man to the other. Whatever Danny was into had probably started right here, with the manager of the Mesopotamian Resort and his well-dressed watchdog. Her instincts told her they had some sort of ulterior

motive for having her stay at the hotel. That there was something else going on here.

A cold knot gripped her stomach. Was she bait in a trap to
catch Danny?

Bartow apparently took her silence as assent. "Is there anything we can do to make your stay with our hotel more comfortable? Anything you want, on the house."

"No, thank you. I won't be staying. I have other plans." Her
instincts urged her to flee, but Cara calmly got to her feet, fingers clenched around her purse. "It's been a long day. I appreciate your time, Mr. Bartow."

Bartow stood as well and came around his massive desk. His
head reached her chin as he stopped in front of her. "I hope your
stepbrother contacts you soon. Not knowing is the worst, in my
opinion."

Uncertain how to reply, she just nodded, then shook his prof-
fered hand. His fingers tightened around hers with surprising
strength as he looked up at her. His eyes were dark and small
and all but lost in the plump flesh of his face. For a moment, she
felt as if she were looking into the gaze of a reptile. Unnerved,
she broke the contact between them; a shower appealed even
more now. "Good-bye, Mr. Bartow. Thank you for your time."

"Miss McGaffigan," he said with a nod. "Mr. Gray will see
you out."

The unsettling Mr. Gray opened the door to the office for her.
"Good day, Miss McGaffigan." He touched her arm as she made
to walk through. "You should stay here at the hotel. Why not? It's
free. You can go to Danny's apartment after you check in."

The world tilted as a wave of dizziness hit. His voice seemed
to come from a long way away, his suggestion wrapping through
her consciousness like smoke. Then everything cleared.

She shook her head. Wow, the stress of all this must be worse than she thought. Now what had she been doing? Oh, that's right. Checking into the hotel. Might as well, since the room was free. Once she'd checked in, she could head over to Danny's place and see if there were any clues to where he'd gone.

With a nod at Mr. Gray, she left Bartow's office and headed for the elevator.

. . . . .

"Do you think she knows anything?" Bartow asked, watching the woman punch the elevator button through the glass wall of his office.

"I'm not certain." Adrian Gray turned away from the hallway where Cara McGaffigan had just disappeared. She'd looked younger than he'd expected.

Bartow paced the room, twisting his fingers together. "I need to get it back, Gray. My numerologist said this is going to be a very unlucky year for me. The Stone is rumored to bring good luck to the possessor."

"So you've said."

"I need the luck to stay in business."

"I understand."

"Damn that kid! How did he know how to get into the safe? Or even that I had the Stone?" Bartow swiped his hand over his face. "I would never have figured Cangialosi had the smarts or the connections to steal it right out from under me." He jerked his head up, his expression approaching panic. "We have to get it back! I'll be ruined if we don't!"

"We'll get it back." Adrian held Bartow's gaze, concentrated. "You aren't going to worry. You're going to leave this to me."

Bartow smiled, tension evaporating from his body like rising steam. "I'm not going to worry. I'm leaving this to you. Security is your job, right?"

"Yes, security is my job."

"So I'm not going to worry," Bartow repeated. "I'll leave this to you." He waved a dismissive hand and returned to his desk chair, hitting a couple of keys on his computer to bring up a screen of financials.

Adrian waited a beat, but Bartow didn't look up. He left the office, his boss buried in reports. The Cangialosi thing might have blown up in his face, but at least he still had Bartow under firm control.

He wouldn't lose command of the situation again.

CHAPTER THREE

Rafe sat at the red light, tapping his fingers on the steering wheel of his SUV. The whole deal with Danny Cangialosi was chafing at him like sand in his shorts. Ever since he could remember, he'd always gotten his man. His gift had never failed him before.

For one moment, he wished he could ask someone about it. But the only people who would understand would be his family, and that wasn't an option. Nope, he was on his own.

Better that way anyway.

The light turned green, and he sailed through it, flicking on his signal to turn into the parking lot of Cangialosi's apartment. With his superpowers out of the picture on this one, he was going to have to track this guy down the old-fashioned way. It would be good for him. Challenging.

Ha. Even he didn't believe it. But he'd do what he could with the tools available. He parked the car and climbed out, then glanced around.

The complex wasn't nearly the dump he had expected, but it wasn't brand new, either. No security to speak of, but not exactly roach central. Cangialosi's file flagged his place as unit twelve, so he made his way over there and stopped before the weathered front door. He swept a hand over the top of the doorframe. His fingers snagged on something sticky. He fumbled around, got a grip on the edge of what felt like tape, and pulled. A piece of duct tape ripped loose, and stuck to it was a key.

Don't have to be psychic for that one. Oldest trick in the book.

Moments later he was standing in Cangialosi's living room.

The place smelled like a Dumpster. According to the file, this guy had been MIA for about three weeks. According to the crusted food on the dishes in the sink, the file was right. The answering machine blinked with fifteen messages.

Quietly, he closed the door and began looking for clues as to where Mr. Cangialosi might be hiding.

* * * * *

What a weird day.

Cara stepped out of the apartment manager's office and walked over to her stepbrother's unit. The complex wasn't the best-kept place in the world, a far cry from her sweet little condo in Western New Jersey. The desert sun seemed to weather buildings faster out west, which was probably why the paint was peeling and the shrubs looked dried up and yellow. It really wasn't that bad; after all, she'd planned to stay here to save money before she ended up in a free room at the Mesopotamian. She still wasn't sure how that had all happened. Not that she minded the swanky hotel; she just didn't want to be beholden to Artie Bartow, especially if he had something to do with Danny's disappearance. Yet for some reason she'd meekly checked into the hotel and hadn't really come out of whatever fog she'd been in until she'd unpacked her suitcases.

Must be more tired and stressed out than I thought. Jet-lagged, too.

She searched out unit twelve. If she knew her stepbrother, there were probably more dishes in the sink than in the cupboard and nothing but old Chinese containers in the fridge.

Maybe she would straighten up the place while she searched for clues to what had happened to him.

Walking toward the door, she dug in her pocket for the key the landlord had given her just now when she'd paid Danny's overdue rent. She hadn't counted on spending that much money—this trip was supposed to be on a shoestring budget—but she couldn't let Danny's place get rented out from under him, even if he had skipped bail and left her own living space in jeopardy. She'd give him an earful when he came back. She could hear the conversation now; she'd try to scold and he would thank her for helping him, giving her those puppy-dog eyes and that lopsided smile. Probably swear to pay her back, too, though she doubted she would ever see a dime. Still, whenever he said he wanted to pay her back, she knew he meant it. It just never seemed to happen.

But he was family, and family looked out for one another.

She started to slide the key in the lock, then paused. The door wasn't quite closed. It stood open a crack.

Had Danny come home? She nearly bolted through the door, then paused. What if it was someone else? Someone who was after Danny? As quietly as she could, she reached into her purse and pulled out the pepper spray that she had shoved in the bag before heading over. Fingers trembling, she eased open the door and silently stepped into the living room.

A man stood by the answering machine listening to Danny's messages. Half of them were from her, and it was weird hearing her own voice pleading with Danny to pick up the phone, to call. Luckily the intruder was busy listening, fast forwarding, listening again, so the hushed whisper of her approach appeared to escape him. He had his back to her, a tall guy with powerful shoulders in a khaki-colored shirt. His sleeves were rolled up to his elbows, exposing tanned, solid forearms. His hair was dark brown, and he wore jeans and black boots. From the trim rear end and the flex of his back muscles beneath the shirt, he looked to be in really great shape. Which meant he might be fast, might be strong. She made a note to stay out of arm's reach as she lifted the little can and pointed it at him.

"That's not necessary," he said without turning his head.

She blinked in surprise, then steadied. "Turn around."

He obeyed slowly, hands spread at mid-chest. "Cara, right?"

She didn't know what surprised her more, that he knew her name or the jolt of stark attraction that nearly knocked her off her feet when she caught sight of his face.

Piercing cobalt eyes, sharp with intelligence, seemed to look right through her. Strong nose, bladelike cheekbones—Native American in there somewhere, she decided—and a mouth that swept into a wicked grin à la Dennis Quaid. He had a great tan, so he either lived in a tanning salon or was a Vegas native.

"Who are you?" she demanded. "What are you doing here?"

"My name is Rafe Montana. I'm looking for Danny. I'm a bail enforcement agent." At her blank look, he qualified. "A bounty hunter."

She frowned. "You don't look like a bounty hunter."

"Maybe if you took those sunglasses off, you would see me better."

She'd forgotten she had them on. No wonder it was so darned dark in the house. Then he took a step forward, and she came to attention. "Bounty hunter, huh? Like a guy who chases down bail jumpers? Who's going to bail you out when I have you arrested for breaking and entering?"

He halted and reached toward his back jeans pocket. "I can show you my license."

"Hey, hey—hold it right there. Hands out of the pockets."

She gestured with the pepper spray and hoped he didn't notice her trembling. "Maybe I should just call the cops and let them sort this out."

"Go ahead." Dropping his hands to his sides, he took another step. "They know I'm here. It's all legal."

"Hey! Stay right there and I won't have to use this."

"Calm down. I'm not going to hurt you. When's the last time you heard from Danny?"

"None of your business."

He sighed. "Didn't you hear what I said? I find people for a living."

"Maybe." Her heart pounded, her mouth dry. "All I know is that you broke into my stepbrother's place."

"I could hand you the phone, and you could call the police. Clear this up."

"Or you could stay right there and I could use my cell." Trying to hold the pepper spray steady with one hand, she rummaged in her purse with the other, keeping her eye on him. Just as her fingers closed around the phone, he moved.

Anticipating a blow, she tried to fire the pepper spray, but he ducked beneath her outstretched arm and grabbed her from behind, pinning her arms. He jerked her right off her feet, her back against his chest. Her purse and phone went flying. So did the pepper spray.

"Hey!" She struggled to pull her arms free. Damn, he was strong. And powerful. And determined, if his unrelenting grip was anything to go by.

"Easy," he said. "I told you I wouldn't hurt you, but with you waving that pepper spray around, I couldn't be sure you wouldn't hurt *me*."

"So you just picked me up off the floor? Great way to make me trust you."

"If I wanted to do something to you, Cara, I could have done it at any time. The pepper spray wouldn't have stopped me."

His voice lowered at the end, almost sexy, triggering a curling warmth between her legs. Holy Hannah, was she getting turned on by the bad guy?

Unnerved by the unexpected—unwanted—attraction, she jerked her head backward and connected with what felt like his chin. She saw stars but was rewarded when he grunted, and his grip around her arms loosened for a second. She jerked free, but he grabbed her shirt and they both went down.

As soon as she hit the carpet, she scrambled forward on her hands and knees. Where was the pepper spray? Had it slid under the coffee table? But he caught her ankle and yanked her flat on her belly. Before she could right herself, he was looming over her on all fours, trapping her. For an instant his hips pressed against her rear. Her stomach did a little flip at the intimate position, muscles trembling with a sudden burst of arousal. He flipped her onto her back, then pinned her down in a primitive move that male had used on female since the beginning of time.

His face looked like stone, his body a cage of lean, hard muscle. He smelled of citrus and sandalwood and fabric softener. Heat swept through her limbs, warmed her belly.

No way. She wasn't going there. She didn't care how good he smelled.

"Let me up." She bucked her hips, trying to dislodge him, and shoved at his shoulders. Her palms tingled at the contact.

"No." He grabbed her hands and pinned them to the floor above her head, then shifted to manacle one hand around both her wrists. "You're not playing nice, Cara."

"Miss McGaffigan to you." The position arched her back, giving her way more cleavage than she had ever intended in her yellow V-neck shirt. He didn't even glance down.

"You can call me Rafe." He yanked off the sunglasses that sat crookedly on her face and tossed them aside. "Let's see what's going on with you."

· · · · ·

Rafe tried to ignore the soft female body beneath his. Tried to pretend he didn't notice how her hips cradled him. Or the way the neckline of her shirt pulled down to reveal a glimpse of really nice breasts and a peek of white lace bra. How her feminine scents called to him, cinnamon and vanilla and something elusive— something *her*—that teased him with possibilities.

The Hunter stirred, lured by the presence of female. Hungry after the most recent burnout. Curious after the vision he'd had of her at Sal's office.

No. This is business.

He shoved the beast back. Once he had regained control, he tilted up her chin with one hand and gazed long and hard into her face.

Her eyes were amber brown and full of annoyance and fear. For a moment he got lost there, lured into warm, sweet caramel. The promise of sex shimmered on the edges of his mind. Then the vision slammed into him like a bullet.

Murder. Death.

Cara's broken body lying at the side of a desert road, her eyes staring sightlessly at the sky as a vehicle burned nearby—he couldn't tell what make or color. There was too much smoke, too much destruction. And the vision was in black and white.

The pain, the grief, slammed him in the gut as the emotions of the future rushed over him. *Death. Murder.* No, no, no. Not Cara. An innocent pawn in an evil game. Used and discarded. A bright light extinguished for greed and power.

The tinny notes of "Rebel Yell" broke the spell.

The connection snapped. Rafe shoved himself off her, breathing hard. He lay there on his back for a second, staring at the ceiling, waiting for the anguish to subside. Cara rolled over and scrabbled across the floor for the cell phone. As she grabbed it, he sat up so he could watch her while he tried to get his equilibrium back. He knew everything about her now, too damned much. Things like she didn't intend to use the pepper spray on him unless threatened, so there was no harm in her answering the call.

But he didn't want to know that she was going to be murdered. He didn't want to be sucked in again, Rafe the do-gooder, using his superpowers to save the world. That was his family's mission, and he had left them to it years ago. He got paid to use his powers now, and he'd sworn he would never go back to the hero gig again. Hadn't Jack's betrayal taught him anything? He was better off sticking it out alone and unaffected.

But here he was, lured by the siren song of an innocent in trouble.

He *knew*—knew with all the certainty that he knew anything—that if he let himself get sucked into this, he'd get too close. He wouldn't be able to avoid it. The vision of her earlier all but confirmed it. He'd known Cara for five minutes and was already drawn to the sweet soul he sensed. He should run like hell.

But he couldn't stand back and just let her die. Damn it.

Cell in hand, Cara sat on the floor Indian-style and flipped open the phone. "Danny?"

Danny.

She met his gaze, then averted her own.

Good. Look away. Don't look in my eyes, remind me of what I saw in yours, of what I have to do.

Listening as she again repeated her stepbrother's name, he

searched the area for the damned sunglasses. Great idea, genius. Take off her glasses, gaze into her eyes. Find out who she really is inside.

Dead. That's what she was, unless he did something about it.

"Danny, I've been so worried. Where—" Pause. "But—"

He stretched out an arm and scooped the glasses off the floor, then got to his feet and took them over to her. As he dropped them in her lap, he avoided looking into those golden brown eyes again.

"Of course I came looking for you." She lowered her voice, snagging the sunglasses without glancing at them. "Look, you have to come back. My condo—" Silence. "Your old boss called me. He said— I'm staying at the Mesopotamian— I will *not* go home. *You* come home. Danny. Danny!" She pulled the phone from her ear and scowled at it. "Crap." Then she snapped it closed and looked up at him.

He focused on her nose, her chin, anywhere but her eyes. "He's alive, then."

"Yes, thank God." She blew out a huge sigh, then frowned down at her phone display. "He's alive, but something terrible must have happened to make him run away like this."

"So you know your stepbrother is okay. That's good news. Now stay out of the way and let the pros handle the rest." *And don't get killed.*

"Pros like you, Mr. Bounty Hunter?" She got to her feet and glared at him, shoving the phone in the pocket of her jeans and hooking the sunglasses in the neckline of her shirt.

He let out a long breath. "It's Rafe, and yes."

"Let's see this ID you were talking about." Wordlessly, he pulled out his wallet and displayed his bail enforcement license. "Looks legit, but what do I know?"

"You know I could have hurt you and didn't." *But someone would, soon.*

"Maybe you need me. Maybe you have to pump me for information or something." She lifted her chin in a clear challenge, her body tense.

Something, indeed. The air between them still hummed with tension.

He shoved his wallet back in his pocket. "You watch too much TV. Did Danny say where he was?"

"See? I knew you needed me for interrogation."

"For Pete's sake!" He focused on her shirt, on the sunglasses that could save his sanity. The cotton fabric clung to her curves in a way he couldn't help but notice. She was no showgirl but had handful-sized breasts and curvy hips that sure packed a punch.

And he had to focus on business. "I need anything you can tell me that will help me find him and bring him back."

"Maybe I'd tell you if you didn't stare at my boobs like that."

"I'm not." Idiot. Of course he had been. He was so damned shaken up by that vision that he was losing his usual discipline. The Hunter jerked at the leash again, wanting to touch her, taste her.

No way. He didn't need that complication on top of everything else.

Forcing his thoughts to business, he glanced around, spotted her purse and the pepper spray, and picked them both up off the floor. He saw her stiffen out of the corner of his eye. Rather than look at her, he called up an image in his head by asking himself where she was and getting the picture as if handed a photo. This way, he could look at her as long as he liked in his mind, just the way he had when she had come into the apartment. It had been pure luck that he had happened to wonder where Cara of the messages was, conjuring her image just as she came in behind him armed with pepper spray.

"What are you going to do with that?" she demanded.

He tossed the purse in her direction. "Here."

She caught it and hooked it over her shoulder. "And the pepper spray?"

"I'll just hang on to that."

"The hell you will!"

"Deal with it. What did Danny say?"

Guarded again, she narrowed her eyes. "None of your business."

This time he made himself look at her. Attraction still simmered, though the shadow of death hovered around the glow of her soul. But he didn't look away. He braced himself for the pain, but it did not come again. Still, that shadow mocked him. "I'll find him, Cara Mia McGaffigan. I'm good at what I do." He handed her the pepper spray. "Watch where you point that next time."

She took the can automatically, her lips parted in surprise. "How did you know my middle name? Did you check me out?"

He pulled out a business card and flipped it onto the coffee table. "Here's my number. Call me if you hear from Danny again."

"Hey!" She gaped as he turned and left the apartment, but he couldn't refrain from the abrupt exit. He should have asked her more questions about her stepbrother. Should have asked her the identities of the people in the photos he had seen scattered around Danny's place.

He should have convinced her to leave Vegas.

She was too sweet to have anyone mad enough to kill her, this soft-hearted girl from New Jersey. So it had to be her connection to Danny that did her in. If she went home, she would be away from the desert, away from whoever was after Danny, and the terrible vision he had seen might not come true.

Ironic how finding Danny was the key to the whole thing,

but that was the one area where his powers failed him. No visions of Danny. Too many visions of his stepsister.

He got behind the wheel of his car and pulled out of the parking lot. The more distance he put between him and her right now, the better he liked it. He would find Danny without her help. He knew where she was staying; she'd told Danny on the phone. And the mention of Artie Bartow made the whole thing stink even more. Artie had never been the philanthropic type. Nope, he was no doubt using the pretty stepsister as bait to get to Cangialosi.

Well, that was going to stop—as soon as Rafe got his bearings back. He would somehow convince Cara to go back to New Jersey, get her out of harm's way. Because if she stayed, he would have to protect her from that gruesome fate he had foreseen. And no way he was playing the hero again.

No way in hell.

CHAPTER FOUR

The next morning dawned as the sun peeked over the desert horizon, casting its infant glow over the city of Las Vegas.

Rafe sat in his *tenplu,* the place of worship and peace he had created in the backyard of his home. He had prepared everything according to the old ways, raking out the circle of sand to get rid of anything that might have blown into it, then carefully setting out his amplifying crystals on the seven flat stone pedestals arranged along the edge of the circle. Tumbled ruby, bright orange carnelian, yellow tiger eye. He held on to the dark green moss agate for a moment, allowing the crystal to vibrate along with his heart, before setting it in its place. Turquoise and tumbled sapphire followed. Amethyst. Then he waited for sunrise.

Clad only in a pair of running shorts, he sat in the middle of the circle, soles of his feet together, hands resting palms up on his bent legs. The sun rose higher in the sky. As the light slowly touched each stone in turn, power hummed to life. Rafe focused on clearing his mind, on breathing, on accepting. Time passed. The clear quartz hanging around his neck grew warm against his flesh as it absorbed and filtered the energy being cast by the other crystals, sweeping it through his own system. He was in a place where hours and minutes did not matter. His body soaked up the power like parched earth to rain.

Once a steady flow had been established, he opened his mind to Ekhia, the center of all life.

Tell me what I need to know.

He had expected some clue to the problem with Danny Cangialosi and his powers. Maybe something to do with the terrible vision he had seen in Cara's eyes. Instead, he got Cara all right. Naked. Opening to him. Welcoming him.

The sizzling sensuality of the vision swept over him, igniting his flesh, soaking into his essence and grabbing control with relentless mastery. His cock hardened instantly, nearly painful in its demand. He could see her so clearly, her nipples shades darker than her dusky skin, her hair flowing over her shoulders, her arms outstretched. Her legs parted, hinting at the warmth awaiting him, her smile sweet and enticing.

Home is where the heart is. Let me be your home.

"No." His voice sounded strangled. He pushed back with his mind, rejecting the vision. He didn't deserve a home. Didn't deserve what Cara offered. He was a loner. It was better for everyone that way.

"I invoke free will," he said. "Not her. Not now." His heart thundered in his chest. His body shuddered with raging desire. A desire that could not be sated. Not with Cara. He had to protect her from what he had seen. He wanted her to live. Which meant he had to stay objective.

That thought brought a change in energy. The vision of Cara melted away. Instead—gunshots. His mother crying out, running toward a doorway beneath his father's protective arm.

Someone had tried to kill her.

The flow of power faltered. His eyes flew open, his breath coming in pants as his pulse spiked. Was she okay? When had this happened?

Last night. She's unharmed. The answers came with a splutter of energy. He focused, balanced out his thoughts so the flow of power stabilized again. He could not risk a backlash.

Instinctively, he reached for his connection to the family. He could sense it, that bond that tied him to the rest of his blood. It was still there; no one had severed it. But where once a strong channel had flowed, now there was only a weak link that coughed and hesitated like a car with a bad carburetor.

"Damn it." Even as the epithet left his lips, the words caused the energy around him to flare with negative heat. He tamped down his annoyance and concentrated on clearing his mind, letting go of fear and frustration and methodically ending the ritual so that all energy released back to the earth in a natural and harmonious flow.

He would have to use the phone.

He stalked into the house. The telepathic connection had been part of him since birth. That it was so weak from disuse—by his own doing—burned him even more. Perhaps if he had stayed connected, he would not have found out about the danger to his mother after the fact.

Was this another indicator of his powers failing?

He snatched up his cell phone and punched out the number he knew by heart, praying they hadn't changed it.

"Hello?" Her voice was thready, shaky, but as dear to him as breath itself.

"Are you okay?" he demanded. His heart pounded, and he tightened his trembling fingers around the phone.

"Rafe?" Hope flavored her tone. "Rafe, is that you?"

Warmth bloomed in the region of his heart. He hadn't realized how much he had missed her voice. "Yes, Mama. It's me."

"Oh, my." A sharp inhalation. "Rafe. Oh, my."

He wished he could see her, to know with his own senses that she was all right. But his abilities had never worked on his family. Visions in the *tenplu* were one thing, gifted by Ekhia, but anything more than that never worked. That meant he needed to rely on simple conversation.

"Are you hurt?" he asked again, rougher than he intended. But he was losing it, desperate for confirmation that she was okay and just as desperate to get off the phone. It was so tempting to slide back into the family fold. Just act like everything was okay. But he couldn't. He was a danger to them, and one phone call couldn't change that.

"No, not hurt, just shaken up. It happened so fast, but I got a flash of danger for your father, so I stopped just in time."

He let out the breath he'd been holding. Thank the Creators for Mama's famous "flashes."

"Dad is right here. Do you—"

"No. I just called to make sure you were okay."

"But—"

"Bye, Mama." He disconnected the call and dropped the phone onto the granite counter. Then he slid to the floor, sitting with his back against the breakfast bar, as wobbly as if his knees had turned to putty. If anything had happened to her . . . He didn't want to even think about it.

But she was okay. Her instincts had saved her life.

He sucked in a long, slow breath. Dad had probably locked her up behind the walls of the compound. No one would get to her there. And his sister, Tessa, would be looking now, actively searching for the person who had put their mother in danger.

Provided her gifts weren't on the fritz like his.

He couldn't help a chuckle at the absurdity of the thought. Tessa must have completed her Soul Circle by now. And even if she hadn't, nothing could weaken or dampen Tessa's abilities. She, out of all of them, had the true powers of a full Seer. She was so strong that people often steered clear of her, put off by the all-knowing confidence of those unusual violet eyes—as if Tessa would read their minds and report their secrets to the tabloids.

But what else could you expect from a direct descendent of the most powerful Seer in Atlantis?

He had made it a policy long ago to steer away from the *A* word when thinking about his abilities. *He* knew the truth, but he had been schooled since birth to keep his heritage a secret. If anyone asked, he was part Native American and part Spanish. He just didn't mention that the Spanish part came from Agrilara, the lone survivor of Atlantis who had come ashore in what was now the Basque area of Spain thousands of years ago.

Agrilara was the reason why his family consistently produced members with brilliant blue eyes, no matter what culture they married into. The blue eyes bred true with the seeing gift and had done so every generation for thousands of years—except in the case of Tessa, who possessed the eerie violet eyes of a full Seer and all the awesome powers that came with it.

Everyone, gifted or not, walked cautiously around his baby sister. Except maybe Darius. Big brother had never been afraid of anything.

He let his head fall back against the solid wood of the breakfast bar. Five years he'd been away, but with the sound of his mother's voice, it seemed like just yesterday. He rubbed a hand over the center of his chest, across the ache that throbbed like a gaping hole. He could recall them all so clearly—good memories.

And bad. Unsteady, he climbed to his feet. That was all long ago. Another life.

But the present wasn't so hot, either. Not with his powers flickering like a faulty lightbulb, a sweet Jersey girl distracting him, and some wacko shooting at his mother.

He realized he was still trembling. Okay, time to get a hold of himself. He picked up the remote from his kitchen counter and pointed it over the breakfast bar at the TV in the living room. The news came on. Setting the device back on the counter, he got out a box of cereal. First he needed food, and then he would get dressed and go track down Danny Cangialosi. More than that, he needed to get back to Cara, to convince her to go home before that horrible image he had foreseen came true.

Maybe instead of puzzling over the instability of his powers, he should start concentrating on what he was given when they *were* working. Like it or not, he had been handed a vision of Cara's death, and it was up to him to do something about it.

The vision of her murder had shaken him. She was too nice a person, too soft-hearted—heck, just too damned cute for anyone to want to hurt her. She had to be tied into this mess her stepbrother was into, even if she didn't know it. And like it or not, Rafe had to protect her from the gory fate he had foreseen.

"Jain Criten, president of the island nation of Santutegi, delivers a speech today to the Association of International Agricultural Concerns at the Mesopotamian Resort in Las Vegas. He will be speaking about the challenges faced by smaller countries in today's agricultural market. The president arrived yesterday and has been enjoying the sights of the city."

Rafe glanced at the TV across the breakfast bar as the pleasant face of Jain Criten filled the screen. The dignitary looked to be in his late thirties, and his casual white suit with the pale yellow shirt made him seem cool, calm, and approachable in juxtaposition to the frantic pace of the airport behind him. His boyish grin invited the viewers to trust him. He wore his dark blond hair in a youthful style that waved back from his prominent forehead, and his green eyes appeared utterly sincere as he replied to a question from a reporter.

Just for the heck of it, Rafe focused on the face in front of him. Concentrated.

Nothing. Just like Danny.

"What the hell?" He set down the cereal box and leaned closer to the TV, but the story changed to a local fire. Frustration burned in his gut.

He yanked open the cabinet door to pull down a bowl. What in blazes was going on with his powers? They had never been so erratic before, always as reliable as the sunrise. He could look at a photo, at film coverage, or best of all, into a person's eyes face-to-face and see what he needed to know.

The only time his powers had not worked had been with his own family. Now suddenly, he couldn't read select people—people who were not related to him in the slightest. People who had nothing in common with each other.

What the hell was going on?

. . . . .

Cara couldn't help but yawn as she walked into the lobby of the Mesopotamian resort. She knew what she must look like—yesterday's clothes, no makeup, hair twisted up haphazardly in a ponytail. She had fallen asleep on Danny's couch last night and, boy, did she look it. She was surprised security didn't stop her as soon as she walked in the door.

The exclusive hotel complex known as the Mesopotamian Resort and Casino had been designed like an ancient city with huge columns of sandy stone enhanced by gleaming marble floors. Fountains graced the sprawling expanse of shops and restaurants, many adjacent to foliage that hid private grottoes with benches for lovers stealing a moment alone. The centerpiece was the huge ziggurat, a temple-like structure with a waterfall trickling down its steep stairs, set in a high-ceilinged lobby that mimicked the night sky. At the base of the ziggurat was the front desk, concierge stand, and bell station.

Bartow had spared no expense to transport his guests to the mystical world of the ancients, though on the other side of the zig-gurat was the entrance to the casino—a very modern setting with flashing lights and human cries of exaltation or dismay.

Cara wasn't a gambler. She worked too hard for her money to take the chance of losing it on the turn of a card or the spin of a wheel. Oh, she might drop a few coins into a slot machine, but she wasn't about to bet the farm, especially now that the business was struggling and her condo was on the line since Danny had skipped bail.

She made her way toward the coffee stand cleverly tucked between two immense statues of ancient gods. Her stepbrother's apartment had revealed no clues to his whereabouts, not even to her, the person who knew him the best.

Unless someone had already found all the clues. Someone like Rafe Montana.

She got in the coffee line, fumbling in her purse for cash. Montana was legitimate, all right. She'd followed his suggestion and checked with the police, then taken it a step further and called Danny's bail bondsman, Sal Fellone. Rafe Montana was a bona fide bounty hunter, and he had an excellent track record of getting his man in record time.

Maybe it would be worth it to talk to him, see if they could work together—only this time without the pepper spray and wrestling.

Though the wrestling hadn't been all that bad, actually.

The thought startled her. Since Warren's defection, no man had coaxed so much as a blip from her libido. But it was easy to forget about Warren here in Vegas, a place that seemed galaxies away from Jersey. Maybe this was just what she needed, a get-away of sorts to put the past year in perspective. And the bounty hunter sure had been easy on the eyes.

"Good morning, Miss McGaffigan." Mr. Gray, Bartow's head of security, slipped into line behind her.

She angled her body so she could see him. She didn't know what it was about Gray, but he triggered her defenses. Was it his dark eyes that saw everything and gave away nothing? His immaculate suit—really, who was that neat? Or maybe the utter stillness of his body?

"Good morning," she said finally.

He didn't look away, kept that dark gaze on her. "Did you go to your stepbrother's apartment?"

She hadn't intended to tell him anything, but the words slipped from her lips anyway. "Yes. It looked like he hadn't been there in days."

The person in front of her moved up, and they both edged forward as well. The counter seemed miles away. Gray gave her a bland smile. "How troubling that a relative could disappear without so much as a note or an e-mail or a phone call." Breaking eye contact, he glanced up to peruse the menu board behind the register.

Dizzy. She shook her head like a wet dog, and the world steadied. Cobwebs in her brain, probably from too much worrying and too little sleep. And Gray—was he fishing? No way was she going to tell him about the call from Danny. Not when her instincts were screaming that this guy was part of what was threatening her stepbrother.

Okay, so she didn't have any hard facts, but everything with Gray and Bartow seemed a little too neat, a little too convenient. And a little too generous. Like calling her to tell her about Danny's disappearance. Offering to pay her way to Vegas—which she'd refused. Giving her the free room in the hotel—which she'd also refused and yet found herself staying in anyway. Picking her up at the airport in the limo. And the way Adrian Gray always seemed to be there, always solicitous, always curious about whether or not she'd heard from Danny.

Yeah, her alarm bells were clanging big time.

She reached the counter and ordered French vanilla coffee. She could feel Gray watching her, and she tried not to squirm.

He leaned closer, brushing her arm with his fingers. When she looked at him, he caught her gaze and held it. "I'm sure you would tell me if—"

A ruckus erupted in the lobby. He whipped his head around, cutting her free of the nearly hypnotic eye lock. A crowd rushed past the coffee stand. Reporters with microphones shouted questions, and cameramen scurried backward with their equipment balanced on their shoulders. At the front of the onslaught was a fair-haired man in a gray suit and a politician's smile, surrounded by muscular young guys in dark suits and earpieces.

The cashier brought Cara's coffee, and she gratefully seized the opportunity to turn away to pay for it. When she faced Gray again, she had braced herself for battle. She nodded toward the melee in the lobby. "What's that all about?"

He frowned first at her, then at the brouhaha. "Jain Criten, a very important guest. Looks like a press conference."

Cara raised her brows. "Don't you have media rooms or something for that kind of thing?"

"We do." His cell phone rang. He glanced at the display, and his lips firmed into straight annoyance. "Please excuse me." He darted out of line and headed toward the lobby, raising the phone to his ear as his long legs ate up the distance.

Glad to be rid of him, Cara sugared and creamed her coffee, then sipped the steaming brew as she made her way to the elevator and rode to her floor. She couldn't wait to step into the hot shower she hadn't gotten yesterday.

But once she opened the door to her room, she stopped dead and realized the shower would have to wait. Again.

. . . . .

Rafe strode into Artie Bartow's office, a pleasant, nonthreatening expression in place. He held out a hand as the casino manager rose from behind his desk. "Mr. Bartow, thank you so much for seeing me."

"I hope this won't take too long. I'm a busy man." Bartow gave his hand one quick pump, then sat down again and gestured at an empty chair. "I've called Adrian Gray, my head of security, to join us. He should be here momentarily."

"Fine with me." Rafe took the chair Bartow indicated.

"While we're waiting for Mr. Gray," Bartow said, "why don't you tell me again why you wanted to talk to me?"

Rafe sat back in his chair and put on his trustworthy-guy face. "As I explained on the phone, I'm a bail enforcement agent. I've taken the Cangialosi case, so I'm talking to all the people who might have known Danny Cangialosi. Naturally you, as his ex-employer, are high on that list."

"Of course, of course." Bartow nodded and steepled his hands. "But I'm afraid I don't know much."

Lie.

Years of practice made it easy for Rafe to maintain his polite expression. "A lot of times people know things they don't even realize. The smallest detail can lead to an apprehension."

"I will, of course, cooperate in any way I can. I just want justice done."

Lie.

Rafe pulled a small notebook and a pen out of his shirt

pocket and clicked the pen. "I've met Miss McGaffigan, Danny's stepsister. She mentioned you contacted her about Danny's disappearance."

"He was my employee, Mr. Montana, even though I terminated him for obvious reasons. I notified his next of kin in hopes she could help us find him."

Truth.

"And you offered her a room here at the hotel free of charge. That was very generous of you."

Bartow shrugged. "I'm a generous man."

Truth. At least as Bartow saw it.

"I would think you would be angry toward Danny and anyone connected with him. After all, he stole from you."

"He did. But it was just a car, Mr. Montana. I'm more interested in Danny learning his lesson than I am about my car being . . . ah . . . borrowed without permission."

Truth. But an odd truth . . . perhaps a hidden meaning?

"I wonder what made Danny take the car," Rafe mused.

Bartow shrugged. "Trying to impress a woman, I heard."

Truth.

"Was anything else taken?"

"No, just the car."

Lie.

"Did Danny—"

The office door opened. Bartow looked up and waved in the man who had entered. "Ah, Mr. Gray, at last. Do come in. This is Mr. Montana. He's a bounty hunter looking for Danny."

Rafe stood and held out his hand. The guy was big, the mega-bucks suit a poor disguise for the military bearing. His black hair was cut in a way that said salon rather than barber, and one glance over Gray's buff physique rated a sure ten on

Rafe's kick-my-ass scale. Went nicely with the don't-screw-with-me attitude.

His eyes were nearly black, and in them Rafe saw absolutely nothing. Just like Danny.

What the hell?

"This is Adrian Gray, my head of security. Mr. Gray, Mr. Montana."

Contrary to Bartow's soft, pampered handshake, Gray's was firm and strong. A guy who knew how to handle himself without posturing.

"You're here about Danny?" Gray asked. He didn't sit, so neither did Rafe.

"Yes. Mr. Bartow was telling me some of what happened."

"He gave the guy a job." Gray's mouth firmed in obvious disapproval. "Promoted him out of the parking garage to be Mr. Bartow's personal driver. And this is how he thanks him."

"So he was your driver." Rafe made a note on the pad, then looked over at Bartow but kept Gray in his peripheral vision. "I'm guessing he had access to the car keys."

"He had access to all my vehicles," Bartow confirmed.

Truth.

Okay, his powers were still working . . . on Bartow, just not on Gray. Which meant the problem might not be with Rafe, but with the subject he was looking at. The mere possibility lifted his mood.

"Makes them easy to steal," he noted.

"We trusted the wrong person," Gray said. "It happens."

"And that makes the sting even worse, doesn't it?"

Gray narrowed his eyes. "I'm afraid it does."

"I have a copy of your statement to the police," Rafe continued, turning his attention back to Bartow. "I'd like your permission to speak to some of Danny's coworkers, see if any of them might have an idea where he is."

"Mr. Gray will see to it."

"I'll set something up," Gray confirmed. "We'd prefer you be discreet about this."

Rafe nodded. "Of course."

Bartow's phone rang. He held up a finger at Rafe as he answered it. "Bartow."

As Bartow continued with his phone conversation, Gray stepped closer, that hard-as-nails stare boring into Rafe. The other man spoke softly, but there was no missing the command in his tone. "When you are done interviewing the employees, bring your results to me."

Rafe blinked at the ballsy demand. "What?"

Gray laid a hand on his shoulder, his clasp firm and his gaze relentless. "When you're done interviewing the employees, bring your results to me."

"Like hell." Rafe shrugged off his grip. "Conduct your own damn interviews."

Gray jerked back, shock flickering across his face before he regained control. "I will . . . that is, I intend to. I thought—" Gray's eyes narrowed.

And Rafe felt it, a touch in his mind equivalent to a mental tap on the shoulder. Instinctively, he slammed his senses closed. His heart pounded in his chest. He hadn't felt anything like that in years, not since childhood.

Only a glint in Gray's eyes indicated that he knew anything had happened. Before Rafe could say anything, Gray's radio squawked. He snatched it up and paced a few steps away. "Gray."

Rafe watched him with narrowed eyes. The guy had been spooked, and he was spooked himself. But what had Gray expected, that Rafe would blindly obey the demands of a total stranger?

Bartow hung up the phone. "My apologies, Mr. Montana."

"That's okay." Still stunned by the mind tap, Rafe strained to hear Gray's conversation, but he couldn't make it out and keep his attention on Bartow at the same time. "You're a busy man."

"I am. So where were we? Ah, yes, you wanted to interview my employees."

"I do. I think it will help me pick up Danny's trail."

"I am certain Mr. Gray can arrange something."

Gray hooked his radio back onto his belt and came toward the desk. "I have to go. A problem with a guest's room."

"Oh?" Bartow frowned. "I wanted you to sit in on this meeting."

"It's the VIP on twelve, sir."

Bartow's eyes widened. He waved a dismissive hand at Gray. "See to it then, and let me know the outcome."

"I will." Gray looked at Rafe, and it didn't take any superpowers to see that the guy was on guard now. "Leave your contact information, and I'll arrange for the interviews."

"Okay, thanks."

"I'll get Mr. Montana's card before he leaves," Bartow said. "You can get in touch with him later when everything is set up."

Gray nodded, then high-tailed it out of the office.

Bartow indicated a chair, the busy man of minutes ago gone as if he had never existed. "Sit down, Mr. Montana. I'm certain you have more questions."

Rafe took a seat and clicked his pen. "I do indeed, Mr. Bartow."

．　．　．　．　．

Cara perched on the edge of the sofa in the luxurious suite, crushing the empty coffee cup between her fingers. She should probably be doing something constructive, like itemizing her belongings. Or mopping up the spilled water from the flower vase. Maybe breathing into a paper bag. Something.

But all she could do was sit there in her suite, broken bric-a-brac strewn all around her, and wait for security.

Someone had broken in. Some lunatic had gotten into her room and ripped open her luggage. Pawed through her things. Knocked the furnishings over in what looked to be a mad frenzy of searching. But searching for what?

Or whom?

What if she hadn't stayed at Danny's last night? What if she'd been here? Her fingers started trembling again, and she crushed the cardboard coffee cup into an even smaller mass.

A knock on the door made her yelp in surprise, and the crushed cup flew out of her hands to land on the floor several feet away. Someone called her name and identified themselves as security—Gray.

"Come in," she replied. The door opened and Mr. Gray stepped in, a uniformed security man behind him.

"Miss McGaffigan, are you all right?" His leather shoe crushed the cup into the carpet as he reached her in three long strides. "Are you hurt?"

She shook her head. "I'm fine. I just came back to . . . this."

He glanced around, and his mouth tightened. "Is anything missing?"

"I don't know. I haven't looked. I just came in, saw this, and called security."

His fierce look softened, and she swore she saw compassion in his eyes. "So you haven't touched anything."

"No. I thought it might contaminate the crime scene or something."

He chuckled. "You watch too much TV."

"Guess so." She let out a breath. "What do we do now?"

"You need to check and see if anything is missing. I'll send Peterson here to take a look at the security tapes for this corridor."

"All right." Dreading the ordeal, she went into the bedroom.

·   ·   ·   ·   ·

Adrian straightened as she left the room. He glanced around at the careless destruction. Anger simmered beneath the surface, and he clenched his jaw. The bastards. Did they think he wouldn't know what they were doing?

"Peterson." He met the security man halfway across the room. "Go down to security and take a look at the tapes for this floor. Let's see who might have done this."

"Yes, Mr. Gray. Do you want me to send a guy up to be on the door?"

"That depends on what we see on the tapes." He met Peterson's gaze and had no trouble snaring his unremarkable mind. "Go downstairs, Peterson. Miss McGaffigan is fine."

Peterson's round features settled into a familiar vacant expression. "Miss McGaffigan seems to be fine. I'm going to go downstairs."

"Yes." Adrian took the man's arm and steered him toward the door. "To security. To look at the tapes."

"I'll check those tapes, sir."

"Thank you, Peterson." Adrian waited until the burly guard had left the room, then turned toward the bedroom. He stepped into the doorway and watched Cara.

She looked so lost, standing in front of the closet with the safe in the back of it standing open, staring at her clothing dumped on the floor. He had thought it would be a good idea to have her here in Vegas, a simple way to draw Danny out into the open. It had been an easy matter to make Bartow invite her, believing it was all his own idea. But now it appeared Cara had become a problem Adrian had not foreseen.

He regretted it had come to this.

"Miss McGaffigan."

She spun to face him, her brow creasing. "I haven't had a chance to check my suitcases, but all my valuables are still in the safe where I left them. It was still locked when I came in here."

"That's good news." He held her gaze, stepped closer. Reached out with his mind. "This has been hard on you."

"Yes." Her eyes took on a dreamy cast, her expression open and malleable. "Very hard for me."

"You're a complication." He came closer and couldn't resist reaching out to smooth a stray piece of hair behind her ear. She made no protest; she was completely his to control. "I'm sorry to do this to you, but I have to make sure you're out of the way. For good."

CHAPTER FIVE

Bartow knew more than he let on.

Rafe got into the elevator after his meeting on the executive floor and punched the button for the lobby. The casino manager had been lying, that much was certain. And Gray—well, there was definitely something weird there. Rafe couldn't read the guy, but then he could turn his head seconds later and read Bartow like a book. So obviously the problems he had been having with his abilities had to do less with him and more with *whom* he was trying to read.

Take Danny, for instance. He could concentrate on him and—

Flash. Danny Cangialosi was walking down the street, hands in the pockets of his hooded sweatshirt.

Rafe's heart raced, and he struggled to hold the vision. Where was it? He'd barely completed the thought before the nugget dropped into his head.

Arizona. Flagstaff.

The elevator door opened to the hustle and bustle of the hotel lobby. A family of six with a screaming toddler waited for him to disembark. Rafe hopped off the elevator and headed for the nearest house phone.

"Cara McGaffigan," he said to the operator, then waited as the line rang.

"Hello."

"Miss McGaffigan, this is Rafe Montana. I have a lead on your stepbrother."

"That's wonderful news."

Rafe frowned. Her voice sounded strange. Flat. Almost disinterested. "I'd like to talk to you about it. I'm in the hotel. Can I come up?"

"If you want. I'm in room 1292."

"All right, I'll see you in a few minutes." He hung up the phone, still puzzled by the lack of enthusiasm in her voice. What had happened to the woman he'd met yesterday, the one who had held him off with a can of pepper spray, determined to protect her stepbrother?

He headed back toward the elevator and managed to slip into a car just before the doors closed on a bellman with a luggage cart.

"What floor?" the bellman asked.

"Twelve."

The bellman punched the number, and the elevator ascended.

Twelve.

It's the VIP on twelve, sir. That's what Gray had said. And Cara was on the twelfth floor.

Coincidence? What were the odds that she was the VIP on the twelfth floor who had needed to call security? Wouldn't she have said something if that were the case?

Unless someone was there with her.

He recalled the tone of her voice. Deadpan. Disinterested. His Hunter instincts flared to life. She was in trouble.

He waited, the Hunter jerking with impatience, the crystal heating against his skin, while the bellman and his luggage cart got off on ten. Then Rafe pounded at the button until the doors closed and the elevator began to rise again. Alone in the car, he opened his senses, little by little, until the Hunter simmered at half throttle. He glanced at the camera in the elevator and wondered if Adrian Gray had something to do with Cara's dilemma.

For all he knew, Gray could be the one holding a gun to her head.

The elevator stopped on twelve and with a soft ding, the doors opened. He sprinted out into the empty corridor, scanning room numbers and signs to find 1292. He came upon it at the end of a hallway, the last room in the corner.

His hands opened and closed at his sides, his senses wide open and revved. He knocked. "Miss McGaffigan? It's me, Rafe Montana."

The door opened almost immediately. "Hi," she said with a vapid smile. "You just caught me." She turned back into the room.

He pushed in, prepared for anyone who might be hiding behind the door or furniture. His senses were all on alert, but the suite appeared empty, though it had clearly been tossed. A search? A robbery? Cara disappeared into the bedroom, and he followed her.

A suitcase lay open on the bed, half packed.

"Going somewhere?" he asked, pausing in the doorway.

She gave him that vague smile and headed into the bathroom. "I'm going home."

"What do you mean, you're going home?" He stepped into the bedroom and frowned at her as she came out of the bathroom with a makeup bag. "What about Danny?"

"Danny can take care of himself." She gave an airy wave of her hand, then dropped the kit into her suitcase. "He's a big boy."

Something was wrong here.

Rafe closed down his Hunter instincts to minimum vigilance,

then grabbed Cara's arm as she started past him again. She stopped and gave him an inquiring look, her expression as placid as a becalmed sea. But her eyes told another story.

Death hovered around her like a dark fog. Nothing had changed there. But now there was more. He stared hard into her eyes and saw some sort of white haze tied around her thoughts, imprisoning them.

It chilled him to his core. She was leaving town? What if she started driving in this weird zombie state and she crashed the car? What if that was the vision of death he had seen?

"I thought you wanted to find Danny," he said, watching for some flicker of emotion. "Have you changed your mind?"

"Yes. Danny can handle his own problems."

Lie. But truth as well. What was going on here?

"What made you change your mind?"

Her smile wavered just for a second. "I just did." She tugged her arm free. "I have to pack and leave."

He followed her back into the bathroom. "Why?"

"Because I do." Picking up her toothbrush and toothpaste, she frowned at him where he stood in the doorway. "You have to move."

That white haze in her mind seemed to flicker. He leaned against the doorjamb and bared his teeth in a smile. "No."

"But I have to leave." She scowled at him. "Please move."

Slowly he shook his head. "No, I won't."

Her fingers began to tremble. "I have to go home."

He gently removed the toothpaste and toothbrush from her hands and tossed them on the vanity. "No, you have to stay and help me find Danny. I think I know where he is."

"You find him. That's your job, isn't it?" She pushed at his chest. "Let me finish packing!"

"I don't think so."

"But you have to!" She shoved at him again, and he took hold of her shoulders.

"Cara, calm down. You don't have to leave."

"I do!"

"Why?" He bent his head so he could look at her eye-to-eye. "Why don't you stay here and find Danny with me? He needs you."

That flicker again. "I have to go home." She jerked out of his hold and stumbled backward. Her elbow struck the towel rack. She hissed and cupped the injured joint with her other hand. For an instant, as he looked into her eyes, her thoughts were clear and frantic, like a trapped animal.

Help me.

Then the haze took control again.

Physical shock. That's what it might take to snap her out of it.

"Come on, Cara." He grabbed her by the arm and dragged her over to the bathtub. She shrieked and struggled, but still he managed to lift her legs over the porcelain edge and get her into the tub. She whirled back toward him, but he blocked her before she could climb out again.

"What are you doing? I have to pack!" The last word came out with a gurgle as he turned on the cold shower full force.

"You need to snap out of it," he said, holding her under the spray.

She shrieked and fought and spat beneath the icy water, but he held her there, preventing her exit with his body. His shirt sleeves got soaked, but it was worth it when she twisted her head back from the spray and glared at him with furious brown eyes.

"What the hell are you doing?" she demanded.

He turned off the water, then stared deep into her eyes, just to be certain. The black shroud of death still lingered there, but whatever had been controlling her thoughts was gone.

Now he just had Cara to deal with, and she was furious.

．　．　．　．　．

"Are you out of your freaking mind?" Her thoughts swimming in confusion, Cara wrapped her arms around her midriff, her body shivering even as her cheeks heated. Her hair dripped, her clothes clung to everything, and Rafe Montana stood there gawking like a teenager at a peep show.

"Here, you're cold." He reached for a towel and wrapped it around her, his touch gentle despite the very male interest in his eyes. Her heart stumbled, but she grabbed hold of herself. Now wasn't the time for romantic fantasies, no matter how comforting his touch. Where had he come from? And how the heck had she ended up in the shower?

She jerked the ends of the towel from Rafe's fingers and wrapped it tightly around her body. *Play it cool, McGaffigan, at least until you know what's going on.* "Of course I'm cold; I'm in a freezing shower."

"I had to snap you out of it."

"Snap me out of what?" She swiped damp hair out of her face. "Is this how you get your jollies?"

"Of course not. Look, I'm sorry, but—"

"Sorry my ass." She stepped out of the tub, her movements stiff from her damp jeans. He assisted with a hand on her elbow, which she promptly shook off as soon as she had gained her footing. "I want to know who you think you are to come to my room uninvited and—"

"You did invite me."

She gave him a get-real look. "I would have remembered if I'd invited you."

"I called you from the lobby to tell you I had a lead on Danny. You told me to come up."

"I would remember that." She stormed past him, soggy sneakers slapping against the tiled floor.

He followed her into the bedroom. "So what *do* you remember?"

She went to the mirrored closet doors and looked at her reflection. Great, she looked like a bedraggled puppy. Wrinkling her nose, she tugged the band from her ponytail, wincing as the elastic snagged in the wet strands. "I fell asleep at Danny's place and came back here this morning." Holding the towel one-handed, she combed her fingers through her hair, then went over to the bureau to grab her brush. Going back to the mirror, she began to pull it through the damp tangles. "I got some coffee in the lobby and came back up here." She stilled as memory stirred.

"What is it?" He came up behind her. "What do you remember?"

"Someone had been here." She lowered the hairbrush. "Someone had torn the place apart." She frowned as she centered on the bed's reflection. "Why is my suitcase out?"

"Cara." He met her gaze in the mirror, his entire demeanor concerned yet in control. His calm soothed her. "You saw the place had been trashed. Then what?"

"I called security." She frowned as she tried to remember. "Yeah, I did. And some guys came up. That Gray guy and another guy in a uniform."

"Then what?"

"I . . . Oh, my God, I don't remember." *Just like the limo ride. Just like the hotel room.* She spun to face him, her pretense of calm shattering like ice. He stood only inches away, a warm, steady rock in the midst of turmoil. So appealing. With one step she could be in his arms, let him make it all go away.

73

No. She didn't know him, and it wouldn't be right to seek comfort there—though whenever she looked into those amazing blue eyes, her instincts screamed she could trust him. But could she trust her instincts?

No way. Not when she couldn't even remember the last five minutes. Warren had taught her what happened when you trusted too fast, too soon. *You're on your own, McGaffigan.*

She took a deep breath. "Look, I'm drenched. Why don't you wait in the sitting room while I get changed, okay? Maybe something will come to me while I'm getting dressed."

"Are you sure?"

The look he gave her said he knew how rattled she was, despite her attempt at cool, calm, and collected. She appreciated his perception and at the same time, resented it.

"I'm sure I really want to get out of these wet clothes." She tried a smile, knew that she failed but pretended anyway. "Please, wait outside."

He looked deeply into her eyes, as if he could see everything she was trying to hide. A thrill of feminine appreciation streaked through her—what woman wouldn't want to be studied so intently? But she was trying to keep from total meltdown here, and his keen examination poked at her fragile pretense of self-control.

"Please," she said again, hating the tiny break in her voice.

He gave a short nod and turned toward the door. "I'll be right out here, Cara. If you need anything at all, I'll be here." He opened the door and glanced back, his hand on the knob. "I mean that. Okay?"

She nodded. "I'll be out in a minute."

He nodded again and left, shutting the door behind him.

For a minute she wanted to run after him, but vulnerability was a luxury she couldn't afford right now. Her gut was telling her to trust him, but too much weird stuff had happened since she'd arrived in Vegas. What if she relaxed her guard with the wrong person? She was a computer geek, not some trained super-spy. She'd probably end up trusting the bad guy—as always.

She rubbed the towel over her hair, regarding her reflection in the mirror, a twist to her mouth. *Sucker.* She'd let smooth-talking Warren sweep her off her feet with all his chatter of mar-riage and children and then stood there like an idiot when he'd dropped her like a hot rock to marry someone else. And now there was the attraction to Mr. Cool-As-A-Cucumber Rafe Montana.

It wasn't enough that she was far from home, that Danny was MIA and her condo was on the line, that someone had trashed her room. No, she had to develop some irrational fascination with a man whose only motivation for helping her find her brother seemed to be money. And yet compared to the other players in this drama, he appeared to be the most honest. Money, she could understand. The puzzling generosity of Artie Bartow and Adrian Gray, that made no sense. Unless they were both full of it and just trying to use her to find Danny.

Now that rang true.

She heard Rafe walking around on the other side of the door, a slab of wood that seemed way too thin when she considered she was about to strip down with him right on the other side of it. But she couldn't allow her thoughts to linger on that. She tossed the damp towel on the bed, then looked her reflection in the eye and put her hands on her hips. "Stop with the fantasies, McGaffigan. Time to get down to business."

She could handle Rafe Montana and this crazy attraction to him. She wasn't about to let a man sneak past her defenses again. As long as she kept her focus on Danny, she'd be fine.

But when she opened the door a few minutes later, fully dressed, and saw him standing there, her pulse fluttered. He really was a seriously hot guy. Then he held out a white mug.

"Coffee," he said. "Crappy hotel room coffee, but at least it's hot." He gave her a crooked grin. "Consider it an apology for the cold shower."

She couldn't say anything for a moment, not when her heart was doing that little flip-flop thing in her chest again, and coherent words would not form on her tongue. He'd made coffee. For her.

She took the mug and studied the creamy beige liquid. The heat from the mug warmed her hands.

"I found the other cup on the floor. From what was left, it seemed like you took it light and sweet, but all they have here is powdered creamer. Hope that's okay."

"Fine," she managed. She glanced at the rug where she'd dropped the cup and saw he'd tried to soak up the drizzle of liquid with the paper napkins from the coffee setup. Wow, a man who noticed things like how she took her coffee or the stain on the rug. Who did something about all of it.

She lifted her gaze to his, recognized the honest compassion in those stunning blue eyes. Her heart did one slow roll in her chest, and she stopped fooling herself.

She was in trouble.

. . . . .

It was all Rafe could do not to wrap his arms around Cara and promise everything would be all right. She looked like the girl next door, all big eyes and caution, and *so* not his usual type. Yet he'd been getting visions of her for a couple of days now, and the Hunter sat up and howled whenever she came near. What the hell that meant, he had no idea, but he had no business dwelling on it. She was in trouble and needed his help, and that had to be his focus.

"Let's go over what happened," he said, gesturing toward the couch. "Then we can figure out what to do next."

"I don't think I can sit still." Shaking her head, she cradled the cup of coffee in both hands and prowled around the room, leaving him to stand as well. "I can't really . . . darn it, why can't I remember?" She glanced over at him. "I've always had a nearly photographic memory. The fact that I can't remember what happened an hour ago . . ." She blew out a sigh and glanced away, sipping her coffee.

"I imagine it's scary." That earned him another wry look. "Let me tell you what I know."

"Okay." She let out another long breath. "Okay, tell me what you know."

"I was in the hotel. I had an appointment with Artie Bartow."

"About Danny, right?"

"Yes, about Danny. I got—" He cleared his throat. "I got some information that makes me think he might be in Arizona. I called you on the house phone to tell you."

That little furrow came back between her brows. "I don't remember that."

"You told me to come on up. When I got here, you were packing to leave."

"No. Impossible." She stopped pacing and shook her head. "I'm not going anywhere until I find Danny."

"You told me Danny was a big boy and could take care of himself."

Her jaw dropped. "You're lying." She stalked toward him, stopping a pace away. "I would never say that! I would never walk away from him, not when he needed me—"

"I know." The distress he saw inside her nearly undid him. "Listen, I think something happened to you."

"Like what? A personality transplant? Geez." She gulped some coffee.

"I think you might have been drugged. Or something."

"Drugged? Who would do something like that?" She jerked her gaze to his, her obvious fear arousing his protective instincts with a vengeance.

"What do you remember?" he asked gently. "You were here with security. Then what happened?"

"Mr. Gray told me to check and see if anything was missing." She shuddered. "That guy creeps me out a little."

"Tell me what happened next."

"I went into the bedroom to check the safe. Everything was still there."

"That's good news. Go on."

"Mr. Gray came in, and . . . then I was in a cold shower." Panic flickered across her face again. "Oh, my God, why can't I remember anything in between those two events?"

"You're doing great."

"Don't placate me, Rafe Montana. I know I'm getting upset. I'm usually the one who calms the upset people, but now I'm one of them." Her pitch rose with each word. She groaned and rubbed her face with one hand. "Listen to me. Two graduate degrees, and I'm falling apart."

"Hey, anyone would get emotional after an experience like this." He took a cautious step toward her. "You'll get through."

She looked up and attempted a smile. "You sound pretty sure about that."

"I'm pretty sure about *you*."

She blinked, and he caught a glimpse of startled pleasure

before she turned away again. "Well, thanks. Maybe I look tougher than I am."

She was attracted to him—big time.

Not the time or the place. Pulling out his pad and pen, he strolled in the other direction. "Back to the time line. Gray wasn't here when I got here. And you were packing your suitcase and insisting Danny could take care of himself."

"That's crazy. It's like I was hypnotized or something."

"Maybe you were."

"So you're saying Mr. Gray is some kind of hypnotist?" She shook her head.

He chuckled at the disbelief in her tone. "I know what it sounds like, but this is Vegas, you know."

"You keep saying that. I guess that theory isn't as wacky as it seems."

"Either the guy is a hypnotist or he gave you some kind of drug to induce submission. I lean more toward door number two."

"Huh. Could be." She glanced over at him, clearly more relaxed now that he had posed a reasonable explanation. "So you figured that the shock of the cold water would snap me out of it?"

He shrugged. "It was worth a try."

"Well, I needed a shower anyway."

Her wry tone and the playful curve of her lips shot an extra jolt of desire through him. Damn, she was cute. She was bouncing back, not letting things hold her down for long. He admired that. "We need to talk about options."

"What options?" She tipped her head back and drained the last of the coffee.

His body tightened as that simple movement pulled her shirt tight across her chest. "It's clear to me that you're in some kind of danger. Someone drugged you—or whatever—to get you to leave town. I don't think you're safe here or even at home for that matter. Not when that's where they wanted you to go."

She lowered the cup. "What do you suggest I do?"

"I think you need to come with me."

She hesitated, and he braced himself for an argument. Then she said, "I checked you out. You have a pretty solid rep for always getting your man." She went over to the coffee stand and set down her empty mug. "So, where are we going?"

"Arizona."

"Right, that's where you said Danny might be." She fingered the unopened packets of sugar left near the coffee pot. "You know, Vegas is a crazy town. All smoke and mirrors." She made an abracadabra gesture with her hands. "And I've got all these people promising me the world so they can find Danny."

"I could promise you the world, but it would be a lie."

"Yeah, you seem like a straight shooter." She nodded to herself. "If you find Danny, you get paid. Cut and dried. At least that's honest motivation."

"It's my job. But I appreciate the faith."

"Sometimes you just gotta jump." Her quick grin struck hard and fast.

Their eyes locked. A vision swept into his mind of the two of them and hot, naked, sweaty sex.

The Hunter snapped, yowled. Wanted.

He looked away and blew out a long, slow breath. If he hadn't already been interested, that sure as hell would have fired up the old furnace. But was that a vision of the future, or just his own fantasies reflected back at him? "Look, if you come with me, you'll be safer than if you stay here," he said.

"Okay."

"You have to pretend to be leaving, pretend to still be under whatever influence they had on you."

"Okay," she said again.

"Go to the airport, and I'll pick you up there."

"Guess I'd better finish packing," she said, and headed toward the bedroom. She stopped just inside the doorway and looked back at him. "Thanks for letting me come with you, Mr. Montana."

"Rafe," he corrected.

"Rafe." Her lips stretched into a smile after forming his name, and she went into the bedroom.

He sank down on the couch, his instincts humming and his body tight. He'd lied to her when he had said he believed it was drugs. He couldn't forget the way Gray had tried to order him to report his findings to him, nor the mental touch. Given the abilities of Rafe's own family, he didn't put it past Gray to have some kind of brainwashing gift. He'd seen too much weird stuff in his own gene pool to doubt that anything existed. But who—or what—was he? Not a Seer. The blue eyes never lied. Maybe the guy was a just damned good hypnotist.

Even he didn't believe it.

The best thing to do was to get Cara out of Vegas and keep her with him. Was Adrian Gray the enemy who caused her to die? Was Rafe saving her life by taking her with him or playing right into destiny's hands?

The conundrum had always made him crazy, which was yet another reason why he had gotten out of the hero biz. He'd always had to decide if acting on his visions helped avoid them or steered him into making them reality. It was always a crap shoot, and someone inevitably got hurt. Bounty hunting was easier, much more straightforward.

At least his powers seemed to be working. He focused on Danny again, hoping to bring up more clues to his whereabouts. But apparently his previous vision had been a one-time sneak peek. When he focused on Danny now, all he saw was a great big nothing.

He blew out a frustrated breath and leaned back on the couch. Oh, joy, playing the odds again. Roll the dice, Montana, and hope nobody gets killed.

Especially Cara.

CHAPTER SIX

An hour later, Rafe hit the button on the slot machine and watched the tumblers spin. Out of the corner of his eye, he glimpsed Cara walking across the lobby from the elevators, dragging her suitcase and carry-on. He had to hand it to her; she played her part with a skill he hadn't expected, smiling with absent placidity at the people around her. She stopped at the front desk, dropped off her key, then headed outside to the taxi stand.

So far, everything was going as planned.

He turned back to the slot machine and hit the button again, watched the machine take his money for the fourth time.

"How's the luck?" Adrian Gray appeared like smoke beside him. The man moved as soundlessly as a ghost, even avoiding the Hunter's detection—a skill that bothered him even more than the mind touch from earlier.

"Crap luck for a crap day." Rafe punched the button again, sent the tumblers spinning.

"Sorry to hear that." Gray looked past him. "I see Miss McGaffigan is leaving us. Did you get a chance to talk to her?"

Rafe had a feeling Gray had viewed the security footage and knew exactly when Rafe had gone to Cara's room and how long he'd stayed. "Yeah, she was a dead end. When I got there she was packing to go home. Says Cangialosi can take care of himself."

"She's probably right about that."

Rafe leaned back and eyed the slot machine. "Seems kind of a waste to fly all the way out here, then turn around and go home."

"When she called me to tell me she was leaving, she indicated there had been some emergency back at her job. A new, very demanding client."

"I see." Rafe didn't need his superpowers to know Gray was lying through his teeth. "I'd hoped she'd be a better lead. I've got zip right now."

"I checked you out, Mr. Montana. You're supposed to be the best."

Rafe scowled, punched the SPIN button again. "Even the best can't do anything without any leads. I was doing this as a favor for a friend, but I don't have time to find a needle in a haystack. Not for the pennies this job would pay."

Gray frowned. "You're quitting the case?"

"You bet I am. I can be making some serious coin chasing real criminals, not some car thief."

"Perhaps Mr. Bartow can make it worth your while."

"You bribing me, Gray? I just brought in a guy who was taking bribes." Rafe stood. "I can't be bought."

"Not a bribe. An incentive."

"Don't dress it up with pretty words." Rafe pointed a finger at the lapel of Gray's Armani jacket. "I don't work for you or your boss."

Gray's eyes narrowed. "Are you certain we can't make an arrangement? We need the best."

"He's a car thief, not public enemy number one."

"Still." Gray lowered his voice. "If word gets out that the thief who stole from Mr. Bartow has gotten away, it would cause considerable embarrassment for him. Surely that is worth your time."

"Breaking the law is never worth my time." Rafe hit the button on the machine to cash out and waited for Gray to try the mind tap again. But it never came.

"Suit yourself," Gray said.

"I usually do."

"You have my number if you change your mind." Gray turned and left, disappearing into the crowded casino.

Rafe glanced at the voucher from the slot machine. A dollar fifty-six left from his five dollar bet. With a quirk of his lips, he sat down at the next slot machine and inserted the voucher. Set up the bet. Hit the SPIN button.

He'd already seen the results, courtesy of the universe.

Whir. Whir. Whir. Stop. The machine began ringing in rapid fire, the tumblers spinning over and over again as bonus round after bonus round hit pay dirt. Rafe watched for several minutes as the numbers added up on the screen. When the machine finally stopped, he hit the CASH OUT button and glanced at his ticket.

Six hundred dollars. That should be enough to get him and Cara to Flagstaff.

. . . . .

Rafe Montana was proving more of a complication than he'd expected.

Adrian Gray swiped his access card and stepped into the private elevator leading to the business offices. When Montana had first shown up looking for Danny, he'd hoped the bounty hunter would track down Cangialosi quickly so they could get the stone back. Then he'd done a thorough background check. Rafe was one of the Arizona Montanas, a family that sat up there with the Kennedys in its status as American royalty. His father, John Montana, ran the biggest security development company in the country.

That pedigree alone would be notable enough in the normal

course of things, but Rafe's resistance to the mind touch had stirred his curiosity. He'd dug into other resources and discovered something even more impressive: Rafe's mother, Maria, was a known descendant of Agrilara, the most powerful Seer in Atlantis. And that turned this into an entirely new game.

He'd seen Rafe's eyes, knew he had to be a Seer as well. But Rafe was estranged from the Montana family, a renegade, which meant he had to be looking for the Stone of Igarle for himself. It was the only thing that made sense. The question was, did the other players in this game know about him as well? If they did, the entire chessboard had just changed.

He would have to step up his strategy ahead of schedule

· · · · ·

Rafe saw Cara standing on the curb watching for him, the late-afternoon sun gilding her tawny hair. Even from this distance, he could make out the concern on her face. But the frown cleared as she spotted him.

"I thought you'd forgotten about me," Cara said, opening the back door of his SUV. Before he could offer a hand, she lifted her suitcase into the backseat, followed by her carry-on. Then she slammed the door and opened the passenger side. "I've been waiting an hour. What took you?"

He heard concern, not petulance, in her tone. "Adrian Gray wanted to have a word with me."

"What about?" She hoisted herself into the passenger seat.

"Wanted to tell me fairy tales about how you had to go home for an emergency. You really had him snowed."

She grinned. "I'm a good actress. I played the lead in *Romeo and Juliet* in high school."

"Well, buckle up, Juliet, so we can get out of this town."

She fastened her seat belt as he pulled away from the passenger pickup zone and headed for the airport exit. "How long does it take to get to Flagstaff?"

"Four or five hours, depending on traffic."

"That's not bad at all. Thank you for taking me with you."

"I couldn't leave you in Vegas. You're safer with me."

"I think you're right." Her obvious gratitude slipped past his defenses and stroked his heart. "But I wanted to thank you anyway. You're the first one who could tell me anything. I've been worried sick about Danny."

"Worried enough that you flew all the way out here to look for him." Rafe glanced away from the road to look at her. "You're a good sister."

She shrugged. "Anyone would do the same."

"I guess." He thought of his own siblings, wondered if they would come riding to the rescue if he needed them. Once upon a time, definitely. Now? He had no idea.

"Family protects each other," Cara said. "And Danny is the only family I have left."

Rafe merged onto the highway and sped up to the pace of the traffic. "Seems like you're the one doing all the protecting."

"That's not true." She sighed. "Well, maybe. Danny's a dreamer. One of us has to keep her feet planted in the realm of reality."

"What do you mean, 'dreamer?'"

Her voice softened, fondness soaking every word. "Danny always has big plans. They just never seem to work out."

"Some people might call that a screwup, not a dreamer."

"He's not a screwup!" He glanced over to see her sitting stiffly in her seat, those eyes hot like melted caramel. "He just doesn't always think things through."

"And what about you? You seem like the type who plans out everything."

She gave a laugh that rang with surprising bitterness. "No one can plan out *everything*."

He wanted to ask who had hurt her, but he didn't dare— didn't dare *care*. Yet despite his resolve, he was drawn to her warmth, in the way that made him want to cuddle on the couch with her and share popcorn from the same bowl as they watched a movie. Maybe make out like a couple of teenagers.

The Hunter stirred, and the image of innocent necking rapidly changed into the two of them naked on the rug in front of a fire, going at it like the last man and woman on earth.

Damn it.

"So what about you?" she asked, her husky voice unwittingly feeding the daydream. "Are you a planner or a seat-of-the-pants kind of guy?"

"A little of both. It's good to be flexible, since life rarely co-operates with our plans." He shifted in his seat and glanced over at her, then considered himself lucky she didn't seem to realize the physical effect she had on him. "So tell me more about Danny. He's your stepbrother, right?"

"Yes, but I think of him as flesh-and-blood."

"No other siblings?"

"No." She shook her head, and the afternoon sun danced across golden strands mixed with brown, glittered off the gold Claddagh earrings she wore. "Danny and I were both only children. His mother passed away, and my father took off right after I was born."

"That's rough. Do you stay in touch with your dad?"

"No. He divorced my mother a couple of years after disappearing, then later died. I never met him. Donald was the only father I really had."

Rafe thought of his own father, tried to imagine growing up

without him. The mere idea made his heart hurt. "Donald was Danny's father?"

"Yes. He was a nice man." Wistfulness softened her tone. "He was a retired policeman."

"Was?"

"He and my mother died in a car crash eight years ago. Danny had just turned eighteen, and I was twenty-one and just finishing college. They hydroplaned after a nasty thunderstorm and went off the road. Mom was killed instantly." Her voice caught.

Sympathy gentled his tone as he asked, "What about Donald?"

"He lived two days, then slipped away without ever waking up." She laid her head back against the headrest. "The worst part was not being able to say good-bye. Or rather, I could say it, but I don't know if he heard me. I hope he did."

"I'm sorry."

"It's okay." She took a deep breath. "That's how I knew Danny was in trouble. Every year on the anniversary of the accident— August nineteenth—he comes back to Jersey and we visit their graves. But not this year. He's never missed the nineteenth, not in all this time." She sniffled and reached for the glove compartment. "Do you have any tissues in here?"

"Somewhere. Watch out for—"

"Oh." She stared at the gun for a long moment, then lifted it with two fingers so she could pull out the fast-food napkins resting underneath it. Shoving the weapon farther into the glove box with one finger, she slammed the compartment shut. "It never occurred to me that you'd have a gun."

"I don't use it much."

"But you have used it."

"Look, some of the people I chase down are dangerous. Murderers, drug dealers, sometimes just crazy desperate."

"You don't have to explain to me."

"Seems like you want me to."

"No, what I want you to do is find Danny, Mr. Montana. And not shoot him."

"I doubt there would be a need." He threw her a quick frown. "And my name is Rafe. Quit that snooty Mr. Montana stuff."

"I wasn't being snooty."

"Look, I know you're worried about Danny. You don't know me, and you know what I do for a living. And you probably watch too much TV like everyone else. Mostly skip tracing is boring stuff. But once in a while there's a nut job who starts waving a gun around, and I have no intention of going out that way. So, yeah, I have a gun. Yeah, I've used it. It's part of what I do."

She remained silent for a moment before asking, "Have you ever killed anyone?"

Now it was his turn to hesitate. Finally he said, "Yeah, I have."

. . . . .

Though she'd expected the answer, Cara was still a little shocked to hear it spoken out loud. Who had he killed? When? Under what circumstances?

She studied the forbidding lines of his profile. His tone sounded so calm and matter-of-fact when he talked about it, but she noticed the way he clenched his jaw, the way he stared straight ahead at the road. However casual the words, she could tell that taking a life still affected him, and that settled her nerves more than any assurances he could have made. He didn't take killing lightly.

"Let's talk about something else," she said.

"Good idea." His tense shoulders visibly relaxed.

"Tell me about you. Where are you from?"

His fingers clenched oh-so-slightly on the wheel. "Here."

"Here as in Las Vegas?"

"That's where I live."

"That's where you live, but is that where you're *from*?"

"What does that matter?"

"Why don't you want to tell me?"

"Because it's not about me. Tell me more about Danny. I need to know all I can so I can track him."

"Mr. Montana . . ." He sent her a warning look and she corrected herself. "Rafe, I'm a woman in a truck with a man she barely knows, headed through the desert. My instincts told me to trust you. Don't make me regret following them."

He sighed. "Okay, I'm a big believer in instincts. I was born in Arizona, but I live in Vegas. I'm twenty-eight, a Scorpio, and I have every Beatles album ever released."

"The digital remasters?"

He slid her a glance. "Of course."

"So far my instincts were right about you." She settled back in her seat. "What else?"

"Isn't that enough?"

"Hardly."

"Too bad. Talk about something else."

The finality in his tone discouraged any further personal questions, though his short answers only made her more curious. But as a woman who had founded her own business, she had learned when to push and when to wait. This was a waiting time for certain.

"What do you want to talk about?" she asked.

"Tell me about you," he said.

"I was born and raised in New Jersey. I'm twenty-nine, a Taurus, and have all the Beatles albums except one."

"Which one?"

"Sorry, I don't know you well enough for that," she said with a mock sniff.

He laughed, and the genuine amusement in the sound had her lips curving as well. "You have a great laugh," she said.

He cast her a glance. "Thanks."

The heat in that one, fleeting look almost melted her into the seat cushion.

"So," she said a little too brightly. "What else do you want to know?"

His lips quirked, but he kept his eyes on the road. "How come you live in New Jersey, but Danny lives in Vegas?"

"When our parents died, we both inherited insurance money. After the funeral costs and settling the estate, there was a little left for each of us. I saved mine until I got my graduate degrees, then used it to start my business, Apex Consulting."

"Right, you said you have two graduate degrees."

"Yeah." She shrugged, uncomfortable as always when the subject of her unusually high intellect came up. She'd learned the hard way that people—especially men—tended to shy away from those they perceived to be smarter than they were.

But Rafe just nodded and said, "So you own your own business. That's an accomplishment these days."

Her shoulders relaxed. "I had to take on partners a couple of years ago to stay afloat when the economy took a dive, but yes, we've managed to keep our heads above water."

"What does Apex do?"

"We write custom computer programs that interface two software packages that normally would not talk to each other. This way our clients can run customized reports using data from two separate applications."

"Sounds complicated."

"Not really. It's more like a Chinese menu. One from column A, one from column B, print report."

He chuckled. "And Danny?"

She couldn't stop the curve of her lips. "Danny headed to Vegas. He was going to win big."

He smiled, shaking his head. "Of course he was. That's what Vegas counts on."

She shrugged. "He blew through the money, of course, but he loves Vegas. He always thinks the next big jackpot is just around the corner and wants to be there to catch it."

"I bet he does." Rafe narrowed his eyes, glanced in his rear-view mirror, then at his side mirror, then back to rearview. He sped up a little, glancing back and forth from the rearview mirror to the road and back. The energy in the truck shifted, growing thick with tension.

Cara felt it, in the ripple of gooseflesh along her arms, the tingle at the back of her neck. "What is it? What's wrong?"

He didn't say anything.

"Rafe. Tell me what's going on."

He glanced behind them again. Sped up.

She clenched her fingers around the armrests of her seat. "Please tell me what's going on. I need to know."

He glanced over at her. "I think we're being followed."

She turned to look out the rear window. A lone sedan kept pace behind them, silver paint gleaming in the afternoon sun. "Who would follow us?"

"Good question. I'm going to keep going for a while, see if they stick. There's a truck stop about an hour from here. If they're still behind us when we get there, then we'll know." He flashed her a grin. "Trust me. I—"

"Do this for a living. Yes, I know. I just hope you're wrong."

His expression sobered. "Me too."

CHAPTER SEVEN

An hour later, Rafe headed for an approaching exit ramp, where a sign promised food and bathrooms. He stopped at the red light at the top of the ramp, glanced behind him at the silver sedan coming over the rise.

"Are they still there?" Cara asked, her voice tight.

Rafe glanced again in the rearview mirror. "Yeah, they're still there."

"Maybe they're not really following us."

He didn't answer. The light turned green, and he gunned it, heading for a flashing neon sign of the restaurant ahead of them. He formed the question in his mind, just as he'd done every few minutes or so for the past several miles.

Who's following us?

The universe remained silent. His mind stayed blank.

This was getting really old.

Rafe pulled into a parking spot and turned off the engine, then glanced over at Cara. Her eyes looked huge in her face.

"Are you sure about this?" she asked.

"It's a long stretch of highway through the desert," he replied, unfastening his seat belt. "That silver sedan has been behind us for a while now."

"That doesn't mean they're following us." She unbuckled

her own seat belt. "The thing about highways is that everyone can only go in one direction."

"Trust me, we're being followed. Let's go inside, get something to eat."

"I could eat." She opened her door as he got out on his side. "All I've had today is a cup of coffee."

"Then we definitely need to feed you." Once she'd closed the door, he hit the remote to lock the SUV. "Maybe we can get a table by the window so we can watch for these guys."

"I feel like I'm in some spy flick," she mumbled as they headed toward the entrance. She reached for the door, but Rafe got there first and held it open for her. She gave him a startled glance. "Wow. A real live gentleman."

He shrugged. "Old habit."

"Good habit." As she stepped through the doorway, he paused on the threshold. The silver sedan pulled into the parking lot. Cara saw them, too. She tensed, then looked at Rafe. "That's them, isn't it?"

"Yup." The Hunter stirred, sensing a potential enemy. Rafe urged her inside with a hand on her waist. "Don't look at them. It's better if they don't know we're on to them."

"What are we going to do?"

"Right now? Eat. And watch."

A dark-haired waitress with a cheerful smile and a name tag reading NANCY appeared in front of them, menus in hand. "Hi there. Two?"

"Yes." Once more he guided Cara forward, this time with a touch on her lower back, inches from her tempting rear end. "Near the window if you can."

"Of course. This way." Perky Nancy led the way into the restaurant.

. . . . .

Rafe Montana had very warm hands.

Twice now he had touched her, just small contacts to ease her this way or that, leaving a pleasant tingle behind and an aura of safety that relieved her tense muscles. He indicated she take the side facing away from the door, then waited until she was seated before sliding into the booth himself. They took the menus from the smiling waitress.

The scents of burgers and coffee wafted through the dining room, and Cara's stomach growled. The lone cup of coffee she'd had before all the craziness had started now proved its inadequacy when she flipped open the menu. "Hey, wow. Breakfast all day."

"Sounds good." He opened his menu but kept an eye slanted toward the door. Moments after they were seated, two men in suits walked into the restaurant.

"That's them. No!" He covered her hand with his on the table, not glancing up from the menu. "Don't look. We don't want to make them suspicious."

"Right." Though she enjoyed the warmth of his skin, she gently slid her hand from beneath his. No use fanning fires when she wasn't sure she wanted to brave the flames. "Tell me again, how do you even know they're looking for us?"

"I've been doing this a long time, Cara." His blue eyes burned with intensity, as if he would make her believe him by sheer force of will. "I have a . . . sense . . . about this kind of stuff."

"Like some kind of superhero?" She chuckled and dropped her gaze to the menu again.

"I'm glad you think it's funny." The barely banked annoyance in his tone had her looking up again. He sat very still, tension rippling over his body. She got the sudden impression of a crouching tiger, waiting to pounce.

"I didn't say it was funny," she replied. "I just wonder if you're overreacting."

"Your stepbrother is missing, and someone trashed your room and tried to brainwash you into going home. Is that over-reacting?"

The reminder splashed over her like ice water, and she carefully closed the menu. "No."

He leaned closer. To anyone watching, they probably looked like lovers murmuring sweet nothings to each other. But there was nothing sweet about the no-nonsense look in his eyes. "For some reason, someone has targeted you. Maybe they think you know where to find Danny, or maybe they want to use you for bait to lure him out. That means that until we sort all this out, everyone is a suspect." He sat back in his seat. "Especially a couple of guys in suits following us for miles."

Smiling Nancy appeared, notepad in hand. "Hi there! What can I get you?"

"I'll take the pancake special," Cara said, never looking away from Rafe.

"Bacon or sausage?"

"Bacon."

"How do you like your eggs?"

"Scrambled. And a cup of coffee."

"Got it." Nancy jotted the order on her pad. "What about you, sir?"

"The same."

Nancy nodded, tucked the menus under her arm and walked away, still scribbling.

Cara sat back in the seat and rubbed her hands over her face. The waitress's interruption had given her the moments she needed to process their situation. "I'm sorry. You're right, you are the professional. I just have a hard time believing any of this is actually happening. I mean, stuff like this doesn't usually happen to me."

He shrugged one shoulder. "Happens to me all the time."

She leaned in. "So you really think those guys are watching us?"

"Yeah. I can see them. Not too subtle about it, either."

She frowned. "You can see them? But you're looking straight at me."

"Peripheral vision," he said. "Yeah, they look like hired muscle."

"Oh." She fought the urge to glance over. "Hired? By whom? Mr. Bartow?"

"Maybe. Maybe someone else looking for your brother. You have no idea what he might have gotten himself into."

She stiffened. "Well, maybe it's that guy Gray. He makes me nervous."

His lips quirked. "Yeah, me too."

"You?" She laughed. "I can't imagine you nervous about anything."

He leaned across the table. "I'm really not Superman," he stage-whispered.

She chuckled again, aware he was trying to make her relax and glad for it. "Thanks for the update."

"But"—his tone grew serious—"I am one of the best in my field. I've been doing this a long time, so you should listen when I tell you something."

Cara arched her brows. "Modest much?"

Nancy came over and set their coffees in front of them. He waited until she left before he answered. "It's not bragging, it's fact. Ask around."

"I did ask." She emptied three sugars and a couple of creamers into her coffee. "Your friend Sal thinks the sun rises and sets on you."

He took two packs of sugar and shook them together, then tore open the tops. "You mean it doesn't?"

"Ha-ha. You're a funny guy."

He dumped the sugar into his mug. "You say that like it's a bad thing."

She couldn't miss the hint of flirtation skimming beneath the words. As a distraction, it worked. "Not at all." She stirred her coffee.

"I'm a firm believer in laughter." He ripped open a creamer and tipped it into his cup. "Life's too short, so laugh while you can."

"Very philosophical."

He shrugged. "What I do can be dangerous. I've learned to live for today."

She cocked her head. "No tomorrows? No plans?"

He shook his head. "I'm an in-the-moment kind of guy."

"I'm not." She blew on her coffee. "I plan everything. I don't like surprises."

"So taking Bartow up on his offer to fly you out here to look for Danny was really out of character."

She stiffened. "I didn't take him up on anything. But I did think it was a good idea, so I bought the plane ticket. Bartow didn't pay for anything."

"Except your hotel room."

"Yeah." She frowned, still disturbed by the situation. "I'm not sure how that happened. I intended to stay at Danny's place while I was here. I don't like to be beholden to anyone. But somehow I ended up in that room, just like I ended up in the limo with Mr. Gray when I had no intention of allowing him to pick me up at the airport."

"Really." A frown furrowed his brows.

"Seriously, do you think Gray is the one who drugged me, hypnotized me, whatever? Seems like whenever he's around, I end up doing things I have no intention of doing."

"Right now, I'm keeping all options on the table."

Nancy returned just then, balancing platters along one arm and passing them out with the other hand. "Here you go. Watch the plates; they're hot."

Cara sat back as Nancy slid the steaming hotcakes and eggs in front of her. Rafe smiled at the waitress, then asked for syrup. As Nancy went off to get it for him, Cara reached across the table and laid her fingers over Rafe's hand. "I think we need to have a plan in place for when we find Danny."

Rafe stilled. Looked from their touching hands to her eyes. The male interest burning there stole the breath from her lungs.

Time slowed, counted by the beats of her heart. Heat rose, shimmered, stretched between them. Her lips parted. His nostrils flared; his eyes narrowed.

She wanted to touch him. The craving tugged at her, urging her to taste, but she resisted. He intrigued her, and after her failed attempt at forever, "in the moment" sounded darned appealing. But she barely knew him, and she wasn't the type to jump into anything without a lot of thought first, especially not with Danny out there somewhere needing her help. She started to slide her hand back, but he caught it, trapped it beneath his large, strong palm.

"Danny's not the only thing we need to talk about," he said.

The challenge hung out there between them, vibrating with tension.

The jangle of her cell phone jerked her out of the moment. Relieved, she dug in her purse for the phone. Unfortunately, it wasn't Danny. She glanced at the display, groaned, and hit the ANSWER button, lifting the phone to her ear. "Hello, Warren."

"Cara, what the hell are you doing in Vegas? I've been calling you since yesterday." Her ex-fiancé's tone abraded like sandpaper on bare skin. She clenched her teeth. She didn't need this, not with her nerves already frayed over Danny, strangers tailing her, and a potent, inconvenient attraction to a way-too-sexy bounty hunter.

"Didn't Mitch tell you?" She kept her tone casual as she started to slide from the booth, but Rafe grabbed her wrist, shook his head.

"Stay put," he mouthed.

She hesitated, tempted to ignore him, but his quick glance at their suspicious followers reminded her to be cautious. She stayed seated.

"Mitch told me you took off for Vegas," Warren said. "What were you thinking, Cara? We need you here."

She turned into the booth, her back to the dining room. "I can't really talk right now, Warren."

"Just tell me—what the heck are you doing in Vegas?"

She bit her lip, braced herself. "It's Danny."

"I should have known." His tone rang with disgust. "Cleaning up after your deadbeat stepbrother again."

"He's family, Warren. I had to come. He needs me."

"What about Apex? The company needs you, too."

"I'm not irreplaceable."

"I promised the Kirby account you would give them your personal attention."

She closed her eyes, rubbed the bridge of her nose. "I've asked you not to do things like that, Warren."

"It gets the signature on the dotted line, doesn't it? Everyone wants personal attention from one of the owners of the firm."

"You're an owner, too. Promise them your time, not mine."

"I'm not a programmer. Listen, Cara—"

"No, you listen. We're equal shareholders in the company. You will no longer promise my services to anyone, do you hear me? Not without talking to me first."

He stayed silent for a long moment. "I can't believe you're forcing me to break a promise, Cara."

She snorted at the dramatic tone. "Well, we both know you're good at that, don't we?"

The instant the words left her mouth, she wanted to call them back. First rule of arguing with Warren: never show your weakness.

"Oh, I see what this is about. Geez, Cara, it's been a year. Are you trying to punish me?"

She inhaled, slowly. "Not everything is about you, Warren."

"But this is. You're still angry at me, aren't you? What did you expect me to do, Cara? It wasn't working with us. I have dreams, needs. I couldn't give those up. I had to move on."

She bit back a sharp reply. She'd had dreams and needs, too. She'd just expected the man who proposed marriage to her to be part of them.

"Cara? Are you still there?"

"Yeah, sorry. I was thinking."

Rafe touched her hand. She glanced at him, and he indicated he was going to the men's room. She nodded as he slid from the booth, then watched his tight, jean-clad butt as he strolled through the dining room toward the restrooms.

She let out a long breath. The man was hot. That lean, easy grace of his led her thoughts down avenues she was trying to avoid. A tingle swept over her, firing up a libido she had thought dormant.

"Cara, are you listening to me? Cara?"

Warren's strident voice cooled her blooming ardor like a bucket of ice water. She frowned at the phone. "Sorry, what were you saying?"

"I said you've got to let me go, Cara. Obsession isn't healthy."

"You're right, Warren." She glanced at Rafe again, considered the possibilities. "Here I am, letting you go." She closed the phone with a click, dropped it into her purse, then picked up her warm mug. The phone started ringing again.

She sipped her coffee and stared out at the dramatic desert view, her lips curving as the phone rang and rang and finally stopped.

Living in the moment didn't seem such a bad idea after all.

· · · · ·

Rafe made his way across the dining room, ignoring the table where his suspected tail sat. He had gotten way too interested in Cara's conversation, way too curious about this guy Warren. He shouldn't care. He *couldn't* care. He'd brought her with him to try to protect her. Nothing more could come of it, no matter how much sizzle flared between them.

He'd been wishing he were somewhere else, longing to get away from her phone conversation and the questions it raised, when one of the guys following them got up to go to the men's room.

He had no doubt that these two were indeed tailing them. Who they worked for, he didn't know, and the universe wasn't sharing. Were they connected to Danny? Or maybe they were under orders from Bartow or Gray. But to do what? Someone had trashed Cara's hotel room, and someone had put a compulsion on her to go home. The same person or different people? How many parties were involved in this mess?

He timed it just right and bumped into the guy in the doorway just as the other man was coming out of the restroom. He gave him a quick once-over and noted the details: about five ten, brown hair, brown eyes, shoulders like a linebacker. Rafe smiled, apologized, and looked into the man's eyes.

Nothing. No images, no facts from the universe. Zip. Just like Cangialosi. Just like Adrian Gray. What the heck was going on here?

The guy pushed past him, and Rafe used the chance to lift his wallet. As the suspect headed back to his table, Rafe ducked into a restroom stall, locked it, and opened the wallet. There wasn't much: a wad of cash, some foreign credit cards, and ID that proclaimed the tail Evan Gerrari, citizen of Santutegi.

He tried again to see something by looking at Gerrari's photo, but he got the same result as before—a big fat nothing.

He glanced over the credit cards, then back at the ID. Santutegi. Where had he heard that name before? It took him a moment, but then he remembered the newscast. The president of Santutegi was in Vegas, going to some convention. Rafe had been testing his abilities and looked at the foreign president on TV . . . and seen nothing. Just like this guy.

His senses tingled, the Hunter stirring as a suspicious pattern began to form. First Cangialosi, then the president—what was his name? Criten, that was it. Then Gray, then this guy. Out of that bunch, two of them had something in common; they were both from Santutegi. What were the odds?

He'd lived in Vegas long enough to know that the odds were always on the side of the house. He'd learned when to walk away from the table, and right now that seemed like a damned good idea. The more distance he and Cara put between them and the Santutegi guys, the better he liked it.

He took the cash and stuffed it in his pocket, then dropped the wallet in the toilet. Leaving the stall, he dropped the credit cards deep in the trash. He washed his hands, then walked out of the restroom. He'd left Cara alone too long.

She still sat in the booth, already halfway through her pancakes, no longer on the phone. She looked up as she saw him, and the sweetness of her smile warmed him. "Hey."

"Hey." He slid into the seat, trying to focus despite his reaction to her welcome. *You're in bad shape, Montana, if one little smile can get you going.* He glanced around as if looking for the waitress, noting that their tails were watching him. Him, not Cara.

"These pancakes are delicious," she said. "I hope yours aren't cold."

"Yeah." He picked up his fork, then leaned forward to snag the syrup from her side of the table. "Listen," he murmured. "I think we need to lose these guys."

She paused in lifting her cup to her lips, but only for a second. She took a sip of coffee, then whispered, "How?"

He poured syrup on his pancakes. "I thought about slipping out the bathroom window to slash their tires, but it's too small. We're going to have to ditch them somewhere."

She finished the last gulp of coffee. "Let me do it."

He cut up his pancakes, still thinking of alternatives. "Let you do what?"

"Let me take care of the tires."

He jerked his gaze up, staring as she calmly popped a bit of pancake into her mouth. "Absolutely not."

"Why not? If you're sure they're tailing us—"

"I am."

"—then let me help. I might fit through the window, and if you stay here to distract them, they may not suspect anything."

"That's a crazy plan."

"You didn't think so when you were going to do it."

"I'm a professional."

"Yeah, but I'm from Jersey." She flashed him a mischievous grin. "Danny taught me a few things."

"Be serious. Have you ever slashed a tire before?"

An enticing little twinkle lit her eyes. "Yes. My boyfriend cheated on me with Andrea Miller in senior year, and I made sure his car stayed in her driveway for her parents to find."

Truth.

He weighed the odds. "I don't want you in danger."

"You won't let me be. Do you have a knife I can use?"

"Yeah. I can slip it to you under the table."

"I have a better idea." Grabbing her purse, she slid out of the booth, then came to stand in front of him, blocking the view of the tails while he slid the knife out of his pocket and palmed it.

"How did you want to do this?" he asked, looking up at her. The white tank top under her plaid shirt really showcased her assets at eye level. His mouth watered.

She bent over, surprising him, her lips hovering above his. "Slip it in my pocket." Then she kissed him.

Heat flared like a spewing volcano, sweeping over him. Her scent wrapped around him, cinnamon and vanilla and delicious female, her curly ponytail sliding forward and tickling his face. He grabbed the waistband of her jeans, tugging her closer, fighting the urge to yank her into his lap and take what he wanted. The Hunter jerked against the leash of his control, wanting woman. Wanting sex.

And Rafe just wanted *her.*

She pulled back from the kiss just enough to murmur, "Put it in, hot shot."

For a moment he thought she had read his mind. Then he remembered—danger, people following them, the knife. He pretended to caress her hip and slipped the weapon into her front pocket.

She straightened, swinging her purse in front of the slight bulge. "This trip is getting more and more interesting, Rafe Montana."

It sure as hell was. It had been awhile for him, and she turned him on like a match to tinder. He wanted to find a motel somewhere so they could get lost in each other for days. He looked in her eyes and saw the truth there: simmering arousal, feminine interest . . . and death.

Damn it. How could he have forgotten that?

"I'll be right back," she said, apparently not picking up on his disquiet.

He watched her walk across the room, ponytail bouncing and that sweetly curved ass swaying with sensual invitation. As she passed the men from Santutegi, he fully expected them to watch her go by. But their gazes stayed fixed on him.

He settled back in the booth, acting like he hadn't noticed them, and dug into his pancakes. He tried to focus on business and not on the arousal still heating his blood. Cara's life depended on his protection, and that sobering reminder helped calm him. Why were the suits watching *him* if they were after Cara?

Unless they weren't after her at all. And that just made no sense.

Where is Cara?

He'd barely asked the question before the vision swelled in his mind. Cara had already slipped out the window and headed over to the silver sedan, staying low and moving quickly. Once she got close to the car, she ducked down into a crouch and hurried to the rear tire. A single jab of his knife did the job. She crept up to the front of the vehicle. A second stab damaged the passenger side tire. Then she scurried back toward the restaurant again, using cars and the shadows of the late afternoon as cover.

By the time Cara finished her mission, he'd cleaned his plate. He got the check from Nancy, went to the register and paid in cash. Then he hung out near the candy by the checkout counter, the picture of the exasperated boyfriend waiting for his girl to come out of the restroom.

Finally the women's room door opened, and Cara stepped out. She saw him immediately and came right over.

"All set?" he asked.

She grinned. "Oh, yeah."

He slid his arm around her waist and guided her to the door, aware that their followers had risen from their table and were headed toward checkout. He and Cara stepped outside, and he took her hand and hurried with her toward his SUV.

"Won't they be suspicious if they see us running?" Cara asked, panting as she tried to keep up with his long strides.

"I'm not running."

"But I am. My legs are shorter than yours."

"Sorry." He slowed his pace so she could keep up with his brisk walk. "Maybe they'll think we're hot to get to a motel, especially after that show you put on."

They reached the SUV and she stopped, looking up into his eyes. "Sorry, it was all I could think of."

Lie. She'd wanted to kiss him, and even though he knew it was a bad idea to get involved with her, he couldn't regret it, either. "When we get clear of these guys, we're going to talk about this."

She studied his face for a minute. "Okay."

Their followers came out of the restaurant. Rafe led her to her side, unlocked the door, and helped her in with a hand on her butt. She raised her brows at him as he closed the door for her, and he shrugged, unrepentant. He was disciplined, not dead.

"We are definitely going to talk," she said when he climbed into the driver's seat.

"First we get out of here." He pulled out of the space, watching their pursuers in the rearview mirror as they discovered their disabled car. He grinned and turned his attention to the road.

"Wow, they're really mad." Cara leaned toward the right, watching the drama in the side mirror. "I sliced the tires on the passenger side. They're not going anywhere."

"You did a good job. That should give us a chance to put some distance between us and them."

She turned toward him, a frown on her face. "Do you think they know we're going to Flagstaff?"

"I think they know we're following Danny." A vision swept into his head: Danny leaving Flagstaff, heading south through the desert in an old Jeep. He tightened his hands on the wheel to control his elation. "Actually," he lied, "I got a call on my cell while you were in the ladies' room. A guy I know saw Danny leaving Flagstaff."

"You've got someone following him?"

"I put the word out. Once we get closer to him, I'll call in my friend Mike Torrez. The law says I need to go through an Arizona agent since I'm licensed in Nevada, and the extra man might come in handy." He sent her a sidelong glance, noticed the way she gripped her purse. "What's the matter?"

"It's bad enough to have one bounty hunter after him. I trust you not to hurt him, maybe to even listen to his side of the story. I don't know what others might do."

"Listen to his side of the story? Cara, he skipped bail. There's nothing he can say to get out of that."

"What if he was innocent of the crime?"

"I told you, that's up to the court. My job is to bring in the guy who cost the bail bondsman a bunch of money when he skipped out on his court date. You told me your condo is on the line for this. Aren't you ticked about that?"

"Of course I am. I plan on having a long talk with Danny when we find him. I just don't want to see him go to jail."

"A long talk? Cara, Danny broke the law when he skipped. He's guilty of that, whether or not he's guilty of the crime he was arrested for."

She was quiet for a long moment. "I thought you might be able to help him," she finally said.

"I'm sorry, Cara, but that's not what I do. Look, I'll put off calling Mike until the last possible second, but I'm a hunter, not a charity worker. The sooner you understand that, the less disappointed you'll be."

CHAPTER EIGHT

Cara didn't know what to say after Rafe's pronouncement. Somehow she'd thought he would help Danny when they found him, not just haul him back to jail. And now the law said he had to bring in another guy? She stared out the window, wondering if she was bringing more trouble to her brother instead of aiding him.

She took a steadying breath. Her emotions were all over the place these days. Between Danny and Warren, the stress alone was enough to raise her blood pressure. And then there was Rafe.

What had possessed her to kiss him back at the diner? She wasn't usually so spontaneous, so forward. But Rafe's talk of living in the moment had energized her, especially after hearing from her ex. After all, why shouldn't she live in the moment, too? She'd spent a lifetime following the rules. Maybe it was time to break some.

But now she regretted making the first move. She shouldn't have kissed him. What if Rafe Montana was the type of guy to help himself to a casual fling and then still throw her brother in jail? She should have waited to be sure rather than jump right in.

So much for living in the moment.

"Cara? You okay?"

She wanted to ignore him, but sticking her head in the sand wouldn't help anyone. No one had forced her to make a move on him; she'd made that foolish decision on her own. "I'm all right."

"Listen, I want you to understand where I'm coming from. I don't want you to get the idea I'm some white knight taking you to rescue your brother."

She gave a laugh. "The last thing I would ever call you, Rafe Montana, is a white knight."

"Good."

She turned to face him. "Though I was hoping you would give him a chance to explain."

"Sweetheart, I don't think you understand how all this works. Your stepbrother broke the law, and as an agent of that law, I am obligated to bring him in. Pretty cut and dried."

"You've never found an exception, huh?"

"No. You break the law, you do the time. Like I said, cut and dried."

"No second chances in your world, Rafe? No forgiveness?"

"I'm no saint, Cara." He slanted her a hard look. "In my world, everything is pretty black and white."

"I'm starting to see that." She turned her gaze out the window at the darkening sky, wondering if she had jumped from the frying pan into the fire.

. . . . .

The sun was setting, turning the desert sky into an explosion of orange and lavender and deep blush pink. The boulders and mesas stood in stark silhouette against Mother Nature's vivid show as Ekhia—the sun—sank deeper into the horizon. Cara had drifted off to sleep about an hour ago, granting him precious solitude at this powerful moment of ending and beginning.

Low in his throat, he crooned a melody ingrained from childhood—the song of farewell to Ekhia, followed immediately by the higher notes of the song of welcome to Ilargi, the moon. The ritual settled his soul, quieted the Hunter and gave him invaluable peace for a few cherished seconds.

"Are you Native American?" Cara's sleepy voice came from the shadows of the passenger seat.

He exhaled, serenity floating away like a dream. "Some. On my father's side."

"I thought you looked it the first time I met you." She shifted, her light hair visible even in the dimness of a highway without street lights. "That was a beautiful song. Does it mean something?"

That she had witnessed his ritual should have disturbed him. In his culture only a mate observed a man's private communion with the elements; only a mate could possibly share in such an intimate moment without disrupting the balance. Had he known she was awake, he would never have exposed his soul in such a way.

Yet she *was* awake, she *had* heard his song, and no sense of violation disrupted his harmony with the universe. Even the Hunter remained quiet. Such a thing had never happened before, and he didn't know what to think.

"It's okay if you don't want to tell me," she said when he didn't answer.

"It's not that." He searched for words. "The song—it's something of a prayer. My mother used to sing it to me."

"It's lovely. You have a nice voice."

"Thanks."

Shuffling noises came from the passenger side, and he glanced over to see her pulling the band out of her ponytail. Her hair settled over her shoulders, curling and waving in every direction. She combed her fingers through it, then started to gather it again.

"Don't." He turned his eyes to the road. "It looks nice that way."

"Thanks, but it gets in a million tangles if I don't keep it under control."

The image of her curly hair spread across his pillow, of Cara out of control, had his hands tightening on the wheel.

"We should probably stop soon," he said, trying to focus on business. "Since Danny left Flagstaff, this trip is going to be longer than we thought. We should crash for the night, start fresh in the morning."

He saw the way she stilled out of the corner of his eye, her hands still tangled in the hair she was trying to tame. "What do you mean, crash for the night? I thought the drive was only a few hours."

"That was before I found out that Danny had left Flagstaff," he said. "I don't know where he's going to land, so this road trip just got longer."

"I see." She finished doing her hair, then settled back in her seat.

He waited for her to say more, but the heavy silence spoke for her. The confines of the SUV's cab seemed to shrink around them, the air filling with awareness.

"We should talk about that other thing now," he said.

She whipped her head around. "What other thing?"

The challenge in her tone stirred the Hunter. He took a calming breath before he replied. "Sex."

"I knew it!"

"We can't ignore this thing between us," he forged on.

"Listen, kissing you in the diner was a mistake," she said. "It was just a way to cover you slipping me the knife. It was a dumb plan."

"It worked. And that kiss was pretty hot."

"You can forget about that. It didn't mean anything."

"Sweetheart, you can lie to yourself if you want, but there have been sparks flying between us since the moment we met."

She shrugged. "It happens."

"Yeah, it does. And I want you to know that when we do stop for the night, we're sharing a room. So get used to that now."

A squeak of outrage came from the passenger seat. "I am not sharing a bed with you!"

"I didn't say that. I said a room." He shot her a quick glance. "There's usually two beds, or I'm fine on the floor. But someone is chasing us, Cara, and we can't ignore security for modesty's sake. This is no time for games."

"I don't play games."

"Good. Neither do I." He caught sight of a neon sign advertising a popular motel, the lettering only half lit. "This place looks good. You hunch down in the seat so they don't see you from the inside. It might be better if I check in alone."

"Good, then you can pay for the room."

He steered the truck toward the exit ramp. "No problem."

. . . . .

Cara did as she was told and scrunched down on the floor of the passenger side while Rafe walked into the motel to register. Her nerves jangled so much that her fingers trembled. She breathed slowly, trying to calm the peculiar excitement flooding her.

So they were stopping for the night. They were both adults. She'd already explained about the kiss at the truck stop, so he knew not to expect her to jump into bed with him. She was a sensible woman and understood the need to stay together for safety's sake, especially since they were being followed by a couple of strangers. She wasn't so naïve to think that a pair of flat tires had completely discouraged them. No, they would probably be back, and she had to agree with Rafe that staying together promised the best protection.

She'd protested when Rafe was around, but now that she hid crouched in the SUV, she couldn't lie to herself. She was attracted to the guy, had been from the beginning.

She hadn't been with anyone in over a year, not since Warren had broken their engagement. Having foolishly made him a partner in the company, she was forced to work with him, but she no longer loved him. Maybe she never had. She'd loved the dream of a husband and children, the longing for a family that she had clung to since her mother died.

When Warren had announced his engagement to Ashley only three months after he'd broken it off with her, all her old insecurities rose like ghosts to haunt her. She could still hear his words the night he'd asked for his ring back. *A man likes to feel like he's needed, babe, and around you—well, I always feel like you're so smart, you don't need anybody.*

Was that why she'd never had a lot of dates? Because the boys always felt intimidated or emasculated by her intellect? Nerd. Geek. Egghead. The names had plagued her since the first day she'd made the honor roll in junior high. Were men really not attracted to intelligent women?

Rafe didn't seem bothered by it.

Maybe that's why she was having such a hard time ignoring this attraction between them. She couldn't deny the physical allure, and here they were, all alone on the road together. She'd mentioned her degrees and her business, and he hadn't seemed to think any of it was at all out of the ordinary. She found that alone very appealing. Yet how much of what she was feeling stemmed from genuine attraction, and how much from worry over Danny? Rafe struck her as a cool place of reason and safety in a world suddenly gone off-kilter, and she didn't want to get intimate with him only to realize she had been using him as comfort. He didn't deserve that.

Which left everything as muddled and confusing as ever.

. . . . .

Rafe climbed back in the truck, the key to room 203—around the back of the motel—safely in his shirt pocket. He glanced over at Cara. She knelt on the floor facing away from the windshield, her arms resting on the seat, her head below the window line. Her ponytail curled along her back, and he couldn't resist trailing his gaze along the blond mass, then farther over her curvy rear end. Her position put her in a provocative pose that grabbed hold of his imagination and wouldn't let go. He could think of any number of uses for such a position, all guaranteed to bring both of them to screaming orgasm.

"Everything okay?" she whispered.

He gave a short nod, not trusting himself to speak. Then he shifted the SUV into reverse and turned his head to look out the rear window as he backed up.

A lime-green Volkswagen flew into the parking lot behind him. He stomped on the brake. Cara cried out, scrambling for balance. The car sped past him, music blaring and its teenage passengers laughing. Once they had passed, he started to reverse again, this time more slowly. Cara grabbed at the console between the seats, trying to regain her position. Her hand slipped, landed on his thigh.

He braked again, the force sending her hand sliding upward. Her fingers halted an inch from his groin.

"Oh, my God. Sorry. Sorry." She curled her fingers into his jeans for an instant while she found purchase, then yanked her hand back. "I lost my balance."

"I know." His gaze was drawn to her mouth as she worried

her lower lip with her teeth, then down to where her tank top pulled away from her breasts. The edge of her lacy bra peeked out. The Hunter stirred, along with his rising sexual interest.

She glanced down at herself, squeaked, and tugged her tank top into place. "What is it with you staring at my boobs all the time?"

He shrugged, a grin tugging at his mouth, and smoothly shifted the SUV into gear. "They're nice."

"Men," she muttered, wrapping her over-shirt more tightly around her.

They made it to the room without further incident. Rafe got out first, opened the door to the room and checked it out without turning on the lights. Empty. Then he signaled to Cara. He opened his Hunter senses wide, alert for danger, as she darted from the truck into the room. When she brushed past him in the doorway, her feminine scent hit him like a sledgehammer: pungent, primal, irresistible.

He breathed in her essence, then stepped into the room and closed the door behind him. His senses were so jazzed he could hear her breathing, her heartbeat. He leaned back against the door, his sharpening eyesight picking out the pale outline of woman in the dark.

"Rafe, aren't you going to turn on a light?"

"In a minute."

She shifted, her clothing gliding over flesh with a soft swish. He wanted to touch her, to sweep away those layers until skin grazed skin. He wanted to bury his face in her hair, inhale the scents that drove him crazy, even now, even from a distance, as he slid into her hot, slick depths. He closed his eyes, rested his head back against the door, willed his senses to return to normal levels. The Hunter fought him, but they'd had this battle before. Always, they struggled. Always, he won.

Except once. And that once had forged the rules he lived by ever since.

"I think there's a lamp over here somewhere."

"Wait, don't—" The bedside light clicked on, and Rafe held up a hand, blinking against the unexpected glare. He had his powers about seventy-five percent contained. The light helped, but the sight of Cara beside the bed, didn't.

She bit her bottom lip again. "Sorry, was I not supposed to do that?"

"I'm in charge of security, Cara." He stalked over to the drapes and yanked them shut. The action gave him the extra moment he needed to regain full control. "You do what I say, when I say it."

"I was trying to help."

"Don't."

"I hate this." She clenched her fists at her sides.

"You can hate me all you want."

"Not you. *This*." She spread her arms. "This whole situation. In my world, I'm the one in charge. I fix the problems; I put out the fires. But out here, nothing makes sense or looks right or is what it appears to be. Even the landscape is different!" She swiped a hand over her face, weariness evident in the movement. "I feel so useless."

The despair in her voice touched him, reaching deep inside to a place he had thought well guarded. He knew he shouldn't go to her. He knew he shouldn't fold her into his arms. But he did anyway.

She fit into his embrace like a key in a lock, her head resting against his shoulder, that soft ponytail curling over his arm. Her quiet hiccup of a sob pierced his heart, sparking his protective instincts. Something about her got to him. Was it her love for her stepbrother? Her obvious loyalty to him? She had flown across the country and taken off with a virtual stranger for parts unknown, all to protect Danny.

Lucky guy.

She sniffled one more time, then pushed back a step, breaking the embrace. He looked into her reddened eyes, swiping a tear from her cheek with his thumb. The dejection he saw tugged at him. And the shadow of death still lingered.

He tightened his jaw. She wasn't going to die, not if he had anything to say about it. He would not let her mission be in vain.

"Get some sleep," he said. "I'll take the bed by the door."

"I need my carry-on," she said. "The little suitcase."

"I'll get it." He headed toward the door, then stopped with his hand on the knob. "Go wash up. You'll feel better." She nodded, and he opened the door.

"Thank you," she whispered.

He gave a jerky nod, then stepped outside. The cooling air hit his heated skin in welcome relief, helping him battle the lingering arousal. He hit the car remote, and the snick of the locks opening echoed through the empty night. He reached for the door handle, then paused, resting his palm against the side of the vehicle. Bent his head.

The past twenty-four hours had doused him and wrung him out: his powers going wacky, his mother being shot at, new players with unfamiliar abilities.

And Cara.

Cara, so pretty and sexy and appealing to him on levels no woman had ever touched. So loyal, so loving, so determined to rescue her stepbrother no matter what. He wanted to keep her close, to bask in her warmth. But the vision of her death haunted him, raising protective instincts he hadn't felt in years. He'd never let anyone close enough. He'd wanted it that way, especially after what had happened with Darius.

He shut his eyes, the ever-present guilt washing over him. Even after five years, it never dissolved, never slipped away. It lingered, coloring everything he did, keeping him at arms' length from other people for fear that the Hunter would win the battle this time. Would succeed in taking another life.

His actions had caused one man's death. Had nearly killed Darius.

That moment had hardened him, changed him. With one accidental death on his conscience and the knowledge that his brother would live, he'd walked away from his family, from their mandate to use their powers only for the good of others. Nothing *good* existed in him. He'd failed at the hero biz, and it was better for everyone if he stayed away. At least then there would be no more accidents for the people he loved.

But now there was Cara, a woman who slipped past his defenses as if they were butter. A woman whose devotion to her stepbrother reminded him what love was all about. A woman who starred in a vision where she'd die violently, a vision that dragged him back reluctantly into the role of hero.

The Hunter relished the challenge; Rafe just longed for Cara.

He sighed, then leaned back against the SUV, looking up at the night sky glittering with stars. It was a lucky thing Ilargi hid half her face tonight, because a full moon would have made things more difficult. The Hunter fought hardest for control during the full moon, and he doubted he would have been able to walk away from Cara under its light. But the relief was only temporary. The full moon would be upon them in another week. He had to get to the bottom of this whole mess and send Cara safely back east before then.

While he still could let her go.

He turned around, opened the door to the SUV and pulled out Cara's carry-on bag. Flipping the lock on the remote, he faced the hotel room door.

It promised to be a hellish night.

CHAPTER NINE

When Cara opened her eyes the next morning, the first thing she saw was the rumpled bed next to hers. The *empty* rumpled bed.

Rafe.

She jerked into a sitting position, looking around the room for him. The lights were off, and the drapes remained shut, though enough sunlight sneaked past the edges for her to see that no one sat at the tiny table beside the TV. The bathroom door stood open. The only sounds that reached her ears were the muffled conversations of people in rooms beside hers, and the distant drone of a TV.

She eased back the covers and got to her feet. Where was he? What about all that talk of protecting her? Of teaming up? Had he left her here to go after Danny himself?

The notion chilled her, and she wrapped her arms around her middle. She hadn't thought Rafe to be the type to ditch her in the middle of the desert, but she'd been wrong about men before. She kept hoping each time would be different. That she'd finally meet a guy who deserved her trust.

She'd kinda thought Rafe might be that guy.

Okay, let's say he *had* left her here to go after Danny on his own. What now?

Phone book. Find a cab company—she winced as she imagined

the cost—and somehow get back to Vegas. Once there, she could formulate a plan.

She spotted the phone book on the table and started toward it. A rustling from outside her door made her freeze. She noticed Rafe's black duffle bag tucked on the far side of the bed just as the door creaked open. Sunlight streamed in behind the silhouette of a man.

"Oh, good, you're up." Rafe stepped into the room and let the door shut behind him. In one hand he juggled a cardboard beverage tray with two cups of coffee in it, and in the other he held a brown paper bag. "I went to get gas and picked up some breakfast."

Breakfast. He hadn't left her.

"I didn't know where you were." The words slipped out before she could stop them, not quite accusing yet way too vulnerable.

"I'm always up early." He went over to the table and set everything down, then turned to face her. "You just wake up?"

"Yeah." She took a deep breath. "Sorry. I didn't know what to think when I woke up and you were gone."

"You were out cold. Didn't you get my note?"

"Note?"

"I left you a note, telling you where I'd gone." His expression sobered as he studied her face. "You thought I'd taken off without you?"

She shrugged and glanced away, the mere idea seeming foolish now. "Like I said, I didn't know what to think."

He went into the bathroom and came back a minute later with a piece of motel stationery, which he pressed into her hand. "I stuck it on the bathroom mirror with some duct tape. I figured that would be your first stop."

His gentle tone only made things worse. She read the note,

her stomach sinking as her own foolishness became even more evident.

WENT FOR GAS AND COFFEE. BE BACK SOON.
DON'T LEAVE THE ROOM! RAFE

She pushed back her unruly hair and made herself look at him. "I feel really dumb."

"You're not dumb."

She couldn't stand the kindness, the patience in his eyes, not when she clearly stood in the wrong. "You don't have to be nice about it. I jumped to conclusions."

"You don't know me that well. It's understandable."

"Will you stop being so sweet about this?" She stalked over to the table and dropped the note on it.

"Sweet, huh?" The obvious amusement in his tone had her looking back at him. "I've been called a lot of things. Sweet isn't one of them."

"I'm sure."

"Look, I'm in this until we find Danny and until I know you're safe. I'm not going to leave you stuck in the middle of nowhere while I go chase my bounty."

"God, it sounds awful when you put it like that. I'm sorry."

He shrugged, but she could tell she'd offended him. "Like I said, you don't know me that well. If you did, you'd know I would never put you in danger. You're under my protection."

"Sorry. I really am sorry." She ran both hands over her sleep-mussed hair. "Look, let me wash up and then I'll come back out here and be a different person."

She started past him, but he halted her with a hand on her arm. He didn't speak until she looked at him. "I don't want you to be a different person."

"Oh, come on." She tried to keep her tone light. "I promise, I'll be better after I have my coffee."

"I don't think you could get much better," he murmured.

That quickly, awareness flared to life. They were alone in a darkened motel room with two rumpled beds only steps away. She was wearing her favorite pink cotton sleep set with nothing underneath, while he was fully dressed. His scent tickled her nose, clean and tangy and deliciously male.

And he was looking at her like she was a dying man's banquet.

The air nearly hummed between them, her blood pounding in her ears. Would he pull her closer? Let her go? The bed was only steps away—but so was the door. His fingers flexed on her skin, then tightened as he drew in a deep breath. Was he going to push her away?

"You're being sweet again," she whispered.

"Truthful," he corrected, then let go of her arm.

The absence of his touch chilled like a winter wind, and she realized she didn't want him to move away. She wanted him closer. *Much* closer.

Stepping in, she raised up on tiptoe and pressed her lips to his.

He didn't respond for about a second. Then a low growl rumbled from his throat, and he dragged her against him, lifting her off her feet as he took her mouth in a hungry, carnal kiss that made her head spin and stars dance behind her closed eyelids.

She gave herself to the kiss, allowing reason to get swept away beneath a wave of hot, honest passion. She didn't want to think right now. She didn't want to analyze. She just wanted to feel.

The kiss seemed to go on forever, or maybe time stood still, she didn't know. Didn't care. All she wanted was more of him— more of his touch, more of his kisses. Just more.

She moaned the word aloud. He turned and took one step, two, then fell on the nearby bed, rolling her beneath him. She wrapped her arms around his neck, crushed beneath the delicious weight of him. She wanted everything, all of him—over her, around her, inside her.

He shoved up her shirt, his hand closing around one breast. She ripped her mouth from his, gasping as his lips closed around the beading nipple. He jerked her shirt up some more, baring both breasts, dividing his time between them. She arched her hips into his. So good . . . but not what she was aching for.

She squirmed against him, trying to get closer. To get *more*. For a few torturous minutes he made her wait, driving her to wild distraction with his lips and tongue and teeth until she was whispering his name in a high, pleading tone. Finally he gave in, easing his hand under the leg of her sleep shorts, stoking the fires higher and higher as he followed the muscle of her thigh upward. When his fingers grazed the moist flesh between her thighs, her mind nearly exploded. Starving for the feel of him, for the taste of him, she tore at his shirt, fumbling with the buttons, finally releasing the top three or four. She swept her palms over his chest—solid muscles, lightly furred. She gave a purr in the back of her throat, threading her fingers through the springy hair, gliding her palms against his warm skin. Holy Hannah, did he feel this good *everywhere*?

Her fingers tangled in a chain around his neck. She followed the warm metal, closing her hand around a slim, rectangular shape with irregular edges. It felt hot, like his skin.

"No!" He tried to grab her hand, but she was tangled in the chain. He wedged his fingers beneath hers. For an instant his palm pressed against hers, the pendant between them.

White light exploded in her mind, heat searing through her body as if she burned alive. Hunger clawed at her, wanting out, wanting release. She struggled for breath, her heart hammering, shaking from the sheer, raw force of what gripped her.

He pried her fingers free.

Cool air flooded over her as he jerked his warm body away. She could breathe now. She could think. She could see—and what she saw was Rafe standing by the bed, rapidly doing up the buttons of his shirt.

"Wow," she whispered.

"Take your shower," he said. "Eat something. We're leaving soon." He headed for the door.

She leaned up on her elbows, blood burning with a kind of hunger she'd never felt before. "Where are you going?"

"I'm going to take a walk around the perimeter and make sure we weren't followed." He paused with his hand on the knob and looked back at her. "Don't leave the room."

Then he was gone.

Cara contemplated the closed door, heart pounding, limbs shaking. She'd suspected Rafe Montana would be an exciting lover, and lordy, how true that was. But what had just happened to her? And why had he left so abruptly? Her body throbbed with unreleased desire, and her mind spun with unanswered questions. She'd thought he'd been right there with her. In fact, she *knew* he'd been turned on. A man couldn't hide it.

Then why had he left? Had she done something wrong? Crossed some unspoken boundary?

Why couldn't men come with manuals? She was great with computers but not so much with humans. Maybe she'd come on too strong. But the chemistry between them flared like a bonfire, and she couldn't ignore it.

Apparently he could.

With a sigh, she forced her trembling legs to stand and made her way to the bathroom. As she turned on the shower, she thought about the chain Rafe wore around his neck and the pendant on it. The heat from Rafe's body made whatever it was feel like it was on fire. The whole experience in his arms had literally made her see stars, had taken her to another world.

She began to strip. She couldn't deny she was fascinated. He talked about business and protection and then kissed her like he would die if he didn't. The whole incident had flared out of nowhere, but when he came back, she expected to be on her game—fully dressed and with clean teeth and hair for one. The man was quite capable of dragging her out of the shower dripping wet and shoving her in the truck—and wasn't that an interesting image?—but she intended to meet him on even footing.

They weren't done yet.

. . . . .

Rafe found a vending machine at the other end of the courtyard and fed it some coins to get a Coke. He didn't usually drink soda this early, but he needed caffeine, and he'd left his coffee in the room.

With Cara.

The Coke tumbled to the bottom of the machine, and he grabbed it with some relief. Even the moment it took to pop the top was a welcome distraction from the memory of her beneath him, his hands on that silky skin.

What the hell was he going to do about this?

He leaned against the wall and took a chug from the soda. He'd spent most of last night on guard in case the tails from Santutegi had gotten their car going, but the hours had passed without incident. Then, as the room had lightened with the approaching dawn, he'd found himself watching Cara. Last night she'd changed quickly into sleepwear and immediately conked out the second her head had hit the pillow. Throughout the night, she'd somehow wrapped the covers around her like a co-coon, with only her nimbus of honey-colored hair spread across the pillows indicating a human inhabited the bed.

For some reason her quirky sleeping habits struck a soft spot in his heart. How did she slip past his defenses so easily? He couldn't allow himself to be distracted, not when she needed protection. Not when the cloud of death still hung over her. But something about her tugged at him, tempting him to mix business with pleasure.

He'd finally given up getting any decent amount of sleep and gotten up early to go next door to the gas station to get food. Best to keep to the basics. Survival first. He'd thought he had it all under control.

Then he'd come back and seen her, standing in those cotton pajamas that clung to every curve, her forehead crinkled in worry that he'd ditched her. Insult fought with tenderness. As if he would leave her. As if he could.

Nope, he was well and truly caught.

His focus stone practically burned a hole in his chest, still humming with reflections of turbulent emotion. He hadn't thought to take it off since things had happened so fast. One min-ute he had been trying to convince Cara he hadn't abandoned her, and the next he'd had her half naked beneath him. He hadn't realized how hungry he was or how much he wanted her, not until the crystal had caught her in its grip and echoed her feelings back at him.

He'd been with a lot of women, many of whom had handled the focus stone, but none of them had ever evoked such a re-sponse from it.

He blew out a long breath and rolled the cold can of soda along his forehead. His entire body still burned, the Hunter very near the surface and howling with sexual frustration. He'd tried ignoring it, but that wasn't working. Every little thing Cara Mc-Gaffigan did caught his attention, enchanted him. He'd had dozens of women in his life, but she left him as rattled as a teenager fumbling with his first bra hooks. With his hormones jacked so high, no wonder her innocent touch on the crystal had nearly sent him straight to orgasm.

This heat between them was dangerous; it could flare up and distract him at the wrong moment. He couldn't let that happen. Better if they went for it, took the edge off. All he had to do was take off the crystal beforehand, at least until they went a few rounds and he was more in control.

He gave a rough laugh as he realized where his thoughts were going. Who was he kidding? He wanted her, and apparently he wasn't above justifying it . . . even to himself.

He plugged more change into the soda machine, grabbed a second soft drink when it tumbled out, and headed back to the room.

Headed back to Cara.

. . . . .

"Mr. Bartow, are you free? President Criten is here to see you."

"I'm certain Mr. Bartow has time for me." Jain Criten eased past the young, busty receptionist blocking the doorway of Artie Bartow's office and smiled at the casino manager, holding out his hand. His bodyguard followed behind and took up a post near the door, his expression both deadly and serious. The pretty brunette cast a questioning glance from him, to Criten, then to Bartow.

"It's all right, Nicki." The casino manager hastily stood and shook hands, then waved the girl away. "Why don't you go get some coffee?" He looked at Criten. "Would you like some, Your Excellency? Maybe your escort?"

"No, thank you. Gadi and I ate earlier." Criten indicated a chair. "May I sit?"

"Of course, of course." Bartow sat as well, the chair squeaking at the rotund man's weight. "Close the door, Nicki," he said. The receptionist nodded and left the office, closing the door behind her.

Criten took the opportunity to snag the newspaper from Bartow's desk, his lips curving as he read the top page. "Checking your horoscope, Mr. Bartow?"

"Crossword puzzle," Bartow snapped, then held out his hand. "May I have my paper back please?"

He was lying. Criten glanced from the blank crossword puzzle to the man's trembling hand and hesitated just long enough to watch panic flare in Bartow's eyes. Then he presented his most charming smile and handed back the newspaper. "Of course."

"Thank you." Bartow stuffed the paper into a drawer of his desk, then faced Criten again, the soul of geniality. "What can I do for you today, Your Excellency?"

"I wish to talk to you about a private matter, not one of state or politics."

"Is something wrong?" Bartow came to attention, his concern seemingly genuine. "Is it your room?"

"No, not at all. The room is most comfortable. I wish to talk to you about security."

"Security?" Bartow glanced at Gadi. "Mr. Gray normally handles security. He should be here shortly, but I can call him in early if necessary. Was there a threat of some kind?"

"Not at all." Criten raised his hand, and Gadi came to stand behind his chair. "I have learned, Mr. Bartow, that there was recently a theft in your organization."

"A theft? Oh, the car." The lie slid smoothly from his lips. "Yes, one of my employees took off with my personal vehicle a few weeks back. It's been dealt with. I'm surprised you heard about it."

"My security team makes it their business to know everything when I am traveling. I don't like surprises."

"Of course, of course." Bartow's smile dimmed a hair. "We tried to keep it quiet. I'm sure you understand. Bad publicity and all that."

"I do understand. I also understand why you lied about the theft."

This time the smile completely disappeared from Bartow's face. "Lied?"

"Your employee . . . this Danny Cangialosi. He didn't steal a car, did he?"

"Yes, he did."

Truth. Interesting. "Ah. Then not *just* a car."

A bit of caution, a hint of possessiveness, flickered across Bartow's face. "Mr. Criten, I believe you have me at a disadvantage."

"This, I know." Criten chuckled. "I am talking about the stone, Mr. Bartow."

"S-stone?" Bartow paled, then glanced around. The glass walls of his office revealed only empty hallways and Nicki's vacant desk.

"The Stone of Igarle. The one you bought at auction on the Internet last month."

"Oh, *that* stone." Bartow laughed, the sound nearly convincing except for the alarm in his eyes. "Not much to it. Looks kind of like a red Egyptian pyramid. A nice paperweight."

"It is much more than that." Criten leaned forward. "I am Selak79."

"Oh!" Bartow's tense shoulders relaxed. "You nearly outbid me."

"Indeed. I lost my Internet connection, or I would have."

Criten shrugged, a mild reaction considering his rage when he'd realized his frustration with the bidding had shorted out the computer he was using, causing him to lose the auction. "I came to Las Vegas prepared to buy it from you."

"Buy it! Oh, I don't know—"

"I was prepared to offer this." Criten took a velvet jewel pouch out of his pocket. Pulling open the drawstring, he tipped a pinkish-orange stone the size of an egg into his hand.

Bartow stood. "That's not . . . it can't be a Padparadscha sapphire? No, it can't be. Not that size."

"It is indeed a Padparadscha. For Santutegi, such treasures are easily obtained." Criten tucked the pouch in his pocket with one hand and admired the sparkling stone nested in the other. "Isn't it stunning?"

"It is. It almost glows from the inside."

"You are correct." Criten shifted his hand so sunlight danced across the faceted surface of the gem. In the center of the stone, a light sparked and grew steadily bigger. "Perhaps you are not aware, but that *paperweight*, the Stone of Igarle, is part of the lost treasure of Santutegi. It has been missing for generations."

"I did not know that." Bartow took a handkerchief out of his jacket pocket and wiped his dampening face, never taking his eyes from the sapphire. "I heard it brought good luck."

Criten shrugged. "Old wives' tales. But I wanted you to see, Mr. Bartow, that the stone means quite a lot to me. It is part of my culture's lost heritage." The sapphire grew brighter in his palm.

"I'm sorry to hear that, Your Excellency, but I paid for it, fair and square. If you have the provenance for the piece, of course I will be too happy to turn it over to you—"

"Provenance!" Criten surged to his feet, the sapphire burning like fire in his clenched fist. "That stone is thousands of years old, crafted by my ancestors. It is mine by right."

Bartow narrowed his eyes. "Like I said, prove it, and the stone is yours."

"You can't give me what you don't have." Criten squeezed his fingers around the gem, his anger stoking the flames. "Danny Cangialosi stole that stone from you. Some two-bit hoodlum. What kind of security do you have here anyway, Bartow? How could you let this happen?"

"Listen, I'm just as upset as you are."

"Hardly," Criten said. "You lost a purchase. I lost my heritage."

"I'm sorry about that, I really am. But I bought the thing fair and square."

"I had hoped we could do business, Bartow." The edges of the stone bit into his clenched hand. "As it stands, I have men on the trail of that bounty hunter and the girl."

"What girl?"

"Miss McGaffigan." Criten gave a harsh chuckle. "Did you really think she flew back to New Jersey?"

"She didn't?" Bartow frowned. "Mr. Gray said she did."

"Then you're both fools. She is going to lead me to Danny Cangialosi and the Stone of Igarle. Then it will be mine."

"Wait just a second—"

Criten slapped the sapphire down on the desk, his palm covering it as he looked Bartow in the eye. "You have no idea what to do with a valuable piece like the Stone of Igarle, Bartow. You with your superstitions and your lucky charms and your horoscopes."

Outrage and embarrassment warred on the casino manager's face. "I don't know what you're talking about."

"The horseshoe over your door? The rabbit's foot on your

keychain? Reading your horoscope as if it's fact and not entertainment?" Criten sneered. "You bought the stone as one more talisman against Fate. No wonder you live in Las Vegas. You worship Lady Luck like a divine goddess."

"You don't know anything," Bartow said, hands fisting at his sides.

"I will make you a deal," Criten said. "I give you the sapphire, and you forget about the stone."

Bartow opened his mouth as if to protest, then closed it and frowned in thought as he regarded the hand covering the sapphire.

"Think of the trouble it will be to hunt down the thief, then reclaim your property without involving the authorities," Criten said. "This way is easier, and you get one of the world's largest Padparadscha sapphires in exchange."

"Maybe."

"Make the deal, Mr. Bartow. Take the sapphire and forget about the Stone of Igarle. Or don't take the sapphire, and I will still claim the stone. Your choice." Criten's lips curved in a mocking smile. "Consult your horoscope if you need to."

Bartow stiffened. "I don't need to. I'll take the deal."

"Excellent." Criten straightened, then removed his hand from the sapphire.

"Dear God," Bartow whispered, his reverent gaze fixed on the glowing pink stone. "Look at the way it shimmers. How does it do that? The cut?"

"Something like that."

Bartow picked up the sapphire and cupped it in his hand. "It's hot. Probably from being in your pocket."

"Probably." Criten waved a couple of fingers, focused his will. The sapphire glowed even more, the light nearly blinding as it built.

"Ow! Oh, it's hot. What the . . . I can't let go!" Bartow

raised his terrified gaze to Criten. "Do something! It's stuck on me! Burned on to me or something!" He turned his hand upside down, but the gemstone still stuck to his palm.

"You shouldn't have outbid me," Criten said, then focused his power and *pushed*.

Bartow screamed in pain as pinkish-orange light surged up his arm from the sapphire, enveloping him in seconds. He shook as if electrocuted, gasping for breath. He clutched his chest with his free hand, wheezing and choking. "Help . . . me."

"Oh, very well." Criten honed the power like a sharpened dagger and stabbed it into Bartow's heart.

Bartow arched his back, eyes bulging, mouth open in a silent scream. Then he dropped to the floor like a brick.

Criten let out a long sigh. "That was exhausting. Shall we try the buffet, Gadi? I need to recharge."

"As you wish, Your Excellency."

"Yes." Criten's lips curved as he regarded Bartow's shoe-clad feet protruding from behind the desk. "As I wish indeed." With a shrug he turned toward the door. "Retrieve my sapphire, Gadi. Now that he's dead, there's no life force for it to cling to. And take care of the girl."

"Yes, Your Excellency."

Criten stepped outside the office and stretched a bit. Manipulating energy always left him ravenous—for both food and sex. The elevator door dinged open, and Nicki stepped out, her purse over her shoulder, a coffee cup in one hand and her cell phone in the other. Her breasts bounced beneath her clingy blouse as she headed toward her desk, tapping the phone's keys with one thumb as she walked toward him, legs that went on for days and a tight little skirt with a frill at the mid-thigh hemline. Her lush dark hair swept over her shoulders, her tongue peeking from between bee-stung lips as she concentrated on her texting.

Criten folded his arms and leaned against her desk. He could think of other things to do with that tongue, and with Gadi's help, she'd be happy to do anything he wanted, for as long as he wanted it.

Sometimes it was fucking awesome to be the boss.

CHAPTER TEN

A towel hastily wrapped around her, Cara darted out of the bathroom still dripping from the shower and dug her ringing cell phone out of her purse. The generic chiming gave no indication who was calling, but her heart pounded anyway. What if Danny had lost his cell or, worse yet, was in jail? "Hello? Danny, is that you?"

"Still chasing ghosts?"

Her soaring hopes crashed back to earth at the familiar, unwelcome voice. "What do you want, Warren?"

"I told you. I want you to come home. I just landed this big account for us, and you're the key to it."

She gritted her teeth and forced her tone to remain polite. "I already told you I can't come home right now."

"Yeah, I know. Because of Danny. Really, Cara, when are you going to understand that you can't keep rescuing the guy?"

She stiffened. "That's none of your business."

"Don't be bitter, babe. It doesn't suit you."

She tightened her fingers around the phone. "Don't talk down to me, Warren. I told you I'm unavailable. Tell Mitch to assign the project to another programmer."

"I can't do that. I promised the client the senior partner would be working on their interface—personally."

"Un-promise them. Have Mitch give it to Rada. She's excellent."

"Rada is not the senior partner of Apex. You need to come home now, Cara. Don't make the business pay for your stepbrother's mistakes."

"I'd say in this case the business would be suffering from *your* mistake, Warren. You shouldn't make promises for other people." She took a deep, silent breath. Counted.

"I'm not the one who goes haring off to rescue a deadbeat relative every time he screws up. You have to choose, Cara—the company or Danny? Because right now it seems the company is all you have. You can't depend on Danny, and you know it."

"Oh, but I can depend on you, is that it, Warren?" She struggled to keep her tone professional and not give in to the ball of anger burning in her gut. "Let's face it, your track record isn't exactly stellar where I'm concerned."

"Oh, here we go. You *are* still bitter. I knew it after you hung up on me yesterday."

"I'm not bitter." Even as she said the words, she caught a glimpse of herself in the mirror across the room. Stiff posture, white-knuckled grip on the phone, jaw clenched.

Well, yeah, okay. Maybe she still harbored a *hint* of bitterness. And disappointment. And some distrust about men.

"If you're not bitter, why are you holding this deal hostage? Prove it, Cara. Come home and take care of business."

She searched for a snappy comeback, but all she managed was, "I can't."

"You mean you won't." He gave a long-suffering sigh. "Think it over, Cara. Decide if your company is important enough to merit your attention. This deal would go a long way toward solving our cash flow problems."

Before she could respond, he hung up.

She stood there, still dripping, staring at the "Call Ended" message on the display. She knew he considered himself the winner of their little skirmish since he'd been the one to end the conversation. Then again, she'd hung up on him yesterday. A small victory.

Talking to Warren always left her battle-weary from the emotional potshots he called conversation. She hated that he could do that to her, force her to play these games that blended striking at weakness with skillfully targeted guilt trips. She wasn't the type to try and one-up anyone, and she found the drama distasteful.

Maybe it was a good thing he'd dumped her, because she sure hated who she had to be when she dealt with him.

That simple truth struck her like a bullet. She didn't want to be this person anymore—argumentative, manipulative, hung up on the past. The stereotypical woman scorned, afraid to trust. She was more than that. She knew she was more than that.

It was time to stop licking her wounds and start living again.

The door opened and Rafe walked in, stopping just inside the doorway. He held two cans of soda in his hands. The door closed behind him with a loud snick. "You're not ready."

"No." She dropped her phone back in her purse. "I'm not."

He took another step into the room. "Everything okay?"

She glanced at those gorgeous blue eyes, gentle with concern. She never felt combative with this man. Challenged, sure, but in a way that excited rather than provoked.

"Cara?"

"Um . . . yeah, everything's fine." She nodded toward the unopened cola in his hand. "That for me?"

"Yeah, I figured the coffee was cold by now." He handed it to her. "I wasn't sure if I should get regular or diet, but you take regular sugar in your coffee, so I took a chance."

"I switch back and forth." She popped the top on the can, using the momentary distraction to get herself under control. *He'd remembered how she drank her coffee.* The notion curled into her heart. Had any other man ever noticed the little things like he did? Even the man she'd thought she would marry?

"So." He waited until she looked at him, then continued, "Was that Danny?"

"No." She shook her head, tried to forget the smug condescension in Warren's voice. Geez, what had she ever seen in him? "Someone from work."

"You know, with people after us and all that, I'd suggest you keep your phone use to a minimum. Unless Danny calls you, that is."

"Right. Good idea." She took a chug of the soda, the caffeine and sugar giving her system a much needed jolt.

He finished his Coke, then walked over to pitch the can in the waste basket near the bed. "I guess we should talk about what happened before I left."

Cara quickly swallowed her mouthful of soda and swiped away a stray drip while his back was still turned. "Okay. Yeah, I guess we'd better."

He turned around to look at her, the rumpled expanse of bed—the scene of the crime—only a step away. "I've been trying to ignore this thing between us, but frankly I don't think we can. Especially after what happened earlier."

"It surprised me, too."

He gave a laugh. "Well, you started it with that kiss. And now . . ." He gave her a quick, hot-eyed once-over that reminded her she was practically naked. "I don't just wonder how you taste anymore. Now I know."

Her breath fled her lungs in a soft whoosh. How was it he could seduce her with mere words?

"And now that I know," he continued, "I want more."

"I want more, too." Was that her voice, all throaty and yearning?

He came toward her, taking his time, as if to give her the chance to flee if she wanted. "There's about a hundred reasons why we shouldn't be together."

"I barely know you," she whispered.

He gave a nod. "Yes, that's one reason. Another is, I'm on a job. I don't like distractions while I'm working." He stopped in front of her. "And you, Cara Mia, are definitely a distraction."

She gave a little shiver; the way he looked at her just melted her inside. "I don't mean to be."

"Yet here we are." He reached out to trail a finger down her throat. "Most guys would take the fact you were waiting for me in a towel as an invitation."

"It wasn't on purpose." She let her head fall back, giving him more access while keeping her gaze on his. "My phone was ringing."

"Yet you're standing here letting me touch you." He stroked his finger over her collar bone, along the edge of the towel. "Who was on the phone, Cara?"

"Is this an interrogation?" She tried for authoritative, but her voice broke as his finger dipped briefly between her breasts.

"Not at all." He smiled, tracing upward, grazing the pad of his finger over the pounding pulse at the base of her throat. Her insides softened; maybe from the tenderness of his expression or maybe from the arousing brush of his fingers on her skin, she couldn't tell. "But something upset you between the time I left and when I came back. The most obvious thing that comes to mind is your phone call."

"I'd rather forget about that."

"Fine, but if you're with me, I can't have people upsetting

you." He cradled her face in one hand, caressed her cheekbone with his thumb. "If we start this, you have to understand that you're mine while we're together."

Cara sucked in a breath at the masterful declaration. "Then you're mine, too."

He smiled. "Absolutely."

She closed her eyes, tempted to throw off her towel and just give herself to him. But there were things that needed to be said before she crossed that line. "I know you're going to take Danny in when you find him."

"That's true. It's my job, and it's the law. But if it wasn't me, it would be someone else. If that's going to come between us, then we stop now and walk away."

"I don't want to stop." She tried to ignore the heat flooding her system as he cupped the back of her neck and stepped closer. "Just promise me you'll give me a chance to talk to him before you take him in."

He gave a nod. "If I can."

"And once Danny is out of trouble, I have to go back to New Jersey. I can't stay here; I have a company to run."

"Let's deal with that when we come to it."

She shook her head. "I think it's better if we talk about it now."

He kneaded her nape, releasing some of the tension in the muscles. "Look, I'm not a long-term relationship guy. You should understand that right off the bat."

"You'd better tell me what that means."

He rested his forehead against hers, locking their gazes. "No other women for me while we're together, no other guys for you, and no expectations of church bells and white picket fences. When one of us wants to end it, we end it."

"Either of us?"

"Either of us. We both take the same risk here."

"What if we find Danny tomorrow?"

"We can worry about that tomorrow. This thing between us . . . it's strong. We can't ignore it. And we have today."

"What if today isn't enough?"

"I like to live in the now. I'm not a settling kind of guy, Cara. If this isn't right for you, then we walk away, no harm, no foul."

"It's that easy for you?"

"Hell, no. I want you badly." He straightened and tried to smile, and the fierce need burning in those amazing eyes made her knees weaken. "But I'm a big boy, and this is about giving each other pleasure, not heartbreak."

"I've never done anything like this before."

"It's your choice, Cara. We can try and ignore this thing like we have been, or we can give into it. Let it burn until it's sated."

"What if it's not sated?"

"Everything burns out eventually." His expression sobered. "I don't want to hurt you, Cara. If this isn't right for you, tell me now."

She studied his features, the sun-bronzed complexion, the sharp cheekbones, the sensual mouth. And those eyes; she always came back to those stunning cobalt eyes that seemed to look right through her and see everything. "I've never met anyone like you."

"I could say the same about you. There's something about you that calls me back even when common sense says to stay away."

The hint of irritation in his words brought a slow, womanly curve to her lips. She'd always been the nerdy geek with her nose in a book, smarter than most of her peers and ostracized because of it. Never had a man looked at her like she was beautiful, sexy, *hot*. Yet that was exactly how Rafe was looking at her, and she reveled in it.

Maybe this *was* what she needed, a passionate affair with a man who reinvigorated her wounded feminine pride. Forget keeping a level head. Just once in her life she wanted to feel instead of think.

She leaned into him. "Let's go for it, for as long as it lasts."

"Are you sure?"

She never looked away. "Yes."

Arousal swept his face, tautening skin over bone, narrowing his eyes and tightening his jaw. Her instincts collided—flee or yield. Panic or passion.

He kissed her. Hunger that had only smoldered now flared to a blaze. She closed her eyes, sinking into the fire, opening, giving, *surrendering*. He slid his hand behind her head, holding her as he took what he wanted from her mouth, offered more. She reached up, wrapping her arms around his neck, seeking the adventure.

Her towel slipped to the floor, and she didn't care. A groan rumbled from his throat as he discovered her nakedness, smoothing his palm along the line of her back, over the curve of her bare hip, her buttock. She curled into his touch, her head spinning. Her insides bubbled like hot wax, and every stroke of his hand only turned up the heat.

He broke the kiss an inch at a time. While she was still catching her breath, he leaned back, taking in every detail of her nudity. Nearly dizzy from his regard, she swept her damp hair back with both hands. The motion lifted her breasts, and he followed the movement, his blazing gaze nearly searing her flesh. She let her fingers trail down her body, skimming her shoulders, breasts, waist, hips, thighs.

"You're killing me," he whispered, and held out a hand.

She twined her fingers with his and allowed him to lead her to the bed, where he urged her without words to lie down. She stretched out on the mattress, inspired by the intensity of his regard to stretch out a little, pose a little. His jaw tightened, and he tugged at the top buttons of his shirt.

"Do you want help?" she asked, arching against the mattress.

He pulled a chain from around his neck and laid it on the nightstand. She caught a quick glimpse of some kind of copper-gold metal and clear crystal, but then he stepped forward to block her view, spreading his hands in wordless invitation.

She scrambled to her knees and unfastened the rest of his buttons, spreading his shirt wide and sweeping her palms along the hair-roughened muscles. "Are you tanned all over?"

"Why don't you find out?"

His teasing grin encouraged her to jerk the tails of his shirt out of his jeans, then tackle his belt. She fumbled with the buckle but finally unfastened it and popped the snap of his jeans.

"Wow. Bad idea." He grabbed her hand and pressed it against his zipper. "We don't have a lot of time," he murmured. "You'd better let me lead today."

She nodded, the hard flesh beneath her palm mute evidence as to her effect on him. Heat raced through her veins, leaving her shaking and hungry and wet. She rubbed her fingers against the bulge beneath the denim and he groaned, then pulled her hand away, putting it on her own female mound. "How about you rub this?"

She tried to pull away, but he kept her hand imprisoned with his own, guiding her fingers, gliding over her damp flesh. Her breath caught. Her eyes slid closed as arousal flared hot and wild. He kissed her, his tongue mimicking the movements of their fingers. Her head spun.

He eased her down on the bed, stroking her and kissing her and short-circuiting her normally busy brain. He caught her nipple in his mouth, sucking with a strength that sent need rippling through her and wrung a cry from her lips. She surrendered, allowing him anything, and he gave it all to her, caressing, nibbling, nipping. So many different sensations, so many surprises, so much emotion welling up inside her like a rising river until a final stroke of his fingers sent her soaring as her body exploded and reality faded away.

She came back to herself moments later. The rustling of clothing had her opening her eyes just as a naked Rafe eased down on top of her.

"My turn," he murmured, then held her head between his hands and kissed her like he had all day.

She relaxed into a puddle again, lost in his kiss, her body humming with the echoes of climax. When he nudged her thighs apart, she welcomed him, thrilled in the gentle tug of her muscles, the sweet, slow stretching as he eased into her body and began to move.

For some reason she'd thought their lovemaking would be frenzied and uncontrolled, but the steady, deliberate coupling devastated any lingering uncertainties about her decision. He staked his claim in an utter, unmistakable *taking* that shattered her from the inside out, from the first moment he slid inside her until the instant he gripped her hard and groaned his own climax, burying his face in her neck.

She went with him this time, sliding over that precipice, stroking the rippling muscles of his sweat-dampened back as her body sang a new song and her essence exploded.

. . . . .

A few minutes later, he lifted his head, sweeping her hair out of her face. "Hey there. You okay?"

She nodded, still floating. How had she lived nearly thirty years and never experienced anything like this?

"I wish we could stay here all day." He brushed a kiss on her lips, then gently disengaged their bodies. "But we've got people after us, and I can't forget that." He sighed and paused, resting his forehead against hers for a second. "I've got to get dressed and start loading up the car."

"Okay." At her nod, he left her, the cool rush of reality chilling her sweat-dampened skin as he climbed out of bed. She glanced at the clock. "Wow, it's later than I thought. I'll get dressed."

"Good idea." He dropped another kiss on her mouth and grabbed his clothes, heading toward the bathroom.

She watched him go, admiring his trim backside as he disappeared into the other room. Holy Hannah, the man was hot. And she could touch that hotness whenever she wanted.

At least until one of them decided to end it.

Shaking her head, she stopped her thoughts right there. She wasn't going to obsess about the future. She was going to try to live in the now for once in her life. And the now required that she get her butt out of bed and get dressed. They still needed to find Danny.

By the time he came back out, cleaned up and dressed, she was standing naked in front of her carry-on suitcase, which she'd opened on the other bed. He came up behind her, trailing a hand down her back to rest on her butt.

"Don't be long," he said. "We're still ahead of our buddies, and I want to keep it that way."

She sighed. "I guess they probably got new tires, huh?"

"I would think so." His expression and tone were all business, but his gentle squeeze of her derriere told another story. "You have five minutes."

She laughed. "Good thing I already took a shower."

He picked up his duffel bag and her suitcase. "You got everything you need?"

"Yeah, I'll be right out."

"Okay." He gave her a stern look, spoiled by the spark of desire in his eyes. "If you're not out there in five minutes, I'm coming in after you."

"And then we really wouldn't get out of here." She made a shooing motion. "Go on. I'll be right there."

He nodded and left.

She turned back to her bag and pulled out clean underwear and clothes, then turned toward the bathroom. Something shimmered in the corner of her eye. She turned her head and saw that Rafe had left his pendant on the table. She hadn't gotten a good look at it before, so she moved closer. It was a simple clear piece of crystal on a goldish-copper chain. Good luck charm, maybe? He hadn't seemed to be the New Age type, but this was the west, and the culture was different out here.

She shrugged and turned away. She'd make sure to give it to him when she went out to the car.

．　．　．　．　．

There was no going back now.

Rafe loaded the bags into the back of the SUV, then headed over to the soda machine for another round of colas. His stomach growled, reminding him they'd never eaten the breakfast he'd bought. But other hungers were well and truly satisfied.

Had taking Cara to bed been the wisest move? Probably not, especially since the shadow of death still lingered in her eyes.

He usually made it a practice not to mix business with pleasure. But something about this woman would not leave him alone, and he'd hoped that a little healthy sex would take the edge off and allow him to focus. But the memory of that cat-and-canary smile she'd been wearing right before he'd climbed out of bed told him he'd been dead wrong. If anything, he wanted her more now that he'd had a taste of her.

But what was done, was done. He'd accept the consequences of his decision. He'd laid it all out for her, and she'd made the choice of her own free will. They would ride this wave as long as it lasted.

And somehow he would figure out how to save her life.

As he got back to the SUV with the sodas, the hotel room door opened, and she exited the room, lugging her carry-on bag with her. He met her as she approached the front of the SUV. He handed her a soda, then took the handle of the carry-on from her. Their fingers brushed. Their eyes met. They exchanged a smile. Without a word he turned away and opened the back hatch to the vehicle, tossing the small bag on top of the other suitcases.

"Thanks for the soda." She came up behind him as he closed the door.

"We forgot to eat." He took her hand and walked her around to the passenger side. "We'll stop and get some fast food some-where."

"Okay."

He opened the door for her and she leaned in to set her soda in the cup holder, then slid back out again. "Oh, you left this inside." She reached into her shorts pocket and held out her hand. The early morning sun gleamed off the clear crystal and orichalcum chain in the center of her palm.

His world lurched. *How could he have forgotten it?*

"Thanks." He tried to keep his tone casual as he reached for it.

"It's very unusual." She closed her fingers just before he snagged it and gave him an inquiring look. "You don't seem like the New Age type."

"It's got sentimental value, and I'd like it back." He stared her down, fighting the Hunter's urge to rip it from her hand. "Please."

Hurt rippled across her face, and she opened her fingers without a word. He reached for the crystal. The instant his fingers touched it where it rested in her palm, a wave of heat swept through him. Roaring sounded in his ears, and his vision darkened around the edges, leaving only Cara shining like a beacon at the center of it. She stumbled back a step with a cry of surprise. He grabbed the chain, yanking it away. The instant it no longer touched her, the world snapped back into focus.

It isn't just me; she feels it, too.

The realization slammed into him. He'd once heard stories of mates using focus stones to center their energies and enhance sex. The clear crystal served as a tool for channeling power, and passion was definitely power. He'd never heard of anyone in recent memory actually trying it, but apparently Cara was tuned into him, and tuned into his focus stone. But that was impossible. They weren't mates. They *couldn't* be mates. He was destined to live alone.

He bought himself a minute while he slipped the pendant over his head, tucking the crystal safely beneath his shirt with a hand that trembled only slightly.

His own hunger for her had made him forget that people close to him tended to get hurt—which is why he took pains to keep everyone at a distance. He'd already seen the vision of her death; he had no desire to be the cause.

She braced herself on the doorframe. "What the heck just happened?"

"You feeling light-headed? You didn't eat this morning." He babbled the first logical explanation that entered his head as he extended a hand to assist her into the car.

She narrowed her eyes and searched his face. "Right. That must be it." Turning her back on his help, she clambered into the car under her own power, fastened her seat belt, then busied herself opening her soda, an unspoken DO NOT DISTURB sign flashing like neon between them.

She hadn't bought it. With a sigh, he closed her door and walked around to the driver's side. She was stewing, and he wasn't used to seeing the animated Cara so very quiet. He wasn't sure he liked it. But maybe it was for the best, at least until that busy brain of hers rationalized the impossible.

He got in the truck, fastened his own seat belt, then started the SUV. The sooner they left this motel—and its memories—behind them, the better.

· · · · ·

"Good morning, Nicki." Adrian Gray paused at the secretary's desk when she didn't respond. The young woman kept sorting through a huge pile of mail, utterly silent. "Nicki?"

Still she did not respond. He crouched down, studied her face. Her waxen skin and the pale shadows beneath her eyes indicated a sleepless night. As she shifted, opening envelopes and moving them to different piles, he caught a glimpse of a bruise on her breast, peeking from beneath the edge of her low-cut blouse. Another on her neck, mostly hidden beneath her dark hair.

He raised his hand slowly and brushed her hair to the side to reveal not just a bruise on her neck, but a bite mark. She didn't stop what she was doing, didn't even seem to notice his presence, much less his touch. She might have been a robot.

Sloppy, greedy fools. Teeth clenched, he moved around her,

checking the other side of her neck. Another mark. Still she kept sorting her mail. Clearly, she had no idea he was even there.

He got to his feet, fists clenched. He glanced down at her hands, saw red, burnlike welts around her wrists. She'd been tied up, used, and sent back to her desk, oblivious to what had happened to her and anything else happening around her. *Ahantzi.* It had to be.

Using the chant of *ahantzi* for the simple expediency of sexual pleasure left a bad taste in his mouth. The ritual should be revered, studied, perfected—used in battle to make one invisible to one's enemies, not for the common purpose of turning a woman into a sex slave. He knew who must have done this. Their carelessness would cost them.

He stepped behind her and rested his hands on her shoulders. "Sleep," he commanded. She slumped forward, scattering her piles of mail. Adrian leaned down near her ear. "When you wake you will remember going to a party last night, one that got a little too wild. You will decide you are hungover and go home immediately." He straightened, then moved down the hall a few paces as if he was just arriving. "Awaken."

She woke up, confusion on her pretty face as she looked around. Her gaze landed on him, and she sat up, sweeping her hair back over her shoulder. "Good morning, Mr. Gray."

"Nicki." He stopped by the desk, gave her a concerned look. "Are you all right? You don't look well."

"I don't feel well." She rubbed her forehead.

"You should go home."

She thought for a moment. "That might be the best idea."

"Go on. I'll clear it with him."

Nicki glanced at Bartow's office door, hesitated, then finally nodded. "Thank you. I really feel horrible."

"Go ahead." He waited while she got her purse out of the

bottom drawer of her desk, smiling in encouragement as she stood, slipped the strap over her shoulder, and started down the hallway. "Feel better!" he called.

She glanced back and waved before heading into the open elevator. Moments later, the doors shut.

Adrian let out a long breath and turned toward Bartow's office. He had taken two steps into the room before he saw the body. A quick visual assessment and many years of experience confirmed that Bartow was dead.

"Careless," he muttered, "*and* stupid." He backed out of the room and took his radio from his belt. "Control, this is Gray. Call 9-1-1. Mr. Bartow has had an accident."

Ignoring the flood of questions squawking from the radio, Adrian sat down in Nicki's chair to wait for the cops.

CHAPTER ELEVEN

Where do we go from here?

Cara glanced at the dashboard clock. They'd left the motel and run through a fast-food drive-through less than half an hour ago, silent except for placing their orders. Neither of them had said a word about what had happened when she'd touched his crystal. And something *had* happened—*both* times—and she wasn't buying his lame explanation.

Blood sugar, my Aunt Tillie.

She crushed the empty wrapper from her devoured breakfast sandwich into a ball and dropped it into the bag on her lap. He couldn't blame blood sugar now, could he? But with the basics taken care of, she wasn't certain how to broach the subject. Heck, she wasn't even certain what to ask. She would have thought she'd imagined the whole thing, except for his reaction. He'd looked kind of stunned and at the same time, horrified. Therefore something *had* happened, but he just wasn't talking.

She slid a glance at him. He stared straight ahead, finishing a breakfast burrito one-handed as he pushed the SUV to the speed limit. The badass bounty hunter was back, the lover of this morning gone as if he'd never existed.

The radio played in the silence between them, and an overly cheerful voice currently speculated on whether the heat index would top one hundred again today. They cut to the news. She struggled to find words to broach her subject.

"So—" she began.

Rafe put down his burrito, leaned forward, and turned up the volume. She narrowed her eyes. Was he trying to avoid the conversation?

The reporter's sober tones filled the car, and as the story registered in her brain, she swallowed the smart aleck remark that hovered on her lips.

". . . since a sniper targeted millionaire John Montana and his wife Maria as they left the William Walters Charity Ball two nights ago. Police are still investigating the incident."

"It was a very close thing," came another voice. "If Mrs. Montana had not turned to go back into the building right at that moment, she could have been seriously injured, if not killed."

"The Montanas have retired to their Sedona estate," the first voice continued. "A press conference is scheduled for later today. Now over to Patrick Manning for sports."

Rafe turned the radio down again. Cara noted the stillness of his features, the way his hands clenched on the wheel. "John Montana. Relative of yours? Rich uncle, maybe?"

"No."

"I thought you said you're from Arizona."

"I am."

"So these people aren't related to you?"

He didn't reply.

She peered at his face. "Rafe?"

He glanced at her, his blue eyes flinty. "Drop it, Cara."

She sank into her seat as he turned his attention back to the road. "I just want to help."

"You can't fix everything."

"I don't want to fix everything!" Frustration burned away any concern about overstepping her boundaries. "If you don't want to talk to me about that news story, you can talk to me about that so-called good luck charm you wear around your neck and the weird thing that happened back at the motel. Don't tell me you didn't feel it, and don't give me any BS about blood sugar. We're sleeping together, buddy, and that should count for something."

"Look, remember back at the motel when we said no expectations? Well, this is what I meant. I'm not a touchy-feely-sharey kind of guy."

"*You* look. In my world, when a woman is intimate with a guy, that means she can know things about him." She shrugged, trying to mask the hurt. "Sorry, I'm new to casual relationships."

He made some kind of growl in the back of his throat, then bit out, "Okay. *One* question."

She weighed the decision, then asked, "Who is John Montana to you?"

"My father."

"Your *father*?" She drew back in surprise. "But this guy—this family—they're like American royalty. I was only kidding about the rich-uncle thing."

"Guess you weren't far off."

"But if you come from a place like that"—she indicated the radio—"then what are you doing running around Vegas catching bad guys? Falling out with the family?"

"Something like that. And that's two questions."

"I can't figure you out, Montana." She shook her head. "You throw it out there, this thing between us. And there I am trying to decide if I want to go for it. Finally I decide, yeah, go for it, and we go to bed together. But now you treat me like I'm some stranger."

"Sorry. I've got a lot on my mind. Like the two guys tailing us. Finding Danny."

She could hear the strain in his voice. "And your mom."

He jerked a quick glance at her. "Yeah."

"Don't look so surprised. If someone took a shot at my mom, I'd be off my game, too." She turned on her side as much as the seat belt would let her. "So are you going to tell me?"

"Tell you what?"

"Why you're on the outs with your family. It's got to be eating at you, especially now."

"No."

She arched her brows. "Why not?"

"Because it's none of your business."

She frowned. "I see."

"Good, then you'll stop asking."

"Look, I was just curious. For God's sake, I'm depending on you for survival in this crazy game. Maybe I want to know a little bit more about you."

He shot her a sharp glance. "You still don't trust me?"

The edge in his voice alerted her that she had hit a serious nerve. "I didn't say that. I know you live and breathe this kind of stuff, big guy, but I'm scared out of my skivvies."

"Nice image."

"I'm just saying, it would give me some peace of mind to know a little bit more about my protector." *My lover.* "I mean, I would never have guessed you were heir to the Montana millions."

He snorted. "Sweetheart, I don't even know if I'm in the will anymore, so I'm not exactly a catch."

"I'm sure you're still in the will. Just because you chose an unusual profession that your family doesn't approve of—"

"That's not it. I'm not part of that family anymore, Cara. End of story."

His gruff words warned her to back off, but she charged ahead anyway. "Of course you're part of the family. How long has it been since you last saw them?"

"Five years."

"Really? Well, that's a long time. I'm sure they've forgotten or at least forgiven after all this time."

His jaw clenched. "No, they haven't."

"How are you so sure of that, especially if you haven't spoken to them in five years?"

"I just know."

"Oh, come on. Surely when they gave you whatever ultimatum, they didn't mean for you to completely disappear off the planet."

"That's where you're wrong, Cara Mia. They didn't ask me to leave." He turned his head, challenge in every nuance of his expression. "I was the one who walked away."

He turned his attention back to the road.

Her lips parted, but words didn't come. *He'd* walked away? How could anyone just walk away from his family? Her throat tightened. No matter how many friends you made, no one could replace family. She would give anything to have hers back.

The silence stretched between them, broken only by the rumble of the engine and the low melody of the radio.

When she could finally speak again, she whispered, "Why?"

"Because I'm a son of a bitch." He glanced at her. Shrugged. "You should probably know that about me—especially if we're going to keep sleeping together."

. . . . .

Cara stayed quiet. She hadn't responded to his crack, just retreated into her own thoughts. Rafe couldn't really blame her. Expected it actually. He knew how crazy she was about family, and the revelation that he had left his behind no doubt disappointed her. Maybe even turned her off about continuing their affair. He shoved back the wave of disappointment. Maybe it would be better that way.

He checked the clock. It was just past noon, and they hadn't stopped except for a bathroom break a few miles back. His stomach growled. If he was hungry, she probably was, too.

He glanced over at her. She'd been nursing that huge bottle of water she'd bought at the rest stop, staring out the window at the passing countryside with a pensive look on her face. "You ready to eat?"

She jumped and dropped the water on the floor. Luckily it was capped, but her face flamed as she unbuckled her seat belt long enough to lean down and scoop up the bottle. Her clothes pulled with the movement, her shorts tightening over her butt, her shirt pulling up to reveal an inch or so of bare skin at her waist. He admired the view and waited for an answer as she sat up, fastened her seat belt again, and flipped her ponytail behind her. "Sorry, I was woolgathering. What did you say?"

"I said, are you ready to eat?"

She nodded. "I'm a little hungry, yes." Her expression, her posture, her tone—everything was as polite as could be.

He hated it, but what had he been thinking? That they could tear up the sheets and walk away with no regrets? No matter what she said, Cara was a forever girl. She deserved better than a few romps with a guy like him, a guy with the kind of baggage that prevented him from promising more than the current moment.

"There's a diner not far from here," he said. "Good burgers. Does that work for you?"

"Sounds fine." She turned her face to the window, ending the conversation.

They didn't exchange another word. Not during the ten

minute drive. Not when he pulled into the diner's parking lot. Not when they both climbed out of the SUV. Cara headed toward the restaurant, ponytail bouncing. He flipped the lock on the remote and followed behind her. He shot one appreciative glance at her butt in those khaki shorts, then pulled his gaze away. He couldn't tell yet if she'd changed her mind about them.

He caught up to her in time to hold open the door. She gave him a little nod and hurried inside. Rafe followed.

Hell, if she was this upset about him not spilling his guts about his family, how would she react if she learned about the rest of it? About his abilities? Probably be ticked that he'd kept that a secret, too. She was already asking too many questions about the crystal. He didn't owe her his life story, any more than she owed him any deep, dark confidences. They just had hot sex between them, and that was it. No commitments, no promises. And he could walk away from sex. Walk away from her.

She glanced at him as they slid into the booth across from each other. Sunlight glimmered off her honey-colored hair, and her light brown eyes had little flecks of green in them. She gave him a quick smile before dropping her gaze to the menu, biting her lower lip as she considered the choices.

Her little white teeth sinking into that soft, pink mouth grabbed his attention like a fist around his cock. When she ran her tongue over that lip, he clenched his eyes closed, then opened them and focused on the menu. He didn't even see the words, just her mouth and all the fantasies he'd conjured over the past couple of days.

Walk away from her? Sure, he could.

·   ·   ·   ·   ·

Just when she thought she had a bead on Rafe Montana, he threw her another curveball. She'd thought she could have a fling with the big, bad bounty hunter, then fly back to Jersey with a few hot memories and no regrets. But his revelation that he had walked away from his family had stunned her.

Dang it, she should have asked about that weird dizziness from the crystal instead. But she hadn't been able to resist; family was her weakness.

How could anyone just write off his relatives like that? His family secrets shouldn't matter, not for an affair that would last only a few days. But she did care, and it did matter.

Which made her wonder—was she really cut out for her new, freewheeling lifestyle? If she wasn't, where did that leave her? She had no husband, no children, just a bunch of debt and a struggling company. Maybe not even a home soon.

And she had Danny.

She seized the reminder, held on to Danny's image in her mind. *He* was why she was here, driving around the desert with this maverick of a skip tracer. She had to find her stepbrother and get him out of whatever jam he'd gotten into. It's what she'd always done. And as long as she focused on that, her world fell into balance again.

"So," she said, breaking miles of silence. "Where are we headed exactly?"

He paused in the middle of biting into his burger, surprise flickering in those bluer-than-blue eyes. He set down the sandwich. "Toward Flagstaff, since that was where Danny was last seen for certain. From there he went south, and we might be able to find someone who saw him." He lowered his voice. "I think we should branch off here and head down old Route 66 to Flagstaff."

"Route 66? Like the song?" She dipped a fry in ketchup and bit into it.

"The same." He stared at her French fry for a moment, then dropped his gaze to his own plate. "I think we'll hit less traffic, and if our intrepid followers are still on our tails, then we might have a chance of avoiding them."

"Sounds good to me."

He nodded and lifted his burger, then paused as she dipped another fry in the ketchup and popped it into her mouth.

"You okay?" she asked after a moment.

"Yeah. Fine." He tore into the burger.

She shrugged and reached for another fry just as her cell phone rang. She dropped the fry on the plate and dug into her purse.

Rafe raised his brows at the ring tone. "Ricky Martin? Really?"

She rolled her eyes and flipped open the phone. "Hey, Maisie."

"Cara, where have you been?" Her best friend's voice vibrated with worry. "I've been trying to call you."

"Sorry. I'm in the middle of the desert. Reception is not so good."

"The desert! I thought you were in Vegas?"

"I was. But we're on the road now, picking up Danny's trail."

"We?"

"Yeah." Cara slid a glance at Rafe, who made no effort to pretend he wasn't eavesdropping. "I've got some help."

"What, like a private eye or something?"

"Or something."

"Like . . . ?"

Cara shook her head, knowing Maisie wouldn't let it go. "A bounty hunter."

"Omigod! Like on TV?"

"Yup."

"You sound weird. He's right there, isn't he?"

"Yes."

"Is he hot?"

"Maisie!"

"Oh, he is, isn't he?" Maisie let out a little whimper of envy. "You have to tell me every detail."

Cara pinched the bridge of her nose. "Maisie, is everything okay at work? Because if you just called to chat, we're in the middle of lunch here."

"Okay, okay. Listen, I have some bad news." She paused. "I don't think you want an audience when I tell you about this."

Cara's stomach dropped. "What do you mean?"

"Seriously, you want to be alone when you hear this." Maisie dropped her voice. "You said you're eating lunch. Can you step outside maybe? Just for a few minutes. I don't think you want Bounty Hunk to see your reaction to this."

"Okay, fine." She slid out of the booth.

Rafe grabbed her free arm. "Where are you going?"

"I'm just stepping outside for a minute."

"Like hell."

"Oooh, was that him?" Maisie squealed.

Cara focused on the determined male in front of her. She'd seen that implacable expression before, but this time she was going to win the battle. "I'll stand right outside the window so you can see me." She lowered the phone, pressing it against her chest. "We haven't seen our fan club since yesterday. I think you can let me have a few minutes of privacy."

"I don't like it."

"I can see that. But we've been constant companions for over twenty-four hours. Is it so crazy to want five minutes alone for a private conversation?"

"Cara, are you there?" Maisie's muffled voice came from the phone.

Cara waited, willing Rafe to agree. They'd been in each other's pockets since yesterday—not to mention each other's beds. She was a person who needed a certain amount of alone time in order to stay sane. Between all the adventure and the sexual tension humming between them, she was about ready to snap.

"Please, Rafe." She slipped her arm from his grip, knowing full well it was only because he let her. "Just for a few minutes. You'll be watching me."

"You're right." He narrowed his eyes. "I *will* be watching. Five minutes, and then I'm coming out there."

"Five minutes," she agreed.

He curled his fingers into the table. "Clock's ticking."

She nodded. "Be right back."

She could practically feel his gaze on her as she walked away. It made her feel safe and tingly all at once. She lifted her phone to her ear as she neared the door. "Maisie, you still there?"

"Wow, all I could hear of his voice was that deep rumbling." Maisie let out a little sigh. "Leave it to you to find a sexy bounty hunter in the middle of the desert."

"I never said he was sexy."

"Hon, you didn't have to. Anyway . . . let me know when you're outside."

"Heading out there now." She pushed open the glass door and started down the walkway toward the window where Rafe sat. "Maisie, you're scaring me. What happened? Did my condo burn down or something?"

"No. Where are you now?"

"Outside." She passed a couple of cars and a huge SUV, Rafe's window only steps away. "Darn it, tell me what's going on."

The voice came from behind her. "Maisie does not know."

Cara spun around. The man smiled even as he grabbed her wrist and ripped the phone from her hand. Heart slamming in her chest, she yanked her arm from his grip and pivoted back toward the door to the diner, but a second man came from the other side of the SUV, gun in hand. She froze.

She recognized them now: their fan club, the two men who'd been following them. How could this be happening, here in a public parking lot? Didn't anyone see?

As if to answer her question, an older man came out the door of the diner. He hesitated upon seeing Cara and her captors.

"You see nothing," said the guy holding her arm.

The old man blinked. A blank expression slid onto his face.

"Go about your business," her captor continued. "Nothing is wrong."

The man turned and trundled past Cara and the two men as if they weren't there, heading for a nearby pickup like he was some kind of zombie. What the—?

Cara cast a panicked glance from one to the other. Who *were* these characters?

"Give it up." The man with the gun smirked. "No one will rescue you."

Rafe will. She held on to the certain knowledge with everything that was in her. Had it been five minutes yet? Or maybe Maisie realized something was wrong?

The other man grinned at her, then lifted his phone to her ear. "Maisie, you will not remember calling Cara or this conversation."

She heard Maisie's voice, far away and flat, as she agreed with the order.

"Hang up the phone and go back to work." He snapped the phone shut.

The second man gestured with the gun. "This way, Miss McGaffigan."

"No."

Gun Guy looked at the one who'd taken her phone. "Evan?"

The one called Evan caught her gaze. Held it. "You will come with us to the car, Miss McGaffigan. Quietly."

Cara shook her head, warding off a wave of dizziness.

"Cara?"

She shook her head again, looked at the man who'd said her name, a young guy. Nice-looking. "Yes?" She pressed her fingers to her forehead. So dizzy.

"The car is this way. You will feel better in the air conditioning." He slipped a hand beneath her elbow and steered her toward the parking lot.

"Air conditioning. Yes, it's hot." She squinted from the man escorting her to the silver sedan. That car looked familiar. Where had she seen it before?

"We need to hurry," he continued. "We don't want to be late."

She shook her head again, trying to clear the cobwebs. "I hate being late."

His friend sprinted ahead of them, clicking his remote to unlock the car. He pulled open the door and started to get in, then froze. "Evan, he's coming."

Evan stopped and looked behind them. Cara looked as well.

Rafe Montana was charging across the parking lot with blood in his eye.

*   *   *   *   *

What the hell was going on here? Why wasn't Cara screaming her head off?

Rafe hurtled toward their two followers. He'd already reached for the Hunter, his focus stone burning against his chest as raw power flooded through it, fueling his muscles, his senses. His sharpened eyesight picked out the immediate threats: the gun, the guy's hand on Cara's arm. Thank the Creators he'd gotten curious, had used his powers to try and see Cara. When he hadn't been able to, he'd opened his mind to the universe—and gotten a vision of the familiar silver sedan in the parking lot. He had a million questions, but they could wait.

Only Cara mattered.

He went for the gun first, but its wielder whipped out of range with a speed that startled him. Rafe reached for the Hunter. More power. Leaped. Threw all his weight at the gun hand.

The guy almost made it out of range, but Rafe caught the edge of his jacket sleeve and jerked. Tore the gun from his hand. Threw it under the car.

The guy snarled and came at him, hands a blur of martial arts moves. Rafe was good, but this guy was seriously trained—like Special Ops trained. Rafe stepped wrong, stumbled. The guy came after him, his punch like a sledgehammer to the gut. Rafe landed on his back. Wheezed. Struggled to suck air into his lungs.

The guy dropped to his stomach on the ground, reached under the car for the gun.

No! Rafe shoved to his side, grabbed the bastard's head seconds before his fingers brushed the gun. Wrapped his arm around the guy's throat and tightened, dragging him back. The guy ripped at Rafe's arm with his fingers, bucking like a landed trout, but Rafe didn't loosen his hold. Lack of circulation won, and his adversary passed out.

Before Rafe could move, the other guy came up behind him, grabbed Rafe by the collar of his shirt, and dragged him backward. Rafe released the unconscious man and twisted and turned, trying to jerk free of the hold. He could see Cara standing by the car, her expression confused.

The edge of his shirt dug into his throat, cutting at his windpipe. He raked at the material, trying to tear it. Then the guy let go. Rafe's head hit the pavement with a thud. Pain blinded him for a second.

The guy grabbed the front of his shirt this time, dragged him to his feet. As Rafe's vision cleared, he met the nearly black eyes of his opponent. Tried to see something.

Nothing.

"Seer," his opponent hissed. "Now you die." He slammed a hard right into Rafe's jaw.

His ears rang, but Rafe managed to rip free before the next one hit. The guy came after him. Rafe blocked blow after blow, but the bastard moved like the wind, his strikes coming seconds faster than Rafe expected. Rafe pulled more power, brought the Hunter in closer, but still he found himself losing ground.

A movement to the side jerked his attention away, just for a second. The first guy had come to and was forcing Cara into the silver sedan. She hit her head as he shoved her into the car, her cry echoing across the parking lot. Rage flared. They'd hurt her.

He spun back in time to block the next punch headed his way. Met his opponent's gaze. This guy wanted him dead, and who knew what they'd do to Cara.

No, *he* knew. He'd seen it. She'd die.

"Like hell." He head-butted his foe, then let the Hunter loose.

. . . . .

He came back to himself minutes later. Both kidnappers were on the ground, unconscious and bleeding. He stood over the guy who'd had the gun. He flexed his fingers, blood from his knuckles oozing, then swept the weapon off the ground. His ribs ached, as did his jaw. And Cara sat in the car, staring at him. In her beautiful eyes he saw that tangle again, the one that held her will hostage—just like in Vegas. But he had no cold shower here.

He glanced at the diner. No one had even come outside during the fight, so he doubted there was any help to be found there.

"Air conditioning," Cara said.

He turned back to her. "What did you say?"

"They told me to get in the car. For the air conditioning." Her voice rose in pitch, distress crumpling her features. "I need the air conditioning. I don't want to be late."

"Of course not." He leaned down, wincing as his ribs protested. "What are you supposed to do, Cara?"

"Get in the car. Turn on the air conditioning." Her dead-blank gaze settled on him, sending a chill along his spine. "I don't want to be late."

He blew out a breath, then said, "This car is broken, Cara. How about my car?"

She frowned. "And air conditioning?"

"I have air conditioning." He reached in and unfastened her seat belt. "Let's go to my car and turn on the air conditioning. Because we don't want to be late."

Her expression cleared. "Yes. Let's go." She held out her hands with the innocence of a child wanting to be picked up.

He helped her out of the car and walked her to his SUV a few spaces away. His legs already trembled, his senses bombarded by the scrape of their shoes on the pavement and the hiss of tires on the nearby highway. He had to snap her out of this trance thing before his burnout hit.

Otherwise they were both dead.

CHAPTER TWELVE

Rafe drove as fast as he dared, struggling to stay conscious as he fought burnout as well as physical discomfort. Add in Stepford Cara sitting next to him, and they would both be sitting ducks unless he figured out how to snap her out of it.

The more he learned about the other players in this game, the more confusing things got. Adrian Gray, the twins back there, the president of Santutegi, Danny Cangialosi. He couldn't read any of them. But Cara, Artie Bartow, the waitress at the diner—no problem. And the guy who'd just tried to kick his ass had called him "Seer." Somehow he knew about Rafe's abilities.

Which made it even more important he break this whammy they'd put on Cara. He could feel his power draining away at an alarming rate, but she was in no shape to drive. Not until he brought her back with some kind of physical shock. They had to keep moving, keep ahead of their enemies, until he could figure this thing out.

His vision blurred. He blinked his eyes. Out of time.

He caught sight of a tiny lot with an emergency phone a few yards down the road. He hit the gas, then pulled in and parked on the narrow strip of blacktop.

Cara glanced over at him. "I don't want to be late."

"We're not late." He glanced at the clock. "See, it's two eleven. We're right on time."

"Oh, good." She beamed at him, her vacant eyes a scary shadow of the real Cara. "We're not late."

"That's right." He swiped a hand across his face, and it came away smeared red. He flipped the rearview mirror toward him and peered at his battered face. A small cut near his eye glistened with clotting blood. Muttering, he leaned across her and popped open the glove compartment to grab some napkins. "Can you hand me that bottle of water, Cara?"

He shut the glove box and realized she hadn't moved. Still bent forward, he turned his head to look at her. She just looked back. With a sigh, he grabbed the bottle of water she'd stashed on the passenger floor earlier and settled back in his seat. Unscrewing the cap, he poured some on his napkins, then used his reflection in the rearview mirror and cleaned off his face.

The water had heated from sitting in the hot car, so it felt good on his wounds, but pouring it over her head probably wouldn't work to break the whammy. It was the shock of the cold that had done it last time. Besides, they were in the middle of the desert, and water was too valuable to waste. And he certainly drew the line at slapping her to snap her out of it.

Stuck where they were, with his strength fading fast, he could only think of one thing that might do it, though it bordered on taking advantage. But he had nothing else.

He leaned over, caught her by the back of the neck, and pulled her into his kiss.

She gave a little whimper—surprise maybe?—but didn't pull away. Instead she sank into him, her lips responding to every unspoken demand. Her compliance fanned desire even hotter, though he knew her reaction had nothing to do with free will. But with the Hunter so close to the surface, and with her scent in his lungs and her taste on his lips, her soft skin beneath his hands, he couldn't control himself as well as he would have liked. He wanted her, wanted to lay her out and have her in every way possible, even though things remained unsettled between them. His hands shook with need, his will weakened by the impending burnout. The Hunter lurked just beneath his skin, eager, desperate, to sate his hunger with her again.

He had to maintain control. He pulled back, looked into her eyes. That white haze was back, wrapped tightly around her will. And the blackness of death loomed larger and darker than ever before.

The kiss alone would not do it.

Weakness dragged at his limbs. Burnout sped toward him like an out-of-control train. Their pursuers would catch up with them soon. Now was their chance to disappear, if only he could snap Cara out of it before he passed out. With shaking fingers, he pulled his focus crystal out from under his shirt.

She watched him, just waiting, like a pet listening for its master's next command. He hated that look on her face. Wanted the fire and complexity that was Cara.

"Hold this." He took her hand and placed the stone in her palm, folding her fingers around it. The crystal was already warm and vibrating from the manifestation of the Hunter only a short while before. Add in some very real, very hot sexual hunger and he was surprised the thing didn't brand her palm. "Here goes," he muttered, then kissed her again.

White energy roared to life, exploding in his head and lighting up his consciousness with dazzling brilliance. She whimpered once, shifted in her seat. He tugged her closer, letting loose his desire, giving the crystal emotional juice to feed on. He slid his hand over her breast, soft and plump in his palm, flicked his thumb over her stiffening nipple. She jolted at the contact, then melted into him, arching her back, offering more.

His instincts screamed at him to strip off her clothes, take what was offered.

Just take it! The Hunter raged just beyond conscious thought, riled up from the recent fight, all jagged edges and blunt, sexual need. *You've already had her once; you can see she wants you.*

He ignored the dark demands, funneling the shadowy power of the Hunter through the focus stone. Each facet cleansed it, filtered it, producing white light, white energy, which rippled into Cara. He knew the second she snapped into the loop. She cried out, tearing her mouth from his, her body stiffening as if in orgasm. He could see the brilliance shimmering through her, chasing away the darkness.

Heal her. Scraping together the last dregs of his vitality, he aimed the power at the bonds around her will. It sliced through them like a sharp knife through soft butter.

The awareness came back into her eyes even as his started to close.

"Rafe! What the . . . ?" She surged toward him, then stopped, caught by her grip on the focus stone. "What's going on?" She dropped the hot crystal against his chest. Stared at it.

"Cara." He pushed the words past his lips as the burnout started to spiral through his body. "I'm going to pass out. You need to drive."

"Where are we?" She looked around. "What happened to the diner?"

"Long story." The words swept out with an exhausted breath. His vision grew hazy. "Fight. You . . . were . . ." He sucked in air.

"I was what? I can't remember anything." Horror swept over her face. "Just like Vegas."

"Yes-s-s." His eyes slid closed.

"Rafe! Rafe, wake up." She shook him. "If you want me to drive, you have to get out of the driver's seat."

"Can't." He couldn't even lift his eyelids. "Burn . . . out."

"Burnout?"

"Fight." His words jumbled together, his lips numb. Blackness blurred the boundaries of his consciousness. "Drained . . . the . . . stone."

Burnout swept over him, dragging him into the unrelenting darkness of oblivion.

. . . . .

Cara stared at Rafe, appalled. What was wrong with him? He'd been in a fight, that much she could see. She pressed her fingers against his neck, got a steady pulse. So far, so good. She tugged his shirt up, looked for gunshots, stab wounds—something that would make a man pass out. Nothing but a few bruises. She jerked his clothes back into place. The crystal banged against her hand before settling against his chest again.

She stared at the clear gem, then lifted it gingerly. It felt hot against her fingers, hotter than a necklace should be from just resting against human skin. He'd said the fight had drained the stone. And . . . was it vibrating?

She dropped it and stared. Remembered that morning in the parking lot. What the heck was going on here?

She struggled to put the pieces together. Apparently someone had managed to drug her or whatever again, because she couldn't recall a darned thing between the time Maisie called and the moment she woke up with her hand around Rafe's necklace and warm, white fire burning through her mind.

White fire. Just like before, in the hotel room, in the parking lot. When they'd both touched the crystal.

She fell back into her seat, staring at the innocent-looking pendant. Okay, now she really was losing it. The thing looked like simple clear quartz. But when she thought back to the moment when they'd been in bed, passion singeing the sheets, and she'd grasped the crystal . . . then again in the parking lot . . .

Brilliant white fire burning through her being. Warmth and affection and hot, delicious desire raging through her. When he'd ripped the necklace from her fingers, the action had left her confused. Bereft. As if their souls had touched, and then he'd backed away.

She couldn't believe she was thinking this. Couldn't believe she was entertaining the notion for the briefest second. But she'd been thinking about it all day, and when she put the facts together, she could only come to one conclusion: this crystal was more than just jewelry.

She'd heard the stories of people focusing mental power through crystals. Chakras and spirit planes and all the other metaphysical stuff. Maybe it wasn't all legends and old wives' tales? People had once thought the world was flat after all. What was fantasy but that which had not yet been explained?

She eyed the crystal. Its glow seemed to be dimming. Was that a bad thing? And somehow she needed to wake up Rafe, to get him out of the driver's seat and find out where they were headed. She shook his shoulder. His head rolled to the side, but he didn't wake. Unease fluttered in her gut. He was really out. What if his wounds were worse than she could see—internal bleeding or something? What if he needed medical attention?

She pressed her fingers against his neck again. His pulse pounded with reassuring steadiness, but his skin burned with fever. She was stuck in the middle of the desert with a very sick man.

"Rafe." She gently slapped her fingers against his face. "Rafe, wake up. You have to help me here."

No response.

She let out a long breath and stared at him. *What now, Mc-Gaffigan?*

Maybe she'd missed something. She bent over him again, shoving his shirt up to his chin in case she missed some injury. The crystal slid with the shirt, then slipped out of the folds, and landed against the back of her hand. At the instant of contact, the crystal sparkled, its glow becoming brighter, the stone heating.

She squeaked in alarm and yanked her hand away. The glow faded instantly. Rafe let out a tiny groan, rolling his head to face her. But his eyes stayed closed.

This was crazy. It seemed like the crystal had something to do with Rafe's condition. And if she touched it . . .

She laid her finger on the stone, watched it glow more brightly. Again, Rafe made a sound.

She fell back again, her gaze locked on the jagged piece of quartz. It looked so normal, but clearly there was something more going on here than met the eye. The world had turned upside down from the minute she landed in Vegas, so why should this be any different? The idea forming in her mind could be categorized as completely nuts, but some of the things that had happened over the past two days didn't exactly fall into the normal column.

"Ok, Dorothy," she muttered. "Let's click those heels." She scooped the crystal into her hand, closed her fingers around it and concentrated, hoping to trigger—whatever. "Rafe, wake up."

Almost immediately, heat seared her skin, as if she held the sun in the palm of her hand. White light flooded her mind, pulsed like a heartbeat. She concentrated hard on the idea of Rafe opening his eyes. Visualized it. *Willed* it to happen.

He muttered, writhed in his seat, gripped the armrests. But still did not awaken.

She hung on to the crystal, the dazzling, faceted energy pulsing more and more brightly. She could practically hear the hum of power, yet instinctively she knew she needed more. What would Rafe do?

He'd kissed her. Intimate contact? Worth a shot. Her hands shaking, her body buzzing with the unbridled energy surging through her, she leaned over, pressing the crystal flat against his chest with her palm, and pressed her mouth to his.

Power crackled like fireworks in her hands, exploding through her mind, hurling her into a crazy kaleidoscope of blinding lights, like riding a roller coaster down Alice's rabbit hole during a psychedelic concert. Suddenly he was there with her, grabbing her head and holding it still as he took over the kiss.

Energy surged back at her as if reflected in a mirror. She took the impact with a soft gasp, allowing him even more access to her mouth in the process. He dragged her against him, greed sweeping over her—from him? Dizzy with wild emotion, she gave herself over to his hands. Burning, burning, her body glowing with heat and want. And more. More.

Inside her. Now. Too many clothes, too many barriers . . .

He shoved her away, his lungs heaving. His fingers tightened around her arms, holding her at a distance when she would have leaned into him again. His gaze, when he met hers, was intense, feral. His voice, a desperate rasp.

"What the hell do you think you're doing?"

* * * * *

It took every shred of control not to strip her naked and bury himself inside her.

He knew she was as turned on as he was; he could feel it through their link, through the stone. But how the hell had this happened?

179

"I didn't know what else to do." She stared at his mouth, licked her lips.

Could she taste him? He clenched his eyes closed, struggled for discipline. "What happened?"

"You were out cold. Something about the stone . . ." She rubbed her thumb along the crystal she still held.

He shuddered. They were so closely linked, it felt as if she stroked his bare skin. "Unless you want to jump in the backseat with me, you need to let go." Bracing himself, he tried to pry her fingers off the crystal. But the first touch of his flesh to hers only stoked the fire. A vision swelled in his mind, the two of them tearing up the sheets—hungry, hot sex. But not here. Not now.

"Rafe." His name emerged as a throaty invitation. Desire shimmered in her eyes.

"Soon, sweetheart. Soon. But not now." He gritted his teeth and peeled her fingers away from the stone.

She fell back in her seat with a soft cry, longing and need still plain on her face as she cupped her hand against her chest. He gripped the crystal in his own fist, focusing on throttling back the power. Layer by layer, he backed it down until only a quiet vibration remained. Then he dropped it beneath his shirt again. Looked at her.

The fading energy had succeeded in calming her as well, though both of them were hair-triggered right now. One misstep, and they would definitely be in that backseat screwing like rabbits.

"So," he said. "Tell me what happened."

"You tell me." She studied him as if she'd never seen him before. "I don't remember anything after Maisie called me. Not until you kissed me."

"Yeah, about that—"

"It was like the hotel, wasn't it?" she interrupted. "Some-body drugged me again. Or something."

"Yeah. Or something."

She narrowed her eyes. "I know you're holding back on me."

He didn't dare tell her the truth. She'd never believe him. "Why would I do that? C'mon, Cara."

She folded her arms. "What is burnout?"

He jerked at the word, then realized he'd betrayed himself when her eyes narrowed. "Where did you hear that?"

"From you. Before you passed out, you said the word 'burnout' and that the fight had drained the stone." She flicked a hand at his chest. "I assumed you meant that stone—especially after this morning."

"No way." He let his head fall back against the headrest, disbelief battling with the evidence in front of him. The fight. The Hunter. He'd hit burnout, passed out.

And she'd somehow recharged the crystal and revived him. Impossible.

He turned his head to stare at her, everything he'd believed for the past twenty-eight years shaken. "How long was I out?"

"I don't know." She glanced at the dashboard clock. "Ten, fifteen minutes."

"*Minutes*?" He rubbed a hand over his face. It normally took hours to recharge his powers. Sometimes a day. How had this untrained woman managed such a thing? He reached for the Hunter, tested—and was awed to find his abilities fully charged. *In minutes.*

Who *was* this girl?

"Yeah, I thought you were never going to wake up," she was saying. "You wanted me to drive, but I couldn't move you."

"Drive. Yeah, let's do that." He started the car.

"Hold on, cowboy. You owe me an explanation."

"We'll talk and drive." He glanced in the rearview mirror at the empty highway behind them. "We have to put miles between us and the Ugly Twins."

She frowned, glancing behind them. "We haven't seen them since yesterday."

"Wrong, sweetheart. They were at the last diner we just left, and they tried to kidnap you."

"What? I don't remember that."

"You don't remember what happened in Vegas, either."

"Right." She swiped her hands over her face. "Okay, I'm officially sick of this. Who keeps messing with my memories? And what is burnout, and why did you pass out like that?" Her pitch grew higher with each question. "And why does your crystal do weird stuff when I touch it?"

He flashed her a quick glance as he pulled out of the emergency lot and onto the highway. "I just thought of a really inappropriate response to that question."

"Oh, please." She snapped on her seat belt and glared at him. "No more joking around, no more half truths. I feel like I've landed in the middle of some sci-fi movie."

"Not quite."

"Well, that just helps so much."

He ignored her sarcasm and hit the gas, cranking the SUV as fast as he dared. The last thing he needed was to draw attention from any cops who might be nearby, but at the same he had to put as many miles as he could between them and the diner.

She seemed to sense his purpose and stayed quiet, but he wasn't foolish enough to think she had dropped the subject. They'd gone at least fifteen miles before she spoke again.

"So, I've heard of people channeling energy through crystals or whatever, but I never actually believed it. I thought it was all nonsense."

"It's not."

"Yeah, I figured. So what's the deal, Montana? Spill."

"You won't believe me."

"Tell me anyway."

"It's a little out there."

"This whole trip has been a little out there."

"Okay." He glanced at her. "I'm psychic."

"I'm serious, Rafe."

"So am I."

"Psychic? You've been in Vegas too long."

"It's true. I specialize in being able to find people. Hence my record."

She opened her mouth—no doubt in advent of some smart remark—then frowned. "Zero percent failure rate."

"Yeah."

"I don't know . . ."

"Look, you asked. I told you."

"You're seriously psychic."

"Yeah."

"And the crystal?"

"Helps me focus."

She hesitated, then shook her head. "No way. There has to be a logical explanation."

"That's all there is. I'm psychic."

"Yeah? Prove it."

He nearly groaned at the challenge in her tone. "What am I, a trained monkey?"

"Look, you just told me something crazy. The fact that I haven't jumped out of the car screaming should tell you how open-minded I'm trying to be. Of course, if you can't do it . . ."

The disbelief in her tone decided him. "I can do it. I just don't like being made to sing and dance on cue."

"Not sing and dance. Use your psychic powers." She leaned back in her seat, her brows raised in mockery. "Tell me, swami. What's my future?"

He pressed his lips together. How could he possibly tell her? "Can't do it, huh?"

He glanced at her. "It doesn't quite work that way. I'm not the crystal ball type. Sometimes I just . . . know things."

Like you're going to die sometime soon unless I can stop it.

"If this gift of yours is so unreliable, then I can't imagine how you actually use it in your work." Doubt rang in her tone. A little bit of hurt, too.

He should have just left it there. Let her believe what she wanted. But he hated that look on her face, that she thought he was putting her on. Damn it, when had he started to care so much? It was never a good idea to get too involved.

Shoulda thought of that at the motel this morning, buddy.

Okay so he *was* involved, enough that she somehow connected to him through his crystal, enough that she had been able to bring him out of a flat burnout and back to full power in minutes. He'd never heard of such a thing, not even about his grandfather, who'd also been a Hunter. Not in the family history. He'd never known it could be done.

"You could just tell me the truth, you know," she said quietly. "You don't have to make things up."

"Okay, fine." He pulled over to the shoulder, shoved the car in park and turned to face her. "Here's the deal. I'm psychic, but my abilities are very specific. Sometimes I just know things. That's totally random. I can also tell if someone is lying to me—every single time. And I can find anyone, alive or dead. I just think about them and know where they are. Every single time."

"Handy in your line of work." The disbelief still rang in her tone, shone in her eyes.

He gritted his teeth. "Try me."

"Okay then. Where's Danny?"

He groaned. "Of course you would ask me that."

"What's the matter, Psychic Man? Don't know?"

"Look, something weird has been going on with your brother. Sometimes I can't see him. I don't know why."

"Try."

"Fine." *Where's Danny?*

Nothing happened. Of course.

She watched him, irritation evident in her tight lips. "Well?"

"Like I said, sometimes I can't see him."

She rolled her eyes. "Of course not."

Her skepticism grated. "Is your cell working?"

"You tell me."

"Geez, woman. I thought I would tell you where Maisie is, and you could call and confirm."

"Seriously?"

"Look, you're the one who wanted the circus act." He turned back to the road and started to put the SUV in drive.

"Oh, hang on." She grabbed her purse and rummaged. "Where's my phone? I was talking to Maisie—"

"At the diner, where the Ugly Twins grabbed you." He rubbed his temple. "They must have taken your cell."

She threw her hands up. "Great! How am I going to get a replacement phone out here in the middle of the desert? And how's Danny going to find me now?" She slanted him a mocking glance. "Unless you can home in on him, Rafe the Great."

"Wish I could. This whole thing would be a whole lot easier." He dug in his pocket and pulled out his own phone, checked the bars. "And I've got no service here."

She folded her arms. "Convenient."

"You know, considering all we've been through, a little faith would not be unreasonable."

"Please. I'm stuck in the middle of the desert with a man who claims to be psychic."

He shoved the phone back in his pocket. "It's not something I advertise. And you asked about the crystal."

"Yeah, tell me about that." She lifted her chin in challenge. "And the truth this time, please."

"Truth. Yeah, okay." He looked her straight in the eye. "I told you I can always tell when someone is lying to me. Give it a shot."

She scoffed. "That's hardly a test. You're going to expect me to lie to you."

"I can't win with you, can I?"

"Not if you keep trying to lead me on like I'm some idiot."

"You're not an idiot. And because you're not, maybe you should try to explain what happened a few minutes ago with the crystal. I know you felt it."

"I don't know what happened. Maybe it was hallucinations. You know, from whatever drugs I was given that caused those blank spots in my memory."

He nodded. "Oh, yeah, sure, that's it. Well, here's a news flash, sweetheart. I don't think you were drugged. I think you were—how should I put it? Hypnotized. Put in a trance. Because before I passed out, I saw something in your eyes, some kind of binding that imprisoned your thoughts. And I think the Ugly Twins may have put it there."

She stared at him for a long moment, then fumbled with the door handle. "Okay, that's it. I'm walking back to that phone and calling the cops. You're nuts."

"Don't be stupid." He flipped the locks, then clicked the switch so that only he could unlock them. "It's nearly twenty miles before you'd get back to the phone."

She rattled the door handle. "Unlock this door right now."

"Be reasonable, Cara. It's the desert. You'll fry out there with no water, no cell phone. I won't let you kill yourself."

"I have water." She grabbed her bottle of water from the floor, cradled it against her like a shield. "I'll be fine."

"It's suicide."

"Oh, yeah? Did you see that in a vision?" She sneered, but he heard the hint of fear behind the bravado, and he hated it.

"No vision needed, sweetheart. It's called common sense."

"Common sense would be for me to take my chances on my own."

He sighed, swiped a hand over his mouth. "I know how crazy it sounds."

"Do you? Do you really?" She clutched the bottle of water more tightly. "Try putting yourself in my shoes and tell me what you would think."

"Cara . . ." He reached for her hand.

She slapped it away. "Don't touch me." She shrank back into the seat, her beautiful brown eyes brimming with confusion and growing fear.

The vision struck like an eighteen-wheeler, knocking him out of the present and into the future. *Cara dead at the side of the road, the desert landscape stark around her. The burning vehicle. The mountains in the distance. The* DO NOT LITTER *sign at the side of the highway. Someone had stuck a smiley-face sticker on it.* The grief roared through him: a life destroyed, a sweet soul snuffed out. Cara.

He heard her voice from far away. "What's wrong with you? Rafe?"

He tore himself from that sweet, caramel gaze, looked out the window at the mountains in the distance. Sucked in air. Fought against the lump in his throat. The here and now slowly slipped back into focus.

And he found himself staring at a DO NOT LITTER sign with a smiley face on it.

CHAPTER THIRTEEN

"Get out of the car!" Rafe jerked his seat belt loose, unlocked all the doors and had his hand on the door handle before he realized she hadn't moved. "Damn it, Cara, get out!"

"Why?" She leaned back in her seat a little, looking at him as if he were insane—probably just an upgrade from what she had been thinking when he'd revealed his powers to her.

"Look, a minute ago you couldn't wait to ditch me."

She jutted her chin at him. "I was mad."

"Just get out of the car."

"Like you said, it's hot and—"

"Get out of the car!"

She flinched. "What's wrong with you?" she whispered.

"We're going to die in the next few minutes, that's what." He leaned over and released her seat belt. "Now, run!"

She narrowed her eyes. "Oh, so . . . what, you had a psychic vision?"

"Yes, damn it." He opened his own door. "Get out and run!"

"You first."

He jerked his gaze to hers. *She didn't believe him, thought he would drive off and leave her standing at the side of the road.* "This is no time to be stubborn."

"How are we going to die?"

The vision slammed into his head again: his SUV exploding

as a hawk swooped through the sky above them. "Car bomb. Now let's *go*!"

She slowly shook her head. "Sorry, Montana, but I'm not falling for these theatrics of yours."

"Screw it." He jumped out of the car and stalked around to her side. The piercing cry of a hawk reached his ears. He shaded his eyes and looked but didn't see anything—yet. If the bird was close enough to hear, then they only had seconds. And Cara was being stubborn.

He jerked open her door, unlatched her seat belt, and hauled her out of the SUV. "Let's go! Run!"

She struggled, yanking at her arm and nearly breaking his hold. He tightened his grip and started to drag her away from the vehicle. She whacked his hand with her water bottle.

"Quit hitting me!" He pointed to a large boulder a short distance away. "Let's get behind that rock, quick!"

"You're nuts, you know that?" she screamed. She smacked his hand over and over with the water bottle, digging in her heels as he hauled her toward the boulder.

The hawk screamed again. Rafe jerked his head up and saw it, a dot in the distance, coming closer. He looked down at Cara, at the fury and fear shining from her eyes. At the doubt. At the shadow of death still lingering.

They had no time.

He reached for the Hunter, opening about half throttle. The surge of power that immediately leaped to his command stunned him. Normally it took days to get this strong again after a burnout. Cara had somehow recharged him to twice the power in a fraction of the time.

He glanced at the bird again, and his now-sharpened eyesight allowed him to see that it was nearly upon them. Then he looked at Cara. Her eyes had gone wide.

"Rafe?" she whispered, uncertainty tingeing her voice.

"Run, Cara," he commanded, swinging her around by her arm and releasing her. "We only have seconds."

She turned to face him. "What's wrong with you? Your eyes . . ."

"Run, Cara!" He grabbed her, spun her around, and shoved her. "*Run!*"

"Is this some kind of sick game?" Damn her, but she whirled to face him again, planting her feet in the sand. "I run and you catch me and . . . what? You rape me? Kill me? Both?"

The hawk shrieked a third time. Too close. Out of time.

"I'm sorry, Cara," he said. And reached for the full power of the Hunter.

. . . . .

Rafe Montana had turned into a woman's worst nightmare—handsome and sexy one moment, then psycho the next.

And now . . . now she didn't know what.

His words of apology had barely registered before he changed. One minute his eyes had burned blue like cobalt, the next they transformed—dilated, something. Because suddenly they were jet black and . . . alien.

He charged at her. She screamed, but he scooped her off her feet in a fireman's carry before she could move. She landed over his shoulder, and her breath whooshed from her lungs. He ran for the rock he had indicated, his hard shoulder digging into her belly. Then they were there, seconds later. He dumped her on the ground behind the rock. Came down on top of her.

And an explosion rocked the silence.

Explosion. Car bomb. He'd been telling the truth.

She would have been killed.

Her lungs heaved against rising sobs. Her eyes stung as the

full import slammed over her. She'd nearly died. He'd tried to tell her. She'd argued, so sure she was right. So sure he was crazy. She squeezed her eyes shut and struggled for breath, laboring beneath the onslaught of emotion and the weight of the male body sprawled over her as smoke drifted to them on the breeze.

He shifted. A warm palm cupped her cheek.

She opened her eyes to see Rafe's face inches above hers. His skin pulled taut across his cheekbones, his austere expression foreign, almost ruthless. And his eyes—those flat, black eyes. She'd expected to see nothing there, yet they burned with hot emotion, stripped down and basic.

She knew how he felt, coming so close to death. When he took her mouth in a hard, hungry kiss, she melted into him, eager. They were alive. By some miracle, they were alive. She shoved aside all the questions and just gave herself up to the heady joy of blood pumping through her veins and the long, lean length of hot-blooded male pressing her into the gritty sand—to the primitive instinct to perpetuate life in the face of death.

Demanding hands shoved her shirt up. Greedy fingers closed around her breast, curling into her bra cup and trying to pull it free. The fully aroused length of him pressed against her thigh through his jeans. His kiss roughened, becoming more insistent, more carnal.

Holy Hannah, he wanted to do it right here in the middle of nowhere. And with the shock of near death vibrating through her body, she realized that she wanted it, too.

She ripped her mouth away, arching her head back and sucking in air. He nipped at her neck, at the same time finally succeeding in scooping her breast out of her bra cup. He pinched her nipple, rolled it between his fingers. Hot pleasure jolted between her legs. He sucked on the flesh of her throat, ripping a moan from her.

She squirmed beneath him, arching her back, wrapping her

arms around him. He knew just where to touch her, *how* to touch her. She shoved her hands under his shirt, sweeping them down to his waist, to his belt. But he grabbed her hands and yanked them away, trapping them on either side of her head with a primitive growl that ignited her juices as he rose over her.

He met her gaze, his eyes still black and burning with a lust that made her quiver. No man had ever looked at her like that. Never. She should make him stop. But he was Rafe, her lover—and he wasn't. But he was. The riddle scrambled her thoughts. She should protest. She should beg him to take her. It was right. It was wrong. It was—

He released one of her hands and jerked down the zipper of her shorts, slipping his long fingers beneath her panties and stroking her wet flesh.

Need weakened her limbs and ripped a choked cry from her throat as her head spun. The ruthless hunger in his eyes—those alien eyes—shook her. What was she doing? This wasn't Rafe—at least not the Rafe she knew. She grabbed his hand, tried to pull it free. When she couldn't, she pressed it hard against her to halt his way-too-delicious stroking.

"Stop," she said. "Wait."

He narrowed his eyes. A frisson of fear trickled down her spine. Would he ignore her and do what he wanted anyway?

She pulled her hand away from his and shoved at his chest with both hands. Her palm hit a hard lump beneath his shirt—a lump that burned like fire.

The crystal.

He flinched backward, looked at her with suspicion. *Somehow the crystal was tied into all this.*

"Rafe," she murmured. She slipped her hand beneath his T-shirt, stroking upward over his lightly furred flesh until she closed her fingers around the sizzling stone. "Come back to me."

He jerked once, but she held on to the stone, and he settled, his expression curious. She closed her eyes and waited for the white light she'd seen before, but it never came. Instead a shadowy cloud swept into her mind, lined with streaks of silver. Need shivered through her, urgent, undeniable. She knew she should flinch away, but she couldn't do it. The dark cloud swept over her, heavy with hunger, laden with lust. With want. With strength. With the seductive knowledge that she could take what she wanted, fulfill her desires, if she just let it in. Let *him* in.

She opened her eyes and looked at him. His pupils still looked dilated, but pure blue ringed them now. His heart thudded beneath her clenched fingers, and his hand still rested between her legs. His breath came in slow, even pants.

He could have been inside her already, soothing the ache of her aroused flesh. Why had she stopped him? She arched her hips, rubbed her sensitive spot against his fingers. Everything throbbed now. She wanted him to pin her down and just screw her blind. Anything to make the burning need stop.

Slivers of silver danced through her mind, weaving through her thoughts, binding any notion of resistance. She was female; he was male. Their destiny lay in sating the painful arousal roiling through both of them . . .

A blast of white light shot through her mind, like a spotlight flooding her vision. She cried out and released the crystal, covering her eyes with her hands. Her body still trembled with sexual hunger. She wanted him so badly her mouth watered.

"Cara?"

She slowly lowered her hands. This was the first time he had spoken since the explosion. His eyes looked normal blue again, his face less taut, more relaxed. This was the Rafe she knew. "Rafe?"

"I'm sorry." He jerked his hands out of her clothing, and she bit back a sob as he rolled off her and sat up. "I can explain."

"Later." She still shook, her skin hypersensitive—to the desert breeze, to the sand beneath her, to the warm sun overhead. Everything amped up her nearly unbearable arousal. "You have to finish this."

"Cara, tell me what's going on. Are you hurt? Did I . . . ?"

"*I ache.*" She arched her hips, closing her eyes. "Oh, God, it's so bad. I've never been this turned on in my life." She focused on her breathing. In through nose, out through mouth. "Please, Rafe. I need you inside me." She opened her eyes and stared right into his. "*Please.*"

. . . . .

Rafe stared down at her with growing shock. He'd come back to himself with the usual abruptness to find his hand in Cara's pants, his crystal gripped in her hand. He was a guy and therefore pleasantly surprised to find his hand where it was, but as the seconds ticked by, he became more aware of the wrongness of the moment. He knew well the sexual hunger that followed the manifestation of the Hunter, and he'd always either handled it alone or sought out company to work off the lingering lust.

That hunger trickled like a stream this time instead of hitting like a tidal wave. Cara had been holding the crystal when he'd snapped back into himself. Had she somehow absorbed that dark energy?

She must have.

"What can I do?" He didn't dare touch her, not when she was so sensitive.

"You need to finish this." Panting, she opened her eyes a slit. "Now that you're back, now that it's *you* . . . please don't leave me like this."

He hesitated. Her arousal coated his fingers, the scent teasing his nostrils. His rock hard erection strained against his jeans.

He hungered to bury himself inside her, but not like this. Not when her desire had been sparked by forces beyond her control. She had not sought the dark energy of the Hunter; it had been inflicted on her.

"Please, Rafe," she whispered. "I can't bear it."

He couldn't leave her like this. "It's okay," he murmured. "I'll take care of it."

He cradled her with one arm as he slid the other hand between her thighs. Gently, he stroked her slick folds. He could sense through their bond how close to climax she was, knew it would only take the lightest of touches to push her over. She moaned, arching into his hand, and he buried his face in her hair, savoring each shudder, each gasp, as he gave her what she needed. The orgasm rolled over her, and she cried out and exploded in his arms.

They stayed like that for long moments, the musky scent of her pleasure lingering between them. A hot desert breeze skated by, bringing the sting of sand and the odor of smoke and fire.

His SUV. Ah, hell.

She stirred in his arms, pulling his hand free of her clothing and shifting to fasten her shorts. He let her go, watching as she visibly gathered her composure. Finally she looked at him. "What the heck just happened?"

No dancing around the truth now. "I told you I'm psychic and that the car was going to explode."

She gave a humorless chuckle. "Yeah. I think you proved that in a big way."

"Okay . . ." He drew the word out. "So if you're not asking about that—"

"I'm asking what happened to *you*." She sat up completely, shoving herself away from him to lean back against the rock. The movement appeared practical on the surface, but he could see the truth in her eyes. She was pulling back emotionally as well. And could he blame her? She'd just come face-to-face with his demon—literally.

"What's the deal with this crystal you wear," she continued, "the one that makes light shows in my head when I touch it? And what the heck happened to you right before the bomb went off? You changed into . . . I don't know what . . . but you weren't you."

"Yeah, that." He rubbed a hand over the back of his neck. "I'm not exactly sure how to explain it."

"Try."

"I *am* trying. Look, no one has ever been able to tap into my power like that, so I'm just as in the dark as you are."

"Great." Her breathing seemed to be calming, and that stubborn look had come back into her eyes. "Let's start with the basics then. What the heck is that crystal?"

"It's a focus stone." He shifted to sit next to her in the shadow of the rock, out of the blazing sun—but took care not to touch her in any way. To respect the distance she had set between them. "I use it to focus my power, to recharge or reach for more if I need it."

"Handy. And that changes you somehow? I mean . . . wow." She let her head fall back against the rock, staring up at the sky as if she would find the answers there.

"Yeah, it can change me, but only if I let it."

She turned her gaze back to him. "That was freaky. You were you, but not you. Your eyes turned all black, and you were like this super strong, primal version of you. Not quite human." Her voice rose in question at the end.

And so it began. "I'm human, Cara. Just more than human, I guess."

"How? I mean, where do you come from?"

"I told you—Arizona." He grinned, but she didn't respond.

"This isn't funny, Rafe. I'm sure that once I can breathe again I'll be pretty freaked out, so you'd better start explaining, like now. What are you? Where do you come from? Was there some kind of experiment? Radiation, pesticides, secret weapons from some past war? Are there more like you?"

Her tone had risen an octave, and he could tell panic was starting to take hold. "Listen, maybe that's enough for now. The rest of the story sounds kind of crazy."

She laughed again, and the harsh sound grated. "We're way past crazy, pal."

"Okay, okay." He reached out and snagged her bottle of water, which lay in the sand a few inches away. "Here, take a drink. Breathe. And I'll explain."

She took the bottle from him, suspicion still evident in her cautious movements, and unscrewed the cap to take a drink. She wrinkled her nose. "Ack. It's warm."

"At least it's wet."

She glanced from the bottle to him, then slowly extended it to him. "Here. If you die from thirst, I'll be stuck out here all alone."

He gave a half chuckle at her grudging words and took a grateful drink of the water. He handed the bottle back to her, and she took a swig, screwed the cap back on, then cradled it in her arms.

"Start explaining," she said.

"If you're feeling up to it, we should talk while we walk."

"Walk!" She sat straight up. "Are you nuts? We should hang out here and wait for the cops to show up. Someone will see the smoke or will have heard the explosion."

"Exactly." He got to his feet. "Someone planted a bomb in my car, Cara. Tried to kill us. Police fill out reports and talk over radios that can be monitored. Do you really want to let the bad guys know where we are? Or worse yet, be sitting here waiting for them when they come looking to make sure the job is done?"

"Geez." She swiped her hands over her face. "This is too much. I need a minute to absorb."

"Come on, Cara." He held out a hand, hoping her senses had settled down, at least for the moment. "I saved your life. Whatever your reservations, please remember that. I won't let anything happen to you."

She looked up at him, hesitated, then took his hand and let him haul her to her feet. "That's the only thing keeping me from hitting you over the head with a rock and running for my life."

"Noted." She dropped his hand as soon as she was steady, and he didn't object. He knew she needed time to accept all this, and he knew, too, she might decide she wanted no part of him anymore—or their affair. Not that it made it any easier as he watched her stalk ahead of him, her cute ass in those khaki shorts giving him all kinds of ideas. The dark energy of the Hunter took a good long while to dissipate, and it had taken all his control not to plunge himself into her after his double dose today. But he'd had years to learn discipline, and survival came first.

She paused at the sight of the burning wreckage. He came to stand beside her, a good foot of space between them, and looked at what was left of his vehicle. "Damn it. I loved that truck."

"I can't believe it," she whispered. "This can't be happening."

"Come on. If I remember correctly, there's a bar down the road. We can get out of the sun while I figure out our next move."

He started down the highway, and she fell into place beside him. "You don't have any superpowers for this kind of situation?"

He barked a laugh. "This is it, sweetheart. We're alive. That's all I've got for now."

"Better than a stick in the eye, I suppose."

"Way better," he agreed.

They walked in silence for a few moments. The afternoon sun beat down on them, and Cara slipped out of her short-sleeved blouse, leaving just her tank top, and started to tie it around her waist.

"Keep it on," Rafe said. "So you don't get sunburn on your shoulders. Sweaty is better than burned."

She stopped. "Is that good advice or some psychic prediction?"

He halted as well. "Good advice. I grew up in the desert; you didn't. You can trust me on this."

"Trust." She shrugged back into her blouse but elected not to button it. "How can I trust you if I don't know who you are?"

"You know who I am."

"Rafe Montana, bounty hunter? Son of John Montana, the billionaire?" She gave a snort heavy with skepticism. "Is that even your real name?"

"It is. And yes, that's my father. But I get my other abilities from my mother." He started walking again, his stride stiff.

Cara wanted to kick herself. She'd ticked him off, and that was no way to get answers. She hurried after him. "Look, I'm sorry for the snark. Really. But this is all kind of overwhelming for me. I mean, power crystals, psychic abilities, someone trying to kill us . . . This may be just another day's work for you, but it's completely foreign to me."

He stopped and bent his head. "You're right."

She came over to him. "Look, I'm sorry about what I said." She laid a hand on his arm.

His head snapped up; his gaze locked with hers. Arousal roared through her like a brush fire—consuming, overwhelming. She sucked in a sharp breath. How could this be, after what had just happened behind that rock? But then she realized that while he'd taken the edge off for her, she had not returned the favor. And he'd apparently gone through that transformation of his twice today. The sexual attraction that had always simmered between them had morphed into a blazing bonfire, especially for him.

Slowly he took her hand. She quivered as flesh met flesh, and he gently removed her hand from his shoulder, lowering it back to her side. His fingers lingered a moment longer than necessary. Then he broke contact.

"The effects of the Hunter are very powerful," he said. "It's better if we don't touch for a while, unless you want to—"

"—do it in the road?" she finished.

He chuckled at the Beatles reference. "Yeah. Basically."

"Gotcha. No touching." She took an extra step away so their bodies wouldn't accidentally brush against each other. "So, what's the Hunter?"

He let out a sigh, then looked her straight in the eye. "Me."

CHAPTER FOURTEEN

"You?" She waited a beat, then asked, "So is that your super-hero name or something?"

He laughed, and the tension visibly left his body. He started walking again, and she fell into step beside him. "Sort of. It's what it's called. What I'm called. Hell, I don't really know what to say about it. Except that it's me, and not me. Maybe part of me."

"Evil twin?" she quipped.

"Sure. Evil twin with superpowers." He shook his head. "Look, I'm messing this up. I've never really had to explain this to anyone before."

"Seriously?" It startled her—humbled her—that he was going to reveal secrets he'd never told anyone. "No ex-wife, fian-cée, best friend?"

"No." He tensed again, rolled his shoulders. "I haven't been that close to anyone for a long time. Years."

"Except your family. No, wait. You're not on speaking terms."

"Yeah. Listen, let me tell this from the beginning or else it's going to get all messed up."

"All right." She could hear the stress in his voice. Had it been the mention of his family that had done it? For some reason, knowing he cared that much about the relatives he'd claimed to have cut out of his life, softened her lingering wariness. "You were saying you get your gifts from your mother."

"Yeah. Well, this is going to sound crazy."

"Crazier than everything else that's happened over the past couple of days?" She laughed. "Go ahead, try me."

"Just don't make a run for it when I tell you this, okay? It's the truth, I swear."

"Just don't tell me your mother is an alien from outer space."

He chuckled. "No, but the truth is kind of close. My mother's family is from Spain."

"Shocking," she teased. "Imagine, you grew up in the western United States and your family is from Spain. I've never heard of such a thing."

"And before that, Atlantis."

She hesitated in her stride, then picked up the pace again. "Atlantis, huh? I don't suppose you mean the casino."

"No, I mean the ancient city that supposedly sank thousands of years ago."

"I see."

He sighed. "This is what I've been told. My mother's family is descended from the survivors of Atlantis. That's where the powers come from. We're Seers."

"Seers, like seeing the future?"

"Some of us."

"You saw that bomb exploding, didn't you? Before it happened."

"Yeah." He hesitated. "I saw it the first day we met."

She stopped. "You saw the bomb exploding the day we met? And you didn't tell me?"

He halted as well. "Would you have believed me?"

She couldn't pretend, even to herself. "No, probably not."

"Well, then." In unison, they began walking again. "Like I told you, sometimes I get flashes of things. It's totally random."

"That doesn't seem fair."

"It's all right. It's more like frosting on the cake. It's not my main power."

"You told me that. Your main power is finding people, you said. But you couldn't find Danny."

"That's right. And I have no idea why."

"Has this ever happened before? Have you ever not been able to find someone?"

"Never. Well, except for my own family. Our abilities don't work on each other."

"Oh, well that's interesting." She shook her head, a smile tugging at her lips. "I can't believe I'm calmly talking to you about Atlantis and psychic abilities. I was never one to buy into that kind of stuff."

"Sorry to burst your bubble, but it's all real."

"Yeah. Wow. My head is spinning just trying to wrap around all this." She unscrewed the cap on her water, then took a sip and offered him the bottle. "So are there other people like you? You know, descendants of Atlantis? Besides your family."

He shook his head before taking a swig of water. "Not that I know of," he said, wiping the excess from his lips with the back of his hand. "I think my ancestor is the only one to have escaped."

"That's wild." She took the water he handed her and screwed the cap on again. "So let me get this straight. You're a Seer, and what you see is people's locations."

"Right."

"And sometimes you see the future."

"Sometimes. A lot of times I just know things about a person. Like the day we met, I just knew your middle name. It just popped into my head."

"Handy. Any lottery numbers ever pop into your head?"

He laughed. "Nice try."

She grinned. "It was worth a shot. So, tell me about this Hunter."

His smile faded. "I'm not sure what to say about him."

"You said he's you, but you talk about him as if he's someone else."

"It's complicated."

"Is it you or isn't it?"

"I've never been quite sure," he said slowly. "My grandfather was the only other Hunter I ever knew, and he died when I was in grade school. He never talked much about it, and my powers hadn't manifested yet."

"So no one knew that you were one, too."

"Right. And when I go full throttle, I never remember anything."

"Wait, back up. What do you mean, 'full throttle'?"

"Okay, I'm jumping ahead. The Hunter is what gives me power. It's what I use to find people, and I can access that power at any time. But I have to be careful and only open myself up partway—I call it half throttle—or else the Hunter literally manifests. I *become* the Hunter—and the me that you see now, Rafe Montana, goes away."

"Goes away? Goes away where?" She stopped and stared at him.

"I don't know." He looked down at the blacktop, kicked a rock into the brush alongside the highway. "It's like I go to sleep, and then when everything calms down, I come back again."

"Wait, wait, wait." She waved her hands in front of her. "This Hunter thing takes over your body?"

"Essentially."

"You're right, this is weird. And complicated. So, when you

come back—you know, turn back into Rafe again—do you remember what happened?"

"No." The word seemed to catch, and he cleared his throat. "I never remember. That's why I never go full throttle unless my life depends on it. I never know what the Hunter will do, and I can't control it."

"So that was what I saw before the car exploded."

"Yeah. You wouldn't move, and I didn't want you to die."

"So you changed into the Hunter to save me. To save us."

"I didn't know what else to do." He looked at her then, regret and—was it fear?—in his eyes. "I hope I didn't do anything . . . that is . . . well, the first thing I remember is my hands—"

"Yeah. Let's talk about that for a minute." Just the memory stoked the embers of desire that still glowed hot inside her. "You—he—didn't hurt me. It's like you were this kind of primitive version of yourself. You didn't say anything, but your whole demeanor changed. Very alpha male, primal even. And your eyes turned pitch black."

"Great. I turn into a caveman."

"Not really. You were also very—um—turned on."

"About that . . . I think you caught some of the backlash from the Hunter."

"Backlash, huh?"

"Yeah." He looked down, rubbed the back of his neck, then glanced up again. "There are side effects."

"Keep talking."

"When I allow myself to go full Hunter, after I come back to myself, I'm usually totally fried. I call it burnout. I pass out, sleep for a day or so. I'm no good to anyone for at least twenty-four hours. That's what happened to me before, when I passed out in the truck."

She frowned. "Then why aren't you still snoozing?"

"Because of you. When you held my focus stone, it did something. Re-energized me. That's never happened before."

"I didn't know what else to do." She shrugged. "You said something about the stone being drained, and I remembered that weird moment in the motel parking lot where both of us touched your crystal. For some reason I thought it would work."

"And it did. Somehow you recharged my batteries. I still haven't figured that out." He started walking again.

"So wait a minute." She hurried to keep pace with him. "You were just the Hunter like fifteen minutes ago when you saved us from the explosion, and you haven't passed out yet."

"That's never happened," he said. "I think that's because of you, too. When I snapped back, you were holding my focus stone."

"Yes, I was. But it was different this time. Instead of bright white lights, there was this dark shadow thing with streaks of silver. And it kind of soaked into me, made me—" She broke off.

"Horny as hell?" he finished.

"Yes." Her face heated, and she didn't think it was from the sun. "I've never felt anything like that before. Such . . . wow, I can't even describe it."

"You don't have to. That's one of the side effects." He actually seemed a little embarrassed. "When I come out of burnout, I have to deal with that, too."

"But we did . . . well, you did. Take care of it, I mean." She shook her head. "This isn't coming out right. You took care of me, but not yourself."

He turned a serious look on her. "I didn't want to take advantage. Neither of us was really ourselves."

She kicked a rock in the road. "I don't know whether to feel grateful or ticked off."

"It's fine. Don't worry about it."

Don't worry about it? She slanted him a look out of the corner of her eye. He had to have incredible discipline to even be walking upright if that kind of sexual heat was still raging under the surface. "Why does that happen?" she asked. "The sex thing, I mean."

"You said the Hunter seemed primal," he said. "What's more primal than sex?"

"I guess."

"I'm sorry you caught so much of it," he said. "But you happened to grab my stone just as the Hunter was retreating, so the energy flowed mostly into you rather than me. And you don't have the experience to deal with it."

"Don't blame me for hijacking your horniness," she snapped. "I had no idea what was happening."

"I'm not blaming you, just stating facts. And what happened back there didn't dissipate all of it, just gave you a little bit of control back. The hunger is only going to grow stronger until we can take some time and get rid of all of it."

"How long does it usually stick around?"

To his credit, he looked a little uncomfortable, though it didn't soften the blow. "Takes me a good day or two to work it off."

"A day or two? You think we're going to stop and have an orgy when Danny is out there, and people are trying to kill us? Forget it. I'm not having sex with you again just because of some . . . some side effect!" She stormed off ahead of him, wishing a car would come down the road so she could hitch a ride. Get away from him, away from all this woo-woo weirdness. She was just a normal woman, for crying out loud.

He caught up to her, his long legs keeping up easily with her shorter, quicker stride. "You had sex with me before, remember? Back at the motel. What's so different now?"

"What's so different now?" She whirled to face him. "How do I know these are even my feelings?"

"Of course they're your feelings. The stone only amplifies what's already there."

"So you're saying I'm some kind of sex fiend now? That's *it*. I am done with all this. I will not be railroaded into sleeping with you again, Rafe Montana. If I have an itch, I can find someone else to scratch it, thank you very much!"

"Are you saying you want to end our affair?"

Her righteous anger dimmed at the utter seriousness of his tone. "I'm saying this affair is more than I bargained for. *You're* more than I bargained for."

"Are you saying you want to end it? Yes or no?"

"I don't know. I don't know *anything* yet. I have to absorb all of this."

"Fine, you do that." He jerked his chin forward, indicating the sun-worn wooden building coming into view at the curve in the road. About a dozen motorcycles lined the parking lot, gleaming in the sun, and an old-style neon sign declared the place as MOTHER'S. "That's where we're headed. If you decide to end it between us, it looks like you'll have your choice of itch scratchers."

He headed toward the bar, not seeming to care if she followed or not.

She trailed after him, unable to stop herself from checking out his tight rear end as he walked ahead of her. Annoyed at herself, she jerked her gaze to the building in the distance. Crystals and psychic powers and manifestations of who-knew-what . . . her whole life had turned upside down ever since her plane landed in Vegas. She longed to get back to Jersey, where things made sense.

Part of her wasn't quite ready to see the last of Rafe Montana, but another part thought she should end the romantic side of things and focus on what was important—finding Danny and saving her condo.

Someone had just blown up Rafe's car, which told her more than anything that the people after them were serious enough to kill. Danny had clearly gotten in over his head this time. She had to find him and help him out of this jam . . . because no one else would. And her best chance of doing that was Rafe Montana. So she had to keep her eye on the goal.

Side effects or not.

. . . . .

Rafe approached the bar, aware of the scrape of Cara's tennis shoes on the sand-dusted asphalt behind him. He shared the same throbbing hunger that she did, but he had more experience handling the effects of the Hunter. He was able to focus that energy on survival—another primal directive. Good thing, too, or else he'd be chasing her like a stag in rut.

They couldn't wander along the desert highway indefinitely. They needed transportation, and they couldn't just call a cab or car service to come get them. Businesses kept records, even if you paid in cash. And he was trying to stay off the grid. Let the guys from Santutegi think they'd succeeded in killing them—at least for a while. By the time they'd discovered the truth, he and Cara could be long gone.

He entered the parking lot and stopped, perusing the various bikes. He found a likely candidate just as Cara caught up with him. Her scent—vanilla and brown sugar—drifted to him on the breeze, stirring up the urges he kept carefully at bay. He glanced at her. Blond strands glittered in her honey-colored hair beneath the sun. Her white, short-sleeved blouse hung open, revealing the matching skintight tank top she wore. The stretchy material cupped her breasts like loving hands, and her khaki shorts made her bare legs look like they went on forever. Sexual fever clung to her like perfume.

He was good in a fight, but he knew that if he went into the bar with her, he'd have a real battle on his hands. Not that the customers in there were criminals or anything, but the majority of them were men, and nothing stirred up male primitive instincts like a woman in heat. Too bad they'd only had enough time to take the edge off. He'd have liked to do more. Much more.

The image formed in his mind: stripping off those shorts and bending her over one of the bikes, then sliding into that slick, warm heat and driving hard and fast until one of them screamed.

A vision of the future? Just the notion made his hands shake.

No, just a normal male fantasy. Now get your head back in the game.

"This place had better have a ladies' room," Cara said.

"Of course they have a ladies' room. Women ride bikes, too."

"Good, because I drank a lot of water."

She started toward the door, but he grabbed her arm and pulled her back. Just the simple touch of flesh on flesh made her freeze. Slowly she met his gaze, her eyes wide with awareness, nostrils flaring. If she had been broadcasting sexual heat on simmer before, now it was at full boil.

"Cara." He couldn't stop himself from stroking her arm before dropping his hand. That bike was looking better and better, fantasy or not. "That place is full of guys, and you might as well be wearing a sign—"

"—that says 'take me, I'm horny?'" she finished.

"Yeah." He cleared his throat, trying to concentrate on their precarious situation and not on her kissable mouth. She'd all but said it was over between them, but until he heard the words, he still considered her his. "Listen, the best plan I can come up with is to broadcast that we're a couple. Hopefully that will keep most of them from trying to hit on you."

"Okay." She studied his face for a moment, then reached out and took his hand, twining his fingers with hers. "I still haven't decided what to do about us. Just so you know."

"I know." He could see the truth, the conflict, in her eyes. He wanted her to choose him, but maybe it was better if she didn't. Safer if she didn't. "Show time."

He pulled her against him, tormenting them both with the oh-so-insufficient contact. Too many clothes, not enough time. He tugged at her ponytail, arching her head back and bending to press his lips against hers. She whimpered, melting into him. Desire clawed at the prison of his will. He wrapped the silky ponytail around his hand and held her fast as he pulled his mouth away. Her eyelids drifted open, blatant hunger shining at him.

He nearly lost it then and there.

"Rafe," she whispered, the word soaked with invitation and need.

"I know." He rested his forehead against hers, inhaling her scent. Then he released her ponytail, one finger at a time, and straightened.

She stepped away from him and sucked in a deep breath. "I don't know if that kiss was such a good idea. I'm feeling even more . . . you know . . . than ever."

"I was thinking it would put my stamp on you, like a no tres-passing sign." He swept his gaze over her. "But you're right. I just made things worse."

"We needed to make it look good." She strode toward the

door of the bar. "Now I have to find that ladies' room or else there's going to be an accident."

"I'm right behind you."

After the bright light of the sun outside, the dimmer lights of the bar's interior took a moment to get used to. Cara shifted from one foot to the other, looking for the restroom sign. Rafe stood very still, studying the clientele.

They had definitely been noticed. It was the middle of the week, so only a handful of customers were there. The volume of rumbling voices decreased as they stepped inside. When Cara squealed and made a run for the back of the bar, eyes followed her. She disappeared into the ladies' room.

Rafe kept a lookout with his peripheral vision as he made his way to the bar. "I'll take a beer," he said to the bartender. The guy looked about his age, but bald as a cue ball. His muscular build strained the confines of his black T-shirt, and tattoos decorated his arms, disappearing beneath the shirt. He had a black mustache and a suspicious look in his eyes.

"What kind?" he asked, distrust heavy in his tone. "And we don't take credit cards, just so you know."

"Whatever's on tap," Rafe said. "I've got cash. Oh, and a glass of water."

The bartender narrowed his eyes, then gave a jerk of a nod and went to fill the order.

Rafe turned and leaned against the bar, checking out the other customers. He visualized the motorcycle he'd picked out.

Where is the owner of the bike?

The vision swelled in his mind, showing him the owner of the somewhat beaten up Harley and feeding him some info about him, just as the guy leaned over to take his shot at the pool table.

He was shorter than Rafe, with a wiry build. A bandana tied around his head kept his long light brown hair out of his eyes as he braced himself, then took the shot. With a hard clack, the cue ball sent the others winging across the table. Two landed in pockets with solid thunks. The shooter straightened and threw his hand up in victory, a cigarette hanging from his mouth. A red-haired woman laughed and clapped, her generous boobs nearly bursting from her low-cut T-shirt as she bounced. When the shooter removed the cigarette to tap away the ashes, the woman jumped up, wrapped her arms around his neck and gave him a hard kiss on the mouth.

Behind Rafe, the bartender slapped a mug of beer and a glass of water on the bar. "That'll be eight dollars."

Rafe turned to meet the bartender's gaze. "How much?"

"Eight."

Lie.

"Pretty steep. Guess I can't afford a tip." Ignoring the bartender's glare, Rafe opened his wallet and counted out the bills. Yeah, the bartender was trying to cheat a couple of outsiders, but making enemies wasn't going to get Rafe anywhere. So he paid the highway-robbery price and picked up his mug just as Cara rejoined him.

"This for me?" she asked, indicating the water.

Rafe nodded and took a healthy gulp of his icy cold beer, then set it down on the bar. "Stay here," he told her, and headed over to the pool table. "Hey," he said to the long-haired shooter. "Eddie, right? Nice shot."

The long-haired guy turned and gave Rafe a narrow-eyed look. "Thanks."

"Listen," Rafe continued, "Dave sent me. Said you were short on cash and might consider selling me your bike."

The conversations around them ceased. Eddie slowly ground out his cigarette in the ashtray on the edge of the pool table, then looked back at Rafe. "That right?"

Looking into Eddie's eyes, Rafe knew he'd hit a nerve. *You might as well have offered to buy the guy's firstborn. But he does need the money.*

"Yeah. Dave knew I was looking for a bike." Rafe lowered his voice. "My girl over there thinks they're hot."

Eddie glanced at Cara, then snorted a laugh. "How much we talking?"

"Depends on how she rides." Rafe smiled, trying to project the right balance of cool and sucker.

Eddie stiffened. "I keep my ride in top condition."

"I know you do, which is why I want to buy her."

Eddie's posture relaxed.

"Maybe you could let me try her out?" Rafe opened his wallet and pulled out the last of the bills he'd won from the slot machine in Vegas. "I've got four hundred cash right here. Consider it part of the down payment."

Eddie glanced at the money, then scowled at Rafe. "You think I'm stupid?"

"Of course not."

Eddie poked a finger in Rafe's chest. "I'm not letting you near my bike until I talk to Dave and he vouches for you."

Rafe held his ground. "So you don't want my four hundred?"

Desperation flashed across Eddie's face, so quickly Rafe doubted anyone but him had noticed it. Then Eddie was Mr. Cool again. "I didn't say that. Said I have to talk to Dave first."

"I don't know if I can wait that long," Rafe said. "There's another guy over in Flagstaff who has a bike that looks good, too. And it's red." He glanced back at Cara, then leaned closer to Eddie and lowered his tone. "She goes for red, but yours is the better of the two."

Eddie hesitated, then shook his head. "Leave me your number, and I'll call you after I talk to Dave."

"Are you sure?" He held up the cash. "Four hundred, just for a test drive. Come on, man. Help me look good in front of my girl."

Eddie glanced at Cara, then raised his brows at Rafe. "You sure she's your girl?"

"Rafe!" Cara cried.

Rafe turned. The two guys from Santutegi were near the bar. One of them dragged Cara toward the front door. The other one smirked at Rafe. "Kill him," he said to the crowd.

Chairs scraped back as men stood. Rafe sprang after Cara, but Eddie grabbed his shirt and yanked him back. He spun around, jerking free of Eddie's hold, then turned back toward the door. But the way was blocked. All the customers in the bar—six, Rafe counted—surrounded him.

"Cara!" he yelled. He charged, but the guy in his way simply shoved him backward with a hand to the chest. Rafe staggered into another guy, who shoved him again. He caught himself against Eddie, who shoved his face close. In his eyes, Rafe saw the white binding around his thoughts he had seen in Cara. He looked around, seeing the same thing in the eyes of all the men surrounding him.

Somehow the guy from Santutegi had put the whammy on the whole crowd.

"This is for thinking I'm stupid," Eddie said, and swung his fist.

Pain exploded in Rafe's jaw. He sucked in a breath, shaking his head until the world settled again.

"Hey!" the bartender yelled.

Rafe exhaled slowly. Good. The bartender was a jerk, but he wouldn't want the place torn up in a fight.

"Outside," the bartender continued. "No way are you getting blood on my pool table."

"Sure thing, Pete," Eddie called back, then nodded to the others.

They picked Rafe up and hauled him out the back door.

CHAPTER FIFTEEN

They dragged him outside to the small patch of land behind the bar and shoved him to the ground. Rafe rolled, avoiding someone's boot as its owner tried to stomp on his head, and got to his feet. He opened his senses half throttle, reaching for the Hunter. He didn't want to hurt these guys; he knew they weren't acting of their own accord. But he wanted to stay alive, too.

His focus stone heated against his skin, responding with a quick efficiency that shocked him. Whatever Cara had done had given the thing a heck of a tune-up. Power flooded his limbs, sharpening his eyesight, his hearing—and his speed. The mob moved in, surrounding him.

What do I need to know?

Knowledge flowed into his mind, and he acted, striking each of the weaknesses as they were fed to him. *Guy on the right—a kick to his bad knee. Behind him—an elbow in the gut since he gets winded easily.* Eddie came at him, and he charged forward, scooping the smaller man over his shoulder in a fireman's carry and dumping him into a pile of empty boxes. A screech behind him warned him, and he whirled in time to catch Eddie's girlfriend as she leaped for him, nails extended like claws. He caught her, spun, and dumped her on top of Eddie, who was trying to get to his feet. The two tumbled backward into the boxes.

That left three guys. The bartender came outside, a baseball bat in his hand and a glitter of mean in his eyes. So four all together, more if the ones he'd gone after got up the gumption to come at him again.

The Hunter tugged at the bonds of Rafe's will, hungry to get loose and take care of the problem. But he couldn't let that happen. These were basically good people; they didn't deserve the wrath the Hunter brought. The best option would be to find some way to break the whammy that held the mob in thrall. He'd half hoped that the physical pain he'd dished out would do the trick, but so far that hadn't worked. But he had to do something; he had to get out of here and go after Cara.

The bartender approached him, slapping the baseball bat against his hand, forcing Rafe to back up. Behind him he heard the creak of leather and the rustle of clothing as the three uninjured bikers closed in.

"You shouldn't have come here, city boy," the bartender said.

"I don't want any trouble," Rafe said. "I just want to leave."

"Too late," said one of the men behind him. "You're ours now."

Rafe glanced around, saw Eddie on his feet dragging his girlfriend out of the pile of boxes. Beside them stood a Dumpster and next to that . . . a garden hose.

The hose was coiled on the ground like a snake, one end connected to an outside faucet, probably for cleaning out trash cans or something. If he could get to that, maybe he could turn the water on the crowd, break the trance like he had with Cara in the shower.

He sure as heck wasn't going to kiss them all.

Someone grabbed him from behind. He jerked away, but only got one arm free. He came around swinging, aiming for the nose of the lanky young guy who still gripped his other arm.

"Hold him still!" Pete yelled, raising the bat. "I'll crack open his skull like a watermelon!"

The truth spoke to Rafe from the bartender's eyes. *He's killed before.*

He reached, opening up more to the Hunter but still not quite willing to go full force. He didn't want any accidents—no innocent blood on his hands. He'd been there, done that.

Never again.

The surge of power gave him the strength to yank away from his captor. He came around swinging and clocked the guy in the mouth. With a cry, the guy staggered backward, blood exploding across his lips. Rafe kept going, kicking one guy on the back of the knee and decking him in the jaw, then socking another in the gut with a hard right.

Pete let out a howl of rage and charged, swinging the bat. Rafe darted out of the way, taking another biker around the gut and slamming them both to the ground. The bat swung harmlessly overhead. Pete stumbled a step, then came back around, raising the weapon like a club.

Rafe rolled to the side, got to his feet. Someone grabbed him by the back of the shirt.

"I've got him, Pete!" Eddie shouted.

"Get him on his knees," Pete snarled.

Another biker came over to help Eddie shove Rafe down on his knees, then pushed his face down into the dirt.

"Just like a real live execution," Pete crowed, glee underscoring his words. "Watch how his head busts open, Eddie. Bet you never seen anything like that."

Rafe tensed his muscles, already regretting what he would have to do as he started to reach for the Hunter.

"Hey! What the—" Pete's words ended on a gurgle.

"All of you," came a familiar voice, "will return to the bar and forget this ever happened."

Eddie loosened his grip, and Rafe stopped the Hunter just before full manifestation. He was able to turn his head enough to see Adrian Gray, standing over a fallen Pete, baseball bat in hand. Gray wore a black T-shirt and jeans that screamed designer badass and an attitude that demanded obedience.

"Who the hell are you?" Eddie demanded.

Gray frowned as he looked from one to the other. "The guy who's going to use this bat on you if you don't let him go."

Eddie chuckled, and the others echoed the sound. "Pal, you look like you lost your golf cart or something. Now turn around and leave. This isn't your business."

"It is when you're about to beat the hell out of my friend."

"Oh, is that it?" Eddie let go of Rafe and stepped over him toward Adrian. "Well, Pete was my friend and you knocked him out cold." The rest of the bikers fell in behind Eddie, splitting up to surround Adrian.

Whatever Gray's game, he'd created a much-needed distraction. Rafe got to his feet and sped for the garden hose.

"Hey!" screeched Eddie's girlfriend. "Where do you think you're going?"

Rafe grabbed the hose with one hand and turned on the faucet full force with the other. He spun to face the mob just as the fighting began.

Adrian Gray moved like a blur—or some kind of martial arts master—and easily took out two of the bikers. Rafe had only a minute to admire the guy's technique; then Eddie's girlfriend leaped on him out of nowhere, locking her legs around his waist and lifting her hands toward his eyes with a snarl. He raised the hose and got her straight in the face with the spewing water, still hot from the day's heat.

She screeched and jumped down, landing on her feet and choking. He kept the spray steady until it ran cold and her crazed expression faded. "What's the matter with you?" she demanded. Her blue eyes shone with anger and confusion, but the binding around her thoughts was gone.

Rafe shoved past her and turned the hose on the other bikers. Gray was doing a fine job defending himself, but as Rafe drenched them, each one in turn stopped fighting, then backed off, looking confused.

"What the hell?" Eddie scowled at Rafe. "What's with the hose? You're nuts, man. No way am I selling my bike to you." He held out a hand to his girlfriend. "Come on, baby. Let's get out of here."

She ran to him and grabbed his hand, then hurried after him as he strode back into the bar. The other bikers looked at one another, similar expressions of confusion on their faces. One by one, they wandered back inside. Rafe leaned down and turned off the water.

Adrian came over, studied his eyes, and smiled a little. "Hunter," he said. "That explains a lot."

Shocked, Rafe struggled to keep his cool. How did Gray know about the Hunter? "I don't know what you're talking about."

"Sure you don't." Gray shrugged. "Okay, you don't trust me. I get that. We can iron that out later. Right now, let's go get Cara." He turned back toward the bar.

Rafe stayed where he was. "Just like that, huh?"

Adrian paused in the doorway and looked back over his shoulder. "You want explanations? Come with me. I'm going to get Cara back from those goons before they hurt her. They've already killed Artie."

"What?" Rafe dropped the hose and started forward. "Bartow is dead?"

"Murdered." Gray stood his ground as Rafe reached him. "Now we can work together and stop the same thing from happening to Cara, or we can have a pissing contest right here."

"You're right about one thing—I don't trust you. So you'll forgive me if I don't just hop into your car and help you avenge your boss."

"Bartow was never my boss; I was the one running things. But there's another party in the game now, and they've changed all the rules."

"What game?" Rafe demanded. "What rules?"

Gray shook his head, exasperation evident on his face. "Look, I'll explain it all in the car—assuming you're coming. Having a Hunter along will certainly make finding Cara easier."

Rafe scowled. He hated not being able to read the guy. He hated that Gray somehow knew about the Hunter. This could be a trap. "Thanks for helping me out there, but I can find Cara on my own."

"I'm sure you can. That heap of burned rubble a couple of miles back was your car, right?"

Rafe clenched his jaw, then nodded.

"Then you might as well come with me. I have a car, and I have information, which you apparently lack. Now we're wasting time. Evan and Mestor could be miles away before we catch up with them." He stepped into the bar.

"Evan and Mestor?" Rafe followed. "Are those the guys who took Cara and put the whammy on that crowd in there?"

"The whammy?" Gray chuckled. "Interesting term, and that certainly explains why they didn't listen to me."

"What's your angle?" Rafe demanded before they stepped into the main area of the bar. "Why are you so concerned about Cara?"

Adrian paused, his shoulders tense. "Because I was the one

who lured her here to find her stepbrother. It's my fault she's in danger."

Rafe nodded. "Finally," he said, "we agree on something."

. . . . .

Cara sat quietly in the back of the silver sedan, staring out the window at the passing terrain. It was all she could do to keep the bland expression on her face and pretend that everything was fine. It wasn't, but her captors didn't know that. They thought she was under their control, like before.

And yet she wasn't.

"You will be quiet and do what you're told."

That's what the one called Evan had said to her, followed by what could only be described as some kind of "push" in her mind. Her immediate internal response had been *No*. And the mental push didn't take hold, just sort of bounced away. She'd realized her advantage and let her expression grow vacant, as if they had succeeded in putting her in a trance. Amazingly, that had worked. They'd put her in the car as if she were a doll, then gotten in themselves and turned back toward Vegas, talking in low, serious tones in some foreign language. And she'd learned their names: Evan and Mestor. She filed that bit of info away for later.

She had no idea how she was able to resist the compulsion this time, when she hadn't been able to at least twice before. Maybe it had something to do with that dark force that had swept through her the last time she touched Rafe's focus stone. He'd said she'd absorbed some of the Hunter energy. Maybe that was helping her now? And if so, how long would it last?

She just hoped it was long enough for Rafe to find her.

. . . . .

They got into the car in silence.

Rafe puzzled over what he'd just witnessed: Adrian Gray easily hypnotizing a bar full of people and convincing them that none of the past hour had happened. Rafe hadn't been affected—on purpose or not, he didn't know. But seeing confirmation of what he'd merely suspected made him wary. Either Gray was serious about working together, or he planned to get rid of Rafe when he was done with him.

The fact that he couldn't read Adrian Gray sat in his gut like cement pancakes.

"I know you have questions," Gray said. "Why don't you locate Cara so we know which way to go, and then I'll answer them."

An olive branch or a trap? He couldn't tell.

"I saw you fighting back there," Rafe said finally. "You're really good."

A small smile curved Gray's lips. "Thank you."

"But if you try to hurt Cara, I'll end you."

Gray nodded. "Understood." He turned the key in the ignition and waited.

Rafe hesitated. Would he be making things worse by leading Gray to Cara? Then again, at least Gray had helped him out of a bad situation, which meant he might not be an enemy, just a man with his own agenda. Gray had earned a point in the trust scale—a very small point.

The devil you know, and all that.

Rafe closed his eyes. *Where is Cara?*

The image solidified in his mind almost instantly. Cara sat in the back of the silver sedan, her expression blank. Rage surged through him. Had they put the whammy on her again?

Then she looked around, a small frown between her brows, and he saw her lips form a word: Rafe.

Stunned, he allowed the vision to dissipate and opened his

eyes as he digested the rest of the information being fed to him. It was almost as if she'd sensed him looking for her.

"Well?" Gray said.

"She's in their car. They're headed back toward Vegas."

"All right, then." Gray pulled out of the parking lot onto the highway and started back the way Rafe had come only an hour ago. "Did she look all right to you?"

Rafe frowned. "Yes, she looked fine. Unharmed, which is lucky for them. Now it's your turn. Start talking, pal."

Gray looked amused, which only irritated Rafe. "What would you like to know?"

"What the hell did you do to those people back there?"

"A simple suggestion to smooth things over. Considering the situation was caused by another Whisperer, I thought it was fitting."

Rafe digested that, then had to ask, "And just what is a Whisperer?"

Gray frowned. "Rafe, how much do you know about your heritage?"

Rafe narrowed his eyes. "You tell me."

"Are you testing me, or don't you know what you are?"

"Why don't you talk to me about what you are instead?"

"You really don't know, do you? That puts you and your family in a lot of danger."

"Wait, what's this about my family?" Rafe turned in his seat. "Start talking, Whisperer Boy."

Gray's mouth thinned, rewarding Rafe with a brief moment of petty satisfaction. "I'm very disturbed by your ignorance, Montana. It does not bode well."

"For you or for me?"

"For all of us." Gray glanced at him, his expression grave. "The very world depends on us."

"Wait a second. How did we go from rescuing Cara to saving the world?"

"Because we are all part of the same whole."

"Yeah, well, I'm not much of a joiner. Start explaining."

Gray slowly shook his head, like a patient mentor dealing with a difficult student. "We're not going to be able to stop Jain Criten until you begin trusting me."

"What does Criten have to do with all this?"

"He's the heart of it. Evan and Mestor work for him."

Rafe settled back in his seat. "Okay, now we're getting somewhere. What does the president of some foreign island want with Cara?"

"Criten is a powerful Channeler, a man on a mission to right what he sees as an ancient wrong. That makes him dangerous. He wants to use Cara to find her stepbrother."

"You lured her out here. Wasn't that your plan?"

Gray shrugged. "I hoped that if he realized she had come looking for him, Cangialosi might surface. I never intended her to get hurt. Frankly, until yesterday I thought she'd gone back to New Jersey."

"Sure. That's why her hotel room was trashed and someone— some *Whisperer*—put the whammy on her to send her home."

"I didn't toss her room; that was Criten's doing. But yes, I did plant the suggestion that she return home. I was trying to protect her." He frowned. "How did you get her to go with you, by the way? I don't recall anyone ever breaking one of my compulsions."

"I'm asking the questions. What's a Channeler?"

"Someone who can manipulate energy and change matter." Gray's jaw tightened. "Look, we need to work together to rescue Cara and recover the stone."

"Stone?" Rafe narrowed his eyes. "That's what this is all about? Some rock?"

"The Stone of Igarle—"

"Geez, it has a name, too? What is it—some huge diamond or something?"

"No, not a gemstone."

"Then what?"

Gray sped up, passing a slow-moving truck. "The Stone of Igarle is very powerful and very dangerous in the wrong hands. I have sworn an oath to protect the stone at all costs."

"Powerful how?"

Gray reached over and tapped the lump beneath Rafe's shirt that was his focus stone. "Powerful like this."

"Hey." Rafe shoved his hand away.

"Relax. I can't use your crystal against you. I am not a Seer."

"No, you're a Whisperer."

"Exactly. And a Whisperer cannot manipulate the powers of a Seer."

"Well, that's good news." Rafe lay his hand against the stone. Power stirred, warming the crystal against his chest. "Why don't you tell me more about you Whisperers?"

"We are the strongest of the Warrior sect of Atlantis," Gray said.

Rafe stared, wondering why he was shocked to hear the *A* word come out of Gray's mouth. "Come again?"

"You and I have a common ancestry," Gray said. "We are both descendants of the survivors of Atlantis."

"Atlantis? Are you nuts?" Then something Gray had said registered. Rafe stopped even trying to play ignorant. "Wait, *survivors*? As in, more than one?"

Gray laughed. "Of course. Surely you did not think your ancestor was the only one?" A glance at Rafe's face had him shaking his head, clearly still amused. "Wow, you did."

Rafe just scowled, feeling five years old again and very dumb.

"Okay, history lesson. And perhaps when you have heard the tale, you will trust me enough to let me help you." Gray kept his foot heavy on the gas, leaving the truck far behind. "Centuries ago in the great kingdom of Atlantis, there were three sects of advanced citizens: Seers, Warriors, and Channelers. Each sect balanced the other to create a perfectly synchronized society."

"And a Whisperer is a Warrior?"

"Yes." Gray nodded. "The Warriors are the protectors of Atlantis. Some of the more advanced ones also possess the Whispering gift—the ability to implant suggestions in others with merely a whisper."

"Doesn't seem too warrior-like to me."

"Imagine," Gray said with a smile, "the effect of such a gift on an attacking force. Or a mob."

"That would take some loud whispering."

"It's just a term, Montana." Gray sent him a glance of annoyance. "Remember what I did in the bar. And what Evan did before me."

"Yeah. Thanks for not including me in your whammy."

"It wasn't my doing," Gray said. "Our powers don't work on other Atlanteans, only humans. I couldn't put a compulsion on you if I wanted to."

"Nice to know." An idea clicked in Rafe's mind. "Wait a second. I can always see anyone, except my own family. Is that why?"

"I would think so."

"And I couldn't read you when we met at the casino."

"Read me?" Gray arched his brows.

Rafe silently cursed himself for revealing that small vulnerability. "I'm a Seer, pal. I *see* things. Except with you and Criten." He frowned. "And Cangialosi. Is he—you know, one of us?"

"Not that I know of." Gray gave a sigh. "It's probably the influence of the stone."

"The Ugly Stone?"

"*Igarle.*"

"The Igarle Stone. And this is some ancient relic from Atlantis supposedly?"

"You know," Gray said, "for a man who can manifest the essence of a primeval warrior at will, you are amazingly skeptical."

So that's what the Hunter was. Rafe bit back the hoard of questions that flooded his mind and asked instead, "So Criten wants the stone, probably for power. What do you want it for?" At Gray's quick frown, Rafe added, "I assume you want it, too, or else you wouldn't be involved in this mess."

"My job is to guard the stone from misuse." Gray jerked his chin forward. "Look, there they are."

Rafe fixed his gaze on the silver sedan ahead of them. The Hunter yanked against the leash, hungry to do some damage. "We have to stop that car without hurting Cara."

Gray gave a slow, deadly smile. "Leave that to me."

CHAPTER SIXTEEN

Cara knew something was wrong when her captors began jabbering urgently in their own language. Mestor was driving and kept glancing in his rearview mirror. Evan, in the passenger seat, turned to scowl out the back window. Keeping her expression serene, Cara glanced behind them.

A black car was coming up on their tail at a suicidal speed, the low growl of the machine's engine indicating the driver had his foot planted hard on the gas pedal. Evan glanced over at Mestor and said something in their language. The car behind them crept a few inches closer—and Cara glimpsed Rafe in the passenger seat. Excitement sparked through her, but she managed to maintain her expressionless demeanor and turned to face front again, as if nothing interesting were happening. But inside she wracked her brain for a way to help Rafe rescue her.

Her kidnappers didn't pay her any attention, no doubt assuming she was still under their spell. The engine of the car behind them roared louder as it crept even closer. Mestor fired off what sounded like rapid-fire questions to Evan, who responded just as urgently. Suddenly Mestor hit the brakes, then the gas.

Cara jerked forward in her seat, then was thrown backward. A squeal of tires sounded from behind them, and she stole a glance out the rear windshield. The black car had jerked to the side and was now coming up beside them. Mestor yanked the wheel hard to the right, nearly striking the other vehicle. Luckily it swerved enough to avoid collision. Evan shouted at his partner, who shot back equally irate responses.

She had to do something to help. Abandoning her pretense, she leaned forward and covered Mestor's eyes with her hands.

He shouted, letting go of the wheel with one hand and clawing at her grip with the other. Evan yanked at her arm, succeeding in pulling one hand away.

"You will let go and sit quietly in the backseat," Evan ordered. That familiar mental push followed his words. For a second the world tilted. What had she been doing again?

The car jolted with a crunch of metal, jerking her attention outside. Rafe stared at her from the other car, his expression deadly intent.

"Sit down," Evan commanded. The mental push came again, like a hand clamped around her will, forcing her to obey.

No.

She shook with effort as she resisted his powers. It was harder this time, as if her ability to resist was growing weaker with every minute.

"I said *sit down*," Evan snarled.

She looked him straight in the eye. "Screw you." Then she turned and raked her fingernails across the driver's face.

Mestor howled, releasing the wheel to grab her hand with both of his. The car veered right, headed toward the shoulder. Evan spat something that sounded like a curse and dove for the wheel.

The black car slammed into them, sending them into the guardrail with a squeal of tires and the sickening screech of metal on metal.

. . . . .

The instant Gray stopped the car, Rafe was out and running for Cara. He had the Hunter at half throttle, but he wouldn't hesitate to go all the way if he needed to rip someone's head off. Cara pushed her way out of the backseat, stumbling toward him and falling into his embrace.

"You okay?" He cupped her face and searched her eyes. She looked rattled, but no compulsion trapped her thoughts. She gave him a shaky nod, and he pressed a kiss to her lips, then hugged her tightly, burying his face in her hair for one, life-affirming moment.

A shout drew his attention. Gray sped past him and leaped at the driver of Cara's car, who had climbed out and was raising his gun to fire. Gray succeeded in knocking the gun from the driver's hand, but the other man darted out of the way with blurring speed. The second captor got out of the car, his forehead bleeding. He locked eyes with Rafe.

"Seer," he hissed, his face twisting with hate. Then he charged.

Rafe pushed Cara behind him. "Get in the car."

By some miracle she didn't argue, just darted for the safety of the black vehicle while Rafe stepped forward to meet his attacker. He reached for the Hunter, allowing the power to flow through him, holding back a breath from full transformation. The other man faltered only for a moment as he got a good look at Rafe's face; then he gave a battle cry and came at him in a blur of movement.

The instincts of the Hunter took over.

. . . . .

Cara opened the door of the black car and jumped into the passenger side, locking the door behind her. Outside, the four men battled bare-handed and with astonishing speed. In that brief moment where Rafe had held her, she'd noticed his eyes had turned nearly black. She knew what that meant now—that he was using the Hunter but hadn't given over completely to it.

Adrian Gray fought alongside Rafe—and she had some questions on how *that* had happened—but even as she wondered about his motivations, she couldn't help but admire the sheer beauty of his fighting technique. All of them moved with stunning, deadly efficiency—striking, blocking, a wicked, lethal dance. Yet Adrian moved a hair faster, his every action measured, controlled.

Mestor matched Adrian, seemed to almost anticipate his moves. At one point he grabbed Adrian by back of the shirt, spinning with an obvious intent to send him flying. But Adrian shifted, flexed, and somehow Mestor stood holding an empty shirt. The startled expression on his face looked almost comical, but he certainly wasn't laughing when a bare-chested Adrian kicked him in the head and dropped him to the ground like a stone. Nearby, Rafe stood over Evan, his knuckles bleeding and ferocity tightening his features. Had he changed over to the Hunter? Cara got out of the car and hurried over to him.

"Hey, hold on." Gray blocked her way, grasping her arms. "Don't get too close to those guys. They're down, but they're not out."

Cara shrugged away from him. "Don't touch me."

He held up his hands in surrender. "Not touching."

Cara pushed past him. "Rafe?" He turned around as she reached him, and she looked into his eyes, noticing there was still some blue around the black. He wasn't fully turned, not yet.

"You should stay back," he said, tugging her backward a couple of steps. "I don't know how long this guy will be out." He looked behind her. "Good job."

Cara noticed then that Adrian had followed her. Gray flashed his movie-star smile. "You, too," he said.

Cara raised her eyebrows at Rafe.

"Yeah, I know," he said in answer to her unspoken question. "I'll explain it all later, but for now, it looks like we're on the same side. Kinda," he added, with a warning look at Gray.

Adrian seemed unfazed by Rafe's distrust. "We don't have a lot of time. As soon as Criten realizes his men are out of commission, he'll send more."

Criten? "Wait—" Cara began.

Rafe nodded. "Agreed. I need to get Cara somewhere safe, where I can plan my next move."

"*Our* next move," Gray corrected.

"Hey, guys—" she started again.

"Look, I appreciate the assist here—"

"You need me, Montana. You still don't know the whole story."

Rafe folded his arms. "Care to enlighten?"

"We don't have time now, but once we've recovered the stone, I will tell you everything I know. I swear it." Gray laid his hand over his heart in an oddly old-world gesture.

Rafe considered him with narrowed eyes.

"*Wait a minute,*" Cara said, pushing between the two. She looked at Adrian. "Criten? Jain Criten, the president of Santutegi, is behind all this? And what stone?"

Adrian glanced at Rafe with a raised brow.

"I'll explain later," Rafe said. "But yes, apparently these clowns work for him. And Danny has some ancient stone that he wants."

"But—"

"We don't have time now." Rafe turned to Gray. "About our next move."

Cara shook her head and turned away as the two began planning. She'd get the whole story out of him as soon as they were in the car.

A hand gripped her ankle and yanked her off balance. She screamed as she started to fall, catching a glimpse of Evan's vengeful expression as he lay on the ground, reaching out his other hand toward her as she tumbled closer. Then Rafe was there, his arms around her, kicking at Evan's gripping hand and forcing his fingers to open.

Rafe dragged Cara out of his reach even as Gray leaped forward and dragged the man to his feet, pinning him against the car. Evan grinned at them over Adrian's shoulder, the expression on his beaten face promising retribution.

Adrian spat words at him—in Evan's language.

Evan jerked his gaze to Adrian's, then glanced down at Gray's chest and paled. *"Leyala,"* he whispered, dread and reverence in his tone.

Adrian released him with a jerk, sending him thudding back against the car. Evan mumbled something. Adrian shook his head. Evan's eyes widened, and he spoke again, louder, his tone more pleading. Again, Adrian shook his head, then turned away. Evan sank to his knees in the sand, his expression one of hopeless despair.

"What did you say to him?" Rafe asked as he came closer.

"Told him his punishment was coming." Adrian shrugged, the muscles roping his arms and chest rippling with the movement. Cara couldn't help but appreciate the beauty of the man— then gasped as her gaze fell on the tattoo over his heart.

"What's that?" she whispered. She'd noticed the tattoo earlier when he'd tried to stop her from going to Rafe. The symbol of three triangles, connected by a circle with a curly line in the center directly over his heart, had struck her as an unusual design, but nothing more than that. Just a tattoo like any other.

Now it had somehow become raised from his skin, like a brand. And it . . . pulsed.

Adrian didn't even glance down; he just looked at Rafe.

"What does *leyala* mean?" Rafe asked, glancing from the weird tattoo to Gray's face.

"Loosely translated, it means 'the loyal ones.'"

"Yeah, okay. What does it mean to *him*?"

"As I said, punishment." Adrian held up a hand as Rafe opened his mouth to speak again. "Look, we have the advantage right now. You're a Seer. Take Cara and find the stone. These two are Warriors—technically." He cast a disgusted glance from Evan to Mestor. "That means they are mine. I will deal with them, then head back to Vegas to keep an eye on Criten and make sure he doesn't send anyone else after you." He pulled out his wallet and handed Rafe a business card. "My cell number is on that. Call me when you have the stone."

"Warriors?" Cara said. "Do I even want to know?"

"Later." Rafe took the card, tapping it against his hand. "You know, one thing's been bugging me since you showed up, Gray."

"Yeah?"

"Yeah. How'd you find us? You said you're not a Seer."

"No, I'm a Whisperer." Gray grinned. "I just called the cops and convinced them to trace the GPS on Evan's cell phone. Then I grabbed a chopper and a rental car to get here fast."

"Nice," Rafe said.

"I do what I can. Now get going. You have a place in mind to take her?"

"Yeah." Rafe looked over at Evan, who knelt on the ground staring at Gray as if he were the devil himself. "You sure you got this? Two to one."

"I'll be fine. Take my car and get out of here. The keys are in it."

"Right." Rafe took Cara's arm and turned her toward Gray's black sedan.

"And call me when you've got the stone!" Gray shouted after them.

Rafe waved his hand in the air, then opened the passenger door for Cara before going around to the driver's side. The keys were in the ignition as promised. As Rafe clicked his seat belt into place, Cara glanced out the window and saw Gray crouching down in front of Evan, placing his hands on either side of the man's head.

Rafe turned the key, and the roar of the car's engine nearly drowned out Evan's bloodcurdling scream. Cara's blood ran cold. Dear God, what had Adrian done? She looked at Rafe, but he gave no indication he'd heard anything unusual, except for the tightening of his mouth. He pulled onto the highway and executed a U-turn right in the middle of the road, not even glancing back to see what Adrian Gray was doing, and headed toward Flagstaff again.

Silence lingered between them as they sped down the highway, passing Mother's and continuing onward. She had a million questions clamoring in her head, but it was only after they'd gone a good fifteen miles or so that she asked the two uppermost in her mind.

"So," she said. "You're going to explain all this, right? The stone, Criten, Adrian Gray, et cetera?"

"Yes, once we're safe." He sent her a reassuring smile, but she could see the tension in his hands gripping the wheel and the way he clenched his jaw. Something was definitely bugging him, something more than simple concern about bad guys.

She knew he wouldn't tell her, not without a lot of coaxing, so she asked her second question. "So where are we going?"

He inhaled slowly. "Home."

. . . . .

Home. Strange how even after five years away, he still thought of the Montana stronghold in Sedona as home.

Rafe could tell that Cara knew something was up, but after he'd told her their destination, she'd just nodded and settled into her seat for the drive. No other questions, just a comforting quiet that he needed right then.

Damn, she was a hell of a woman. He'd never met anyone like her.

When he was younger, he'd imagined he would marry someone like her, have kids, pass on the family legacy. Then came the incident where his actions had caused the death of one good man and almost killed Darius as well. The event had torn apart his family. It had become clear to all of them that he had no control when the Hunter manifested, and until he did—if he *ever* did—he was a danger to everyone. So he'd left.

Hell, they'd *wanted* him to leave.

But in the past few hours he'd learned a lot about his heritage— provided Adrian Gray wasn't full of it, which was still a remote possibility. But the idea that he wasn't quite alone anymore, that there were other descendents of Atlanteans out there, perhaps even other Hunters, filled him with a hope he'd thought long dead. He might be able to learn more about his abilities and how to command them. A personal quest, as it were. But it would take all his faith to let down his guard enough to work with others, even those with the same power. To get past the fear that he would, however inadvertently, hurt one of them.

He couldn't help thinking about Cara. She'd come face-to-face with the Hunter and walked away unscathed. She'd not only handled his focus stone but actually used it to help him come out of burnout. Yet despite that—or maybe because of it—she wasn't even sure if she wanted to be with him anymore, so it was no use fantasizing about a future with her. But finding other Atlanteans to learn more about himself and his abilities? He could do that—far away from those he loved.

And yeah, here in the quiet of approaching dusk, he could admit, if only to himself, that Cara fell into that category.

They'd get to Sedona just after sunset, and he didn't know what kind of welcome he'd get when he showed up on the doorstep of the Montana residence. The family credo dictated they use their powers to help those in need and never for personal gain, so while he knew they wouldn't turn Cara away, he wasn't so certain about himself. That had always been a bone of contention, and he'd broken the cardinal rule when he'd run off to Vegas and become a bounty hunter, using the Hunter gift to make a living. The family would probably give them shelter, and he doubted they would bring up old family business in front of an outsider—but he also doubted they'd break out the fatted calf. Best thing to do would be to stay as short a time as possible—just regroup and get out.

But before he left, he would find out how much of the stuff Gray had told him was true, or if his parents had ever even heard of some of the things he'd said. There was still a chance he was being played, and the fact that he couldn't read Adrian Gray left him without his usual defenses. He didn't like it. How did normal people survive without knowing what others were thinking?

Cara had gotten really quiet, and one glance confirmed she'd dozed off. Good, she probably needed the sleep after the afternoon they'd had. He turned his attention back to the open road stretching before him, and started down the familiar route that would take them home.

. . . . .

Cara awoke to a keening melody that prickled along her skin, raising goose bumps along her arms and warming her heart. Through the foggy lethargy of sleep, she realized it was Rafe singing. She turned her head to look at him, his profile solid and familiar against the dramatic orange and pink of the sunset. They were going uphill, and towering trees—evergreens, it looked like—blocked more and more of the sky.

The road seemed to cling to the side of the mountain, winding upward. Rafe slowed as they came to a turn, then surprised her by taking a left up a hidden driveway. She glimpsed stone pillars as they headed even further up, blanketed on either side by evergreens. They curved again, and suddenly the road—driveway?—was blocked by a huge iron gate. The song dying on his lips, Rafe coasted to a stop in front of a speaker box, opened his window, and hit a button.

"Yes?" came a tinny voice after a moment.

"Rafe Montana."

"One moment." A click and then silence.

Rafe sighed and glanced over at her. "Oh, you're awake."

"Yup." She sat up, rolling her head to stretch her stiff neck muscles. "So, this is the old homestead?"

"Yeah." He tapped his fingers on the steering wheel, then looked at the speaker with obvious impatience.

"Think they'll let you in?"

He barked a laugh. "Fifty-fifty shot."

"Those aren't bad odds."

He shrugged, stared harder at the speaker box. Suddenly the gates began to roll open. She'd expected some sort of dramatic creaking, but the well-maintained machinery didn't make any noise other than the hum of the motor that drove it. As soon as the opening was wide enough, Rafe drove through. They eased around another curve in the driveway. The trees fell back, opening to a stunning view of mesas and sunset—and the house.

The place was a mansion. The darkening sky stretched like a velvet cape overhead in the clearing where the house sat, the stars becoming visible as the sun sank farther beneath the horizon. They passed a four-car garage, and she got impressions of huge windows and elegant terraces as they pulled into a circular drive with a fountain in the middle of it. Rafe stopped the car in front of the main entrance and turned off the ignition.

He sat for a moment, staring at the closed door of the house.

Cara touched his arm. "You sure about this?"

He shrugged. "We have no choice. No way anyone is getting to you here." He gave her a weak smile, then opened his door.

Cara climbed out on her side, smoothing her clothes and finger-combing strands that had escaped her ponytail. "This place looks like a vacation home for the royal family, and I look like a bum."

"You look fine." Rafe came around the car and took her hand. "Come on. We'll take them on together."

He's just as nervous as I am. The realization calmed her, and she walked with him as he climbed the steps and pressed the doorbell. A hum of energy tingled along her fingers where he touched her, reminding her of the sexual heat still simmering between them. The energy of the Hunter still lingered, uniting them in a way she had not expected.

But chemistry had never been their problem. They had that in spades. Lies of omission, *that* had been the problem.

She didn't know what to expect when the door opened—maybe a butler or maid, given the sheer luxury of the place—but she certainly hadn't anticipated the huge, long-haired man who appeared. He filled the doorway, his massive shoulders nearly touching the doorframe on either side. His dark hair fell to his shoulders in an elegant, pricey cut designed to look casual, and his neatly trimmed mustache and goatee lent a devilish edge to his good looks. Leaning on a cane, he stared at Rafe.

Rafe stared back. "You're walking."

"You son of a bitch." The big man punched Rafe right in the mouth. Rafe stumbled backward, nearly tumbling down the steps. The other guy tilted off balance, his cane clattering to the ground as he grabbed for the doorjamb. Cara leaped forward and shoved her shoulder beneath his arm, giving him support as he found his footing.

He looked down at her, surprise flickering across his face. He searched her eyes as if he could see into her very soul, then slowly smiled. She got the impression of warm approval, like she had passed some kind of test.

"You got it?" she asked. He nodded, and she bent down to pick up his cane and hand it to him.

Rafe came forward, swiping the blood from his mouth with his hand. "Cara, meet Darius—my brother."

CHAPTER SEVENTEEN

"Your brother?" Cara looked again at the bigger man. Darius topped Rafe by a couple of inches and had the broad chest and shoulders of a bodybuilder, compared to Rafe's leaner, sleeker physique. But the resemblance was obvious in the stunning blue eyes and narrow-eyed glower Darius turned on his brother— an expression she had seen many times on Rafe's face.

"Maybe this was a mistake," Rafe said. He met his brother glare for glare. "I thought this was a place we could come to get help. Guess I was mistaken."

"That's rich," Darius said, "coming from you."

"Okay, that's enough." Cara stepped between the two men. She looked at Rafe. "You said this was the safest place you knew, and with people trying to kill us, I'm thinking you might be right." Before he could respond, she rounded on Darius, taking satisfaction in the momentary disconcertion that flashed across his face. "And you. This is how you treat the brother you haven't seen in years? Don't you know how hard it was for him to come here?"

"Cara—" Rafe protested.

"What do you mean, people are trying to kill you?" Darius asked.

Before she could answer, the sound of running feet reached them from inside the house. A blond woman with a killer tan and a swimmer's athletic build pushed past Darius. "Rafe!" She cast a quick, apologetic smile at Cara and then launched herself at Rafe, wrapping her arms around him in a bear hug. "You're late."

"Tess." Rafe hugged back, his expression surprised and pleased at the same time. "Guess you knew we were coming."

"Of course." She kissed his cheek, then pulled away to turn to Cara. "Sorry, I'm rude. I'm Tessa, Rafe's sister."

Cara took the hand extended to her, arrested by the genuine friendliness of Tessa's greeting—and by her stunning eyes. Their violet hue startled her; she'd never heard of anyone with eyes that color, except for Elizabeth Taylor or a heroine in a romance novel. The perception and knowledge there unsettled her, making her feel like Tessa could see all her innermost secrets.

And maybe she could.

"Nice to meet you," Cara said finally.

"Come inside. Pay no attention to Mr. Crabby here." Tessa brushed past Darius and entered the house, signaling they should follow.

Cara glanced at Darius, uncertain, but Rafe stepped forward, urging her on with a hand on the small of her back. "Go on, Cara. No one argues with Tessa."

Darius stepped backward into the house, extending his arm in an exaggerated invitation to enter. Cara moved past him, Rafe right behind her.

"Get the door, Dar," Tessa said, then led the way through the open foyer with its curving, iron-wrought staircase, past the living room with the big-screen plasma TV and leather couches and into the dining room. The huge table was set for a meal. "Sit down, you two. Dinner's in an hour."

"Six places," Rafe said.

Tessa laughed. "Like you said, I knew you were coming. Come on, sit down."

"Do you mind if I use the bathroom first?" Cara asked.

"Heavens, what am I thinking?" Tessa pointed down the hallway. "Right down here, first door on the left."

"Thanks." Cara set off down the hall, eager to get the grime of the afternoon off her skin.

Rafe watched her go, missing her as soon as she was out of sight. Her presence served as a buffer, holding family drama at bay. Tessa's bubbly welcome aside, the greeting he'd gotten from Darius was more in line with what he'd expected. He'd done a lot of damage before he'd left, and he knew he'd hurt people, especially his parents. Waiting for them to appear, his confidence dripped away like an ice cube in the summer sun.

He just hoped their dedication to the mission trumped their anger at their son.

"I like her," Tessa said, drawing his attention back to her. She pulled out a chair and sat, gesturing for him to do the same. "You two have been through a lot today."

"How much did you see?" Rafe asked, sitting down. He didn't dare touch the snowy linens on the table with his dirty hands.

"A lot of it was murky. I saw an explosion." Tessa's expression grew distant as if she were looking inside herself. "I saw Cara in danger. I knew you were coming because you were in her thoughts. She thought of home and family and safety. She trusts you."

"An explosion?" Darius said from behind him. "That sounds like you."

Rafe turned his head to see his brother standing—*standing!*— in the doorway. "You going to sit down before you fall down?"

Dar's lips tightened, indicating a direct hit, but Rafe felt no triumph. Just the sight of his brother on his own two feet, cane notwithstanding, squeezed his heart. The last time he'd seen

Darius, big brother had been in a hospital, with a prognosis of permanent paralysis for the rest of his life.

Leave it to Dar to flip off the doctors by managing to walk again when they'd said he never would.

"You two never change." Tessa shook her head.

"Where's Mama and Dad?" Rafe asked, ignoring Darius as his brother claimed a chair at the head of the table.

"In the *tenplu*. You arrived in the middle of the sunset ritual, so they stayed behind to channel the energy back into the earth properly while I met you at the door." She rolled her eyes at Darius. "I was trying to head off El Cranko over there."

"You didn't participate?" Rafe asked, a little shocked. Darius fervently embraced their beliefs and had always been eager to participate in the rituals since before Rafe left.

"I was told my energy was disruptive," Darius said with a curl of his lip.

"Strange how that started as soon as I told you Rafe was coming home," Tessa said.

"I'm touched, Dar." Rafe put a hand over his heart.

"Screw you."

Tessa gave a sigh and sat back in her chair just as the sound of footsteps echoed from the stairs. "Mom and Dad are coming."

A few moments later Maria Montana walked into the dining room, then hesitated just inside the doorway. His father appeared behind her, a big, broad-shouldered man with the black hair and copper-toned skin of his Native American and Hispanic ancestors. John Montana placed a supporting hand on Rafe's mother's waist and stared at Rafe with unreadable dark brown eyes. Rafe knew that look; he'd seen it many times as a kid when he'd pulled some stunt. It usually promised some uncomfortable man-to-man discussion and a realigning of Rafe's priorities.

He'd seen it again on the night he'd left for good, mixed with the overwhelming grief of disappointment.

Rafe stood, trying to ignore the elephant in the room. Cara was what mattered, and he knew that no matter what their feelings about him, his family would do the right thing by her. "Hello, Mama."

She approached him slowly. "Rafael. What brings you to my home?"

My home, not just home. The lob hit him squarely in the heart, squeezing like a python. But what had he expected?

"We need help."

She tilted her head to the side, her coffee-colored hair flowing with the movement. "We?"

"Rafe has a woman with him," Tessa said.

"She's in danger," Rafe added.

"So you brought her here, to us." His mother folded her arms and studied him with narrowed eyes. "I thought you no longer wanted anything to do with our ways, our mission."

"That's not true, not exactly."

"Then explain it—exactly." His father came to stand behind his mother, protectiveness radiating off him in waves, from his don't-screw-with-me glare to his stiff posture. "How is it that what we do was not good enough for you five years ago, but now suddenly you show up on our doorstep, asking for our help?"

"I needed someplace safe. And Atlantis is a part of this." Rafe lifted his chin and met his father's gaze head on. Thanks to Adrian Gray's explanation, he now knew why he'd always been able to read his old man but not the rest of his family. His father was human; the others had Atlantean blood. And Dad's emotions were coming through loud and clear. Disappointment. Anger. And . . . hope?

Answering hope bloomed in his heart. Maybe this would work out after all.

"Oh, so now it becomes clear," his mother said. "Atlantis. Suddenly you need us, and we're supposed to forget the way you just left, with no word to anyone. No calls, no e-mails. Nothing. But we're supposed to help you now."

He glanced at his mother, at the fury in blue eyes so like his own, and some of his optimism faded. "Not me. Help Cara. Or is your anger at me more important than the mission?"

"Don't you speak of the mission!" his mother hissed. She surged forward, but his father's hands on her shoulders halted her. "You turned your back on us, just ran away at a time when we needed you most. When Darius—" She choked to a stop, her eyes gleaming with tears as she took a deep, shaky breath. "You had the promise to be great, and you threw it away."

"I wasn't great," Rafe said. "I was young and reckless and nearly got Dar killed."

"So you left. Just like that." His mom snapped her fingers. "Can you imagine what it is like to be a mother and to not know the fate of your child?"

"Mama—"

"I'm not finished." She glared at him, her mouth quivering. "How could you take off like that, leaving us to wonder if you were dead or alive? Your phone call a few days ago was the first time we've heard from you in *years*."

His gut churned. "I'm sorry."

"Sorry! You rip out my heart with such careless disregard, leave your brother struggling for life, and you're *sorry*?"

"I don't know what else to say. You made it clear you wanted me to go."

"*We* made it clear . . . ?" She shook her head, her lips pressed in a line.

Tessa broke the tense silence. "There was an explosion. Rafe nearly got killed."

His mother paled. "What?"

"What explosion?" his father demanded. "When?"

"That would be my car," Rafe said. "It was a bomb. Today."

"Someone put a bomb in your car?" His mother raised a trembling hand to her mouth, then launched herself into his arms. She hugged him with surprising strength, and he closed his eyes, absorbing the familiar citrusy scent of her shampoo. "Thank the Creators you're all right."

"Who would do something like that?" His father stepped forward, his fists curling. "One of those criminals you're always chasing?"

"You know about that?"

His mother pulled out of his arms. "Of course we know. You couldn't be bothered to call home, so we hired a private detective. We are well aware of how you have been using your gifts."

The censure in her tone made him wince. "I didn't have much of a skill set when I left, Mama."

"Which is why you shouldn't have left at all. You should have trusted us to help you."

"Let's not get into that," Rafe said. "Dar was in critical condition, and you forbade me to complete the Soul Circle. After what happened, I didn't see that I had any other choice."

"You weren't ready for the Soul Circle," his mother protested. "We were trying to look out for you."

He shrugged. "I can take care of myself. It's better this way."

"For whom?" his father demanded.

"For everyone."

"Not for me," his mother said. "I don't know if I can ever forgive you for putting us through that, the not knowing."

The quiet words sliced through his heart like an arrow, silent and fatal. His faint hope of redemption went up like tissue paper caught aflame, burning to ash in an instant.

He'd always wondered what would happen if he came home. Now he knew.

He forced himself to speak despite the tightness in his chest. "History aside, let's focus on what's happening now. Last week someone shot at Mama, and now my car was blown up. According to what I've learned, it was the same man behind both."

"What? Who?" his father demanded. "I've had people tracking the sniper, but they haven't gotten anywhere."

"What people?" Rafe asked.

John hesitated before admitting, "I called in the Team to investigate."

Rafe tensed. *The Team.* Of course, that's who he would call. "That was probably the best option at the time," he said calmly, tamping down bitter memories of the past. "But they wouldn't be able to track these guys. They're like us. Apparently we're not the only descendants of Atlantis out there."

"What kind of crap is that?" Darius jerked forward, gripping the edge of the table. "What the hell has happened to you, man? Why would you screw with us like that?"

"It's true," Rafe said. "Think about it. Could our ancestor really be the *only* one to survive the destruction?"

He glanced at his mother, but she stood silent and pale, her eyes wide with some emotion he couldn't read.

Dar sucked in a breath. "Mom? You know something about this?"

His mother turned toward his father and fumbled for his hand. Still she did not speak.

"We both do," his father said, his voice rough as he twined his fingers with his wife's.

"Mom?" Darius sank back into his chair. "What's he talking about? Did you lie to us?"

"Back off, Darius," his father said.

"We can't back off," Rafe said. "These people tried to kill two members of our family. They won't stop, unless we stop them. We need to know everything you know."

"It's all right, John." His mother let out a long, shuddering breath and patted his father's arm. She finally looked at her children, each in turn. "Your father is just keeping a promise to me. It was to protect you."

"What promise?" Tessa asked. "What's happening? How come I haven't seen anything?"

"Protect us from what?" Darius demanded.

"Your brother is right, Darius." Maria looked at Rafe as she said it. "These evil men are like us, descendants of the survivors of Atlantis. That's why you can't see them, Tessa. They nearly destroyed my family when I was a child. They want to kill every Seer until none are left."

Tessa made a quiet sound of distress, raising her hand to her mouth as if to hold back more.

"Why didn't you tell us?" Darius asked. "Why didn't you warn us?"

"I thought we'd finally escaped them. Your father helped me all these years and swore to me he would never reveal the truth to you unless we did it together."

"Dar is right. You have been lying to us." Betrayal burned an acid hole through Rafe's heart. "I could see when we were children, but now that we're adults? We deserve to know about any danger threatening us. And the truth about our heritage."

His mother raised her chin in a proud tilt he used to call "the Spanish aristocrat" when he was a kid. "I did what I felt was best, Rafael. The best I knew how." She softened her tone, though her eyes stayed steady and hot. "You can't know the horror of being hunted, of being exterminated like rodents. I did not want that for my children. Not ever."

"That explains it," Darius said, his voice rough. "That explains the darkness I sometimes felt from you."

"You should have told us," Tessa whispered, face white with shock. "Both of you."

"It doesn't matter now," Rafe said. He looked around at his family, his emotions a frozen block of ice. The secrets his parents had kept could mean death for all of them, and they would need his help. "They've found us. Perhaps if we had known to watch for them, this could have been avoided. But now to make things worse, they're also looking for Cara's stepbrother. He's on the run, and apparently he has something these guys are after—something called the Stone of Igarle."

His mother gasped and steadied herself on the edge of the table. "No. That's impossible."

Rafe wanted to reach for her, but his father jumped forward to assist her into a chair. Once she was settled, his father pulled out a chair for himself and sat, sliding his arm around her—the very picture of unity. Rafe hesitated before seating himself across from them. "So, you've heard of this thing?"

"In legends. Ancient texts." She glanced at his father. "It's one of the Stones of Ekhia."

"The Stones of Ekhia?" Just uttering the name sent a prickle along Rafe's spine. "What are those?"

His mother folded her hands, but he could still see the tremor in her fingers. "According to the scrolls I have in the vault, the Stones of Ekhia were the central source of power for Atlantis. The Seers used the stones to talk to the Creators." She waved her hands as if dismissing the idea. "But they've been lost for eons, since the cataclysm. They may never have existed at all, just myth."

"What if they're not? These goons tried to kill me and kidnap Cara to get to her stepbrother. Supposedly he has this stone."

"No," she whispered hoarsely. "How could it possibly exist and we do not know about it? Our ancestor Agrilara was the *apaiz nagusi,* the high priestess. If anyone could have saved any of the Stones of Ekhia, she would have been the one."

"I don't know how they would know about it," Rafe said. "Maybe these Atlanteans have access to some ancient records that we don't have. Whatever the case, there are some big-deal people chasing this thing. The president of Santutegi sent the goons who blew up my car."

"Cara's coming," Tessa said, seconds before the sound of approaching footsteps reached them.

"Quiet now," his mother whispered. "We will talk more of this later." She sent a hard look around to each of her children to emphasize her order.

"Mama—" Rafe began.

"Later!" Maria hissed.

Cara appeared in the doorway of the dining room and hesitated when she saw his parents. "Hello," she said.

Rafe could practically hear the mental closing of doors as his family put on their game faces for the non-Atlantean. He'd started to tell them she already knew about them, but he supposed they would discover that soon enough. He got up and went to Cara. As he led her toward the table, he could feel her reticence. She knew she'd interrupted something. His Cara was no dummy.

His Cara. When had that happened? "Mama, Dad, this is Cara McGaffigan."

"Hello, Cara. I'm Maria Montana." His mother held out a

hand. Cara took it, and his mom looked deeply into her eyes. "It's *very* nice to meet you, dear. So sorry about the circumstances."

"Nice to meet you," Cara replied.

His dad stood and offered a hand. "John Montana," he said, shook, and sat.

She offered him a smile. "Hello."

"Over here." Rafe steered her toward the empty chair between him and Darius. "I was just telling everyone what we've been through over the past couple of days."

"Lordy, I must have taken longer in the bathroom than I thought. But I couldn't help washing up once I caught sight of myself in the mirror." Cara wrinkled her nose and sat down in the chair Rafe held for her. "So everyone is filled in? The explosion, Adrian Gray, and the whole thing?"

Rafe shook his head. "I didn't get there yet."

"Who is Adrian Gray?" Tessa asked. She focused on Cara, got that distant look on her face, then said, "Oh. Nice-looking guy."

Cara stiffened, and Rafe reached out to cover her hand with his. "Tess, don't pull things out of Cara's mind without asking."

"Oh!" Tessa winced. "Sorry. I told you I was rude."

Darius leaned forward. "Hold on a minute. She knows?"

"She knows about *me*," Rafe clarified.

Cara looked around the table. "Let's get this out in the open. I know you're all descended from a survivor of Atlantis and that Rafe is psychic. I assume the rest of you are as well."

"Rafael!" his mother chided. His father narrowed his eyes.

"Just hold it." Darius slapped both hands on the table. "This day just keeps getting worse. What happened to keeping our abilities secret? No offense," he said to Cara, "but we don't know you."

"Darius," Tessa said softly, "I know you must have seen what I did in Cara."

His brother's mouth tightened, and he slouched back in his chair, folding his arms across his chest.

"I apologize for my children," Maria said to Cara. She sent Rafe a warning look.

"Don't apologize for me, Mom," Darius said. "Apparently this lady knows everything about us, thanks to Rafe. It's dangerous, if you ask me."

"Chill out, Powderpuff," Rafe said. "Sorry to be cramping your style, but we need a place to spend the night and regroup, a *safe* place. We've got to get ahead of these guys. Then we can stop them for good. I think we *all* want that."

Darius scowled. "Listen up, Roid Rage. You may have led this danger right to us. Did you think of that?"

"Of course I thought of it." Rafe tightened his fingers around Cara's. "But I also brought new info, things you might be interested in hearing."

"Like what?" Darius challenged.

"I already told you that there are other Atlanteans." Rafe calmly met his mother's furious glare. "But some of them have powers other than Seeing. Some can manipulate the wills of others."

"What kind of BS is that?" Darius demanded.

"It's true," Cara said. "I've met these men. I've experienced their power for myself." She caught and held Darius's gaze. "Look into my eyes and tell me if I'm lying."

Darius clenched his jaw. "By the Creators, does she really know every damned thing about us?"

"About me," Rafe corrected. "Though now she's getting a feel for what a sweet, sensitive guy you are, bro."

"Screw you."

"Enough." Maria's tone brooked no disobedience. She looked from one son to the other, her gaze coming to rest on Rafe with heavy meaning. "This is astonishing news, and we need to hear your brother out. *After* dinner."

"I have some questions for you, too," Rafe said, hating himself as his mother flinched. "About Atlantis," he continued, "and anything you know about this stone. These guys are still after us, and I feel like I'm fighting blind."

His mother relaxed and nodded. "I will consult the scrolls."

"Just like that?" Darius demanded. "He has no respect for our ways, Mom, and you would open up the archives to him?"

"He's your brother. And we may need him now, more than ever."

"He didn't complete the Soul Circle. He rejected our beliefs and left."

"He's still one of us," his mother said. "This is my decision."

Darius used the edge of the table to get to his feet, then snagged the cane hooked over the arm of his chair. "Just make sure he doesn't sell our secrets to the tabloids."

Rafe rolled his eyes. "Don't be an ass."

Darius started toward the door. "Don't sell out your family, and I'll think about it."

Only his brother's lurching gait held Rafe back from going after Darius and making him eat those words. The click of the cane and the shuffle of shoe soles echoing back from the hallway served as a bucket of ice water on his fired-up ego. Darius had a right to his suspicions—and to his anger.

"You know, you two must be hungry," his father said into the suddenly silent dining room. "Why don't you get washed up and then we'll eat? We'll all think better on a full stomach."

"Good idea." Rafe turned away from the doorway and raised his brows at Cara. She nodded. Fatigue shadowed her face.

"Cara, that shirt of yours has half the desert on it," his mother said. "Why don't we throw your clothes in the washer before we eat? I'm sure Tessa has something you could borrow."

"Rafe still has clothes in his room," his father said.

"I would love a shower," Cara said, "if Tessa doesn't mind me wearing her stuff."

"Of course not," Tessa said, getting up from the table. "Come on, I'll show you where you can change." As she passed Rafe, she gave him a cheeky grin. *One room or two, big brother?*

"One," Cara said, rising from her seat.

Everyone froze and stared at her.

Cara hesitated. "Is that a problem?"

"Come on." With a warning look to his family, Rafe took her arm and led her from the room. Tessa followed a few moments later, but hung back as if to give them privacy.

"What did I say?" Cara murmured as Rafe hurried her toward the stairs. "Will it offend your parents if we share a room?"

"It's not that," Rafe said as they started to climb.

"Then what?" Cara whispered, clearly confused.

They reached the landing, and Rafe paused, glancing back at his approaching sister. "Look, you didn't do anything wrong. They were just . . . surprised."

"At what? Your sister asked a question, and I answered her. I know she was talking to you, but—"

"No," Rafe said. "It's because when Tessa asked the question—"

I did it without words. Tessa reached them and smiled, completing his sentence, though her lips never moved.

"—she did it telepathically," Rafe finished. "And you heard her."

Cara opened her mouth, then slowly shut it again. "Oh," she said finally.

"Yeah," Rafe agreed.

"I'll get those clothes," Tessa said, brushing past them. "Your room is the same, Rafe."

And welcome home, Big Brother.

CHAPTER EIGHTEEN

Tessa kept her promise, showing up at Rafe's bedroom door to drop off sweats and a T-shirt for Cara moments after they reached the room themselves. His sister winked at him and disappeared down the hallway. Rafe slowly closed the door, glad Tessa hadn't sent him any more telepathic comments. Being back here, in the house where his life had changed so drastically, he was one wise-guy remark away from ripping something apart.

How many years had he longed to know more about his abilities? Had wished there were others like him? Now to find out that there were . . . Not just other Atlanteans with abilities like his own, but different types of Atlanteans with different types of abilities—and some who wanted him dead just because he was a Seer.

How could his parents keep such a secret?

The rage slid up on him like an assassin, hooking its claws into him and garroting him until he could barely breathe. He'd imagined coming home a thousand times. Visualized his first conversation with his parents, with Tessa, with Darius. Always he'd expected feelings of guilt. Sadness. Regret. Not another betrayal. And not this killing rage that nearly blinded him.

He stared at the door. Inhaled. Exhaled. Opened his fingers, closed them into fists around the borrowed clothing. He'd controlled the Hunter for years now, never harming anyone more than necessary. This should be no different. But this fury didn't feel like the Hunter.

It felt like *him*.

"Are those for me?"

He'd nearly forgotten Cara. He blew out another long, slow breath, turned and handed her the shirt and sweats. "Yeah, sorry. You can change in the bathroom." He pointed to the adjoining bath.

She didn't move, just stood there watching him. Waiting for . . . what? Why didn't she go change? His bedroom seemed smaller with her in it, closer. More intimate. As if he could whisper from across the room and she would hear him.

He wondered what she would do if he kissed her now.

The idea appealed, a possible channel for these dangerous emotions threatening to break free. Break *him*. Something had to give. Something *would* give. It was just a matter of when and where.

She'd said she wasn't sure if she wanted to keep sleeping with him, but he'd seen the truth in her eyes. *Her brain is trying to rationalize everything, but her body and heart still want you.* She'd opened up completely when they'd been together in the motel room, holding nothing back, and he'd reveled in the honesty, the sincere caring that shone from her eyes when he touched her. It seeped into his blood like potent wine, making his head spin. He craved more. Needed more . . . needed *her*.

"So you want to fill me in now?"

Her innocent comment brought a graphic image of *filling her* to his mind, but he forced himself to think. She wasn't talking about sex.

"About what?" Rafe turned away and went over to the bureau, giving himself a moment to calm down before he jumped on her like a ravenous wolf. Opening a drawer, he pulled out a pair of battered gray sweats. "Wow, I can't believe these are still here."

"Don't change the subject," Cara said. She set the clothes down on the bed. "There were so many undercurrents in that dining room I could have sailed away on a raft."

"Yeah, I guess so." He opened another drawer, pulled out a dark blue T-shirt.

"So give me the scoop."

Rafe studied the shirt for a long moment before he trusted himself to meet her gaze. Even windblown and dusty, she still looked hot to him. Then he looked into her eyes, saw the compassion and sympathy there, the willingness to listen. The noose around his neck loosened ever so slightly. He was being an ass, all tangled up in the barbed wire of his emotions, looking to escape in the sweet oblivion of her arms. That wasn't fair, not to her and not even to him. He'd handle things alone, just like he always had. If he told her this new piece of it, he'd have to tell her all of it, and he couldn't bear seeing the tenderness in her eyes turn to horror. "I don't want to drag you down with ancient history."

"Can't be that ancient," she said. "Seems to me some wounds just never healed."

He gave a short, harsh laugh and shrugged a shoulder. She had no idea how open and bleeding those wounds were now. "Yeah, I guess we should have all gotten over it by now. Don't worry about it."

"Clearly whatever it is, it's still bothering you." Her soft tone wrapped around him like a cozy blanket, as warm and delicious as hot chocolate and homemade cookies. "You can tell me, you know."

Did she have to be so damned *sweet*? So accepting? It would be way too easy to lower his already crumbling defenses, to tell her everything and seek the comfort she offered. But if he did that, if he stripped himself vulnerable, how would he ever build the wall back up again? How would he survive, especially here, in this house, surrounded by the people who'd witnessed his greatest shame? By the parents who had just confessed their betrayal?

He chanced another look at her. *Yeah, she's sweet, but she's stubborn, and she won't let up. Tell her something, anything. You don't have to tell her the whole story. Just enough to satisfy her curiosity.*

"I never intended to come back here. But I did and I saw everyone and—" He broke off, crushed the shirt between his hands. "I don't belong here anymore, and it's awkward. That's all."

Typical Cara, she cut right through his bullshit. "How long have you been gone?"

"A little over five years."

"Why'd you leave?"

He unclenched his fingers and smoothed the shirt. "It's a long story."

She crossed her arms. "We've got time."

"They're waiting dinner on us."

"Give me the *TV Guide* version." Her lips curved. "I'm a good listener."

"I'm sure you are." He couldn't tell her any more of it; she would hate him. She was his last island of peace in this mess, and he was too selfish to cut off his access to her.

She came over to him. "I can tell you're all churned up about something. You might as well get it out." She laid a hand on his arm.

The solid foundations of his defenses turned to putty beneath her touch, melting fast, like rock candy in hard rain. He wanted to rest his head on her shoulder, set down his burdens for just a while, just long enough to soothe the battered wounds of his heart.

But if he surrendered, they would both end up casualties.

"Look, Cara, you don't have to do this." He pulled away from her and tossed his shirt on top of the bureau with the sweat-pants. "This is old business." He gave her a thin smile. "Family business."

"Oh, I see." She took a slow step back, her pain obvious though she tried to hide it. "Family business. Right. And I don't understand family—because I haven't got one." She marched to the bed and snatched up Tessa's borrowed clothing, then started toward the bathroom.

Damn it. He'd hurt her. Hell, he'd *meant* to hurt her, to push her away because he couldn't bear to see the disgust in her eyes if he told her the whole truth. Well, he'd succeeded, and her re-action sliced through his gut like a finely honed Japanese sword. The fury he'd been battling turned inward, changing to disgust. All she'd done was open that soft, mushy heart of hers to him, and he'd kicked her away.

"Cara, wait. *Wait.*" He grabbed her arm before she reached the bathroom. "Okay, you want to know what's wrong here? It's me."

She shook him off. "What are you talking about?"

"Darius," he said. "I'm the reason he can't walk."

"In case you missed it, he *is* walking."

"Yeah, he's walking all right . . . with a cane." Once he started, the words poured from his lips like an overflowing river. "Last time I saw him, he was in a hospital bed and the doctors were saying he'd be paralyzed for life. *For life.* And it was my fault."

She tilted her chin, lips pressed together. "How did it hap-pen?"

"He was shot, nerve damage near the spine."

She folded her arms, crushing the borrowed clothes to her chest. "And you pulled the trigger, right? That's why you feel so guilty?"

"Of course not," he snapped. "But someone else did—because of me." He gave a harsh laugh. "Because I was trying to show off. Impress my dad so he'd give me a job."

"Oh, Rafe."

The sympathy in her voice ripped the wounds anew. "Don't do that. Don't talk to me all sweet and understanding, like you can feel my pain. I told you, I'm a son of a bitch, a bad bet. It's probably better if you do walk away from me. From . . . us."

"What kind of job?" she asked, ignoring his rant.

He scowled. "It doesn't matter."

"What job, Rafe?" she pressed. "It must have been really important to you."

"It was, at the time." He shrugged, realizing that was the truth. "My dad's company specializes in security, but not just gadgets. He also has a special team on the payroll that takes on private contracts. You know, like kidnappings and other things where the victim doesn't want the cops involved, at least not right away. I thought, with my abilities, I would be a good fit for the Team."

"Where does Darius come in? Does he work with this team, too?"

"Not usually. Dad asked him to get involved that day. We needed a diplomat type to negotiate with this guy who'd kidnapped the daughter of one of Dad's friends."

"So Darius is a negotiator?"

That surprised a laugh from him. "You could say that. Dar is an empath."

"Oh. So he . . . what, knows what everyone is feeling?"

"Yup. Even us. Out of my entire family, he's the only one whose powers work on us as well as normal people."

She chuckled. "Now I get why you call him Powderpuff."

"Well, he's all touchy-feely. Poor bro got the girly power." Rafe grinned at her, and for a moment, perfect accord held them fast, then faded slowly like the vibration of a harp string.

"So why the big fuss over you wanting to work for your dad? Seems to me most fathers want their sons to come into the family business."

And just like that, the harp string snapped.

"My parents were against me going to work for the Team. It's against our . . . their . . . beliefs to use our abilities for profit. If I worked for the Team, I'd be getting a paycheck for using the Hunter."

"So wait, wasn't Darius working for the Team? Why would it be different for you?"

"Once in a while Dad would ask one of us to pitch in, whoever had the best ability for the job. But it was totally on a volunteer basis."

"From what I've seen, your abilities would be perfect in a lot of cases, especially kidnapping. I bet you could locate the victim like that." She snapped her fingers.

"You'd be right, and I did. But I didn't want to just be a volunteer. I wanted to make this my career. I'm not suited to a regular job. Dar and Tessa both have jobs within Montana Security, Tessa in public relations and Darius in research and development." He shrugged. "I need to be active. I can't sit behind a desk all day."

"So it seems like working for the Team would be a perfect fit."

"Except for the profit part of it. And my parents would not budge on that."

"So what happened? I take it you didn't just accept their decision, since clearly there's some kind of rift between you."

"You'd be right. And this is where you find out what an ass I can be."

"Oh, good. Normally it takes much longer. I like to know what I'm up against."

Her wise-guy comment surprised a laugh from him, and the chokehold loosened a little more around his neck, giving way to a glimmer of hope. She hadn't run yet.

Maybe she wouldn't.

"Like I said, I was trying to impress my father—or at least Mendez, the Team leader. I knew where they were keeping the girl, and I went charging in there in full Hunter mode, with some idea about rescuing her. When I came back to myself, all hell had broken loose."

"Oh, no." She took a step forward, her face soft with concern. "How bad was it?"

"The kidnap victim was okay, and the scum who took her was all right—by some miracle—but Dar was critically injured." He clenched his fists and swallowed hard as he remembered again the sight of his brother on the floor, blood pooling from his injuries. And the other man . . . waxy skin, eyes wide with shock, staring at nothing. "One of the Team members was dead— Mike Hennessy. He had a family."

Without hesitation, she tossed the clothes on the bed and wrapped her arms around him, squeezing tightly. "How awful," she whispered. "I'm so sorry."

The simple gesture tore away the last of his restraint. He buried his face in her hair, holding on as the rest of it came pouring out. "I was twenty-three and preparing to walk my Soul Circle, but after the incident my parents wouldn't sanction it. Everyone completes the Soul Circle at twenty-four. It's a rite of passage, a graduation that shows we've mastered our abilities. But they wouldn't let me do it."

"Wasn't there some other way you could still do it?"

"No." His voice caught, and he squeezed his eyes shut and forced the rest of the words out. "My mother is the head of our religion, and only she can preside. I already felt crushed that a man died, and that Dar almost had. What I did was stupid. I was young and thought I knew everything. I had the best power, the strongest power." He took a deep, shaky breath. "That day I learned how dangerous I could be. I left that night, just took off. It was better for everyone."

She'd been stroking his hair, but now her hand stilled. "You explained to your parents why you were going, right?"

"No." She started to pull out of his arms, and he scrambled to add, "Look, they weren't going to listen—"

"So you just left? With your brother fighting for his life and a man dead?" She narrowed her eyes and stepped back, leaving his arms empty and cold. "Did you ever contact your family, let them know why you took off? Or to say you were sorry?"

"No. I keep telling you, it was better this way."

"Better for whom? For you, certainly, since you didn't have to face the consequences of your mistake." She crossed her arms, her eyes flinty. "You screwed up and left your parents to clean up the mess."

"It wasn't like that." But even as he said it, he realized the truth. *Yes, it was.*

Her next words came like bullets, fast and hard. "You went haring into danger, causing injury and death. That's bad enough, and maybe things would have smoothed out eventually if you'd stuck around. But you caused all this chaos, then *just left,* with your brother in the hospital and your parents having to make explanations and reparations on your behalf. Did it occur to you how all this would affect them? I'm sure they were worried about your brother and maybe even you, too, since apparently they had no idea where you were or what had happened to you. My God, Rafe, what were you thinking?"

"I was thinking I was dangerous! Damn it, I got one man killed and nearly did the same to my brother." He turned away from her, swiping his hands over his face. "Do you have any idea how that made me feel? What if it happened again? I had to get as far away from them as I could, as fast as I could. I had to learn control—before someone else died."

Her silence weighed on the room like a heavy wool blanket in August. "You have to fix this," she said finally, her voice soft.

He turned to face her. "I don't know how."

"You need to figure it out. This is your family, Rafe. You can't take them for granted." She stepped closer, her expression intent. "Do whatever you have to do, no matter how uncomfortable or demeaning it might feel, to make them understand that you are truly sorry for what you did."

"I *am* sorry. Damn it, I went away to protect them."

"I guess you need to tell them that." She gave him a small smile. "You mind readers need to get used to verbalizing things like the rest of us mortals. I think you're all spoiled."

"We can't read each other, except for Dar. Makes things awkward sometimes. Confusing."

This time she chuckled. "Welcome to the human condition. Normal people have to deal with that all the time."

"I don't know how you do it."

She shrugged. "We have no choice, so we deal. And back when all this happened, maybe you felt you had no choice either, to do what you did. But you're older now, and you need to start dealing with this. It's been too long."

"There's more." He longed to have her arms around him

again but stayed where he was. "All my life I thought my ancestor was the only person to escape Atlantis. Today Gray told me I was wrong, that there are lots of us. And not just Seers. There are other kinds of people with other kinds of abilities."

"Gray," she said. "Gray is like you?"

He nodded. "Apparently there's a bunch of Atlanteans who hate Seers, want to see us dead. I just found this out today. My parents confirmed it."

She frowned. "I thought they had told you that your ancestor was the only one to escape."

"They did. They lied. We've been in danger all our lives—they knew it—but they never told us. Not even when we were old enough to defend ourselves."

"Oh, Rafe." She let out a gentle sigh. "They love you. I don't need psychic abilities to see that. I think you and your parents need to sit down and talk all this out. Make them see your side. And you try to see theirs."

"You inspire me to fix things. I want to. I do." He rubbed the back of his neck. "I just don't know where to start."

"You could start with 'I'm sorry.' Then go from there and listen to their side."

"You make it sound easy."

"Admitting you made a mistake is never easy. Maybe your mom is feeling that right now." She came toward him, a calm force of encouragement soothing his battered emotions. "That you want to fix it at all is a step in the right direction."

"What if they don't forgive me? What if I can't forgive them?" The words slipped from his lips before he could stop them, stripping him bare before her all-too-perceptive gaze.

A smile quirked one side of her mouth. "They love you, Rafe, and you love them. Even I can see that, and I'm an outsider."

"You're not an outsider." He pulled her into his arms, staring into her eyes, overwhelmed by the force of his own words. "You're inside me, Cara. I fought against it, I tried to resist it, but somehow you're inside me." He rested his forehead against hers, closing his eyes so he wouldn't know if she lied. He needed the lie. "Why did you tell my family we wanted one room? You said you weren't sure if you wanted us to keep sleeping together."

"That's still true. But the way everyone was ganging up on you, I thought you needed someone on your side. You're a good man, Rafe, not the monster you seem to think you are. Whatever control problem you have with your power, I have faith you'll master it." She pulled back, her expression serious. "I saw your Hunter, and you didn't hurt *me*. You saved my life. That gets you big points in my book."

Truth. Not pity. He nearly staggered from the relief of it. "So you're sleeping in my bed because of gratitude?"

"No, I'm sleeping in your *room* to show solidarity. A lot's happened, Rafe, and I have a lot to process. I haven't decided any more than that." She stepped out of his arms. "Now I've got to get in the shower or we'll never get to dinner. And I'm starved."

"Okay." He stood there, empty arms dangling at his sides, and watched as she retrieved Tessa's clothes from the bed and headed for the bathroom. She was sharing his room to take his side. He didn't have the heart to remind her that in a family of psychics—one of them an empath—there was no fooling any-one. He wanted her with him too badly. "Cara."

She paused in the doorway and looked back at him.

"Thank you," he said.

She gave him one of her sunny smiles, chasing the shadows from his soul. "Any time."

She went into the bathroom and closed the door, leaving him alone with the terrible truth he had only just acknowledged himself.

He was in love with her.

"Ah hell." He rubbed his face with both hands and sank down on the bed to wait for his turn in the shower.

. . . . .

Cara retreated to the privacy of the bathroom, her heart aching for Rafe. Since she'd met him, she could tell he had some demons haunting him, and now she knew what they were. When she'd decided to go to bed with him, she'd wanted adventure, and boy, had she gotten more than she'd bargained for! Psychic abilities and energy crystals and transformations into . . . whatever. Yet at the heart of it, he was just a guy who'd made a huge mistake, and his family hadn't forgiven him for it. Heck, he hadn't forgiven himself.

She stripped off her dirty clothing, grimacing at the sand that fell from the garments and sprinkled across the pristine marble floor of the spacious bathroom. Rafe's old room looked like a luxury suite in a high-priced hotel, complete with a huge bed and a balcony overlooking the stunning Arizona landscape. And the palace that passed for a bathroom . . . She doubted the Romans had had such luxury. Gleaming black tile shone against ivory porcelain with fluffy white bath towels, gold-accented fixtures and floor-to-ceiling mirrors. She grimaced at her reflection; she really did look like she'd lost a battle with a sand heap.

She had her choice of a multi-head shower or a deep spa tub. In the interest of time, she selected the shower. Throwing her bra in the pile, she rinsed her panties in the sink. She had no other underwear, but she could wash the delicate nylon with soap and water and dry it with the hair dryer so she could wear them again. The plan took minutes and worked perfectly, and she draped the mostly dry undergarment over the rack shared by the thick, cream-colored towels.

She picked up her clothing and started to fold it. As she shook out her shorts, something fell out of her pocket and fluttered to the floor. Slowly she bent and picked it up. It was a photograph, one she'd been carrying with her since she'd found it on the fridge in Danny's apartment. She'd been looking at it that morning and had shoved it in her pocket when they'd stopped for lunch—and thank God she had, otherwise it would be toast like everything else she owned.

Danny smiled at her from the photo, giving a thumbs-up to the camera. Beside him was a guy she didn't know, and the two of them stood in front of a convenience store called Winner's Circle, each holding one end of a single lottery ticket.

How many times had she seen that surefire grin on Danny's face? That eternal optimism that *this* time was the big payoff he'd been waiting for his whole life?

Her eyes stung, flooding with moisture before she could stop it. Her throat clogged. She choked a sob, covered her mouth and fell back against the cool black tile, knocking over a shiny black tissue dispenser sitting on the edge of the vanity. Would she ever see Danny again? What would she do if the people who had been chasing them found him first?

She couldn't lose him. She couldn't face the rest of her life alone. And her only chance of finding him was a psychic bounty hunter with demons he couldn't control.

Rafe knocked on the door. "Cara, you all right in there? I thought I heard something."

She picked up the fallen dispenser and grabbed a tissue to wipe her face. "I'm fine," she called back, hoping her voice sounded normal. "I'll be out in a couple of minutes."

"Okay. Let me know if you need anything."

"I will."

Cara set Danny's photo on the vanity and got into the shower, flipping the faucets on full blast. The blessedly hot water poured down on her, wiping away the grime of the day.

And the tears that continued to trickle down her cheeks.

.　.　.　.　.

Night had fallen by the time Adrian got back to the Mesopotamian. He'd checked in with the staff, then made his way to Jain Criten's penthouse suite. He didn't have to wait long before Criten and his entourage returned from their evening adventures. The stunned expression on the foreign president's face when he entered his suite and noticed Adrian waiting for him, was worth the two hours he'd been cooling his heels.

"You." Criten stopped right inside the door, and his two security guards rushed forward.

Adrian stood and murmured a threat in the Atlantean language. The two guards stopped cold, then glanced at their boss in uncertainty.

Criten came toward him, casting a disgusted look at his security detail. "So," he said. "A surprise. Mr. Gray, is it not?"

"That's correct. I'm the head of security for the Mesopotamian."

"I know who you are." Criten dismissed his bodyguards with a wave of his hand. The two men took up sentry duty close to the door, and Criten sat down on the comfortable leather sectional. "What can I do for you, Mr. Gray?"

"It's what I can do for you."

"Indeed?" Criten leaned back, crossing one leg across the other, stretching his arms across the top of the couch.

"I came to return something of yours."

"You intrigue me, Mr. Gray. I don't recall losing anything. Are you certain it's mine?"

"Absolutely."

"How hospitable of the head of security to take the time to return missing items. Show me. Don't keep me in suspense." Criten smiled, his teeth white in his tanned face.

Adrian unclipped his radio from his belt. "Control, this is Gray. Peterson, bring them."

"Got it, boss," came the hiss of the reply.

"Very cryptic," Criten said as Adrian put his radio back on his belt. "You know, you remind me of someone. Have we met?"

"Maybe a long time ago." A knock came at the door.

"That was quick," Criten said. He caught the eye of one of his bodyguards and jerked his head toward the door. The guard checked the peephole, then frowned at Criten. "It's hotel security."

"Well, let him in," Criten said.

The bodyguard frowned as he opened the door to reveal Peterson standing in the hallway. The security guard's worried expression eased as he saw Adrian. "Here you go, boss."

"Thanks, Peterson. I've got this."

Peterson nodded, then shoved two men through the doorway, one of them stumbling into Criten's bodyguard.

"Evan!" The bodyguard steadied his friend and closed the door in Peterson's face. "Evan, it's Gadi. What happened to you?"

Evan simply stared at the table lamp, unresponsive.

"What's wrong with them?" the other bodyguard asked, snapping his fingers in both men's faces. Neither so much as flinched. Both seemed focused on the light fixtures.

Criten slowly stood. "What is the meaning of this?" he whispered.

"These men have been judged."

"Judged?" Criten spat. "I am the only one who should judge them. They are *my* employees!"

"Then you should keep a closer eye on them."

"How dare you?" Criten whirled toward him, clenching his hands at his sides.

"I dare," Adrian said, "because no one else can." He took a step toward Criten. "These men tried to commit murder."

"That's an outrageous claim!"

"We both know they were acting on your orders," Adrian said.

"I think you should leave." Criten pointed at the door. "I will address this with your state department tomorrow."

"No, you won't." Adrian took another step closer. "We have our own laws, don't we?"

"Get out."

"Of course." Adrian gave a nod and headed for the door. The bodyguards made a path for him. He paused in the doorway and looked back at Criten. "Do yourself a favor and forget about the stone." He glanced from one bodyguard to the other. "The stone and the Seers are both under the protection of the Leyala."

The door slammed behind him. He allowed himself a small smile and headed for his office.

. . . . .

"The Leyala!" Gadi hurried forward, his face pale with terror. "Your Excellency, what are they doing here?"

"A good question." Criten narrowed his eyes at the two employees Gray had returned to him, both reduced to drooling idiots. Of course he was familiar with the Leyala, the Warriors who policed the Warrior sect. Since the Warriors were the strongest and fastest of all the sects of Atlantis, someone had to stand as judge and jury in the event one of them went rogue—and so the Leyala had been born. "As I recall, an entire temple left the island about twenty years ago. They disagreed with my father's policies. I wonder if this fellow was among them. He would have been just a child."

"What do we do with Evan and Mestor, Your Excellency?"

"Once the Leyala has enacted judgment, there is no turning back, correct?" At Gadi's nod, Criten shrugged. "Dispose of them then. I'm certain that's what they would have wanted."

Gadi swallowed hard, but nodded.

"Your Excellency." Marcus came forward, a cell phone in his hand. "I found this in Evan's pocket. It's not his."

Criten took the turquoise-colored phone with a skeptical glance. "I should hope not." He powered it on and pulled up the contacts list. Slowly he smiled. "Well, well. This is Cara McGaffigan's phone. Even in defeat, Evan did well for us." There was a new text message, and he opened it. A delighted smile spread across his face. He flipped through the contacts again, found the number for Home and called it, listening to the answering machine that picked up.

When the beep sounded, he disconnected the call and summoned power, gathering energy from the air around them. A soft glow covered his hand and the phone in it. Motioning for quiet, he dialed the number where the text message had originated.

Danny Cangialosi answered on the first ring. "Cara, my God, where have you been?"

Criten filtered his voice through his power, manipulating the tones and pitch to match the voice on Cara McGaffigan's home answering machine. "Danny, I'm so sorry. My phone went dead and I had to get a new charger, and I just got your text. I can have the money you need wired to you, just tell me where."

"I'm in a small town called Benediction in Arizona. There's a Western Union in the grocery store here. You can send it there."

"Are you okay, Danny? I'm worried about you."

"I'm fine. Just send the money so I can pick it up in the morning. I'm running low. I'll text you the info, and if it's not there by noon, then I'll know you changed your mind."

"Maybe I should come out there. I can help."

"By the time you get here, I'll be long gone. Don't look for me, Cara. Just go home to Jersey, and I'll be in touch when things settle down." He hung up.

Criten closed the phone and looked at Gadi. "Arrange for a private plane to fly to Benediction, Arizona, tonight. Danny Cangialosi will be picking up a wire transfer there tomorrow morning."

Gadi nodded. "Yes, Your Excellency. We'll go get him."

"No." Criten held up a hand. "We'll all go. I'm tired of incompetence. Arrange for appropriate accommodations in whatever decent-sized city is closest to the area."

"Yes, Your Excellency."

"And see to those two before you go." Criten waved a hand at Evan and Mestor before slipping the phone in his pocket and heading toward the bedroom.

By tomorrow morning, the Stone of Igarle would be in his possession. By tomorrow night, the bounty hunter and his entire family of Seers would be dead. And then he could begin his search for the last of the Stones of Ekhia.

After centuries, justice would finally come to pass for the Great Betrayal.

CHAPTER NINETEEN

The tension at dinner could have smothered all of them.

Cara swallowed the last bite of her meal—simple tacos with fresh tortillas and refried beans—and reached for her iced tea. She'd hoped that Rafe's emotional confession in the bedroom would have given him some release, but in the presence of his family, he once more took shelter in a shell of reserve. He exchanged small talk with his father, punctuated by awkward silences, and otherwise focused on his food. Maria chatted with Tessa about a shoe sale she'd seen at the mall, but the stiffness of her shoulders indicated she wasn't as relaxed as she pretended to be. Darius scowled and ripped into the soft tacos as if he were a lion with a freshly killed gazelle.

Cara looked from one to the other. Their polite imitation of a family eating dinner together tore at her insides, ripping open old wounds that left her throbbing. Where were the good-natured debates, the ribbing, the laughter? This wasn't a family. This was a ragtag bunch of survivors from a long-ago war. She didn't know how long she could stand it. Didn't they realize how lucky they were to have one another? Didn't they know it could all be gone in the blink of an eye?

Darius threw his taco down on the plate. "Cut it out," he snapped. "You're spoiling my appetite."

She jerked as she realized he was talking to *her*. The entire table grew silent, everyone looking from her to him with wariness and uncertainty. It ticked her off. Why did they stare at her as if *she* were the one who had done something wrong?

Rafe put down the glass he had been holding. She could tell he was about to get up and charge to her rescue—heck, maybe even leap across the table at Darius for all she knew—but she caught his eye and shook her head. He hesitated, then sat back in his chair, folding his arms, his eyes mere slits as he stared at his brother. His entire posture said he was ready to defend her if necessary, and a trickle of warmth curled into her belly.

His silent confidence gave her courage. She turned to Darius. "Don't you know you're not supposed to point out the elephant in the room?"

Tessa's eyes widened, and Rafe glanced down, a grin tugging at his lips. His parents exchanged a look of surprise. Darius just scowled at her, then picked up his taco and took another bite, chewing and watching her with the intimidation of the lion she'd just compared him to.

Well, she wasn't about to be the gazelle.

She pulled the napkin from her lap and dropped it on her plate. "Don't try and glare your way out of this, Darius. I'm sorry you can feel my feelings, but at least they're honest. And I can't stop having them because you don't like it."

"Try," Darius bit out.

"Watch how you talk to her," Rafe growled.

"Or what?" Darius challenged. "You'll kick my ass?"

"He won't," John Montana said. "But I might. You don't speak to a guest in our home like that."

Darius opened his mouth as if to argue, then shut it, clenching his jaw. "Sorry," he muttered.

Maria pushed back her chair with a sigh. "Rafael, if you're done I have some things from the vault to show you."

Darius clenched his hand into a fist but said nothing.

Rafe stood up, setting his napkin beside his plate. "Cara, you coming?"

His mother stopped short on her way out of the dining room. "Rafael, you know—"

"I'm fine here," Cara interrupted, not missing the relief that flickered across his mother's face. She gave him an encouraging smile. "I'm going to have some more tacos."

"If you're sure." Rafe flicked a narrow-eyed look toward his brother.

"I'm fine. You can tell me about it later."

"All right." He came over and dropped a quick kiss on her lips. "This won't take long."

Her mouth tingled from his kiss as she watched him leave the room with his mother. Sneaky guy. Apparently he'd decided their earlier talk meant the door was still open to continue their affair. And he wasn't wrong. She'd just wanted some time to get used to all this supernatural stuff, to decide that this Rafe, the real Rafe, was the guy she wanted as her lover. And from his new determination to fix things with his family, she knew he was.

"Oh, for pity's sake. Get a room already." Darius shoved his plate aside and lurched awkwardly to his feet, reaching for the cane hooked over the arm of the chair.

Tessa sent a teasing grin her way. "Nothing's private here, remember?"

Cara's cheeks heated, and she darted a quick glance at Rafe's father, who studiously built another taco and avoided her gaze.

Darius stomped past her, the click of his cane on the hardwood floor echoing the heavy tread of his footsteps. Cara watched him, her heart going out to his struggle. How difficult it must have been for a man so obviously strong and healthy to have to learn to walk again.

Darius spun around to face her, nearly upsetting his balance. "Don't pity me," he snarled, his blue eyes fierce. "Don't you dare pity me."

"Pity and sympathy are two different things," she returned. "I can't help but feel for your situation. It can't have been easy."

"It wasn't."

"He only started walking with the cane a few months ago," Tessa said. "Before that he was in a wheelchair."

Darius shot his sister a hard look. "Can it, Tess."

"Hey." John looked up. "I know this is hard for you, son, but you've got to keep hold of your temper."

"I'm in no mood for any *fatherly* advice tonight, Dad. After what you and Mom pulled, I think I have a right to be ticked off."

John pressed his lips together and rubbed the bridge of his nose, but remained silent.

"You should have seen Darius right after the accident," Tessa confided to Cara in a dramatic stage whisper. "He was horrible. But he's been so much better over the past couple of years, at least until Rafe came home."

"But he didn't *come home*." Darius turned his narrow-eyed glare from his father to the two women. "Isn't that right, Cara? He just stopped here to regroup after you two almost got killed by the bad guys. He has no intention of *coming home*."

"I don't know what he intends," Cara said. "I can't read his mind. Or his emotions."

Darius jabbed a thumb at his chest. "Well, I can. And I can tell you that he has no intention of staying here. We're just a rest stop on his latest mission."

"If you know so much about what he's feeling," Cara shot back, "then you know how torn up he is over what happened. He was trying to prove something and it backfired."

"He was being a hotshot as usual," Darius snapped. "Trying to show off. And we all paid the price."

"He was young and stupid, and he knows it," Cara replied. "He wants to make amends but he doesn't know how. Some empath you are, if you can't see that."

"Oh, I can see it. I know he regrets what happened. And yeah, he was young and an idiot. We all do stupid things at that age."

"You did," John said.

"But at least I knew to say I was sorry." He looked from one to the other, his expression daring them to comment. "He never said he was sorry. Not to me."

He left the room, leaving awkward silence in his wake.

Rafe's father sighed. "Sorry about that, Cara. I appreciate what you're trying to do."

"I just don't understand." She tore her eyes from the empty doorway where Darius had disappeared. "I'm no empath, but I can tell clear as day that strong emotions are running here. Why aren't you all trying to sort things out? Why did it take five years for Rafe to come back here before any of this was addressed?"

John remained silent for a long moment, making her wonder if she had overstepped. Finally he said, "There's a lot more going on here than a simple mistake. Rafe's actions cost a man his life and challenged the very foundations of my family's beliefs. Maria was very firm in her decision that Rafe wait to complete his Soul Circle. The ritual would give him even more power, and if he couldn't control what he already had—" He pressed his lips together. "My wife and I disagreed on this point, but as *apaiz nagusi*—the high priestess—she has the last word in these matters. I'm the outsider here." His lopsided grin echoed Rafe's. "As are you."

"I get that, but did you explain that to Rafe?" Cara asked. "He seems to think you held him back as punishment."

"No, no, not at all! Maria just wanted to slow things down, to make sure Rafe really was ready." His expression grew grim. "The Soul Circle is just a formality for most people, just a challenge to test the mastery of their gifts. But in Rafe's case—"

"The Hunter might take him over," Tessa cut in, her expression uncharacteristically sober. "The essence that is Rafe would be gone, possibly for good." She looked at her father. "Guess someone should have explained the danger."

"We didn't have time. He left so abruptly."

"You have time now." Cara sat back in her chair, regarding father and daughter. "I lost almost every member of my family over the years. Danny is all I have left, and if we can't find him . . . if something happens to him—" She choked back the words before the tears could take hold and cleared her throat. "Sorry. I lost my cell phone earlier today, and I haven't been able to call Danny. Not being able to contact him . . . It's got me a little upset."

"That's understandable," Tessa said.

Cara looked from daughter to father. "You all need to fix this. Rafe needs you. He's been alone way too long, and stubbornness is no reason to lose the people you love."

John nodded. "I told my wife she should let Rafe try, that perhaps he needed the control of the Soul Circle to manage his abilities, to keep this from happening again. Maybe I should have argued harder, but she understands my children's gifts far better than I do."

"Her father was a Hunter like Rafe," Tessa added. "My dad figured she knew what she was doing."

John gave his daughter a look of mild annoyance. "It's sometimes irritating to have a child who can read your thoughts."

"Apparently not all of them, or I would have honed in on the secrets you and Mom were keeping."

John blanched. Tessa put her hand to her mouth, regret flickering in her eyes.

"I bet that was fun during the teenage years," Cara said, trying to lighten the mood.

John tried to smile. "Completely took away the intimidation factor." He looked back at his daughter. "I'm so sorry we kept things from you, kitten. We were only trying to protect you."

"Oh, Daddy. I know you meant well." Tessa got up and hugged him. "And you *can* be very intimidating, especially when you really are angry. You only have trouble when you're bluffing."

Cara's heart turned over at the easy affection between father and daughter. She'd had a taste of that with Donald, Danny's father, but it had been taken away far too quickly. Far too abruptly.

She got to her feet. Her emotions were running close to the surface today. Nearly dying obviously did that to a person. "Thank you for dinner," she said, "but I should get to bed. It's been a *really* long day."

"Of course." John stood, his arm slipping around Tessa's waist. "Do you remember the way? Tessa can show you."

"No, I'm fine. If you see Rafe, just let him know I went up."

"Sure thing," John replied. "See you in the morning."

"Don't worry, Cara." Tessa's face took on a faraway expression, and for a moment it seemed as if her eyes glowed. "Everything will work out for the best. The final battle is coming, and all will be resolved. For better or worse." Her eyes closed, and she sagged in her father's arms.

Cara took a step forward. "Is she okay?"

"Just a prediction. Happens all the time." John watched as Tessa's eyes fluttered open. "Good morning."

"Wow." Tessa straightened, putting a hand to her temple. "That was a doozy."

"Are you all right?" Cara asked.

"Fine. It happens." Tessa gave a tight smile. "But maybe I'll go meditate for a while."

"I'll walk you there," her father said.

"Thanks. I don't want to end up passed out in the yuccas again. Good night, Cara. Sleep well." She headed out of the dining room, her father beside her with his arm around her shoulders.

Cara watched them go, humbled by their love for each other. Maybe even envious. And more determined than ever that Rafe mend the rift with his family, before it was too late.

· · · · ·

Rafe followed his mother to the staircase leading up to the third floor. She ascended ahead of him, her feet quick and sure. He followed more slowly. Memories assaulted him as he took hold of the smooth oak banister and began to climb, images from childhood and from the last time he had ascended these stairs. Tonight elegant light fixtures lit the way, but that day—that terrible, awful day—bright sunlight had streamed through the windows that stretched up toward the cathedral ceiling, false brightness illuminating a house heavy with grief. His stride faltered. A man had died that day, and Darius nearly so.

His fault. All his fault.

He struggled to breathe as he made himself continue to the top of the stairs, not from exertion but from the sheer bombardment of emotion that swamped him. All these years, he'd thought he was handling it. All this time, he'd thought he'd moved on. But the pressure in his chest and the lump in his throat told him he'd been fooling himself. The wound was as fresh today as it had been five years ago—perhaps more so from the thick scar tissue that had formed over it, and made worse by his parents' deception.

By the time he got to the third floor, it was all he could do to keep walking forward. His instincts screamed at him to go back the way he'd come, to get Cara and leave. What had he been thinking, coming back here? What had made him think he could be here, even for a minute, and have it be okay?

But he knew he had to do this. Had to keep going, to make things right again. It was past time, and he wasn't a kid anymore.

He paused outside the door to the *tenplu*. Beyond the portal lay his family's most sacred place, the consecrated circle where they all performed their energy rituals. He knew the layout by heart. As soon as he stepped through the door, the circle would stretch before him, five, maybe six feet from the door. To his left, an alarmed door that led to the rooftop garden where they grew flowers and herbs and recharged their focus stones beneath the blessed sunlight. And straight ahead, beyond the boundaries of the circle, was the vault.

He hadn't been allowed in the vault when he'd lived at home; he would have only been welcome there when he completed his Soul Circle at twenty-four. Since he'd left home at twenty-three, that day had never come. Frankly, after all that had happened, he was surprised his mother had summoned him to this place. He would have expected her to keep him far away from his family's treasures.

Gathering his courage, he opened the door and walked into the room, then stopped. When had they moved so much greenery into the *tenplu*? Planters ringed three of the four walls, all of them full of flowers bursting with color. His mother stood at a planter right near the door to the greenhouse, watering her favorite birds of paradise: tall, orange flowers that resembled open-beaked birds because of the way the sharp petals bloomed.

Nostalgia gripped him by the throat. How many times had he seen her like this, puttering around the garden?

"Give me a minute," she said. "My babies were thirsty."

He nodded, unable to speak. What was he doing here, mere feet from the sacred place where he'd thought he would some-day complete his Soul Circle? He wanted to leave, but he knew he would find no solutions that way. He had to stay here and confront what he had done—as did she. Only then did they have a chance at mending this horrible rift.

At least, that was what Cara believed.

Part of him doubted it could be done. There had been too much hurt on both sides. Surely the best thing was to stay apart. He actually took a step backward, and she jerked her gaze up to his, her eyes narrowing.

"Don't you even think of moving another step, Rafael Jude Montana."

He froze, the use of his full name as effective now as it had been when he was ten and had sneaked a lizard into Tessa's room. "I shouldn't be here," he said.

"That, young man, is not your decision." She plunked down her watering can—pink with butterflies—and yanked at the chain around her neck, tugging a familiar pendant from beneath her pale blue shirt. The chain glittered reddish gold even in the ar-tificial light, the setting ancient, the large crystal clear and deftly faceted as it settled against her chest. "I am the *apaiz nagusi*; I am in charge in this place."

He nodded his head. "Yes, Mama."

She came toward him. "Have you forgotten our ways al-ready?"

"Of course not. But I have questions."

"About the stone."

"About the stone. About Seers. About Atlantis." He barely got the last word past his lips.

"Yes." His mother sighed and glanced down for a moment before meeting his gaze again. "I have something to show you." She turned and walked through the circle of the *tenplu,* her focus stone glowing softly as she passed each of the markers that denoted the chakras. Halfway through the circle she stopped and looked back. "Are you coming?"

He wanted to refuse, uncertain of his welcome. No matter his mother's affection for him, the circle would not accept the unworthy, even if he was the son of the current priestess. That alone would assure the power contained therein would not kill him, but it could knock him unconscious for several hours. Still there was no defying his mother, not when she had that determined set to her mouth. Bracing himself, he stepped into the circle.

His crystal heated against his skin—not a searing, get-thee-from-my-presence burn but the slow glow of an old friendship rekindled. He let out a measured breath. She gave a short nod and led the way through the circle to the other side of the room.

His heart pounded as he followed, and he didn't take a substantial breath until he crossed the boundary on the other side unscathed. With a look that clearly commanded him to follow, his mother led the way to the steel door in the middle of the wall—the vault.

He had never been this close before. The reinforced portal had a hand plate next to it and some kind of peephole. She laid her hand on the plate, then leaned in to look through the peephole. A pale blue light shimmered across her eye, and small

LED lights on both panels went from red to green. The locks on the door snicked open.

High-tech biometrics. Probably one of Dad's gadgets. As his mother pushed open the heavy door, he glanced down and saw an identical eye scanner and hand plate lower down, about four feet from the floor.

Wheelchair height.

"For your brother," his mother confirmed. "Of course he doesn't use it as much now, not since he started walking again."

"Yeah." He tried to swallow past that damned lump in his throat again. "How long has he been out of the chair?"

"About nine months or so. He never gave up, always swore he would walk again. He spent a lot of time meditating, working with healing energy." Her lips curved. "That stubbornness of his came in handy this time."

He just nodded, his vocal cords unresponsive, as his mother stepped into the vault and flicked on a light.

He almost expected laser beams or a three-headed dog to come after him as he crossed the threshold. But nothing happened. She went to one of the many long, slender drawers lining the walls of the vault and opened it.

"This is what I wanted to show you." She moved aside so he could see inside the drawer. Lined side-by-side on black mountings were clear blocks of some kind of glass, and preserved within each block were documents—ancient sheets of some kind of curling parchment yellowed with age. "This is our history, Rafe—all that is left of it, anyway. And here is the one about the Stones of Ekhia."

The document illustrated three pyramid-shaped stones being set into some kind of triangular frame. Another sketch showed hands hovering over the stones, and in a third, the stones seemed to change, become clear, with power streaking from one to the other like a ricochet, meeting in the middle, then shooting skyward. Descriptions accompanied each picture, though he could not understand the strange alphabet to read them.

But a symbol in the corner of the parchment caught his eye. Three triangles connected by a circle with a wavy line in the middle. The same design as Adrian Gray's tattoo.

"What does it mean?" he whispered, uncertain whether his hushed tones were due to reverence or emotional overload.

"Much of our written language has been lost over the ages," she said, regarding the parchment as if she could will its secrets to reveal. "My grandmother's mother used to speak of a great wrong done to the Seers, a wrong that resulted in the destruction of our perfect utopia and the theft of our heritage."

"What wrong? By whom?"

"Someone who wanted the power of the Seers." Her lips curved in a sad smile. "Of course we cannot give our powers to anyone; it is not our choice. But the legend goes that this evil being—some say he was of Atlantis and others say he was a foreigner—tried to seize the key to the power of the Seers by force and the backlash of its misuse destroyed the city."

"The key being the Stones of Ekhia?"

"So legend has it."

"The thing about legends is that they become enhanced over time." He eyed the parchment again. "For all we know, this could be a picture of the pyramids of Egypt."

"I don't think so." She closed the drawer and moved to a cabinet hanging on the wall in the middle of the vault.

"Why? Because of the stuff you never told us? About the other Atlanteans?"

She paused with her hand on the handle of the cabinet, her back to him, her shoulders tense. "From what I was told by my grandparents, the people hunting Seers have something to do with the one who destroyed Atlantis. That's all I know." She shook her head and opened one of the cabinet doors. "I prefer not to think of that time. We have been safe all these years, but those men murdered my mother."

"I thought your mother died in a fire."

She glanced at him over her shoulder. "Who do you think set the fire?"

He hadn't put the pieces together. With one simple question, she cast a new light on a childhood story. He'd always known his grandmother had died in a house fire. But knowing that the fire had been deliberately set by a group of people who wanted to exterminate Seers gave the old tale a sinister twist.

"I want you to see this," she said, opening the other cabinet door so that the entire contents were revealed. "It was the last relic our ancestor saved as Atlantis was sinking into the ocean."

He'd expected shelves or more documents. Instead the shallow cabinet functioned more as a showcase, lined with royal blue and covered in more of the glass. Shining brightly against the lining was a triangle of the same reddish-gold metal as the chain around his neck—orichalcum. The thing had to be over a foot long, solid throughout, and in each corner of the triangle were indentations of a smaller triangle about the size of a woman's palm, as if something was supposed to be fitted there.

"What is that thing?" he whispered.

"Legend says this was a frame for the Stones of Ekhia." She shrugged. "But as you said, legends become distorted over time. Before today I'd assumed the stones were another myth. But somehow our ancestors used this frame and the stones to communicate with the Creators. And now someone else wants that power."

"You should have told us."

She stiffened and whirled to face him. "I was trying to keep us alive. I made the best decision I could at the time."

"But our lives were in danger. Every minute, someone out there wanted to kill us. And we didn't know. Do you realize how dangerous that was? We could have done something—"

"Don't you mean *you* could have done something? Even after all that's happened, you still want to be the hero, Rafe."

"No," he said. "I don't. But I can handle this thing, so why not let me try?"

"Because you have no control." She slammed the cabinet doors closed and turned back to him. "When the Hunter comes, Rafael Montana goes away. You have no knowledge of what happens during that time, and that is dangerous. Can we trust your other side to make the right decisions?"

"I don't have to go full throttle. I can use my powers without losing myself. So you can trust me—the side that is Rafe Montana—to make the right decisions."

"How can you say that?" She marched out of the vault, implying with one hard look that he should follow. "You had not transformed yet when you decided to interfere in the Quintana matter, so it was truly you who made the decision to charge in there like some superhero. Darius had the situation under control." She waited for him to exit the vault, then pushed the heavy door closed, and turned to face him. "A man died, and your brother almost did as well. All because you wanted to be a hero."

"I wanted to work on the Team. I was trying to show Dad—and Mendez—what I could do."

"And so you did. But at what price?"

Her judgmental tone grated. "Maybe if I'd known there were other Atlanteans out there, I could have found someone with a similar power to train me over the years. Then maybe no one would have died."

She gave him the aristocrat look again. "So you are saying it is my fault?"

"I'm saying you judged me and excommunicated me unfairly."

"We did not send you away, Rafael. You did that to yourself." She let out a slow breath. "This has been a very long day. Perhaps we all need to sleep on what we have learned."

He hesitated. Fueled by righteous anger, the Hunter chafed to continue the fight, but his other self recognized the wisdom in a strategic retreat. He gave a nod. "Agreed. I'm beat."

"Then we will talk about this tomorrow." She led the way through the temple.

He followed, a million questions in his mind, scraping his churned-up emotions like sand in a windstorm. But she was right. Enough secrets had been dragged into the light today. Better to go back to his room and think about the next step.

"By the way," his mother said, pausing in the doorway leading to the hall. "I like Cara very much. It's about time you took a mate."

"What? A mate?" Her words literally stopped him in his tracks. "I mean, we have a thing going, but—"

His mother shook her head, an amused smile playing around her lips. "Have you forgotten my power, Rafael? *Ezkonta.* Matchmaking. I knew as soon as I looked into Cara's eyes that she was your mate. And it's a good thing, too. My father told me that Hunters need mates to balance them and keep them grounded in the here and now. She can be a great help to you."

"She's not my mate. She can't be."

"Are you sure?"

The question echoed back to him off the temple walls as she disappeared into the hall, leaving him alone to wrestle with the answer.

CHAPTER TWENTY

Rafe entered the silent bedroom. He didn't turn on a light; he felt at home in the dark.

He could make out Cara curled under the covers of the bed, her blond hair flowing across the pillow and gilded by the soft glow of the moonlight. Unable to look away from her, he slipped his T-shirt over his head, barely aware of what he was doing. He'd walked into this room with his emotions scraped raw from interacting with his family, but for some reason seeing Cara in *his* room, in *his* bed, soothed the sting with a salve of pure male satisfaction.

It made him think about what his mother had said. Made him want it to be true.

His mate.

What would it mean, to have a mate? He sat on the edge of the bed and bent down to untie his sneakers. He'd been alone so long he could hardly wrap his head around the idea of a woman just for him, a woman who would wait for him and sleep with him and hold him. A woman who would stay with him and not fear him. He'd never dared dream of such a thing before.

Still couldn't dream it now. Not when he was still a danger to the people close to him.

He set his sneakers aside and stripped off his socks, dropping them on top of the shoes. Maybe he was reading too much into it. He knew there was something special about Cara, but hell, anyone would know that within thirty seconds of meeting her. She was so warm, so loving, so damned loyal. If his life were different, if *he* were different, he'd give serious thought to a long-term relationship with her. As things stood now, he was lucky she was still talking to him.

He was lucky anyone was still talking to him.

The covers behind him rustled, and her small hands slid around his waist. She snuggled closer, her hair brushing his arm. "Penny for your thoughts."

"They're not worth that much." He turned his head just enough to inhale the lemony scent of her shampoo. "I thought you were asleep."

"I tried. My brain wouldn't stop."

"Make it. You need to rest." He covered one of her hands with his. "It's been a long day."

"I can't. I can't stop thinking about Danny." She buried her face in his back. "Those jerks took my cell phone. I haven't been able to call him."

"You can use mine."

"You don't understand. I don't know the number. It's in my contacts."

"It'll be okay."

"Usually I just memorize phone numbers, but Danny's been through so many phones over the past couple of years that I couldn't keep them straight anymore."

"Cara, not knowing his phone number doesn't make you a bad sister."

"Feels like it." Her voice sounded muffled against his skin.

"Hey, cut that out." He twisted around to face her. "I'm a worse family member than you are, and I *know* my family's phone number."

"*You* cut it out." She shifted back a little, giving him more room on the bed. In the sleep shorts Tessa had lent her, her legs seemed to go on forever. "Your family is still here. There are issues to be worked out, sure, but they're all still in your life."

"Just like that, huh?"

"Not quite." She touched his hand. "How did it go with your mom?"

"Okay. Or maybe not okay. I don't know. It's confusing."

"That comes with the family package."

"What I need is an instruction manual."

"It's not that hard. You're both angry, both feel betrayed, and both love each other."

"Betrayed!" He scowled. "I didn't betray them."

"You went away."

"To *protect* them!"

"And your mother kept her secret to protect you." She raised her gaze to his, her eyes luminous in the moonlight.

"That's different." Even he could hear how halfhearted that sounded. "My 'betrayal,' as you put it, saved their lives. My parents not telling us of a threat this dangerous did the opposite. It put our lives in danger."

"Oh, yeah, I can see that." She glanced around the bedroom. "Living in a castle in the middle of the desert with enough security to put Fort Knox to shame. I can see how that would paint a target on your back."

He tugged a lock of her hair. "Quit with the sass." Instead of releasing her, he let his fingers linger on the silky strands. She didn't push him away.

"Just saying it like it is." She closed her eyes as he slid his fingers deeper into her hair and stroked. "Might have helped if you hadn't left this amazing fortress to run off into the big, bad world. Probably gave your mom some bad moments."

"I'm not going to win this argument, am I?"

"We're not arguing. We're discussing your perspective."

"Oh, yeah?" Winding her hair around his hand, he tilted her head back and leaned in until his mouth hovered above hers. "My perspective says you're in my bed."

"Yeah." He dipped his head to nibble her neck, and a slow, shuddering sigh slipped past her lips. "I am."

"So what does that mean?" He nipped her jaw and raised his head to look at her, caressing away the sting with his thumb.

"Does it have to mean anything?"

"With you, yeah. You're not the type for one night stands, no matter what you try to tell yourself."

"Well." She tilted her head, her hair falling away from her shoulder and giving him more access to her neck. "Technically, this is a second night stand. Already I'm breaking the rules."

"Yeah, you're a real rebel." He took advantage of the unspoken invitation, gliding his tongue along the sweet flesh of her throat. He couldn't get enough of the taste of her, and her tremor of reaction shot straight to his groin.

She stroked her palm along his arm. "I'm on your side, Rafe. You can talk to me."

"Enough talking for tonight." He took her hand and tugged it lower so her fingers brushed the cotton of his sweatpants and the stirring hardness beneath it. "Show me how rebellious you are."

Her lips curved. Instead of yanking her hand back, she traced the stiffening contours. "You don't scare me, Mr. Bounty Hunter, even if you are mad at just about everyone in this house."

"Not you." He swept his hand under her loose T-shirt, up along her ribs, and cupped her bare breast in his hand. "Does this feel mad to you?"

No, it feels like you're hurting. He wouldn't admit it, but she could sense how deeply his feelings for his family went. Had she really believed he'd simply walked away from them without a second thought? He cared *too* much, and for a man more comfortable with action over words, that had to bug him.

He stroked his thumb over her hardening nipple. "Stop thinking so loud."

"I'm not." The words slipped out on a sigh as he pulled the shirt over her head and tossed it aside, leaving her clad only in her shorts.

"I can practically hear your thoughts in my head." He pulled her down on the bed and rolled onto his back, arranging her limbs until she straddled him, his hard cock nudging her butt through the thin layers of clothing. With his hands around her waist, he leaned up and took a nipple in his mouth.

She whimpered, arching her back as her eyes slid closed. Heat shot through her body, pooling between her thighs. She fell forward, catching herself with her hands on his chest. Her thumb nudged the crystal.

White light streaked through her mind, followed by a wave of arousal so primitive that she nearly came right there. She shook with the hunger rippling through her body, the tightening of her nipples, the moisture between her thighs. She rocked against him, imagining riding him, imagined that hard cock sliding inside her. She was already so wet, so ready.

He released her nipple on a groan, arching his hips. "You want to play, baby? I'm game." He tugged at her shorts, and she wiggled to help him get rid of them. He threw them aside and slid his fingers between her legs, stroked the damp flesh. She shuddered.

"You're so ready for me." He shoved at his sweatpants. She helped, jerking the pants down his legs with hands that trembled. He kicked his legs free, and she tossed the garment away, returning quickly to stroke his newly freed erection.

He groaned, arching his back. "You're killing me."

"I hope not." She brushed a teasing kiss on the smooth head of his cock.

He grabbed the back of her head. "I have an idea."

"So do I." She flicked her tongue against him, his groan vibrating straight to her core. "Betcha they're the same."

"I think I like your idea better."

"Let's see." She took him in her mouth, savoring the strength of him against her tongue. She teased him with mouth and fingers until his hands fisted in the sheets, her name a plea on his lips as he begged for release. She pulled back seconds before he got one. "Was that your idea?"

"It's a damn good one, whose ever it was." He blew out a hard breath. "You drive me crazy, woman."

"Good."

"Come here." He dragged her up and over him. "If I'm right, this should blow both our minds." When she straddled him, he took her hand in his, wrapped it around his crystal, and slid inside her in one swift thrust.

Her brain exploded, colors and light nearly blinding her mind's eye. Passion rushed through her like liquid fire, surging into him and bouncing back at her. Heat seared her where their bodies touched, and his every move stoked it higher. Waves of hot and cold rippled along her skin, the flesh prickling with exquisite sensitivity. She didn't think she could handle it all; she couldn't breathe. Surely she would burn alive from it. Surely she would die.

The orgasm flared up out of nowhere, melting rational thought and turning her inside out, stretching her across eons, shaking her free of the fetters of humanity. She went up in flames like a phoenix reborn. She screamed, but he swallowed the sound with his kiss; controlled the flames before they devoured her.

And she let herself fall.

. . . . .

Rafe stirred before Cara. He turned his head slowly, not wanting to disturb her where she dozed on top of him, and checked the bedside clock. Only an hour had passed. His mind argued that it was impossible so little time had gone by. His body insisted he had just run twenty miles across the desert at high noon. The symptoms fit: drenched with sweat, trembling muscles, hard to draw a breath. And tired. Bone tired.

But satisfied. Hell, yes, utterly, completely satisfied. He'd surely never come so hard in his life.

He glanced down at Cara and saw she'd released his focus stone. The crystal glowed in the darkness, clearly fully charged from the energy of their mutual, mind-blowing climax. He lifted the stone, enjoyed the vibration against his fingers. Oh, yeah, he was loaded for bear. Probably a good thing with this enemy out there who wanted to kill him.

Cara stirred against his chest. "Mmm. What time is it?"

"Late." He stroked her hair. "Sleep, baby. Nothing's going to happen tonight."

"Too bad."

"Like you could go again."

"Maybe." Her lips curved into a mischievous smile, and she drifted back to sleep.

She fit against him like she'd been made for him. Everything about her called to him, lured him, made him want her. If ever a true mate existed for Rafe Montana, she was it. But his life was in danger—and perhaps always would be. How could he ever give her what she deserved?

He lay awake for a long time, wondering how he had fallen so hard in love so quickly . . . and how in hell he would ever be able to let her go.

. . . . .

Cara awoke the next morning to sun streaming into the bedroom and an empty pillow beside her. She stretched, enjoying the ache in her muscles and the memory of how it had gotten there. Their hands linked together, the crystal burning between their palms . . . Like a couple of mirrors in the sun, they had reflected arousal back and forth, each time stronger, each time hotter, chasing each other toward the blinding pinnacle of pleasure, each touch, each stroke, like a whip to bare flesh. The pleasure had torn through her like lightning, ripping a scream from her throat, burning away anything had she had been before and leaving someone completely new, completely *his*.

And he'd been right there with her, his heart open to her as they both soared high and plunged into the sun.

It didn't surprise her that Rafe was up and gone already. He tended to slip away before things got too serious. She didn't hold it against him. He'd revealed more to her last night than he knew, his crystal a looking glass into his emotions. She hoped that when all this was over, he'd want to stay together. She knew they lived lives on opposite coasts, but they could work it out somehow. This kind of thing came along once in a lifetime, and she wouldn't give it up without a fight.

She sat up, pushing her hair out of her eyes. Rafe thought he was a bad guy, but he was wrong. Hopefully they'd stay long enough with his family that everyone would see the big-hearted, honorable man she did. The man she had somehow fallen in love with.

Yeah, she'd gone and done it. Never mind that she'd only known him a couple of days. Never mind that the guy was some kind of psychic superhero. She could cope with all that. The real terror was that he was also related to one of the richest families in the country. How could a computer programmer from Jersey hope to fit into the level of society the Montanas called home?

She shook her head. One night of orgasmic bliss, and she was already planning the wedding. She had to keep her feet on the ground. She knew Rafe believed he had to stay a lone wolf to protect those closest to him. She got that; it was a noble idea. But everything she'd seen said Rafe had more control than he thought. Now he just had to realize it, and maybe she could help him.

Provided he didn't shove her on a plane to Jersey once all this was over.

She pushed aside the covers. First order of business was get cleaned up and dressed and find some breakfast. Or lunch, she thought as she caught sight of the clock. She'd slept a lot longer than she'd expected.

She spotted her T-shirt on the floor. Sliding naked from the bed, she pulled it over her head and headed for the shower. As she passed the dresser, she noticed her own clothes, clean and folded, sitting on top of it. And on top of *those* was a cell phone.

The phone was brand new, shiny, and black. She picked it up and turned it on, puzzled. She couldn't remember Danny's number, so what good did having a phone do? But someone had left it here for a reason. She started pressing buttons. When she hit the one labeled CONTACTS, she almost dropped the phone as she scrolled down the list: Apex Consulting, Canzo's Pizza, Danny, Maisie . . . *These were her contacts.*

How . . . ? She shook her head. She didn't care how. She knew Rafe or his family had somehow done this, and she'd find out the means later. For now she hit the contact for Danny, listening as the phone dialed.

It went right to voice mail, but it was nice to hear his voice, even in a recorded message. Choking back tears, she left a message for him to call her, set the phone back on the bureau, and scooped up the clothing.

A nice hot shower and a good cry, and she'd be all set to face the day.

. . . . .

Darius stood in front of the fridge. Holding on to the door, he leaned inside to grab the milk, but the door swung wide. He tilted, off balance, and struggled to retain his grip on the gallon jug.

"I got it." Rafe grabbed the milk with one hand and stabilized the fridge door with the other.

Darius scowled and looked down at both their hands on the milk jug. He jerked his hand free, lurched away from the fridge, and followed the line of the counter to the small table in the breakfast nook, where his cane rested against the wall. "Make yourself useful and bring the milk over here."

Rafe closed the fridge door. Any other time he would have given Darius a hard time for talking to him like the hired help, but he figured he deserved that and more. He watched Dar sit down at the table, a box of cereal and a bowl already set out. He swung by the cabinet to grab a second bowl, then headed over to the table where his brother was already pouring his cereal.

He set the milk down between them and pulled out a chair, scowling at the little brown sticks and balls in Dar's bowl. "What's that, twigs and berries?"

Darius reached for the milk. "High fiber."

Rafe wrinkled his nose. "Got any of that other stuff around here? The one with the multi-colored O's and the little marshmallows?"

Darius paused before pouring and looked at him with that

older-and-wiser look all older brothers were born with. "Don't you have any respect for your body?"

"Yeah, which is why I feed it good-tasting stuff instead of hamster food like that." Rafe snatched a twig thing out of Darius's bowl seconds before the milk hit it. He popped the cereal into his mouth. "Not bad. Who knew hamsters lived so well?"

Darius set down the milk. "I just wanted a quiet breakfast. And now there's you."

Rafe shrugged and poured some of the high fiber stuff into his own bowl. "Good thing I came when I did, or you might still be on the floor covered in milk."

Dar's mouth thinned, and he dropped his spoon in the bowl with a clank. "What the hell do you want? Haven't you caused enough trouble?"

"I don't think that exposing the truth is trouble. Mom and Dad shouldn't have hidden that from us. I like to know who my enemies are."

"Me, too."

His brother's snarl sucked the air out of Rafe's optimism balloon. He set down the box of cereal and looked Darius in the eye. "I'm not your enemy, Dar."

"You sure about that?"

"What kind of question is that?"

"A legitimate one, seems to me." Darius leaned back in his chair.

"I'm your brother, damn it. I screwed up, okay? I know I screwed up." Rafe glanced at the cane leaning against the wall. "I would take back every minute of that day if I could. I'm so sorry, Dar. Seriously."

Darius stayed silent for a long moment, then reached for his spoon. "Seems a little late for an apology."

"I know it must seem that way, and I'm sorry about that, too."

"You left." Darius fixed him with a hard stare. "You didn't know if I would live or die, but you left anyway. What kind of brother does that?"

Rafe curled his hands into fists. What had he expected, that Darius would just shrug and tell him to forget about it? "I had to go."

"You couldn't stick around for the funeral maybe?" His brother spooned a big scoop of cereal into his mouth and chewed.

"Cut it out."

"If you'd hung out, maybe you would have gotten my car if I hadn't survived."

"I don't want your car."

"Maybe my comics. You always drooled over those." Darius took another spoonful of cereal.

Rafe stared at his own bowl, his appetite gone. "Dar, quit it."

Darius swallowed. "If I were a quitter, I wouldn't be walking."

"I'm glad, really glad, that you're a stubborn cuss. It killed me to see you in that hospital bed."

Darius scoffed. "When did you ever come see me in the hospital?"

"The night I left."

The quiet words made Darius pause with the spoon halfway to his mouth. Slowly he set it down.

"I sneaked into the hospital that night before I left town. You were still unconscious from the surgery. I slipped past security and the nurses and sat by your bed for a good hour, talking to you telepathically."

Darius narrowed his eyes. "You're telling the truth. I can feel it."

"Of course I'm telling the truth. Why would I lie?"

"I don't know, Rafe. Why do you do anything?"

"I'm not the selfish prick you think I am." Rafe leaned closer. "I left because I knew I was dangerous. Hennessy died because of me, and you nearly did, too. What else was I supposed to do? I had to get away from the people I loved to keep you all safe. But before I left, I came to see you in the hospital to tell you I was sorry."

"You couldn't have told me when I was awake?"

He could see the struggle in Dar's face, as if he wanted to believe but didn't dare. "There wasn't time."

"Why do I think you're full of it?"

"I left you the healing crystals."

Darius bit back whatever smart remark he had been about to deliver. "I thought Mom did that."

"No, that was me." Rafe glanced down at his cereal. "It was my fault you got shot. I had to find a way to help you get better but still leave so everyone could be safe. That was the best I could do."

"The nurses kept moving the crystals off the bed." The amusement in Dar's voice had him looking up. "You should have heard Mom arguing with them."

Because he actually could imagine it, Rafe couldn't hold back a smile. "I guess she won."

"She started out telling them it was a religious ritual, and when that didn't work, she kept upping the amount she pledged to donate to the place. There's a wing with her name on it now."

Rafe chuckled. "She is a force, that's for sure."

"Yeah."

Their laughter died. Rafe looked his brother straight in the eye, all his remorse open for him to see. "I really am sorry, Dar.

I did a dumb thing and you paid the price. I hope you can for-give me."

"I don't know." Darius toyed with his spoon.

Rafe's heart sank. "I understand. I just wanted you to know how sorry I am."

Darius nodded but didn't look up.

Rafe pushed back his chair and stood. "You can have my bowl of twigs. I'm not hungry."

When Darius remained silent, Rafe turned to leave. He'd got-ten halfway across the kitchen when his brother finally spoke. "Rafe."

He paused. "Yeah?"

"There is something you can do."

He turned to face Darius. "What?"

"Actually, there's a couple of things."

"Name it."

"Well, my car needs detailing."

Concern gave way to confusion. "What?"

"And my laundry's piling pretty high."

"Laundry? Doesn't Lupe still do the laundry?"

"And then there's one last thing only a brother could help with."

Only then did Rafe spot the gleam in his brother's eyes. He folded his arms, scowling to hide the stupid, hopeful grin that wanted to explode across his face. "And what's that?"

"Well, you're aware I have mobility issues, and sometimes there's a few places I can't quite reach in the bathroom. . . ."

The laugh burst from his lips. "Forget it."

Darius smiled. "You'd leave me with dirt in sensitive places?"

"In a heartbeat. Now eat your twigs."

"That's cold. Now be a good boy and get me a cup of coffee.

It should be done brewing, and it's hard for me to get it myself without spilling it."

Rafe glanced at the coffee pot and the tower of disposable cups and lids stacked beside it. "Yeah, I can see that. Still take it black?"

"Always."

Rafe poured the steaming coffee into one of the disposable cups just as their father walked into the kitchen.

"Bring your breakfast into the dining room," John said. "I'm calling a family meeting."

CHAPTER TWENTY-ONE

Rafe carried both cereal bowls into the dining room, and Darius followed with his coffee. Their mother was already sitting at the table, nursing a cup of coffee. Tessa breezed in with smiles for everyone before she sat down at the table and grabbed a banana from the fruit bowl. Moments later Cara appeared in the doorway.

"I'm sorry," she said, glancing over the gathering. "I'm interrupting."

"Not at all," his father said. "Did you get your new cell phone?"

She nodded and held it up, a hint of a blush sweeping her cheeks. "Yes. Do I have you to thank for that?"

"I just called in a favor with the cell company, and this morning they sent a new one over and deactivated your old one. Darius was the one who told us how upset you were about being out of contact with your brother."

Cara shot a surprised look at Darius. "Thank you. It means the world."

Darius just shrugged.

"Come on in," Rafe's father said, gesturing. "This meeting involves you, too."

She frowned but slipped the cell into her shorts' pocket and came into the room. Rafe reached over to pull out the chair next to him. Their gazes met for one second of white-hot heat before she accepted the seat. Rafe draped his arm along the back of her chair, his fingers grazing her shoulder, content to just touch her.

John rested his hands on the back of an empty chair in front of him. "Thank you all for coming."

"What's this about?" Rafe asked.

"Patience, Rafe," his father said.

"Got a date?" Darius drawled.

"No, but I planned to get on the road today." The silence that fell and the sober expressions that accompanied it had Rafe looking from one to the other. "What? I still have to find Cara's brother."

"*We*," Cara corrected. "*We* have to find Danny."

Rafe touched her hand. "No, you're staying here, where it's safe."

She started shaking her head before he'd finished his sentence. "I'm going with you."

"No, I'm not taking the chance."

She yanked her hand from his grasp. "This isn't up for debate."

"You're right. I can move faster without you, so you're not going. Period."

She paled. Before he could say anything further, his father cleared his throat, drawing the attention of the entire room. "If I could get in a word?"

"Sorry, I should have asked. She can stay here, right?" Rafe looked from one parent to the other.

"Of course she can stay," his mother said.

"In fact," his father added, "that's exactly what I wanted to talk to all of you about."

"Rafe's love life?" Darius gave a quick laugh.

"No. The enemies Rafe and Cara brought to our attention."

At his father's serious tone, Darius sobered.

"Your mother and I had a long talk last night." John glanced at Maria, who gave a nod of agreement. "We realize now we might have made the wrong decision in not warning all of you about these extremists who are trying to kill Seers." Voices erupted, all three siblings trying to be heard. John raised his hand until they quieted. "We thought we were protecting you, but now we realize we left you unprepared for this threat. And that was a big mistake. I make my living as a strategist and security specialist, and I ignored my instincts. That stops now."

John looked from one face to the other. "I called this family meeting because we need to neutralize this enemy, especially now that they're after a source of power that might prove dangerous."

"What do you mean?" Tessa asked.

"The Stones of Ekhia," their mother said. "According to Rafe, they exist. And if these men get their hands on them, it could be disastrous."

"Disastrous how?" Darius asked.

"According to the scrolls," Maria said, "misuse of these stones led to the destruction of Atlantis."

"Which means they're too dangerous to leave out there in the wrong hands. We have to get them first." John's fingers tightened around the chair back. "We need to bring them here to keep in the vault for safety."

"There are three," Maria said. "Cara's brother apparently has one of them. We will find him and retrieve the stone. We'll have to search for the other two. They could be anywhere in the world."

Rafe shook his head. "No, it's too dangerous. They already tried to take you out once, Mama. I don't want to give them another shot at it."

"None of us do," John said, "but your combined powers are stronger than one man alone. We have a better chance of success

311

as a group, and everything your mother has read says these stones actually belong to the Seers. That's us, and yes, I am including myself in this." His gaze touched on each of them in turn. "It may take years or even lifetimes to recover all three stones. We *all* have to make the commitment now to find the Stones of Ekhia and stop these people from doing some serious damage to the world."

Rafe hesitated. "I'm in," he said finally. "I'm not real comfortable with amateurs putting themselves in danger, but I want this to end. And you're going to need my expertise."

"Amateurs?" Darius growled.

"I spent the past few years tracking fugitives," Rafe told Darius. "That trumps your lab experiments."

"We welcome your experience," his father said before Darius could respond. "Now we need to lay out the plan to find Cara's brother and retrieve the first stone. That should stop these people for now."

"Why's that?" Rafe asked. "What good is just one?"

His mother answered. "Because all three are needed to trigger the power. By capturing one, we keep these men from doing that much."

"I know I don't have the same powers as the rest of you," John said, "but my business is security and troubleshooting. Between our two skill sets, I believe we can do this. As your father— and husband"—he looked from one face to the other—"I will protect you with every resource I have."

Before anyone could respond, the doorbell chimed.

"That's probably Mendez," John said. "We'll need his team."

"I gave Lupe the day off," Maria said, scooting her chair back.

"I'll get it, Mom." Tessa jumped from her seat and jogged from the room.

Darius frowned. "Doesn't feel like Mendez."

Cara's eyes widened. "Could they have found us here?"

"It has to be Mendez," John said. "He's the only one besides us with the security code to the gate."

"I said it doesn't feel like Mendez. It's someone else." Darius shoved his chair back and reached for his cane just as Tessa's cry of alarm echoed through the house . . . and was abruptly silenced.

Rafe leaped to his feet, dragging Cara from her chair. "Mom, Cara, into the kitchen."

"But—" Cara protested.

Rafe leaned close. "I want you safe. Grab a weapon—a knife, a frying pan, something. And don't come out until one of us comes for you." He pushed her toward the kitchen. "Dar, go with them."

"You're not sending me off with the women," Darius snapped.

"They need someone to protect them." As his mother grabbed Cara's hand and raced for the kitchen, Rafe reached for the Hunter. His crystal responded with unusual speed, warming and pouring power through his veins in seconds. "They won't be expecting you, Dar, and Dad and I need to move fast."

"Do it," their father said, pulling a handgun from the small of his back and clicking off the safety. "It's a good plan."

"Fine." Darius swung around toward the kitchen. "But I don't like it."

"Noted," John said.

"Let's go." Rafe opened up to half throttle and pivoted toward the front hall. He skidded to a halt as a figure filled the doorway, one arm locked around Tessa's waist, and the other hand clamped over her mouth.

"I'd like to point out," Adrian Gray said, shuffling into the room with Rafe's struggling sister, "that I did ring the doorbell."

"Damn it, Gray," Rafe said. "Couldn't you have just called?"

"Rafe, you know this man?" His father had not lowered his weapon.

"Yeah, he helped me and Cara get away from the men trying to kill us. John Montana, meet Adrian Gray."

"Pleasure," Adrian said. "I'd shake hands, but I'm afraid to let go of this one." He contemplated Tessa. "She bites."

"Get your hands off my daughter," John demanded.

"As long as she promises to be a good girl. I like my fingers right where they are."

"Tessa, when he lets go, you come here to me, understand?" John said.

Tessa nodded. Gray released her, and she ran to her father, who pushed her behind him with one hand, still aiming the gun with the other.

"Why didn't you call?" Rafe asked again.

"Criten's gone," Gray said.

"Gone? When? Where'd he go?"

"Last night. And as for where, according to my sources"—Gray glanced at the gun still pointed at him—"here."

"Here?" John demanded. "To this house?"

"To Sedona. He chartered a private plane."

Rafe swore.

"Sir?" Gray addressed John. "I'd appreciate it if you lowered the gun."

"Too bad."

"You might as well do as he says," Rafe said. "He could have taken it from you whenever he wanted. He's a Warrior."

"A what?"

"A Warrior. Adrian here is Atlantean, just like us. Some kind of superpowered fighting machine."

Gray winced. "A simplified but fairly accurate description."

314

Tessa poked her head from behind her father. "I don't care if he's the Terminator. That doesn't give him permission to barge into our house."

"Might I remind you again that I did ring the bell?" Gray said. "You're the one who screamed."

"Only because you tried to push past me."

"Because you wouldn't let me in, and I have important information for Rafe. I'm sorry if I scared you."

"You don't scare me."

Gray gave her a slow smile. "Are you sure about that?"

"Hey, hey." John's protest drew Gray's attention. "How did you get past my security system?"

Gray shrugged. "Lucky."

"That's the most sophisticated system in the country," John said. "I know because I developed it. You'd need more than luck."

"It is impressive," Adrian agreed, "but it's not hard for someone like me to get past it." He glanced at Rafe. "Criten's men might be able to get in eventually, but it would take them a bit longer."

"That's comforting."

"No, it's not." Tessa stepped out from behind her father, fists clenched at her sides. "I don't like any of this. And I don't like you."

Gray shrugged, not seeming the least bit disturbed. "I grow on people."

"Like mold, I bet," Tessa muttered.

"Okay, cut it out," Rafe said.

"I know you don't trust me." Adrian looked from father to son, ignoring Tessa. "But I can be an asset against Criten. He surrounds himself with Warriors. I'm your best bet at taking them out."

John shook his head, clearly about to protest.

"I believe him." The voice came from the kitchen doorway. Darius leaned against the doorjamb, arm lowered to his side and a gun clutched in his fist. "I can feel his sincerity."

"Dar . . . ?" Rafe gestured at the gun, raising his brows.

"We keep guns secured around the house," Darius said, never looking away from Adrian. "Comes from having a paranoid father."

"Security conscious," John corrected.

"The legs aren't so hot, but the hand-eye coordination is perfect," Darius added.

"He's an amazing shot," Tessa said to Gray. "So don't move too suddenly."

"Look, this man did help us get away from those guys yesterday." Cara stepped past Darius into the dining room. "When the chips were down, he saved our lives. And he did have some kind of power over Criten's men."

"Completely neutralized them," Rafe said. "That's his car we drove here. He took the other guys back to Vegas in their vehicle." He looked at Gray. "I would have returned the car, you know. You didn't have to come all the way out here."

"Where Criten goes, I go. He checked out of the hotel before dawn and headed to this area on a private plane. I followed as soon as I could, but he had a few hours' lead on me." Gray looked from one to the other. "I'm here to help."

"You have an agenda," Darius said.

"Of course," Gray agreed. "Doesn't everyone? Luckily, my agenda is the same as yours."

"And that would be . . . ?" Maria came out of the kitchen, fixing Adrian Gray with her aristocratic look.

Adrian bobbed his head in what could only be described as reverence. "To see the Stones of Ekhia successfully returned to the Seers, *Prestulana*. To put an end to *Mendeku*."

His mother sucked in a breath. *"Mendeku?"*

"What's '*Mendeku*'?" John asked.

"Blood vengeance," Maria whispered, her face pale.

"Sworn upon the Seers by the descendents of Selak and all who follow him," Gray confirmed. "Including Criten."

"Selak?" Rafe repeated. *"Prestulana?"*

"Selak, he who destroyed the great city of Atlantis," Adrian said. "Criten is his many times over great-grandson. And *Prestulana—*"

"Great Lady," Maria translated, her voice soft. "I have not heard that in many years, not since my grandmother was alive."

"So you're here to help." John glanced at his sons. When both nodded, he lowered the gun. "Guess we can use all the help we can get."

"We're going after the stones," Rafe said. "Starting with the one Danny has."

The doorbell rang again.

"That's Mendez," Darius announced.

"I'll let him in," Tessa said. She sent Adrian a glare that had him moving from the doorway. "I'm sure *he* knows how to act around a woman."

The corner of Adrian's mouth lifted in a half smile as he held Tessa's gaze for a moment, clearly speaking telepathically. She gasped and darted from the room.

Rafe frowned. "Do I want to know what you said to my sister just now?"

"Don't know what you're talking about," Gray answered.

Rafe narrowed his eyes.

"Rafe, you're vouching for this guy?" John asked.

Rafe hesitated, but finally nodded. "Yeah."

"All right, that's good enough for me." John jerked his head at the table. "Everyone sit down. We need to get a solid plan in place before we go chasing after Cara's brother."

Rafe's mother sat down next to Adrian. "You have knowledge of our history that we lack," she murmured.

"I can say the same of you," Gray replied. "Perhaps we can fill in the blanks for each other."

"I look forward to that." She pursed her lips. "My daughter doesn't like you."

"She'll get over it."

A mysterious smile curved her lips. "Well, you certainly have your work cut out for you."

Even as Rafe puzzled over the cryptic conversation, Tessa came back with Rodrigo Mendez. The leader of the Mountain Security troubleshooting team was in his late thirties with a military buzz cut and a don't-screw-with-me expression. Rafe didn't move a muscle as the guy's dark-as-hell stare fell on him. His father had told them he'd involved the Team when someone had tried to shoot his mother. Mike Hennessy, the guy who'd died during Rafe's little stunt five years ago, had been under Mendez's command.

He still blames you. He doesn't want you here.

He didn't even need the universe to confirm the assessment. It was written in every molecule of Mendez's body, shining like a beacon from his eyes. *Note to self: try not to piss off the ex-Marine this time around.*

"Mendez, thanks for coming." John shook the team leader's hand.

"Certainly, sir. What's the op?"

"We're searching for a fugitive." He indicated Cara. "This lady's stepbrother jumped bail and is hiding somewhere in the area."

"Is that why he's here?" Mendez indicated Rafe with a jerk of his head. "Heard he was a bounty hunter now."

"Yes, my son brought Ms. McGaffigan to us." John ignored the attitude. "We believe her stepbrother is in possession of an item that has interested a very dangerous group of people—the same group that took a shot at my wife a few days ago."

Mendez looked at Cara. "Have you been in contact with your stepbrother, ma'am?"

"He called once," Cara said. "That was a couple of days ago. I lost my cell phone for a while and just got a new one, so I don't know if he's tried to get in touch with me again."

"We might be able to trace the phone if it has GPS or trace the signal to the nearest tower," Mendez said. "I'll put Weatherly on it."

"Sounds good," John said.

"I'll get my team assembled." Mendez left the room.

"How much does he know about us?" Rafe asked.

"I haven't told him anything," their father said, "but he doesn't ask questions, either."

"Let's keep it that way," Gray said.

"I was planning to."

A few minutes later, Mendez came back into the room, three armed, black-clad men following him. "This is Weatherly." He indicated the thin young guy right behind him who carried a laptop bag over his shoulder and two silver cases that looked like electronic equipment. "Ms. McGaffigan, let's see if we can find your stepbrother."

CHAPTER TWENTY-TWO

Jain Criten sat outside on the balcony, sipping his mimosa over the remains of a five-star breakfast, and watched the world awaken. The spa in Sedona boasted individual luxury villas, and the view from his included the pool, a meditation garden, and more green trees than he'd ever expected to see in the desert. In the distance, beyond the lush tree line, rose two majestic mesas of red stone, lines of white and gray threading through them, capturing the glow of the rising sun.

Gadi had done well.

There was something about this place that energized him, something that ignited the power within him and sent it racing through his veins, intoxicating him like hard liquor. Was it the sun, so strong in this part of the world? Or maybe it was Sedona's famous vortex energy. The so-called power of the vortexes had attracted all types of New Age people to the area, many of them setting up shop in town. Given the way his power sparked and shimmered along his skin, practically visible, he had to believe the stories that vortex energy thrived in this area.

He wondered if he could tap it. Use it to enhance his own powers.

A sparrow fluttered to a landing on the back of the empty chair across from him. He watched as it considered the scraps of food on the table, turning its head from side to side as if gauging the risk.

With a half smile, he ripped off a piece of croissant and threw it on the ground. The bird leaped into flight and followed, landing inches away, then hopped closer to the bread, always cautious. Just as it got near its goal, Criten flicked his fingers. The food jumped a foot away.

The sparrow hesitated, then hopped toward the bread again. Criten flicked his fingers again. Red sparks trailed in the wake of his hand as the bread jumped again. Power hummed beneath his skin, rushing to his head. He could feel the vortex energy nearby, strong and masculine, sweeping through him, stealing his breath and leaving his flesh tingling. Closing his eyes, he reached for it.

It surged into him like a dam that burst, saturating his senses with glorious power. The bird chirped, and he opened his eyes, grinning as he aimed his hand at the piece of bread and let go.

Energy gushed from his hand, red as blood and just as draining. He tried to control the flood, but it poured from him, blasting the bread into cinders, leaping to the bird. The sparrow let out a peep of alarm, leaped into flight. Sparks ignited its feathers, the flames overtaking it with a soft whoosh, snuffing its life in seconds. The carcass hurtled to the ground, blackened and smoking.

He tried to stem the flow, but still it bled from him, using him as a conduit and burning a deep groove into the tiles of the balcony.

Would he die here, victim of his own power? He'd come so close to finding the stone, to tracking the girl—

A vision exploded in his mind. The girl. The house. The men. The plan. Never before had he seen so clearly. Information flooded his mind. Overwhelmed his nerve endings. Blurred his vision.

"*Baku*," he whispered, closing his hand into a fist. "Enough."

Gradually he managed to slow the flow of energy, from a river to a stream to a trickle. By the time he'd stopped it completely, he'd slid to the floor, curled into a ball, his palms burned and blistered as he tried to breathe.

The vortex energy had run rampant through his system, sublimating his power pathways for its own. But even as it had warped his Channeling abilities, it had somehow enhanced his small, often intermittent gift of Seeing—at least while the energy held him in its grasp. He'd seen Cara McGaffigan and the Montana house, the men who worked for the Montanas and the plans they made even now to recover the stone. He'd seen the vault of treasures in the house and Cara McGaffigan opening that vault for him.

He'd seen enough to know he'd be triumphant today.

He was not blind to the irony that, even as *Mendeku* demanded the death of Seers, the only other being who could use the Stones of Ekhia was a Channeler with a minor Seeing gift. That family secret, passed through the generations, was the reason why only his ancestor Selak had been able to use the stones. It took the exact combination of the two gifts at particular strength for a non-Seer to even activate the stones. For anyone else, even their strongest Channelers and Warriors, such action would result in death.

It had taken these many generations for another like Selak to be born—himself—to at last bring to fruition the possibility of claiming the power that should belong to all Atlanteans, not just Seers.

Cradling his injured hands to his chest, he called to Gadi

telepathically for help. He would take back the stone today. He'd seen it.

And the universe never lied.

. . . . .

"Got him." Weatherly turned to look at Mendez. "Cangialosi activated the phone, made a call, then turned it off. But I got a ping."

"Where is he?" Mendez asked.

Weatherly grinned. "Here in Sedona."

"And I found that foreign national." A man they called Murray stepped forward and handed Mendez a paper. "Also in Sedona. President Criten is staying at Los Robles Resort and Villas. He checked in last night."

"Well, well. Looks like a party." Mendez handed the paper to Rafe's father.

"Can you tell where Danny is?" Rafe asked. He'd tried a couple of times over the last hour to find Cara's stepbrother, but his senses had only given him the same big nothing.

"Just within a certain square-mile range." Weatherly pulled up a map on his laptop and pointed. "It's a pretty big chunk of area."

"We could take some men and split up the grid," Rafe said. "We'd find him faster with more feet on the ground."

Mendez's mouth thinned. "Maybe you should leave this to us, son." Distrust came off him in waves.

The universe confirmed it for him with one glance in the team leader's eyes. *He doesn't want you anywhere near this op. He thinks you're reckless and dangerous.*

Well, maybe he was both those things, or had been. But not today. There was too much riding on this one.

"I know you don't trust me much," Rafe said. "And I might not trust me either, not after what happened. But I've been working in bail enforcement for over five years now, and my record is solid. You can't afford *not* to take me."

Mendez leaned in. "Wanna bet?"

"Rigo." Rafe's father spoke quietly, but the word might as well have been a shout in the now silent room. "He will be an asset."

Mendez gave a short nod, but he didn't seem convinced. "If you say so."

"I do." John looked over the rest of the group. "We'll go in pairs to cover more ground."

"I'm going." Rafe's mother stepped forward. "You may need me, John."

For the stone.

Rafe didn't know if his father heard the mental message she sent to them or if he just trusted his wife, but John nodded and said, "You'll be with me, Maria."

"I'll go with Rafe," Darius said, drawing surprised glances. He bared his teeth in a sardonic smile. "I want baby brother where I can see him."

"Nice," Rafe said. He threw sarcasm behind the word, but only to hide his startled pleasure. Either Darius had truly forgiven him, or he really did want to keep an eye on him. Maybe even both. But either was preferable to the way things had been before.

"I thought I would go with Rafe," Cara said.

"No," Rafe said. "I want you to stay here, where it's safe."

"But—"

"He's right, Cara," John said. "We're all trained for this sort of thing. You're not. I think you should stay here."

"I'll leave a couple of men behind," Mendez said. "Weatherly and Murray, you run the base here and stay with the women."

"Yes, sir," both men answered.

"What do you mean *women*?" Tessa asked. "I'm going with you."

Mendez frowned. "I know you're very capable, young lady, but we have enough people to run the search. Three teams—"

"Four," Adrian corrected. "I'm going, too."

Mendez's frown deepened. "And you are?"

"Adrian Gray. I've got training that will be useful."

"He's right," Rafe said. "We can use him."

"He got through my security like it was nothing." Rafe's father scowled at Gray, but he couldn't hide the hint of admiration beneath the annoyance. "We should take him."

"Then I'm going with *him*," Tessa said. "If he's such a bad-ass, I should be perfectly safe." *And I can keep an eye on this guy. I don't trust him.*

Gray sent her a look of amusement, letting everyone know that he, too, had heard the telepathic part of Tessa's remarks.

"Fine." Mendez shook his head. "Big show for one small-time punk, but if he leads us to the shooter, let's do it. Harmon, you're with me," Mendez continued. "Weatherly, assign everyone an area."

"Yes, sir."

. . . . .

While Weatherly printed off maps and Maria made coffee, Cara leaned over and whispered to Rafe, "Can I talk to you for a minute? Alone?"

"Sure." He glanced around, then stood up as she did. "We'll be right back," he said to his father, who waved as he listened to whatever Mendez was telling him.

Rafe took her hand and led the way out of the dining room, through the kitchen and out onto the patio. A wrought iron table and chairs complemented the tile work, and flowers surrounded them, some in planters and boxes and others in beds. Before them stretched a huge, natural rock swimming pool. Tall trees surrounded them, but the house stood high enough on the mountain to see the stunning red rock formations in the distance. He never got tired of looking at that view. He hadn't realized how much he'd missed it living in Vegas.

"If this was my house," she murmured, "I'd eat breakfast out here every morning. The sunrise must be amazing."

"It is. But you didn't pull me out here to talk about the scenery."

"No." She turned her gaze from the view and looked at him. "When all this started, it was just you and me looking for Danny. Now we have a SWAT team, and your family and Adrian Gray, a guy I don't know if we can trust a hundred percent. I'm worried."

"Mendez's men aren't SWAT."

"I know, I know. But they're a special team, right? The one you wanted to join?"

He gave a short nod. "Yeah."

"So we have a special troubleshooting team—men with guns. And Adrian Gray. We don't even know if he's one of the good guys."

"For now he is."

"He may be after the stone."

"It's possible."

"I don't want Danny hurt. You can take your stone back—"

"It's not *my* stone."

"—and you can even take Danny into custody. I just want

him to be okay." She stepped closer and locked her gaze with his. "I want to be there when you bring him in."

"No. It's too dangerous."

"I need to see him, to talk to him."

"You can do that, but after he's safely in custody."

"He won't hurt me."

Her plaintive tone struck a nerve. "Cara, you have a blind spot about this guy. He's taking advantage of you, and it ticks me off."

"You've said that before." She turned away, folding her arms, and stared at the mesas in the distance. "I'm not stupid. I know I let Danny get away with too much. But what am I supposed to do?"

"Say no once in a while."

"Easy for you to say."

"Easy for you, too. One simple word."

She bent her head. "I'm all he's got." *And he's all I've got.*

He heard the thought as it drifted through her mind, and it made him ache. He came to her and rested his hands on her shoulders. "He needs to learn how to solve his own problems, and he can't do that with you wiping his butt all the time."

She spun to face him, her mouth falling open. "I do not—"

"You keep riding to his rescue."

"Because he needs help."

"Sometimes the best help you can give is to let someone fall so they learn to get back up again."

"Tough love and all that?"

"Yeah. So no, you can't come along."

"Fine." She laid her hand on his chest, right on top of the crystal, and stared into his eyes, her own intense. "Promise me you'll look out for him. Don't let them shoot him."

"Nobody wants that. But if he starts shooting first—"

She gave a shaky laugh. "Danny hates guns. Won't touch them."

"Then everything should be fine."

"Promise me anyway."

"I promise."

"Okay." She let out a slow breath. "Thank you."

He laid a hand over hers, and the crystal beneath started to warm. *His mate.* All she had to do was come near him for fireworks to happen. When she was close, he could think of nothing but her.

And that could get us both killed.

Which was why he had to let her go. As much as he longed for exactly what she represented—a partner, a home, the possibility of a family—he couldn't let her take the chance. Sure, she had seen the Hunter, but what if he had to fight, to kill, and she got caught in the crossfire?

"You must be pretty happy," he said. "It's almost over. You'll be able to go home soon. Get back to your life."

"What?" She looked as if she'd been smacked. "What are you saying, Rafe? What about us?"

He forced himself to keep the casual tone. "That was the deal, right? We rip up the sheets for a while until one of us decides it's time to end it."

"Is that what you're doing by leaving me behind?" She stepped back from him, dropping her hand so they no longer touched. "Have you decided to end things? *Now?*"

"Maybe it's time." He didn't step toward her, made no move to touch her again—and it was the hardest thing he'd ever done. "I have to take your brother back to Vegas. I just figured you wouldn't want to be sleeping with the guy who's going to turn Danny in."

"What about what you said the other night . . . about me being inside you? All that poetic, passionate talk?" Her voice broke, her eyes shimmering. "Was that all to keep me in bed with you?"

"No, of course not." He forced a smile. "I'm really fond of you, Cara. We had a great time together, and I'm more than willing to keep going until you fly back home." He slid his gaze down her body as if she were a prime cut of meat. "You are seriously hot, and I want nothing more than to keep you in my bed. But your life is on the other side of the country, and mine is here."

"What if I decided to move?" She jutted her chin at him, still fighting. His little tigress. "I own my company. I write software for a living, for God's sake. I can work anywhere. And I may have lost the condo anyway. So, what if I came out here? Would you still want to end it?"

"You'd be willing to do that?" For a second he was tempted. They could give it a try. He could find a way to keep her safe.

"I would, if you give me a good reason to come."

He looked into her eyes, saw the hope and longing and, damn it, the love. He remembered the vision of her death that had haunted him until they'd survived the bomb. If just the vision had tormented him, what would he do if something happened to her for real?

He couldn't be that selfish, not until his powers were more under control. Maybe if he found other Seers, someone to learn from, he could master his abilities. Maybe then they could be together. But that was a long way off. Maybe years.

He studied her face, sketching every detail into his heart like scrimshaw. He couldn't ask her to wait for him, and he couldn't coax her to go home. His Cara was loving enough to want to be with him and help him while he learned and stubborn enough to resist any suggestion to go where she'd be safer. Therefore, it had to be her idea to leave.

"Rafe? Are you going to answer me?"

He shook his head, played the part. "Sorry, babe, I was thinking."

"It took that long for you to think about this?" Her incredulity raked across his raw emotions, drawing blood.

"Rafe." Darius called out to him from the doorway. "We're moving out."

"Okay." Rafe dropped a kiss on Cara's head. "You stay here with the security guys. We'll bring Danny home soon." He turned and headed for the house.

"Rafe!" When he glanced back, she said, "So that's it? We're done?"

He shrugged. "I'm game for another ride, but we have to say good-bye some time."

He turned his back and jogged toward the house, quickly enough to escape her whispered reply, but not fast enough to escape the words as they slipped into his mind. *Wrong answer.*

His heart cracked, but he held it together. It was better this way. *She* would be better this way—home, safe, and far from him.

He reached Darius, who didn't move out of the doorway. "What the hell are you doing?" his brother muttered.

"Nothing."

Darius narrowed his eyes and glanced from Cara back to Rafe before moving to let his brother through. "You're an ass."

"Yeah," Rafe said. "I know."

. . . . .

Cara stood on the patio and stared at the stunning landscape without really seeing it, a throbbing ache where her heart used to be. What had she expected? Rafe tended to slip away before things got too serious, and now he'd done exactly that. She'd thought she could change him. She'd imagined she could make him believe again.

She lifted her head and focused on the mesas, blinking back the sting of tears. He hadn't exactly kicked her to the curb, after all. He was still interested in a sexual relationship, but nothing more than that. And that wasn't enough for her anymore. Heck, it never had been, but she'd deluded herself into thinking it was, just to be with him.

Which was worse? The lies Warren had told her to weasel his way into the company, or the painful honesty Rafe offered, which fell so short of what she wanted?

Her cell phone rang, vibrating in her pocket. She jumped at the sound, then slid the device out and glanced at the number. Warren. Without a second thought, she clicked the IGNORE button and slid the phone back in her pocket. Warren and his manipulations seemed very far away and unimportant now. Maybe they always had been, but she simply hadn't realized it. She would deal with him when she got back to Jersey.

Her phone rang a second time. Muttering, she took it out of her pocket again. Her thumb hovered over the IGNORE button until she realized this was not a New Jersey number. It was a Nevada number. Danny?

She picked up the call. "Hello?"

"Cara, hey, it's me." Danny's voice swept through her, a soothing balm to the sting of Rafe's lack of commitment. "Listen, change of plans. I need you to cancel that money transfer you sent to Benediction. I can't pick it up, so I need you to send it to Flagstaff instead."

Her relief at hearing his voice evaporated as the meaning of the words sank in. "Danny, what are you talking about? What wire transfer?"

"The one we talked about last night. Listen, I know I've

borrowed a lot of money from you already, but this is life and death—"

"Danny, I didn't talk to you last night. I lost my cell phone and only got it back this morning."

He gave a rough laugh. "Come on, Sis, this is no time for jokes. I know your voice. You agreed to send me twenty-five hundred dollars."

"I'm not joking." Her stomach lurched, and she forced herself to overcome the urge to panic and speak calmly. "Listen to me, Danny. There are some very bad people after you."

"Yeah, I know. I owe this guy some money. But I've got that all worked out. I can pay him back and you, too—"

"No, these people are not from your bookie. They want the stone."

She could practically hear his panic in the pause that followed. In the forced normalcy he tried to inject into his voice. "What are you talking about, Cara? What stone? These are Tornatelli's guys."

"No, they're not. Danny, you know I love you, right?"

"Yeah, yeah, sure. I love you, too."

"I'm telling you this to save your life because I love you. The people chasing you are after that stone you took from Bartow's safe. I can help you, but only if you trust me."

"Aw, come on, Cara."

She heard a sound behind her and turned to see Murray in the doorway. He gave her a hand signal to indicate she should keep Danny talking. Obviously they were tracing the call. She nodded.

"This is it, Cara," Danny was saying. "This is the big score. Bartow really screwed me over by having me arrested for a little joyride, so I figured he owed me, you know?"

Damn it. She squeezed her eyes shut. When had Danny become someone who disregarded the law for his own selfish purposes? Had she had a hand in that by bailing him out so many times, by not letting him take the consequences of his irresponsible actions?

"This thing is going to fix all that," Danny said. "And I'm going to pay you back every dime I owe you, Cara, with interest. You can buy one of those big houses in Bergen County, way nicer than that condo."

"I appreciate the thought, Danny. I really do." She didn't mention the condo, afraid her anger about it would come through. "But these men are dangerous. They've already killed Artie Bartow."

"Bartow's dead?"

"Yes. Now listen to me. I can help you, but you have to trust me."

"I don't know. Maybe I should keep moving. Bartow's dead. Holy crap." Agitation edged his voice.

"Danny, there's a reward for the return of the stone." She winced as she lied, but she knew him like no one else. He was about to run, and she didn't know if she would ever find him if he did.

"A reward?" The panic still lingered, but interest edged his tone.

"Yes. You know John Montana?"

"The millionaire? Yeah, sure."

"Well, that stone is a family heirloom that was stolen years ago. He's offered a reward for its return. You could claim that, Danny."

"Seriously? How much of a reward?"

"A quarter of a million dollars." She crossed her fingers as she named the dazzling figure. "And since the stone was stolen to begin with, I bet there would be no charges against you."

"Yeah. Yeah." She could practically hear him thinking. "I would be like a recovery expert or something. An innocent bystander."

"Exactly."

"So how would I do this? Claim the reward, I mean."

"Well, I'm at John Montana's house in Sedona," she said.

"His house? Seriously? How'd that happen?"

"I met his son in Vegas. It's a long story."

"Wow, Cara. A millionaire's son? Way to go, Sis."

She shook her head at the admiration in his voice. "Tell me where you are, Danny. I could send one of his security staff to pick you up. This guy has personal jets and helicopters, the works. His guy could bring you back here to the estate."

"An estate, huh?"

"Yeah."

"It must be really slick."

"It's gorgeous. You should see the pool."

He went silent for a moment, then said, "So they wouldn't press charges? And I'd get the reward?"

"Yes." She gripped the phone hard, willing him to agree.

"You know I skipped bail, Cara."

"I know."

"I guess I'd have to go back to Vegas and take care of that, huh?"

"Yes. But with all that money, you'd be able to hire a really good defense lawyer."

"Yeah, and maybe Montana would be so grateful to me that he'd help me out with that, right?"

"I don't know if he'd pay for a lawyer for you, Danny—"

"No, no. I could handle that part if I have this reward money. But maybe he could give me the name of a good one, you know?"

Her heart nearly leaped from her chest at his reasonable

tone, his responsible thinking. "I think he would be happy to recommend someone, Danny."

"And he's a good guy?"

"Yes, John Montana is a really good guy."

"And what about his son? What's up with you two?"

"I'll tell you about it when I see you."

"Yeah, I want the story on that. I don't want to see you screwed over again like that jerk Warren did to you."

She laughed, part relief and part pain. "We'll talk."

"Yeah, okay. So you won't believe this, Sis, but I'm in Sedona, too."

"No way!"

"Way. But I know how smart you are, and I bet you knew that already."

"Okay, you got me. I knew you were close. But Danny, those bad guys really are after you, and they will kill to get the stone. I don't want that to happen. I can't lose you, Boo." Her voice trembled on his childhood nickname.

"Yeah, I'm not crazy about getting dead, either. The reward deal sounds a lot easier than trying to sell this rock."

"Tell me where you are," she said, "and I'll send someone to get you."

He rattled off the details, then said, "I can't wait to see you, Sis. I missed you."

"Missed you, too. See you soon." She ended the call, then swiped away the tears streaming down her cheeks before heading back into the house.

Danny was finally coming home.

. . . . .

Danny ended the call and stared at his phone for a minute. Was he a sucker for giving up the big dream for a sure thing? Once upon a time he would have thought exactly that, but now it seemed smarter to turn over the ruby, take the reward money from John Montana, and go back to Vegas to face the music. He was getting too old to keep chasing a dream that seemed impossible to grasp. He needed to make a change, and this seemed like the perfect time.

His phone dinged and he looked at the text message Cara had sent him. *Black SUV license plate MNTNS-5. Guy's name is Murray.*

Okay, that was his ride. He got off the outside bench where he'd called Cara and turned to go back into the tour center to cancel his Grand Canyon reservation.

"Danny Cangialosi?" Two guys in suits blocked his path. He looked from one to the other. They were both dark-haired, dark-eyed, and built like tanker trucks.

"Sorry, no." He tried to step around them.

One grabbed his arm and snatched the cell phone out of his hand.

"Hey!" Danny jumped for the phone, but the second guy yanked him back.

First Guy brought up the text message. "They're coming for him. Black SUV."

"Where are they meeting you?" Second Guy shook him. "Talk."

"Get the hell off me." Danny struggled, but the guy had a grip like a vise.

"Hold him." First Guy shoved Danny's phone in his pocket as Second Guy jerked his arms behind his back. First Guy did a quick pat-down, then gave a satisfied grunt as he discovered the stone in Danny's sweatshirt pocket. "Got it."

"Hey, that's mine!" Danny fought harder to get free.

"Is it, Mr. Cangialosi?" A third man stepped into view,

blond with a thousand-dollar suit and a politician's smile. "Is it truly?"

"Who the hell are you?" Danny demanded, fear curling in his gut at the look in the newcomer's crazy green eyes.

"My name is Jain Criten." First Guy handed the ruby to Criten, who smiled as he studied it in his gloved hand. Who the hell wore gloves in the desert at this time of year? "Normally we would kill you where you stand, Mr. Cangialosi, but luckily for you, we need you breathing for a while yet." He glanced at First Guy. "Do it." He turned away and headed toward a sleek town car parked nearby.

First Guy locked eyes with Danny. "You will take us to Cara McGaffigan."

Danny blinked and shook his head. Dizzy. Must be stress. Or the heat.

"Where are you taking us, Danny?" a voice asked.

He glanced up at the big man in front of him. "To see Cara. Isn't that what you wanted?"

The guy smiled and nodded. "Exactly so."

CHAPTER TWENTY-THREE

As soon as Mendez radioed them that Danny was coming in, Darius pulled into a shopping center parking lot to make a U-turn. Rafe had expected to drive, but his brother had made the argument that he'd be of more use driving in the search than riding shotgun. And given Dar's specially outfitted van with its hand controls on the steering wheel, Rafe couldn't argue. Rafe could run if needed, and Dar could drive. Worked out for all of them, provided his moody brother didn't decide to leave Rafe stranded somewhere just for kicks.

Rafe's cell phone rang just as they were pulling out into traffic. "Hello?"

"Rafe, it's me." Just the sound of Cara's voice made his pulse skip a beat. "Danny just called me."

He ignored the pang in his chest and focused on business. "Yeah, Mendez just radioed us. Said Murray went to pick him up and bring him back to the house."

"That's right."

"Good work, Cara. How'd you get him to come in?"

She cleared her throat. "Um . . . I told him there was a reward for the stone and that no one would press charges." Her voice roughened. "I hated lying to him, but I was worried he would run again."

He wished he were there to hold her. "How much of a reward?"

"A quarter of a million."

"Wow. No wonder he's coming in."

"I know, I know. But I didn't know what else to do." *What to do about us, either.* He picked up the thought in her mind, though he doubted she was aware of it.

This is for the best, he reminded himself. "Sounds like you did just fine."

"I just hate lying. I hate manipulating him. It's not my style."

"I know." His voice softened despite his determination to push her away. "This was one time where Danny really did need you to save him, Cara, and you did it."

She let out a long, soft sigh. "Thanks. It helps that you said that."

"Listen, all the search teams are heading back. We'll get this all squared away, and then we can all get back to our normal lives."

"Yeah." The word caught, and she cleared her throat. "That will be good. See you later."

"See you." But the call ended before the words left his lips. He looked at the phone, watching as the call info disappeared and went back to the date and time display.

"You're breaking her heart, you know," Darius said.

"I know."

"She's the best thing that ever happened to you."

"I know. But she's better off without me."

"Maybe." Darius shrugged, his gaze on the road. "But if you're stupid enough to let her go, I guess we'll never know."

"Guess I'm not as smart as I should be."

"I usually love it when I'm right." Darius turned the van toward home. "But not this time."

. . . . .

"They're here." Weatherly looked away from the video monitors and smiled at Cara. "Let's go meet them at the door."

As soon as the words were out of his mouth, Cara turned and raced for the front door. Everything with Rafe had fallen apart, but if she could help Danny out of this jam, then everything else would work out okay. She had to hang on to that.

It was all she had left.

She flung open the front door as the SUV stopped in front of the house. Men got out of the car—more than there should be. Murray, Danny, two men in dark suits and a third man, blond and smiling with black gloves on a warm day.

"Ms. McGaffigan," the blond man called out. "At last we meet. I'm Jain Criten." He signaled to one of the dark-suited men, who took her brother's arm and led him toward the door. The other turned to Murray, pointed a gun, and shot the security man point-blank in the head.

A scream rose up in her throat as Murray crumpled. She clamped both hands over her mouth, folding into herself as bile leaped into her throat. He'd killed him. Sweet, geeky Murray. Just killed him. Just like that. As if Murray were nothing.

Weatherly came up behind her. "What—"

She shoved him away before he could be seen. "Run! They killed Murray. Call for help. Go!"

Weatherly pulled his gun. "I'm not leaving you."

"Go. Please!"

"Now, now, Ms. McGaffigan." Criten signaled to the guard behind him. The man charged into the house, shoving Cara aside and disarming Weatherly before she could blink.

"Please don't kill him." She turned pleading eyes to Criten as he reached the doorway. "Please."

"How sweet." Criten tilted his head. "Gadi, let him live for now. He might be of use."

Gadi nodded and stared into Weatherly's eyes. "You work for President Criten now. You will obey his orders without question."

"I work for President Criten now," Weatherly repeated. He nodded at Criten. "Sir, how may I be of assistance?"

"Stand guard here at the door. If anyone tries to come in, kill them."

"Yes, sir." Gadi handed back Weatherly's weapon, and he immediately took a position at the door.

"And you, Ms. McGaffigan." Criten turned his eerie green eyes on her. "You will take me to the family *tenplu*. To the vault that holds the treasures of Atlantis."

She opted for ignorance. "I'm not sure what you're talking about."

"Stop with the games. Or Danny here will die."

Cara glanced at her stepbrother. He just smiled at her, a goofy grin she knew so well, clearly under the same kind of mind control she'd experienced herself. "Hey, Sis," he said.

He sounded so normal, except for the dazed look on his face. She swallowed past the bitterness in her throat. "Hey, Danny," she managed, then looked at Criten. "I think what you want is upstairs."

Criten swept a gloved hand toward the stairs. "Lead the way."

She turned toward the staircase and started upward, sending one, desperate heartfelt thought out into the universe. *Rafe, it's a trap. Stay away.*

·　·　·　·　·

Rafe, it's a trap. Stay away.

Cara's voice echoed loud and panicked in Rafe's mind. He frowned. *Where is Cara?*

He could see her at home, going up the stairs. Danny was there. And other people, but he couldn't get a fix on them. And she was terrified.

"Something's wrong," Darius said.

"There are people at the house. I can't see them."

"Criten?"

"I don't know, but Danny's there, too."

Tessa's voice sounded in his mind. *Rafe, something's wrong. Cara's in danger.*

I know. She reached me.

Has to be Criten. Adrian's mind voice sounded strong and in control. *What's the plan?*

Rafael. His mother slipped into his thoughts. *Your father says for all of us to meet at the old mine. He'll explain when we get there.*

"Dad wants us to meet at the old mine," Rafe told Darius.

"I heard. Listen, these men that are with Cara . . . one of them is borderline crazy. Obsessed or something. I felt it even this far away, and then it just cut off, like a switch."

"Thanks, Dar. Just what I needed to hear." Rafe reached for the Hunter. His crystal responded as quickly as before, fully charged with a bright, vibrant energy that made the hair on his arms stand up.

"Don't amp up too fast," Darius said. "You're a little too close for comfort."

"It's okay, Dar." Rafe thought of Cara, reached for her. Stopped.

"Not to harp on ancient history," Darius said, "but the last time you powered up around me, it put me in the hospital."

The words sliced like a dagger through an old wound. "What choice do I have?" Rafe demanded. "I get that you still don't trust me. Sorry. But someone has Cara. Do you expect me to sit this one out?"

"No."

"Good. Because you would be disappointed."

"I figured."

They didn't say anything else until they arrived at the old mine. Everyone else was there already except Tessa and Gray, who showed up as Darius and Rafe were climbing out of Dar's van.

"It has to be Criten," Rafe said as everyone gathered outside the blocked entrance to the old mine. "Dar could feel him."

"Just for a second," Darius said. "The guy's nuts."

"Obsessed," Gray corrected. "He lives and breathes *Mendeku.*"

"What the hell does that mean?" Mendez demanded. "My men are in there, too."

"Blood vengeance," Maria said. "He hates our family."

"So this is definitely the guy who hired the shooter?"

"Most probably," John said. "Rigo, I trust you and Lee here to keep what you're about to see to yourselves." Both men nodded, faces grim.

"Why are we here?" Rafe asked. "Cara's in the house with this maniac, and I've got to get there."

"He'll be expecting us to come in the front door," his father said.

"Well, yeah," Darius said. "How else do we get in the house?"

Their father indicated the entrance to the mine. "Right here. With your mother so worried about the people hunting her family, you don't think I would build a house without an escape route, do you?"

Mendez slowly smiled. "You built a secret tunnel?"

"You bet I did. And this is how we're going to get into the house and take these guys by surprise."

Rafe grinned. "Dad, you're brilliant."

"Why, thank you." John smiled and swept a hand toward the mine entrance. "Let's go. The secure door is just a short way down the passage. It's all been reinforced, so don't worry about cave-ins."

As Mendez and Harmon led the way into the mine, Rafe's mother came up to his dad and gave him a big kiss. "I'd forgotten about this. Thank you, darling."

"Anything for you, my love."

The *tenplu* was on the third floor. Cara stepped inside, scanning the room. It had to be the oddest place she had ever seen. To the left was a door to what looked like a rooftop garden. For an instant she considered running for it, but even if she could somehow get through it, where would she go? The roof was a dead end.

The rest of the room had a massive pit of sand stretched along the length of it, like a piece of the desert indoors. Short stone pillars stood in a semicircle, different-colored gems gleaming from each of them in the sunlight that streamed in through the glass roof. Plants thrived all around the room. On the other side, a heavy vault was built into the wall.

"How quaint." Criten looked around with a smirk. "A monument to our lost culture. And there lies the vault that holds the lost treasures of Atlantis. I find it hard to believe the Seers were so foolish as to leave it unguarded."

"Allow me, Your Excellency," said the man who'd killed Murray. At Criten's nod, he stepped into the sandpit. He'd gone two steps before a loud hum rose from the pillars. The stones glowed in a rainbow of hues. Power surged from one to another in a visible arc, met at the center, and blasted as a single stream into the bodyguard. He went flying from the pit and lay crumpled on the ground, motionless.

"What?" Criten surged forward but stopped short of stepping in the sand. "An Agrippa Boundary? No one has seen one of those for centuries."

Criten reached into his pants pocket and pulled out a pyramid-shaped gem. It glowed blood red in the sunlight against his black glove, and Cara swore she could see patterns swirling in it like fluorescent dandelion seeds. It seemed to vibrate.

"I underestimated these Seers," Criten murmured. "They have technology long forgotten by my people. The stone senses it. But no matter. The key to an Agrippa Boundary is the right energy." He turned his cold green stare on Cara. "You will attempt the crossing."

"I can't do that!" Her mouth went dry, and she held up her hands in protest. "I'm not like you guys. I'm just a normal person."

"You will try, or Danny dies."

"Okay, okay, hold it." She lowered her hands and considered the sand, her mind racing. "Let's say I make it to the other side. What then? I can't open the vault."

"I think you can." He gave her a slow, terrible smile that made her stomach sink. "Go."

"But—"

Criten nodded at Danny in the grip of the remaining bodyguard. "Gadi, kill him if she fails."

Gadi caught Danny with an arm around his throat. He whipped out a handgun and held it to Danny's temple.

Cara sucked in a breath, her knees going wobbly as she fixed her gaze on the weapon. One wrong move, one wrong *breath*, and they would snuff out Danny's life in a single shot. Just like Murray.

Her heart pounded so hard she could barely breathe. She

turned her gaze to Criten, struggling to keep her expression calm. "Wouldn't it be easier to just hold us hostage in exchange for whatever it is that you want?"

"What I want? I already have the prize." Criten held up the stone. "Thousands of years we have been searching for this. And now it is mine."

"If you've got what you want, then why not leave now, before they catch you?"

"Because it's not enough." Criten approached her, his steps graceful, his body swaying as he tilted his head at her. "I want what's inside that vault, and I want the Seers dead. Only then will my mission be complete." He shoved her into the sandpit with a hand to the chest.

She screamed as she stumbled backward onto the sand, then froze, bracing herself for laser beams or whatever. But nothing happened.

"As I suspected," Criten said, his fingers clenching around the stone. "You mated with that mongrel Seer, didn't you? His energy is all over you. The boundary recognizes you as one of them." He narrowed his eyes. "Now go open the vault, and maybe your stepbrother gets to live."

Her spit dried up at that look. He intended to kill her. Probably Danny, too, when they no longer needed him. She was no match for the two of them, she had no weapons and Danny was in la-la land. All she could do was drag things out long enough for Rafe to find them.

She turned to face the vault and started forward. She could see from here there was a keypad and a hand scanner of some kind. How the heck was she supposed to get past that? She passed the stone pillars without incident and reached the other side. Now that she was closer, she spotted the eye scanner, too. All John Montana's best toys. Dandy.

She glanced back at Criten. He watched her with an obsessive intensity that made her hair stand on end. He waved her onward. After one quick glance at Danny to reassure herself, she walked up to the vault and studied the security devices.

"Open it!" Criten barked.

She was going to die. There was no way she could open this door, no way she could save Danny or herself. But she could buy some time. Maybe Rafe had gotten her message. Maybe Tessa had seen something wrong or Darius had felt her terror. Maybe Mendez had gotten suspicious when Murray didn't answer the radio.

Maybe, maybe, maybe. No guarantees, just like life.

She inhaled deeply to calm her thundering heart. She should have argued with Rafe's decision to end their affair. Fought for him. God knew she loved him enough.

Stalling for time, she let out a long, slow exhale, then punched the digits of her birthday into the keypad with trembling fingers. She put her hand in the hand thing and looked into the eye thing.

The lock clicked, and she jumped.

"I knew it!" Criten crowed. "I knew you would be the one to open the door!"

Cara took the handle and started to pull the heavy door open. After just a few inches, she stopped, her eyes widening as she glimpsed what was in the vault.

"Hi," Rafe said. His blue eyes had turned nearly all black, his face the hard, edgy mask of the Hunter. "You're going to want to get out of the way."

She stepped back, and he exploded from the vault, racing across the sand for Criten. Adrian Gray surged out behind him, Mendez and Harmon hard on his heels, weapons drawn and aimed across the room. The rest of Rafe's family poured from the vault.

Cara fixed on the weapons. "Wait!" she shouted. "He's got a gun! He's going to kill Danny!"

Too late. Adrian charged forward at the same time Mendez and Harmon fired at Criten and his goon. The bullets stopped halfway across the pit, as if they had lost all momentum, then dropped harmlessly into the sand. Seconds later the crystals on the pillars hummed, and energy darted from column to column, forming a wall of power that shot forth, slamming into Adrian's chest and flinging him backward to the edge of the sand. He gasped for breath and struggled to sit up, then fell back. Tessa flew to his side, casting an urgent look at Cara. Grasping him under the arms, she and Cara dragged him out of the pit to safety near the vault door.

Cara swung to Mendez. "They've got a gun to my brother's head, damn it!"

Criten's laughter carried to them across the room.

．　．　．　．　．

Rafe got to Criten in seconds, the bloodlust of the Hunter flowing through his veins. He'd opened it up as much as he could without losing control. He reached Criten and punched him in the face.

The instant his fist connected, the power of the Hunter drained from him, cutting off like a plug pulled from the outlet. Criten still fell backward. His lip still split open. But Rafe stood stripped of his power, just a man. He reached for the Hunter again. No response.

Criten got to his feet, a crafty smile curling his mangled lip.

Superpowers were gone. No more Hunter. And Criten knew it. But Rafe still had his fists and years of experience chasing scumbags. And if that's what it took to stop this nutcase, so be it.

"Problem, Seer?" Criten swiped his bloody lip with his thumb and held up his other hand. A ruby-red pyramid sparkled in the sunlight. Criten grinned and licked the blood off his thumb.

"Won't be once I beat the crap out of you."

Rafe grabbed the wrist of the hand holding the stone and twisted as hard as he could. Criten howled in pain, his fingers springing open. The stone went flying and hit Danny in the chest before clattering to the floor. Rafe nailed Criten with a blow to the jaw and another to the cheek. The president fell backward, but then stopped, floating in midair. Smiling, Criten straightened as if by invisible strings, raising glowing red hands that sparked like live wires.

"Thank you for that. The stone was suppressing my abilities. But not anymore." He fired a burst of red energy toward Rafe. "The vortex . . . such a rush!"

Rafe braced himself to be hit with a blast, but instead flames burst up without any tinder, encircling him, consuming the very air around him. His breathing seized as the oxygen bled away. He could see Criten's grin on the other side of the wall of fire.

He struggled to understand. Atlanteans couldn't use their powers on one another directly. But indirectly . . . setting fire to particles in the *air* instead of Rafe himself . . .

He reached for the Hunter again. This time his focus stone heated as expected, pulling power for his use, thinning the force of the flames. His breathing eased.

"Now, now," Criten said. "None of that." He stretched out his hand and snapped his fingers closed into a fist.

Rafe's crystal cooled as quickly as it had heated, his power draining into the wall of flames, flaring them higher and hotter. *Impossible.*

Criten laughed, his hands glowing red, his eyes impossibly green. "I'm a Channeler, you fool. We command the energies of this earth!"

Rafe struggled for breath. He could not let this madman kill everyone he loved. His parents. His siblings. Cara . . .

He couldn't let that happen. No matter what it took.

. . . . .

Criten was killing him.

Cara charged across the sandpit, ignoring the shouted warnings of Darius and Rafe's parents. She could see Rafe's face through the wall of fire, see him trying to gulp air, his throat working.

She launched herself at Criten, ducking under the red glow of his hands and tackling him around the waist just like Danny had taught her during his football phase. Criten went down, his power shooting toward the ceiling, his curses ringing in her ears.

A bellow of rage echoed through the room. She glanced up to see Gadi turning his gun on her. She caught a glimpse of Danny's face—the alarm, the awareness—before he knocked the bodyguard's arm to the side. She dove to the ground as the gun fired. The bullet pinged off a planter, shattering it. She chanced a look back just as Gadi backhanded her stepbrother, sending him flying across the room. Danny slammed into the wall with a horrible thud and slid to the ground, motionless. Cara scrambled to her feet, ready to defend herself against Gadi, Criten, whomever.

But Gadi had stopped. He stood staring across the sand, his face white, his eyes wide with terror. His whole body shook, and he dropped the gun, clamping his hands over his ears and whimpering like a child lost in the dark.

Cara followed his gaze across the pit . . . to Darius.

Rafe's brother stared at Gadi, unblinking, his focus unnerving in its intensity. She had no idea what he was doing, but she could sense he had somehow taken Gadi out of the mix.

Criten stirred behind her, and Cara glanced at Rafe, imprisoned in a box of fire. She had to get him out of there before Criten got his bearings back. Running to the sandpit, she scooped up sand in her cupped hands and ran back to throw it on the flames.

The sand hissed and sizzled as it hit the fire, but it did nothing to douse the flames by so much as a flicker.

Don't let him win, Rafe, she whispered in her mind. *Fight! Do whatever it takes, but don't let Criten win.*

. . . . .

Don't let him win.

Rafe seized on Cara's mental whisper, clinging to it. He wouldn't go out like this. His stone was ice cold, but still he tried to run power through it, jump-start it. He searched for the Hunter. For something . . . *anything* that could free him. And touched . . . a mating bond.

Where everything else had been taken from him, the mating bond shone silver in his mind, glimmering, entrancing, leading him straight to Cara. Leading him home.

He remembered the first time he'd seen her, in the vision at Sal's. *Come with me. Let me make you whole.*

He reached for the mating bond and, through the flames, saw Cara's eyes widen as she felt it. Then she smiled as she gave him full access to everything she had.

Power surged into him, his crystal flaring with dazzling strength, feeding his body a steady stream of white-hot energy fueled by his bond with Cara. Sounds sharpened around him, smells. Smoke from the flames, his own sweat. He saw his parents running across the boundary, his mother running to Danny's crumpled form, his father pointing a gun at Criten.

Criten laughed and with a wave of his hand, turned the gun

into a bouquet of flowers before flicking his father aside like a toy with a surge of power.

Criten turned toward Cara, his hands glowing red as blood.

Rafe opened to the Hunter almost all the way, holding on just enough to keep himself in the picture, and leaped at the wall of fire.

Only to bounce back, his hair singed and his skin stinging, his lungs about to burst as the oxygen burned away. *I'm not strong enough.*

Cara's voice slipped into his mind. *We need the Hunter* now, *Rafe.*

He could see her, backing away from Criten. *It's too dangerous. I can't control it.*

Trust yourself, Rafe. We need you. Take what I have and use it to kick this jerk's ass!

The surge of energy and love that flooded to him through the mating bond nearly buckled his knees with the force of its power. Did he really have a choice? The Hunter was the only thing that might stop Criten, might save his family.

Or kill all of them.

Now you decide to be all cautious? Darius's sardonic tones flooded his mind, and he could see his brother on the other side of the flames, having crossed the boundary to stand over the weeping Gadi. *I can't hold this bodyguard forever. If you're going to do it, now's the time, bro.*

Rafe bowed his head. No choice at all. Clenching his trembling hands into fists, he closed his eyes and opened up completely to the Hunter.

．　．　．　．　．

Criten came after Cara. He threw some kind of energy balls, one after the other, spheres of red, angry power. She tried to dodge them. One struck her shoulder, burning through clothing and flesh like hot acid. She fell to her knees, gasping for breath, nearly blinded by the agony. She reached for the wound, touched it, and nearly blacked out.

"Cara!" Rafe's mother appeared at her side. "Stay down," she ordered, then faced Criten. She barked a word, something foreign and musical, and the Agrippa Boundary flared, sucking in Criten's energy balls as fast as he could throw them, disintegrating them.

"So," Criten snarled, lowering his still glowing hands. "The head bitch finally makes an appearance."

"You can leave now under your own power," Maria said, staring him down, "or you can leave with the coroner. Your choice."

"Someone will definitely die here," Criten said. "But it will be you, Seer. You and your spawn."

"Perhaps you should speak to my son about that," she said.

And Rafe leaped through the flames with a roar, flinging Criten across the room with one swing of his arm.

．　．　．　．　．

Rafe had become the Hunter. Cara blinked teary eyes and breathed slowly, trying to ignore the searing pain of her shoulder and arm. She recognized that impassive expression, the blackened irises she could see even from this distance. More than that, while he still pulled energy from her, his own had changed. The black and silver of the Hunter swept through her instead of the silver and blue of Rafe. She welcomed it. The impassive, unemotional warrior that was the Hunter helped her keep it together in the middle of what had become a battlefield.

"Oh, my," Maria murmured as the Hunter went after Criten. "Maybe this wasn't such a good idea."

"He won't hurt us," Cara said as Maria helped her to her feet.

Rafe's mother shook her head as she watched the entity that looked like her son pull Criten up by his shirt and pummel him with machinelike efficiency, before dropping Criten's groaning form to the ground. "You've never seen him like this, my dear. Last time—"

"Last time he was still a kid and still new to what he could do." Cara peeled back one side of what was left of her shirt and winced at the burned flesh of her shoulder. "And, yes, I have seen him like this. When his car exploded, he changed." She looked up and held Maria's gaze. "And he saved my life."

Maria gave a nod, but Cara could tell she wasn't quite convinced.

Cara looked over at Rafe. He stood over Criten's fallen, bleeding body, breathing hard. Their bond flickered for a moment. "He's weakening." She started for Rafe.

"Cara, no." Maria caught her uninjured arm. "Don't get too close. Wait until he changes back."

Cara shook her head. "He won't hurt me." She pulled her arm loose and headed across the room toward Rafe.

He seemed to sense her coming. This time that flat, black alien gaze didn't throw her. This was a part of Rafe. He'd saved her life. Again.

"Hey," she said as she reached him, then frowned as she noticed how he held his arms a little away from his body. "What happened to your hands?" She took them in hers, hissing in sympathy as she saw the burns on his palms.

He pulled his hands free, then frowned and pointed at her shoulder.

"Yeah, he got me, too." She laid her hand on his forearm. "Come see your mother. She's worried about you."

He looked past her, then back.

She urged him with a jerk of her head. "Come on. Come see your mom."

He didn't respond, just turned and headed toward Maria. Cara shook her head and followed. "We really have to work on communication," she mumbled.

They were halfway across the room when Maria screamed. Cara whirled to see Criten on unsteady legs, glaring at them with enough hate to set them on fire where they stood. Criten glanced over at Maria's flowers and jerked his hand. The birds of paradise popped off their stems and flew across the room toward them, glowing with red light as their spiky petals became razor sharp blades.

"Farewell, Seers," Criten gasped, sinking down to his knees.

Cara dodged to one side, then the other, but the swarm of blades changed directions with her. Her strength flagged. Her breaths came quick and fast. She stumbled.

Rafe stepped in front of her. His body jerked once, then again and again as the deadly blades found their target in his flesh. Someone screamed. He staggered.

The bond between them flickered again.

"Where . . . are you getting . . . this power?" Criten panted. He narrowed his eyes, focused on Cara. "Ah." He raised his hands.

Energy built up in the room like a static storm, making Cara's hair stand on end, pressing against her lungs and making it hard to breathe. A panel of glass shattered in the atrium roof, raining shards down on all of them. She hunched down and covered her head as splinters sliced at her exposed arms. People cried out. The power intensified with an audible, growing hum. She looked up, shaking off the glass bits. Criten had fixated on her, his entire form glowing demonic red. The energy writhed around him like snakes. His features twisted into a sneer, his eyes narrowed on her, gleaming with glee and pure, murderous menace.

She raised her chin and stared him down.

The bond with Rafe flickered, then kicked in at full force. Energy drained from her to him in one quick flood, leaving her empty and trembling. She whimpered and slumped to the floor as the pain in her shoulder roared to life again. In front of her, she saw Rafe straighten to his full height, flex his shoulders and charge at Criten. She wanted to shout a warning to him, but her vocal cords wouldn't work. She simply did not have the strength. She could only lie there, limp and fading, as Rafe used their combined life forces to slam his hand into Criten's chest, sending him flying across the room. Criten hit the wall with an audible crack. His smirk faded to stunned surprise as he slid like a broken doll to the ground.

Rafe turned toward her. Took one step. Another. Stumbled. Fell to his hands and knees. Tried to rise again . . . and keeled over like a felled tree.

She fought to stay conscious, to make sure he was all right, but this time her body won. Exhaustion hit her like an ocean wave. Reality faded to distant sounds and cloudy images.

Then, finally, to nothing at all.

CHAPTER TWENTY-FOUR

"Today, deadbeat dads. Is this one man the father of the children of these *six* women? Stay tuned after the commercial break."

Rafe winced at the overly loud commercial jingle that followed the words. Swallowing spitless in a desert-dry mouth, he forced his eyelids open, then groaned at the brightness of the room and shut them again.

"So, Sleeping Beauty awakes." Darius's voice had Rafe turning his head and squinting at his brother.

"What happened?" he managed.

"Well, first of all, let me express my delight that this time it was you who ended up in the hospital and not me." Darius grinned. "Payback and all that."

"Hospital?" The proof came at him in a rush: antiseptic smells, the beeping of medical machinery. The fact that his chest ached as if he'd hugged a hand grenade. That he wanted to sleep for a week. *Burnout.* "What happened to Criten? Is everyone okay?"

"Yeah, everyone's fine." Darius sat back with a creak of the plastic chair and turned down the sound on the TV with the remote. "You went all Roid Rage and kicked some Criten ass. No casualties, though Criten had to be taken out by ambulance. Apparently you fractured his neck, but it didn't kill the son of a bitch."

Rafe closed his eyes as relief swamped him. "How long?"

"How long have you been in the hospital? Two days."

Rafe licked his dry lips. Wanted to ask about Cara. Didn't. She was probably gone by now. Darius had said no one was hurt. So she must be okay. Probably back home in New Jersey . . .

"Oh, man, you're breaking my heart." Darius waited until Rafe opened his eyes again and looked at him. "Why don't you just ask about her, bro?"

Rafe scowled. "Stop reading my feelings."

"I can hardly help it. You're shoving them in my face." Darius shook his head and reached for the plastic pitcher on the bed tray. "I don't know who I like better, the jerk who thought he had all the answers or the guy with the hair shirt and all the guilt."

The sound of water being poured into a plastic cup had Rafe's salivary glands jumping to life with painful intensity. "Bite me," he managed.

Darius grinned and offered the water. "No way, you already have enough holes in you."

Rafe took the water and almost dropped it. Only his brother's steady fingers around his kept him from dumping it all over himself like a baby. He sipped, the liquid seeping into his parched mouth like ambrosia from the gods.

"Easy there." Darius set the cup on the tray. "The nurses said the meds would make you super thirsty, but you shouldn't go too fast." He chuckled. "Though if you need more help, I think some of them would be happy to assist you with any number of needs."

"No thanks." His voice sounded raspy. He cleared his throat. "So what happened? I remember you and . . . well, you . . . telling me to go all the way Hunter. Then nothing. As usual."

"You can say her name, you know."

Rafe ignored him, staring at the now-muted talk show on the TV.

The silence stretched for a moment. "Well, you beat the hell out of Criten, which he deserved, by the way," Darius said. "The ambulance took him to the hospital—"

"This hospital?" Rafe jerked his head around, and he winced as his muscles protested the movement.

"No, some private hospital. Doesn't matter anyway. He's gone."

"Gone?" Rafe struggled to sit up, gritting his teeth as his battered body objected. "Gone where?"

"Beats me." Darius reached for the bed control and eased Rafe into a better sitting position. "Dad wasn't too pleased when we were told some government types took off with him and those bodyguards of his. Diplomatic immunity or some garbage."

"Figures."

"Exactly." Darius glanced at the TV and scowled. "Two of those women are lying. He's not the father of their kids, and they know it."

"What? Oh, man, are you still hooked on those talk shows where everyone airs their dirty laundry?"

"Hooked is a strong word." Darius shrugged. "I like to hone my abilities that way."

"I think it's just your softer side showing."

Darius sent him a warning look. "You want to make your stay here longer, keep talking like that. Now why haven't you asked me about—"

"So what did you do to that bodyguard?" Rafe interrupted. He knew Darius wanted to talk about Cara, but he wasn't ready yet. Couldn't bear to hear that she was gone.

"The bodyguard? Something I learned when I was doing all that studying about my abilities. You know, when I was researching how to heal myself?" Dar waved his hand. "Never mind. Anyway, I learned that I can augment the emotions of another person. Even overwhelm them with that emotion if I need to."

Rafe stared at his brother. "No way."

"Yeah, well, that guy was worried about his boss, so all I did was blow it out of proportion. Next thing I knew, he was crying like a little girl. And of course, you went all badass and did the rest of the heavy lifting."

"And everyone is okay."

"Yes. Though that Adrian Gray guy? He slipped out before the ambulance arrived. Something about not wanting to be there when the cops came."

"Figures." Rafe closed his eyes and braced himself to ask the question burning in his heart. "And Cara? What about her?"

"What about me?"

He heard her voice, and when he opened his eyes, even saw her standing in the doorway of his room with two cups of coffee in her hands. But it wasn't until she smiled and sent a little pulse of reassurance along their bond that he realized she was truly there.

"You didn't leave," he said.

"Good observation." She strolled into the room as if nothing had happened, all blond and cute and sexy in jeans and a green top. The heavy weight crushing his heart lifted. She was all right. He hadn't killed her. She hadn't left.

But what that meant, he had no idea.

· · · · ·

She was shaking. Rafe was wrapped in bandages with an IV in his arm, and he looked a little pale. But those stunning blue eyes were open and alert and still made her weak at the knees when he looked at her. The two-days' worth of scruff added a bad-boy attractiveness that she was trying to ignore. The man had come near death, and here she was lusting after him.

Get a hold of yourself, McGaffigan.

She came into the room and handed one of the cups to Darius, delaying the moment of truth a few seconds longer. "Sorry, it's not the best coffee in the world. Maybe your mom can make another donation and get a real coffee shop put in around here."

"Maybe." Darius set down his coffee and stood, grabbing his cane from where it leaned against the wall. "I'll be back in a little while. I think you two need to talk."

He lurched out of the room before either of them could respond. Cara scowled after him. So much for a buffer to help with the awkwardness. She glanced from the TV and back to Rafe. "Maury? I didn't think you were the type."

"Darius. It's a thing." He took the remote and turned off the TV. "They said you were okay. You don't look okay."

She stretched out her arm so he could see the healing cuts. "Just scratches mostly. Broken glass. The thing that really smarts is the burn I got on my shoulder. Nothing a bunch of gauze and antibiotic cream won't fix, but it really hurt when it happened." She sipped her coffee.

"How'd you get burned?" he demanded. "And what glass?"

"Long story."

He narrowed his eyes. "I love stories."

"Yeah, me too." *The heck with it.* She set down her cup beside Darius's and moved closer to the bed, curling her hand over the bed rail to resist touching him. "I especially like the fairy tale you told me about wanting to break up."

"About that . . ."

"Yes?"

"I was full of it." He took her hand and entwined their fingers, meeting her gaze with a candid vulnerability that melted her heart. "The truth is, I was scared. Ever since Darius was injured, I've been convinced that I'm dangerous to anyone who's close to me."

"No kidding."

"Okay, well, that was why I said the things I said." He tightened his fingers over hers, his body stiffening as if preparing for
rejection. "I was trying to make you go away to keep you safe.
But then all this happened. When I touched Criten, I lost my
powers. And you still got hurt."

"We took Criten down. Together." She gave him a look. "Or
are you going to pretend that whole mating bond thing doesn't
exist?"

"No, it exists. I guess it saved our butts." He sighed and
rubbed the back of her hand against his beard-roughened cheek.
"But I wouldn't blame you if you wanted to catch the first plane
back to Jersey."

"Stop trying to get rid of me. There are no guarantees, Rafe.
I realized that when I thought Criten was going to kill me. And
if that bond thing we have doesn't convince you we're meant to
be together—"

"Who am I to argue?" He shook his head. "What I'm trying
to say, Cara, is that I love you. I'm not perfect—"

"Really?"

"I have a temper, and I can be a jerk sometimes."

"I may need smelling salts for the shock."

"But no one will ever love you like I do. You're the only
woman for me. Please stay with me. Help me learn to love you
like you deserve."

She'd thought she could be strong and in control and talk
rationally about their relationship, but what woman could resist
such a plea? She leaned closer and brushed her lips against his.
"Just try to get rid of me. We'll compare scars some night and
play twenty questions, and I'll tell you everything that happened while you were out of touch."

"You'd better." He tugged on her hand. "Why don't you climb up here with me?"

She arched back. "What? No, I'll hurt you!"

"Come on. No one's looking."

"Behave yourself!"

"Don't you love me?"

"Of course I love you—" She scowled as a wicked grin swept across his face. "That's cheating. I had this whole speech prepared for when I told you I loved you, and now you ruined it."

"You can still tell it to me."

"Nope. You ruined it."

"Come on. What were you going to say?" He lifted her hand to his lips and nibbled on her fingers.

Her pulse fluttered. "Can't you act sick?"

"Tell me, sweetheart. You know you want to."

She looked away from that too-seductive gaze and tried to ignore the tingling along her limbs. "It might have been something about how I called my partners and made arrangements to open an office of Apex on the West Coast."

"That's good." He flicked his tongue against her palm, grinning when she gasped. "What else?"

"Um . . . Danny turned in the stone to your dad, and your dad is helping him get a good defense attorney."

"Good news. What else?" He gently pulled her closer until she was bent over the bed.

"I got my condo back," she whispered. "I'm selling it to buy controlling shares in Apex."

"I like it." He rubbed his nose against hers. "And?"

"I have to go back to Jersey to close the deal. You can come, and maybe we can rent a really hot car to make Warren weep with envy."

He grinned. "Lamborghini okay?"

"Yes." She traced his lips with one finger and looked him straight in those gorgeous blue eyes. "And I love you. I love Rafe Montana, the Hunter, all of it. I want to stay with you and stand by you while you figure all this stuff out."

He looked hard into her eyes, and a smile crept across his face. "Truth," he murmured, and kissed her.

I first got the idea about the descendents of the survivors of Atlantis from a story I heard in my freshman Spanish class. My teacher spoke of Spain and specifically of the people of the Basque region, whose native tongue is unrelated to any other language on Earth. The legend goes that the Basques are actually the descendents of the survivors of Atlantis, which is why their language is so unique. I therefore used vocabulary from Euskara Batua, the standardized language of the Basque people, as the basis for my Atlantean language. Any errors in meaning are completely mine and meant in the spirit of entertainment.